A
DESIRE
FOR
VENGEANCE

By L.R. Puttock

A Desire for Vengeance

For Jayne, Jennie, Robb

and

Millie

Prologue

The Klotjevac Gorge, Bosnia-and-Herzegovina, June 1992

Ibrahim emerged from the trees onto the sloping, stony beach and shivered. It was early morning and it would be some time before the sun was high enough to spread its warmth on the little beach at the bottom of the gorge.

The "beach" was in reality a small semi-circular cove on the right bank where the Drina River meandered to the left. After the headlong rush though the confines of the upper gorge, the river widened here and slowed its pace. Herons, egrets and spoonbills browsed in the shallows, while swans and geese patrolled the deeper waters offshore. As Ibrahim watched, a black cormorant dived effortlessly below the surface, leaving barely a ripple. Moments later a flotilla of greylag geese overran its position. Then something on the beach caught Ibrahim's eye and his jaw dropped in surprise. He looked around for his cousin. Mustapha was eleven years old – ten months younger than Ibrahim. He had been right behind as they descended the steep slope from their hamlet through the pine forest to the river, but now he was nowhere in sight.

'Mujo? Where are you?'

It was not always so tranquil here. In the spring, the melting snow from the mountains further upriver turned the Drina into an angry raging torrent that inundated the beach. At those times, it was dangerous to go near the water, but now, in the summer, it was a good place for fishing and sifting through the flotsam left stranded on the little beach. Mostly, the boys would collect driftwood to take home to fuel the kitchen stove, or sometimes there would be plastic containers, useful for storing anything from water to engine oil. Once, after a big storm in the mountains, they found a whole tree at the water's edge.

Lately, however, the discoveries had been considerably more macabre in nature. In the past few weeks, the presence of human remains in the shallows alongside the beach had become an almost daily occurrence.

The boys' initial shock had soon given way to morbid fascination, and in defiance of their parents' strict instructions to stay away, they would come early each morning before the adult men arrived to take the morning's crop of bodies away for burial.

Affording these erstwhile living, breathing human beings the same dispassionate interest that they might show to the decomposing corpse of a stray dog, Ibrahim and Mustapha ghoulishly examined the wounds that had so cruelly ended their lives. Some of them had had their throats cut, leaving great gaping wounds that left the heads lolling at unnatural angles. Some had been shot, leaving large exit wounds in the head or torso. The wounds always were white and bloodless, scoured clean during their passage downriver. With some victims, the cause of death was less obvious and the boys speculated at the manner of their demise. Perhaps she had drowned; perhaps he had been strangled, another clubbed to death.

Although it had so far not intruded into their remote hamlet, which nestled on the slopes of the Zvijezda Mountain, the boys were well aware of the vicious civil war that was ravaging their country. They had heard the elders telling of the massacres in the town of Višegrad, ten kilometres upstream. They heard how the *Chetniks* were daily bringing truckloads of Muslim civilians to the two bridges that spanned the Drina, slashing throats or shooting their helpless victims before dumping the remains into the green waters below.

The current carried the corpses through the gorge. Only a small proportion came to rest in the little cove. Most continued their journey further downstream to Lake Perućac. So many bodies had been drawn into the sluices of the Bajina Bašta hydroelectric power station that the superintendant of that facility telephoned the Višegrad authorities begging them to reduce the number of bodies thrown into the river.

'Mujo! Where are you?'

'I'm here, Ibro.' The younger boy emerged from behind a tree, zipping the fly of his denim jeans. 'I needed a piss.'

'Come here!' urged Ibrahim, pointing to where the wavelets lapped against the stony beach. 'Look at that.'

There were three bodies today; two were adult males, fully clothed, and lay in the shallows, their limbs moving with the rhythm of the eddying current. The third was female, blonde – and stark naked. She lay face down on the shingle, a few feet from the water's edge. It was as if someone had pulled her from the river before abandoning her lifeless body on the beach.

Something about this body struck both boys with awe, and they stood rooted to the spot for half-a-minute or more. Eventually, curiosity overcame fear and they inched down the beach. Ibrahim fell to his knees and studied the body closely.

She was young and beautiful, probably not much older than his brother's wife, who was nineteen; but this girl was much prettier. Her eyes were closed and her wet blonde hair covered her face. Her skin was very pale, unbroken by blade or bullet, but the otherwise perfect skin of her back was marred by a number of small, red injuries, like small burns, but regularly circular in shape.

Ibrahim reached out with his fingers. The skin was pale and cold, but soft and smooth. Lost in his own little world, he jumped with surprise when Mustapha suddenly spoke from close beside his ear.

'Let's turn her over and see her tits.'

'Okay,' the older boy agreed. Grinning lecherously, he slipped one hand under the bent right knee while his cousin took hold of the corpse's right wrist and they pulled together. The body rolled smoothly onto its back and Mustapha let the limp arm flop down onto the stones.

Ibrahim had never seen a naked woman before, not even his sisters – well, not since they got big enough to be interesting, anyway. Guiltily, he allowed his eyes to feast on the sight. The breasts were small but firm and tinged appealingly with rose-pink nipples. Further down, the wispy pubic hair was the colour of straw. There were cuts and bruises on the face, and several more clusters of those curious circular injuries around the stomach and breasts, but these were the only blemishes on an otherwise perfect body. What a pity that it had been damaged, desecrated, turned into dead meat.

Almost of its own accord, Ibrahim's hand reached out and gently squeezed the nearest breast, and the boy marvelled at the feel of the cold, soft, pliant skin beneath his fingers. His heart started to beat faster and the blood-rush was pounding in his ears as, consumed by devilment and lust, he traced his fingers across the woman's stomach toward the gossamer strands of golden pubic hair.

Then, unexpectedly, the body moved.

With a drawn-out, wheezing gasp, the young woman's chest rose sharply. Her hands flapped up and down like the wings of an injured bird, the palms slapping loudly on the damp shingle. Fighting for breath, she rolled onto her side and retched.

Ibrahim yelled in fear and surprise and leapt to his feet. Overbalancing, he stumbled backwards and tripped over one of the bodies at the water's edge, landing on his backside in the water. The movement caused the corpse to turn over, and the sightless eyes stared at him in silent accusation.

Mustapha had already disappeared into the trees at the top of the beach. Terrified, Ibrahim rolled to his feet and ran after his cousin, but before he reached the trees, he heard the woman call out, in a language he did not understand. Then she repeated the appeal in his native Serbo-Croatian.

'Wait! Do not leave me! Help me! Please come back!'

The desperation in her voice made Ibrahim stop and turn back to face her. The woman had raised her upper body, supporting herself on straight arms, seemingly oblivious to her nudity. He could see her small pert breasts peeking out at him from between her arms and he felt his body react. The frightened child in him wanted to run away but the emerging man was transfixed.

'Please help me!' the woman repeated before another fit of coughing wracked her body.

The spell was broken. 'I'll get help,' he shouted. 'I'll get my mother and my sisters. Wait. I'll be back soon.' Then he turned and ran into the trees.

The woman watched the boy disappear and then she collapsed onto the stones. Curling into a foetal position, she lay coughing and wheezing as her body continued to purge the green river water from her lungs.

Chapter 1

The Wirral, Cheshire, 4th September 1992

The opening credits of the late-evening news faded from the screen to be replaced by the face of the anchorman, his grim expression forewarning his viewers of the portentous news that was about to follow. As the final strident notes of the theme music faded, he began to speak.

'Good evening. In the last few minutes police have identified the woman gunned down in London's West End, this afternoon, as the veteran BBC broadcaster and war correspondent Jane Badell.'

The anchorman was replaced on screen by a close-up of a middle-aged woman with collar-length grey hair, facing the camera with piercing blue eyes. His voice continued in the background. 'Miss Badell was shot twice in the head from point-blank range as she sat in her car in Hans Place, Knightsbridge. Police say she had just returned to her car after shopping in Harrods department store, nearby.'

The woman's picture faded and the anchorman reappeared in the foreground. The murdered broadcaster's face now appeared on a screen behind him.

'An eyewitness said Miss Badell was shot by the pillion passenger on a red motorcycle that pulled up alongside her car while it was still at the kerbside. He fired two shots through the driver's window at point-blank range and then the motorbike was driven away at speed. Both riders were wearing black motorcycle leathers and full-face helmets with dark-tinted visors.'

The camera angle changed and the anchorman turned smoothly to face his viewers again.

'Fifty-seven year-old Jane Badell was well known for her broadcasts from war zones and trouble-spots around the world for more than twenty years. Most recently, millions of viewers watched her nightly broadcasts from the besieged Bosnian capital, Sarajevo, during the first few months of the civil war. She announced her retirement from broadcasting on her return from the Balkans, following an incident in which several members of her film-crew were killed.

'Police are baffled by the apparently motiveless murder and are appealing for witnesses.' The anchorman paused and shuffled his papers before moving on to the next story.

'In other news, the trial of the alleged members of a Provisional IRA cell continued in Liverpool, with a female MI5 officer giving evidence from behind a screen.'

Lieutenant Colonel Charles Harris, Royal Engineers (retired) sat in his favourite armchair near the window. The beige and green Regency striped curtains were drawn against the early autumn night, isolating the living room from the outside world.

He raised his glass to his lips, took a sip of whisky and wiped his grey moustache with a forefinger.

'Terrible business! Gunned down in broad daylight. In Knightsbridge, of all places!'

'She'd just left Harrods,' his wife added. She sat in the twin of Charles' armchair, positioned to one side of the Georgian-style multi-paned double-doors that led into the dining room, beyond which lay the back garden. Beside the chair, a mahogany standard lamp threw its light across a copy of *Country Life* on her lap. 'You'd think one would be safe around that part of London, wouldn't you? I don't know what the world's coming to, I really don't.'

'To think of all those dangerous places she's been reporting from, for all these years, without a scratch,' said Charles, 'only to get shot dead in the centre of London on a Friday afternoon. It doesn't bear thinking about.'

'Sandra, whatever's wrong? You've gone as white as a sheet!' Grace Harris always insisted on using her stepdaughter's full Christian name, which the younger woman referred to as her "Sunday name". Since childhood, everyone else had called her Sandy.

Sandy did not reply. As the news programme began, she had been sitting on the sofa in an attitude of boredom and apathy. Barefoot, with her shoulder-length blonde hair tied back, she was wearing a short-sleeved, V-neck, black cotton tee shirt and figure hugging, faded blue denim jeans. Her legs were drawn up under her and her cheek rested on the knuckles of her balled left hand. As the story of the broadcaster's murder unfolded, however, she sat forward, literally on the edge of her seat, both hands clasped to her mouth, her mind refusing to accept what she was seeing and hearing. Now, as the broadcast continued with the next story, she sat stunned, shocked, dumfounded, and tears were running down her cheeks.

'She's crying,' said Grace. 'Why is she crying? Sandra, whatever is the matter with you?'

'Stop it,' Sandy snapped, wiping tears from her cheeks with a tissue. 'Leave me alone. I'm trying to think.'

'Sandra, I don't care for your tone!' Grace turned to her husband for support. 'Charles, she shouldn't be speaking to me in that manner.'

Charles sighed and tried to restore calm.

'Leave her be, Grace. You can see she's upset.'

'I can't think why, Charles. The way she's carrying on you'd think she knew the woman. Honestly, I don't know; I really do not understand.'

'Grace, leave it!'

'Well, Charles, I'm sick and tired of her attitude, I really am! She's been so sullen and moody since she got back from Africa. She refuses to tell us anything about it; in fact, she hardly even speaks to us'

'Grace...'

'And why has she taken a clerical job? She's hardly making good use of her degree by processing tax forms, is she! What a waste of a good education! She's so ungrateful for all the sacrifices we made for her. Why can't she be more like her sister and enter one of the professions? She could be a lawyer, like Samantha, or a doctor, a . . .'

'Grace, for God's sake, will you please drop it,' Charles insisted. 'Please!'

'Well, there's no need for you to raise your voice, Charles! I...'

'Please stop arguing!' said Sandy above the raised voices. 'And please don't talk about me as if I wasn't here.'

Sandy's parents looked at her as if they had forgotten she was in the room.

'Now, if you'll excuse me,' Sandy added, keeping her voice calm, 'I'm going to my room.'

Sandy closed the door quietly behind her, fighting the urge to slam it.

'Well, what do you make of that?' An astonished Charles asked his wife.

'I don't know,' said Grace huffily, and then added, 'I do wish she wouldn't yell at us as if we were all denizens of some grubby council estate in Toxteth!'

***

Sandy bolted up the stairs, two at a time, and into her bedroom. She closed the door behind her and sat on the bed. She needed to call in urgently, but should she do that first or should she tell her parents what was happening? Should she tell them the truth or continue with the subterfuge? So far, it had been easier to let them believe the cover story about working with Christian Aid on a famine relief mission in Eritrea. Jane's death changed everything. Now the killers would most likely come after her and if they did, her parents would be in danger as well.

In fact, it was surprising that the two hits had not been coordinated. Surely, they would know that Jane's assassination would be sensational news – and that Sandy, therefore, would be forewarned. Unfortunately, she had no weapon with which to defend herself. It had never occurred to her that she would be in danger in England. Had she thought it likely, she would have drawn a personal weapon from the armoury. On second thoughts, after the way the debriefing went, they probably wouldn't have allowed her anywhere near a firearm.

Perhaps she was being paranoid. Perhaps she was not at risk after all. However, she could not afford to take the chance. She should call in, but the telephone was downstairs in the hall and there was no extension upstairs. Her parents would wonder whom she was calling. They might even overhear what she said. No, she decided; she would have to tell them first. *God, their lives will never be the same again!*

She must go downstairs, now, and tell them the whole story – well, obviously, not the *whole* story. Not only would it be too shocking for them, there was not enough time. She nodded determinedly. She would tell them just enough to . . . *God! What a mess!*

***

Charles stood up and headed toward the door.

'Where are you going, Charles?' Grace asked.

'I thought I'd go and talk to her. See what's troubling her.'

'She just needs to grow up, that's all. She's arrogant and self-centred. She thinks of no one but herself and her attitude is appalling. If you continue to go running after her and pandering to her, she'll never be any different.'

Charles shook his head. Grace was being unfair. Sandy was a changed person since returning home from Africa. No longer the confident, exuberant, devil-may-care character she once was. Now she was withdrawn, distant, introverted. There was a time that they could discuss almost any subject in a forthright, no nonsense manner. Even with personal matters, she would often listen to his advice, even if she didn't always take it. Now it was different. Lately, she had retreated inside herself, stonewalling any and all attempts to get her to open up about what was troubling her. Charles was at a loss. How could he rebuild the relationship they once had? Did he do something to lose her trust? What must he do to regain it?

He had just reached the bottom of the staircase when the doorbell interrupted his thoughts.

'Who on Earth can that be at this time of night?' he muttered to himself.

He turned to open the door.

***

Sandy heard the doorbell and felt a precognitive dread. The hairs on the back of her neck rose. A shiver ran down her spine. She rushed out of the bedroom and down the first few steps of the staircase. She opened her mouth to tell her father not to open the door, but was too late.

Sandy saw him stumble backwards. Three figures rushed through the doorway into the hall. Each was dressed head-to-toe in black and wore a balaclava ski mask. Each carried a semi-automatic pistol fitted with a suppressor.

Sandy's training immediately took control of her actions, quashing her natural instinct to rush to her father's aid. Unarmed and alone, she could not hope to take on three armed X-Rays and win. She slunk further into the shadows at the top of the stairs and, like a five-year-old peeping at guests arriving for a grown-ups' party after bedtime, she observed through the balusters.

So far, the only sound had been that of her father's initial cry of surprise. Then the first intruder covered the old man's mouth with one gloved hand and held the pistol to his head. The second aimed his pistol up the stairs and the third calmly

A Desire for Vengeance

closed the front door. At that moment, the living room door opened and Sandy's stepmother appeared.

'What on Earth . . .'

The second X-Ray whirled around and viciously jabbed the muzzle of his gun into Grace's solar plexus, cutting off her words as if turning off a tap. Winded, her knees buckled and she might have fallen had the man not caught her and manhandled her back inside the living room. Then, still holding the gun to Charles' head, the first intruder forced him to follow his wife.

The third intruder remained in the hall. He held his pistol in a two-handed grip and looked up the stairs. He was looking straight at her. Surely, he could see her. How could he not see her? She forced herself to remain absolutely still and silent, her eyes averted to avoid direct contact with his.

For the moment, she was trapped. She had to remain motionless. Any movement, no matter how slight, would draw the eyes of the gunman and she would be finished. Suddenly, the living room door opened and one of the X-Rays appeared in the doorway. Using hand signals, he motioned for the third man to search upstairs and that he would check the kitchen. The distraction gave Sandy the opportunity to retreat silently to her bedroom.

Sandy had no doubt that she was the target. For the third time in as many months, Death was coming to claim her. Her mind struggled to come to terms with the speed of events. In just a few seconds, intruders had invaded her home and were holding her parents at gunpoint in their own living room. She had just seconds before they came looking for her. What could she do? She considered surrendering herself in the hope of saving her parents, but dismissed the idea immediately. If they were going to kill her, they surely would not leave her parents alive to tell the tale. No, if she had any hope of saving their lives she had to fight back – but how? Surprise was her only advantage. So far, the intruders did not know where she was or that she was aware of their presence. Desperately, she looked around the room for something – anything to use as a weapon. Then an idea struck her.

As a child, at boarding school, much to her stepmother's disapproval, Sandy had taken up archery. Although it was more than five years since she had last used the bow, all of the equipment was still in her room, stored under her bed. Kneeling on the carpet, she swiftly pulled out the old bow and a quiver containing six aluminium arrows.

It was a novice's bow, a simple fibreglass shaft, some sixty inches in length, with a plastic handle in the middle and a maximum draw-weight of thirty pounds. The bow was unstrung for storage, with the string notched onto the top end of the bow with the remainder wrapped around the shaft. Sandy shook it free as she stood up and attached the string to the other end. Immediately transforming what was essentially a fibreglass stick into a weapon capable of propelling a missile accurately to a target over a hundred yards away.

Sandy reviewed her preparations. There was no time to strap on the wrist-guard so she left that lying beside the bed. What could she do to distract the X-Ray – take his attention long enough to give herself a slight edge?

Coming to a decision, she quickly turned on the radio and turned the volume up louder than she would normally have it. She stuffed one of her pillows inside a red pullover and placed it upright in a chair facing her dressing table, with its back toward the bedroom door. Then she removed the shade from her bedside lamp and turned it on. Finally, she turned off the main ceiling light and moved to the furthest corner of the room.

***

There were six doors leading off the landing. From the mission briefing, he knew that four led to bedrooms, one to a bathroom and the last was an airing cupboard. He knew the first door on the right at the top of the stairs was the target's bedroom. Through the small gap under the door, he could see that the light was on in the room, whereas the landing was in semi-darkness, only partially illuminated from the hall light downstairs. He could hear the radio playing loudly enough to have drowned out the commotion downstairs when the team forced their way in. He grinned. This was going to be easier than expected. A "southpaw", he held the gun in his left hand and raised his right to knock gently on the door.

***

Even above the sound of the radio, she heard the creak. The last-but-one step before the landing always creaked – even if one tried to avoid it by treading on the outside edge. Someone was on the landing outside her room. She laid an arrow on the bow and nocked it onto the string at a point marked by a few twists of red cord. Holding the bow in her left hand, she stood with her feet shoulder-width apart, her left shoulder facing toward the bedroom door. She grasped the string with three fingers of her right hand – her forefinger above the arrow, the other two below, and the little finger curled into her palm.

There was a polite knock on the door.

'Come in; I'm decent,' Sandy called lightly, affecting an unconcerned tone as if she expected it to be one of her parents knocking.

The doorknob turned. Sandy drew the bow. Her right hand was under her chin with the string touching the tip of her nose and the cleft of her chin. Without conscious thought, she kissed the bowstring – the time-honoured method of checking position before loosing the arrow.

***

He pushed open the door. His eyes were accustomed to the gloom of the unlit landing and he squinted at the brightness of the unshaded bedside lamp. His eyes picked out the shape wearing a red pullover in front of the dressing table, but he immediately discounted it. Holding his pistol in a two-handed grip, he quickly scanned the room looking for the target. He almost missed the figure with a most unexpected profile, standing motionless in the corner. Only when his brain finally registered what his eyes were seeing did his smile fade. He gasped in alarm and took a step backwards, instinctively turning his head away even as his finger tightened on the trigger.

***

Sandy loosed the arrow in the same instant that the intruder fired. The bullet buzzed within inches of her left ear and slammed into the wall behind her, showering her head with particles of plaster and wallpaper.

The arrow leapt from the bow at nearly a hundred miles an hour and was still accelerating, a fraction of a second later, when it entered the intruder's throat. The momentum took it clean through his larynx to sever the spinal cord and exit through the back of his neck. Only the fletchings were still visible from the front, nestling beneath his chin like a snazzy red and white bow tie.

For a moment, the man stood still, his eyes wide open in shock. Then, as if the weight were suddenly too much to bear, the hand holding the gun dropped to his side and he fell to his knees, tipping forward to land flat on his face, his blood seeping into the beige wool/acrylic carpet.

Sandy dropped the bow and knelt beside the dead man. Prising the gun from his hand, she recognised it as a Russian Tokarev 7.62mm semi-automatic. She flipped out the magazine. It was a nine-round magazine and although he had only fired once, she could see through the holes in the side that there were seven rounds left. That made sense. It was standard practise to load one less than the maximum into a magazine. It preserved the strength of the spring and reduced the likelihood of a misfire.

Seven rounds were better than nothing, but not enough for the job in hand. She slammed the magazine back into the handle and winced as she pinched the skin on the edge of her palm between the two metal parts, scraping off a half-inch flap of skin.

Tucking the gun under her armpit, she sucked on her injured right palm as she felt in first one then the other side pocket of his bomber jacket with her other hand. In the right-hand pocket, she found a second magazine for the Tokarev with eight rounds, and a quick-release five-round clip for a revolver. Running her hands down his left calf, she found his back-up weapon, a black Smith and Wesson 0.38 revolver with a full five-round chamber. So now, she had two pistols and a total of twenty-five rounds of ammunition. Better – much better!

Sandy glanced at the clock radio on her bedside table. It was not yet twenty past nine. It felt as if an hour must have passed since retreating to her bedroom, but it was less than three minutes. She stood up and looked down at the dead man. Clearly, his companions would be expecting him either to return downstairs, with Sandy as a captive, or alone to report her dead. When he failed to show up one of the others would come looking for him. In that case, she could deal with him, leaving only one more in the living room. Sandy brightened; things were looking more hopeful now.

***

Charles Harris was on his knees with his hands on his head. Grace was sitting in her armchair looking pale and frightened. The television was still on and the weather forecaster was predicting a clear night with the prospect of a light frost in some areas.

Charles shook his head. If this was a robbery, they were handling it in a strange way. None of the intruders had spoken a word, not even to ask where the valuables were. They were communicating with each other entirely by hand-signals. It was clear that these men, whoever they were, had undergone military training at some time. Only one of the gunmen was in the room now. He was standing beside the door leading to the hall, covering Charles and his wife with his semi-automatic. The other two must be searching the house. Charles thought of Sandy and fretted about what they might do to his beautiful, vulnerable daughter when they found her.

Charles' attention and concern switched to his wife. She seemed to be struggling to breathe properly. He wondered if the vicious jab in the chest had caused some damage. Perhaps she was about to have one of her asthma attacks. Then, almost as if prompted by his concern, she clutched at her chest and began panting and wheezing.

'She's asthmatic,' Charles told the guard. 'She needs her inhaler.' To Charles' outrage and astonishment, the man simply shrugged and held a finger to his lips. 'Don't you understand?' Charles said, rising to his feet. 'She needs her inhaler! It's in the drawer over there in the sideboard,' he explained, pointing.

The man waved his gun, clearly indicating that Charles should kneel again. Charles hesitated, expecting the man to go to the dresser to get the inhaler, but he did not move.

'Look, this is ridiculous,' said Charles and taking care not to appear in any way threatening to the gunman, he strode purposefully toward the dresser.

This time the intruder did move. He lunged at Charles and attempted to grab his arm. Charles shrugged him off and tried to continue on his mission of mercy for his wife. The masked man swung the gun at Charles, catching him on the temple. Charles reeled from the blow and, clutching his head, fell across the sofa where Sandy had been sitting earlier. Seeing her husband collapse from the blow, Grace tried to scream, but it was no more than a slightly louder wheeze ending in a deep, bronchial cough. Fighting for breath, she tried to get up from her seat but the gunman pushed her back down again. Grace resisted, struggling and slapping at him with her hands.

Charles realised that with his attention – and both hands – fully occupied trying to subdue Grace the gunman was suddenly vulnerable. Ignoring the throbbing pain in his head, he leapt upon the intruder, pinioning his arms from behind.

Despite his age, Charles was fit and strong. Since retiring, he had devoted his energies to his garden, relishing the physical challenges of turning the soil, laying a patio and a hundred other tasks that kept him feeling young, supple and strong. Consequently, although much older than his adversary, Charles hoped that surprise might help him overpower the younger man and wrest his weapon away, giving him the means to rescue his wife and daughter from this terrible situation.

The intruder reacted quickly to Charles' assault. Throwing himself backwards bodily, he forced the older man to retreat several steps. Determinedly, Charles latched two hands around the gunman's right wrist, trying to shake the weapon from his grasp. Unfortunately, his opponent was stronger. He twisted in Charles' grip and elbowed him in the midriff. Winded, Charles' hold on the man's wrist weakened and the intruder wrenched it free. Grabbing the front of Charles' cardigan, the intruder started to push him back toward the sofa.

Having recovered enough to be aware that her husband was losing the fight, Grace grabbed the mahogany standard lamp, from beside her chair, and swung it down violently at the intruder. The stem struck his shoulder and the lampshade spun across the room. The bulb shattered against his cheek and fragments of glass dug into the flesh through the wool of his balaclava.

Automatically, his free hand went to his cheek and, seizing the opportunity, Charles made a renewed effort to take the gun. Remembering his unarmed-combat training from many years before, he grasped the barrel and twisted the weapon sharply to his left, forcing the man's trigger finger back against the knuckle. The intruder yelped with pain and suddenly the gun was in Charles' possession. Charles turned the weapon and pointed it at its owner, but he was too slow. In one fluid movement, the intruder dropped to one knee, produced a small black revolver from beneath his trouser-leg, raised it and fired twice. Both rounds hit Charles squarely in the chest, throwing him backwards. He crashed into the television and dropped onto the floor. His last thought as he lost consciousness was that he had failed to protect his family.

Grace screamed.

***

The leader was searching the kitchen and utility room. He made sure that the doors to the garden were locked and removed the keys to ensure the target could not escape that way. It was then that he heard the thump from the floor above and looked up at the ceiling as if he could see right through it. No other sound followed. He would have expected some squeal of alarm from the girl at the very least. More likely, with her history, she would try to resist, but even she would not be able to do much against a big man pointing a semi-automatic in her face. Still, the ensuing silence was puzzling. Perhaps he should just go and check.

Passing through the doorway from the kitchen to the hall, he heard the unsilenced pistol shots from the living room, followed by the old woman's scream.

Quickly but cautiously, he entered the room and swiftly took in the scene before him. The old man was lying by the window with the television on the floor beside him; the woman was sitting in her chair, covering her ears with her hands as if to block out the sound of her own screaming. His teammate was standing indecisively in the middle of the room, revolver in hand. He appeared to be in a state of shock. The leader swiftly reached a decision. He snatched the revolver from his companion and fired two shots into Grace's head. She stopped screaming and slumped back in her chair.

With his ears ringing from the screaming and the unsilenced shots, the leader told his number-two to cover his back while he went upstairs to find the missing man.

***

Sandy heard the reports from two shots followed by her stepmother's screams. Taking a gun in each hand, she ran out of the bedroom and started down the stairs. As reached the half-landing, there were two more shots, and the screaming stopped abruptly. She knew immediately that her father and stepmother had been murdered. Shocked beyond comprehension, she hesitated in mid-step, wondering what to do next.

Suddenly, the living room door opened and instinctively Sandy shrank to a crouch behind the balusters. A black-clad man emerged into the hall. He held his pistol in a straight-armed, two-handed grip and sidestepped toward the bottom of the staircase. The muzzle followed his eyes as he scanned the hall and stairwell. With her heartbeat pounding in her ears, Sandy took two deep breaths then, holding the third, aimed the Tokarev through the gap between two balusters and fired two shots, rapid-fire.

The X-Ray's reflexes were impressive. He was diving to the floor before she fired the first shot. Rolling onto his back, he returned fire. Meanwhile, his companion also fired from his position in the living room doorway. Sandy cried out involuntarily as the baluster beside her left thigh snapped like a twig. Two more rounds thudded into the wall behind her.

Sandy fired another two shots to keep the men's heads down and retreated up the stairs to the landing. Two more rounds buried themselves into the wall before she turned the corner and was, temporarily at least, out of their line-of-fire.

This was a good defensive position. The X-Rays would have to storm up the stairs to get to her, exposing themselves to her fire as they came. There were only three rounds left in the Tokarev, one in the chamber and two more in the magazine, so now might be a good time to swap it for the full one. She laid the revolver on the carpet, then ejected the almost empty magazine and quickly replaced it with the spare. She now had fourteen rounds in two guns. With the Russian semi-automatic in one hand and the revolver in the other, she sat on her haunches and waited to see what the X-Rays' next move would be. She did not have long to wait.

A black cylinder landed on the half-landing three steps down from her position. She recognised it as a thunderflash stun-grenade. Knowing that the device had only a two-second fuse, she turned and leapt through the open door into her bedroom. The grenade exploded with a deafening roar and a blinding flash of light. Had Sandy remained on the landing she would have been deafened, blinded and totally disoriented, unable to resist as the X-Rays sprinted up the stairs to capture or kill her. By diving into her room, she had saved herself from the full impact. Even so, her ears were ringing from the blast. The X-Rays could be charging up the stairs right at this moment, but she would be unable to hear them.

She tried to kick the bedroom door shut but it caught on the outstretched arm of the man she had shot with the bow. To give the others something to think about, she fired four shots from the Tokarev through the open doorway in the direction of the stairwell. Then, grabbing the dead man's sleeve, she dragged him far enough into the room to allow her to slam the door shut. She looked around the room for something with which to barricade the door and her eyes settled on her bed. It had a heavy wrought-iron frame and was standing against the wall adjacent to the door.

That'll have to do!

Grunting with the effort, Sandy dragged the bed around and jammed it against the door. Then she turned off the bedside lamp and retreated into a corner from where she could cover both the door and the window that overlooked the back garden. Bending her knees, she braced her back against the wall and prepared for the next assault.

With her ears ringing and the smell of cordite in her nostrils, Sandy performed a mental audit of her situation. There were six rounds remaining in the Tokarev and another two in the original magazine – which, she suddenly realised, she had left on the landing when she dived back into her room. At least she still had the revolver, loaded with five rounds plus another five in the spare clip.

She tried to work out what the X-Rays would do next. Clearly, their intention had been to carry out this operation with minimal noise to avoid arousing the neighbours. The four unsilenced shots in the living room and her stepmother's screams had put paid to that. From that moment, they appeared to have thrown all caution to the winds. The use of the thunderflash showed just how desperate they were to kill or capture her before the police arrived. The explosion must have sounded to the neighbours as if World War III had broken out. Surely, someone must have called the police after that.

What would she do now if the positions were reversed? The obvious answer would be to lob another stun-grenade through the window and then break the door down while she was incapacitated. What could she do to counter that eventuality? She pulled the duvet from her bed, ready, if necessary to wrap that around her head. She had no idea how effective it would be, but it might help reduce the effects.

Suddenly, the door rattled in its frame as one of the men put his shoulder to it. Sandy fired a shot through the door to dissuade him. The rattling stopped but he returned fire. Two bullets splintered the wood before thumping harmlessly into the bedroom wall opposite. The sound of heavy, clumping footsteps on the stairs told her that at least one more X-Ray had entered the house. The odds were not improving.

Sandy considered her options. To try to make a defensive stand here in the bedroom would be to die like a rat in a trap. The only other way out was through the window into the back garden. That, too, was risky because surely they would have stationed at least one more member of the hit team in the back garden. He could easily pick her off as she was clambering out of the window. Taking care not to become too easy a target, Sandy cautiously opened the window and looked out.

It was dark outside, but light from the kitchen window bathed the part of the back garden nearest the house. Beyond its reach, however, deep shadows formed, providing ample concealment to any intruder. Her eyes scanned the garden trying to spot anyone lurking in the shadows, but she could see no one.

Sandy flinched and ducked as two more shots came through the door. Then the X-Rays started hammering on the door with their pistol butts, trying to batter through the oak panelling. Sandy knew that once they had made a hole large enough to see her it would all be over. To stay here was to die. She had to take her chance with the window. She had to go. Now!

At that moment, Sandy noticed that her feet were bare and she stooped to pick up a pair of trainers. Unable to spare the time to put them on, she tied the laces together with a bow and hung them around her neck. The hammering on the door continued and the panelling was starting to splinter. They would be through very soon. She fired two shots through the door and smiled grimly when someone cried out in pain on the other side.

Cautiously, she looked out of the window again. If someone was out there, she needed to keep his or her head down. Unscrewing the suppressor from the Tokarev, she fired the last three rounds through the open window, the reports shattering the peace and quiet of the genteel suburban neighbourhood.

Dropping the empty Tokarev on the floor, she transferred the revolver to her right hand and climbed out of the window. She held onto the sill with her left hand and slid down on her stomach until her arm was at full stretch. Then, as the last echoes of the shots faded away, she let go of the sill and pushed away from the wall with the knuckles of her right hand. Her body turned in mid-air as she dropped the remaining eight or nine feet to the sun terrace. Bending her knees to absorb the shock, she parachute-rolled and came up on one knee, raising the revolver ready to respond if anyone fired at her.

Nothing happened. Incredibly, it seemed the attackers had neglected to have anyone cover the back of the house, after all. Thanking her lucky stars for their incompetence, she ran quickly to her right, past the French-doors and ducked around the side of the house. Noises from above told her that the X-Rays had finally forced their way into the bedroom.

She was now on the blind side of the house and shielded from view, but she had to keep moving. She leapt at the six-foot fence bordering the neighbouring garden and, pivoting on her pelvis, she placed her gun-hand against the far side of the fence and executed a half-somersault, landing lightly on her feet on the other side.

What little noise she had made prompted frenzied barking from Barney, the neighbours' Dalmatian, who was evidently in their kitchen. Sandy hoped that the noise would curtail any pursuit by her assailants, but she was taking no chances.

The grass was cold and damp as Sandy ran swiftly and silently on bare feet to the end of the garden. Crouching as she ran, she stayed close to the boundary fence to avoid being spotted by anyone positioned at her bedroom window. At the bottom of the garden, she slipped behind a stand of eight-feet-tall rhododendrons, and, making as little noise as possible, scrambled over the back fence. On the other side, she ducked into a narrow space behind a summerhouse.

Chapter 2

The mission had been a disaster from the start, the leader reflected. First, there was the pile-up on the M6 that put them over an hour behind schedule. Then there was the presence of the parents. According to the briefing, they should have been out playing Bridge and should not have been in the house after seven-thirty. He grimaced as he remembered his shock when the old man opened the door. The hastily revised plan to take the parents as well as the girl fell apart when his idiot number-two allowed the old man to jump him and take his weapon, necessitating the shooting of both parents. To make matters worse, the girl had somehow managed to kill the man given the simple task of escorting her downstairs. How the fool could have allowed her to get the better of him with a bow-and-arrow was beyond comprehension.

Well, whatever had happened, it was irrelevant; they were now a man down and the target was in possession of a handgun. It was obvious that their chances of completing this mission successfully were receding fast. They would be lucky, now, to escape without further casualties, and to avoid the police.

The leader had left his number-four with the vehicle – a nondescript white van, parked outside the house – to act as lookout. Number-five was supposed to be watching the back garden and should have killed or captured the target when she jumped out of the window. When he had looked out, just seconds later, there was no sign of either of them. The only way to find out what had happened to number-five was to go through the French-doors into the back garden. If he moved quickly enough he stood a good chance of getting out to the garden without getting his head blown off.

Like the rest of the team, the leader carried a Russian Tokarev 7.62mm semi-automatic pistol and had a 0.38 Smith and Wesson revolver in a holster strapped to his calf. He slipped the locking catch of the French doors with his left hand – and swore at the pain. Wrapped in a soiled handkerchief, his left hand hurt like a bitch. One of the last bullets fired through the door by the target gouged out a great chunk of skin between his thumb and forefinger. He was lucky. A fraction to the right and could just as easily have killed him. The pain steadied his resolve and, with his heart racing, he nodded to his number-two to cover him as he burst through the doors.

Expecting to come immediately under fire, he threw himself down, rolled twice to his right, to throw off the target's aim, and then lay prone on the sun-terrace, sweeping the garden with his eyes – and the Tokarev. He saw a figure detach itself from the shadows further down the garden. He almost fired, but just in time he realised that it was not the target running toward him, waving and pointing towards the fence to his right, but the team member assigned to cover the back – the missing number-five!

What the hell was going on?

***

Sandy sat with her back against the wall of the summerhouse, recovering her breath and listening for sounds of anyone approaching, but she heard nothing. Even Barney had stopped barking.

She took the trainers from around her neck and put them on. It took longer than it should have because her hands were shaking so badly. When she finally finished tying the laces in a double-bow, she checked herself for injuries. She had a minor laceration on the heel of her right hand, from where she had fallen forward on the terrace, and she had a graze on the inside of her right arm from scrambling over the fences. She had gotten away remarkably lightly – unlike her parents.

Tears welled in her eyes as her mind grasped the enormity of the evening's events. Her father and stepmother were dead. Dead! And it was her fault. She was to blame! She should have ushered them upstairs and called for support the moment she saw the news about Jane. Resolutely, she forced those emotions back into that other compartment in her mind. There was no time for grieving or self-recrimination now. That would have to come later. She raised her head sharply. She could hear a siren. It was far away but getting closer all the time. That, at least, must drive the X-Rays away.

Sandy shivered in the chill evening air and wished she were wearing something more substantial than the thin cotton tee shirt. She briefly considered taking shelter inside the summerhouse, but she knew she could not stay here. With three dead bodies in the house, the police would soon be combing the gardens, particularly the sheds and outbuildings, in search of suspects. Sandy had to avoid the police. If they found her, there would inevitably be questions. Who? Why? Soon the Press would be involved and the whole story would be in the public domain. It could cause a major international incident. At the very least, it would embarrass the British Government. Either that or the Service would deny all knowledge of her; paint her as a delusional lunatic and throw her to the wolves.

No, her first priority was to evade capture. She had done it before, both in training and for real in Bosnia. There was a procedure for emergencies such as this, drummed into every officer during training. She had to find a phone and call in. They would come for her and take her to safety. Before she could do that, she had to put distance between herself and the scene of the incident as quickly as she possibly could. The fact that she could regard the brutal murders of her father and stepmother as an *incident* was testament to the way her mind had been trained to work in such an emergency.

The wailing siren was coming closer and closer, until it stopped as the police arrived outside the house.

Barney started to bark again.

***

The van was two streets away when, with blue lights flashing and siren wailing, the first police car sped by in the opposite direction. Another followed seconds later. The leader sat in the cab alongside the driver; the rest of his team were in the back. The two that were still breathing sat on the floor with their backs to the sidewalls and avoided looking at the corpse of their colleague. They both looked up like startled rabbits when they heard the sirens so close, then the sound faded into the distance and they relaxed.

'That was close,' one remarked to break the uncomfortable silence.

His companion merely nodded and stared unseeingly at the lock mechanism on the rear doors. Fifteen minutes later they were on the M53 speeding southwards.

***

Wearily, Sandy clambered to her feet and, keeping to the shadows, approached the back of the house. The Fletchers lived here, she remembered. A nice, retired couple, just like her parents. Just like nearly everyone else in this exclusive neighbourhood of substantial detached houses, each with a large back garden and manicured front lawn. Dare she bang on the window and ask for their help? They would help her, unhesitatingly; they had known her since she was eleven years old. No, the risk was too great. Her mere presence in their house might just condemn them to death. Cautiously, she skirted the house and approached the side gate. A six-inch galvanised steel bolt secured the gate, preventing it from being opened from outside. Fortunately, there was no padlock securing it, so she eased it back as quietly as possible and lifted the latch.

The Fletchers' driveway opened onto the turning circle at the end of a cul-de-sac called Britten Close. Tall sodium street-lamps bathed the area in a warm amber glow. There was no one in sight and all was peaceful as the inhabitants sat snugly in their living rooms behind drawn curtains. Apparently, the sounds of the gunshots she had fired from her bedroom window and the subsequent police sirens had gone unnoticed here.

Checking again that she was unobserved, Sandy quietly closed the gate behind her and hurried to the main footpath. Suddenly realising that she was still holding the revolver in clear view, she concealed it under the front of her tee shirt and folded her arms across her body to hold it in place.

Sandy walked quickly along the footpath toward the open end of the cul-de-sac. She could hear more sirens now, seeming to come from all directions and converging on this normally tranquil suburban neighbourhood. This was a major concern. It would not be long before the police broadcast her description. Twenty-four years old, five-foot-eight, slim with blonde hair and blue-eyes. Dressed as she was in a light tee shirt and jeans and no coat, she would not get far on foot before someone noticed her.

Just then, a car turned into the road and stopped thirty yards ahead. Sandy slowed her pace and lowered her head but watched closely. A man, suited and carrying a briefcase got out of the passenger side and approached the nearest house. The driver, however, remained in the car. As she got closer, Sandy could see that the driver was speaking into a microphone. Clearly, the car was a minicab. Probably, it had brought the suited man from the railway station, two miles away. Her heart beat faster. This was her way out, but how best to approach it? She had a gun. It would be an easy matter to hijack the vehicle, but what would she do with the driver? Obviously, she could not kill him, and wherever she might leave him, he would soon raise the alarm. The police – and the X-Rays – would have a trail to follow.

She could simply ask the driver to take her somewhere, anywhere away from here, but she had no money. If she ran off without paying, he would probably inform the police and once again, there would be a trail to follow. Before she could formulate a plan, she had drawn level with the cab. Impulsively, she reached out and grabbed the rear door handle. It was unlocked so she dived into the back seat, sliding quickly across so she was sitting directly behind the driver, making it difficult for him to get a look at her.

'Hey,' the driver protested in an accent that was an uneasy marriage of Scouse and the Indian sub-continent, 'I'm not for hire.'

'Why not, you're a cabby aren't you?' Sandy challenged, affecting a strong Belfast accent to disguise the modulated tones that betrayed her middle-class breeding and private education. She looked away as the middle-aged driver strained to look at her over his shoulder.

'Yes, miss, that is true, but I have another fare to collect. I'm not free. I'm very sorry.'

'Well,' Sandy said sharply, 'you can drop me on the way, can't you?'

The driver waggled his head in that uniquely Indian manner. 'Madam, I am not supposed to pick up passengers from the street. My licence only allows pre-booked passengers.'

'Look, mate,' Sandy replied in a pleading tone and thickening the accent even more, 'I'm here now. I need a ride. I had a row with my boyfriend and he dumped me in this God-forsaken hole and drove off with my coat and my handbag. I've got no money, I'm cold and I need help.'

Sandy prepared herself for his response. He may simply refuse her request or he might agree and demand payment in kind. Her training dictated that providing a sexual service would be preferable to using the gun to force the issue. A five-minute blowjob would almost certainly guarantee his discretion, especially if he was married. Using the gun, however, would ensure that the story would be in tomorrow's newspapers. Nevertheless, with all that had happened tonight, if he dared to ask for sex, she would beat the bastard senseless and lock him in the boot of his own taxi. To her relief, her concern was ill founded.

'Okay,' he replied after a moment's thought. 'Look, I have to go to Wallasey to collect my next fare. I can drop you off anywhere you like on the way.'

Sandy breathed a sigh of relief. Wallasey was far enough away from here.

'Thanks,' she said, 'that's great. I've got friends in Wallasey.'

At Sandy's request, the cabby dropped her near a phone box on the outskirts of the town. Before she got out of the car, he reached awkwardly behind his seat and handed her a few ten-pence coins and a five pound note.

'You'll need coins for the phone,' he said.

Sandy could not tell him that the number she was going to call required no money.

'Thanks,' she said. 'What's the fiver for?'

He indicated a pub opposite the phone box. 'You can buy yourself a drink in there while you wait for your friends. It's too cold to stand around outside without a coat.'

His generosity brought tears to Sandy's eyes. 'Thanks. That's really nice of you. I really appreciate you helping me.'

'No worries,' he said. The words sounded odd in his accent, reminding Sandy of the movie, *Crocodile Dundee*. He went on, 'I have a teenage daughter. I would like to think that someone would do the same for her if she was in trouble.'

Sandy felt choked with sudden emotion. 'You're a good man. Thank you.'

Sandy watched the cab drive away before she entered the phone-box. She punched a six-digit number on the keypad. The phone was answered on the first ring.

'Yes?' A single word uttered by a male voice, giving nothing away.

'Caesar officer in flight. Need urgent assistance.'

'ID, please?'

'Curlew.'

'Ah yes. The shootings on The Wirral.'

'You know already?' Sandy was surprised at the speed with which news of the incident had circulated.

'Yes, it was flagged up when the police responded to the call. All Service officers' addresses are monitored for incidents. You're listed as non-operational. What happened?'

'Three-plus X-Rays attacked the house; one eliminated; one possibly wounded.'

'We have only two elderly civilian casualties,' he said.'

Sandy swallowed hard to clear a lump in her throat. 'My parents.'

'I'm sorry.'

The compassion in those two words almost caused her to break down, but she steeled herself and replied, 'But there was also one X-Ray down, a definite kill.'

'Then they must have cleaned up before they left,' he said tersely. 'What is your status?'

Sandy considered the question. Red would mean that she was in immediate, life-threatening danger, or seriously wounded. A Condition Red would precipitate armed response from police or the SAS within minutes. Orange meant she was in imminent danger of discovery or capture. This too would probably result in a helicopter scramble. If blue or green, she would not be calling for assistance.

'Yellow,' she replied. This fitted the bill – out of immediate danger but in need of support.

'Stand by.' A few seconds silence, then, 'We have your location as Leasowe Road, Wallasey, Wirral.'

Sandy read the location notice fixed to the back wall of the telephone kiosk. 'Correct,' she confirmed. 'I'll wait in the pub opposite. It's called The George.'

'The George,' he repeated. 'Are you armed?'

'Yes.'

'Someone will be with you in thirty minutes.'

'Thanks,' she said, but the phone had already gone dead.

Even though the revolver was slim and compact, it was still too bulky to fit inside the pockets of Sandy's tight jeans, so she jammed it into the waistband in the small of her back. It was uncomfortable but at least the tee shirt hid it from view and it should stay in place as long as she was careful how she moved. She pushed open the door of the pub and a wall of sound assailed her senses. The voices of the predominantly young, predominantly male customers competed with the thumping base and strident electro-synthesisers of the "Garage" music playing on the jukebox. The air was thick with smoke and the smell of sour beer. There was a large central area where most of the clientele stood in closely packed but distinct groups, each customer clutching a pint of lager or stout in one hand and, many of them, a cigarette in the other. A lot of the men (and a few women) sported replica Liverpool F.C. shirts as they stood around talking up tomorrow's big home-match against Chelsea. A few tables and chairs were set around the edges of the room, occupied mainly by couples, or groups of young women.

From the moment she walked in, Sandy became aware of nudges and whispered comments between many of the men. Sandy was a beautiful young woman, a classic English rose with fine bone structure, skin like porcelain and sparkling blue eyes. Her features were further accentuated by her tied-back, natural blonde hair. Her looks could open many doors and soften the hardest male heart, but at times like this her beauty made it hard to blend into a crowd, especially when wearing a tight tee shirt with her nipples protruding through the material because of the cold night air – despite the fact that she was wearing a bra. She ignored the comments, some admiring, some crudely suggestive, and pushed her way through to the bar. Immediately a youth of nineteen or twenty, wearing a Liverpool shirt, sidled up to her.

'Buy you a drink, luv?' he asked.

Sandy sighed with frustration and adopted a broad Liverpool accent, the better to fit in. It would also distance her from the Ulsterwoman that the taxi driver would remember if questioned.

'I'll get me own, thanks,' and then to the barman, 'Large scotch and a bottle of Diet Coke, please.' She sensed the youth watching her as she downed the scotch in one and then filled the glass with the Coke. Sandy heard him order three pints of lager as she walked away from the bar. She found a seat where she could watch the two entrances, and tried to ignore the admiring glances. She prayed that none of the young men would pluck up the courage to talk to her, but her prayers went unanswered. The lad that had spoken to her at the bar approached her, placing his glass heavily on the table.

'Mind if I join you, like, luv?'

She looked up at him. He was slightly the worse for wear. His eyes lacked focus and he was swaying on his feet. Rejecting him would show him up in front of his mates, who, she could see, were avidly watching his progress from across the room. If she embarrassed him, he might cause a scene and draw unwelcome attention from everyone within earshot.

'Alright then – if I can 'ave a fag,' she replied, laying on the Scouse accent with a trowel. She took one from a proffered pack of *Players* and waited for him to light it. She inhaled deeply. It was her first cigarette since giving up smoking in Sarajevo, four months before, when the price of a pack of black-market *Marlboros* rocketed to forty US dollars.

The boy sat down beside her. Strangely, he was, after all, a welcome distraction. His overtures prevented her from brooding about her parents and Jane – and the others. He made the time pass more quickly and she acted her part, reposting his chat-up lines and parrying his clumsy attempts at physical contact.

Eventually, a woman appeared in the doorway. She was taller than Sandy with a wiry build and frizzy strawberry-blonde hair tied back in a ponytail. They made eye contact and recognised each other immediately.

'Oh, look,' Sandy said, maintaining the Scouse accent and stubbing out her second purloined cigarette. 'Me friend's here, now. I gotta go.'

'Can I see you again, like?' the youth asked, slurring his words, his face showing his disappointment after such a promising start.

'Yeah, o' course,' Sandy promised, forcing herself to smile. 'I'll see yuz here again tomorrow night or maybe Sunday.'

The boy brightened at the prospect. 'Right, see you then, then.' He reluctantly left the women and returned to suffer the jeers and catcalls of his friends.

Sandy stood and greeted her rescuer. 'Hello, Maggie,' she smiled through eyes once more clouded with tears.

'Hello, Sandy. Come on; let's get you out of here.'

The two women left the pub together as the boy's friends taunted him mercilessly. The last distinct word that Sandy heard from the group was "lesbian".

Chapter 3

The Director General of the Secret Intelligence Service, MI6, traditionally bears the code-name C, after the organisation's founding chief, Captain Sir George Mansfield Smith-Cumming, RN, who used that single letter as his signature. The current C was James Barrington. He had succeeded to the post only six weeks earlier, following the resignation of his predecessor, Sir Vivian Webber, in the aftermath of the ill-fated covert mission in the Balkans. Sir Vivian had subsequently died of a sudden heart attack, a few weeks later.

Five-foot-eleven with a slim build, Barrington wore his wiry grey hair short and sported a bristling silver moustache, making him look older than his fifty-two years. He was here at the request of his opposite number, the Director General of MI5, also known as K, after their founder, Major General Sir Vernon Kell. Under normal circumstances, Barrington would be dressed in a smart business suit for a meeting such as this, but given the lateness of the hour and the urgency of the situation, he was dressed casually in a tweed jacket and brown corduroy slacks.

Barrington looked impatiently at his watch. It was two-thirty on Saturday morning and the idiot security guard was making a point of thoroughly checking his ID. Having rushed here from his crash pad in Battersea, he was less than impressed at the delay.

'I'll get someone to escort you, sir,' the officer said at last, handing back the ID.

'I know the damned way, man! I've been here a hundred times before, as well you know!'

The security guard was unfazed by Barrington's tone. 'Yes, sir. Nevertheless . . . Sam, please show Mister Barrington to the DG's office.'

Fuming, Barrington followed the second security guard to the lift.

'Here we are, sir,' said his escort as they reached the door to the holy-of-holies – the DG's office.

'Thank you,' Barrington replied tersely as he knocked and entered.

'Oh, hello James,' said K. 'How good of you to come. Do come in.'

Above average height and pencil-thin, fifty-seven year old Amanda Gillette was everyone's idea of a girls' school headmistress. Her thin, angular face, close-trimmed hair, the colour of stainless steel, and gold-rimmed spectacles made her appear severe and humourless. It was an appearance, though contrary to her true nature, she made little attempt to dispel. She was standing in the centre of the room, wearing a plain navy-blue dress and a white knitted cardigan.

'Quite all right, Amanda,' replied C, covering his ill humour with urbane charm. 'What's this all about?' It was then that he noticed another person was already in the room with K.

Neil Mitchell-Hunter, the Director General of the Covert Surveillance Resource Service or CSR was sitting on one of two red sofas, set at right angles around a square coffee table.

Aged fifty-five, he was five-foot-nine, twenty pounds overweight and wore his sparse, sand-coloured hair combed over a bald pate. To Barrington's irritation, Mitchell-Hunter, in contrast to himself and K, was dressed immaculately in an expensively tailored grey lambs-wool suit, a blue silk shirt and a yellow silk tie with blue diagonal stripes.

As Director General of CSR, Mitchell-Hunter's code-name was Eagle.

CSR, usually pronounced phonetically as "Caesar", had its origins in the Special Operations Executive (SOE), an organisation founded during the Second World War to train and supply agents to help organise and inspire resistance groups in France, Norway and other countries occupied by the Nazis. At the end of the war the bulk of SOE officers were absorbed into MI6, but at the behest of Winston Churchill, a nucleus of specialists secretly formed a new intelligence-gathering and special operations organisation that could augment, or work independently of their more famous cousins, MI5 and MI6.

Since the creation of MI5 and MI6 in 1910, successive UK Governments had continually denied their very existence. The Security Service Act of 1989 changed all that, officially acknowledging MI5 for the first time. Another Act of Parliament was due to follow a few years later that would legitimise MI6. The Government's intention was to open the security and intelligence services to public scrutiny and accountability. Whilst MI5 and MI6 were to be demystified and shown to be accountable to the rule of law, CSR was deliberately excluded from the legislation. Unknown, unchallenged and unaccountable to Press and public, even its finances were concealed within the accounts of the Cabinet Office as "Supplementary Services".

CSR officers specialised in under-cover, close surveillance operations. They would infiltrate into the world of their targets. They might spend weeks, months or even years living among anarchists, terrorists or even animal rights activists, gathering intelligence and passing information back to their controllers. It was a highly dangerous role, during which time the under-cover officer would be in constant danger of discovery, perhaps leading to physical harm, even death. CSR operatives had been active during many national emergencies, starting with Palestine in 1948, continuing with Suez in 1956, the 1962 Cuban Missile Crisis and, of course, Northern Ireland. Infiltrating the ranks of Britain's enemies – and occasionally her allies (as in the case of the Cuban crisis), the intelligence they passed back to the Government helped shape the United Kingdom's policies, actions and reactions during those dangerous times.

Other CSR specialists had been instrumental in neutralising certain individuals, at home and abroad, individuals whose very existence was deemed contrary the safety and security of the realm. An IRA bomb-maker met his own maker due to a flaw introduced into his device courtesy of a CSR mole. Others met with car accidents or died from carbon monoxide poisoning when their gas heaters suddenly developed faults. The CSR "black ops" teams were boundless in their creativity.

'Good,' said K. 'Now that we're all here, let's get started, shall we? James, come and sit down. Help yourself to coffee,' she said indicating a Thermos jug and some mugs set out on the small table. 'Neil, perhaps you'd like to tell us why you wanted us to meet here tonight?'

Eagle crossed one leg over the other and cleared his throat. 'Thank you, Amanda. This evening, or rather, yesterday evening, one of my junior officers went berserk, killing one of my men and wounding the other. She also shot and killed her own parents before escaping.'

'Oh my goodness,' said K. 'How terrible. What prompted her to do it, do you know?'

'I sent two officers to bring her in following the assassination of Jane Badell, yesterday afternoon. Instead of coming quietly, she produced a gun and started shooting.'

'What connection did she have with Jane Badell?' asked K. At that very moment, MI5 officers were working with police trying to establish a motive for the reporter's death. Her work reporting conflicts abroad, particularly her most recent time in Bosnia suggested that it might well be the work of foreign agents.

'Our girl knew Badell, personally,' Eagle explained. 'I simply wanted to get to her before the police did. As you know we – all of us – like to keep this sort of thing in the family.'

K nodded. 'True. Do you think she may have known something about the hit? We are currently under the assumption that it was ordered by the Yugoslavian government.'

'You may be right, there,' C chipped in. 'Belgrade considered Badell's broadcasts from Sarajevo to be biased against the Bosnian Serbs and critical of the JNA's continued involvement in that theatre.'

'Yes, I know,' said K. 'The JNA[1] were supposed to have pulled out in early May.'

---

[1] The Jugoslovenska Narodna Armija or JNA was the national army of Yugoslavia. Most of its officers and men were ethnic Serbs.

'But,' C continued, 'Badell's crew filmed MiG's with JNA markings bombing the Muslim enclave of Žepa in June'.

'It seems the Serb nationalists tried to wipe Badell's team out,' added Eagle. 'Several were killed but Badell and her cameraman escaped.

'So, it looks like yesterday's assassination was just a pointless act of revenge,' said K.

The two men shrugged their shoulders at the speculative comment.

'Perhaps they wanted to eliminate a potential eye-witness if and when Slobodan Milosević ever goes on trial in The Hague,' Eagle suggested.

'How is your officer involved in all this, the one that was the subject of tonight's incident?' K asked again.

Eagle frowned. 'It has been suggested that she may have been involved in Badell's assassination,' he explained. 'And her actions last evening do seem, unfortunately, to support that hypothesis.'

'According to our CIA contacts, Amanda,' C added, 'there was a traitor in Badell's team, presumably a Serb sympathiser.'

'But what has that to do with Neil's officer, James?' asked K. 'Does she have any connection with Yugoslavia?'

'Yes, she was one of four Caesar officers in Badell's team in Sarajevo,' Eagle replied.

'They were there to apprehend a Serb officer – a suspected war criminal,' C added.

'My goodness, you kept that well under wraps. Was Jane Badell aware of this?'

'Of course she was aware; she was one of our most useful agents.'

K's jaw dropped. 'Jane Badell, the BBC war correspondent, worked for SIS?'

C shrugged his shoulders and smiled crookedly. 'Yes, she's been working for Six for nearly twenty years, since the Yom Kippur war, in fact.'

'Well, I'm astonished!' said K. 'I had no idea. Were you aware that she was in danger?'

'There were hints coming out of a source in Belgrade,' C replied, 'but we believed it was all hot air. We certainly didn't think that the Yugoslavs were in any sort of position to mount such an operation in London.'

'That falls into my domain, James,' said K. 'Had you passed the intelligence to MI5 we might have been able to save her.'

'As I said,' C stressed, 'there did not seem to be much point. We know differently now, of course.'

'Tell me more about this escapade in Bosnia,' said K.

Eagle and C exchanged glances. For a moment neither man spoke. K's frustration mounted.

'Well?'

It was C that finally replied.

'When the Croatian war broke out in June last year, the UN immediately started taking an interest. The Security Council passed a resolution banning the trade in arms to any of the combatant republics. Unfortunately, this didn't stop the fighting. In October, they started sending envoys, including our very own former Foreign Secretary, Lord Carrington, to try to negotiate a peace settlement, but to no avail. By November, with the fighting spreading in area and intensity, the UN was desperate for information from the ground. We sent a couple of our chaps who were based in Zagreb, to have a nose around. They were kitted out with a white Land Rover with UN markings, British Army uniforms with UN blue berets; the lot.'

'But surely, the UN didn't have people on the ground at that time,' said K.

'Correct,' C agreed. 'The first contingent didn't arrive until a month or so later. It was a risk, but a risk committee, headed by Sir Vivian himself, concluded that the worst that would happen, if our men were caught, was that they would be drummed out of the country.'

'And what did happen?'

'A unit of the Croatian Serb rebel militia, backed by a column of JNA regular infantry and armour, was rampaging through the hills in north western Croatia. Our people were tracking them but keeping out of sight. Most of the towns and villages capitulated fairly quickly, offering little, if any, resistance. But one village, which apparently contained a sizable detachment of Croatian paramilitary police, offered serious resistance and caused some casualties amongst the militia. The JNA brought the tanks up and pounded the village. It was a pile of rubble before they stopped the shelling, by which time all resistance had long since ceased.' He paused and sipped his coffee before continuing.

'Our chaps had set up an observation post from where they watched the action. Then, after the village had fallen, they saw members of the militia herding over a hundred prisoners, including women and children from surrounding farms and hamlets, into a field on one of the farms. It was pretty obvious what was going to happen and our men tried to do something about it.'

'My Goodness!' said K. 'What did they do?'

'It seems they thought the best course of action was to alert the commander of the JNA unit in the hope that, as a professional soldier, he might be able to prevent a massacre by the militia. They communicated their intentions back to base by radio. And that was the last we heard from them.'

'Another team was sent out to find out what happened. They tracked down a couple of kids – teenagers – a boy and a girl who had somehow avoided the round-up, and they got the story from them.

'Basically, it seems our men did as they planned and waltzed into the JNA command post. The teenagers saw the JNA vehicles turn up at the farm with our men following in the UN Land Rover, but by then, the deed had been done. The captives had been slaughtered with hand-grenades and machine-guns, and the militia were finishing off anyone still breathing with knives. Whether or not it had always been the intention, or if the fact that the massacre had already occurred prompted it, we don't know, but the JNA commander ordered our men shot, there and then. The JNA armoured column included a bulldozer, which they used to gouge a trench in the field before pushing the bodies, including those of our chaps, into it and covering them up.'

There followed a long silence as the three directors general contemplated the awful outcome of a valiant attempt to save the lives of innocent civilians. Then C broke the silence again.

'Sir Vivian was absolutely shocked and furious when he found out what had happened – as indeed were we all. Sir Vivian ordered that the name of the JNA commander be discovered. He turned out to be a Lieutenant-Colonel Antonije Szopienice, a Bosnian Serb from the southeast of the country near the border with Serbia. He was a professional soldier who joined the JNA as a subaltern, straight out of university. In 1989, he was an aide to the Military Attaché in the Yugoslavian Embassy in Washington DC, but was recalled at the start of the Croatian emergency. Now, he's a brigadier-general in the army of the breakaway Bosnian Serb state, Republika Srpska.' C looked up but when no questions or comments were forthcoming, he carried on.

'Sir Vivian authorised a mission to capture or kill Szopienice. It was designated Operation *Cevapi*. However, by the time *Cevapi* was ready to get off the ground, our target had disappeared from the Croatian theatre. He surfaced again a month or so later in the Bosnian capital, Sarajevo. By then the Bosnian Government had declared its intention to hold a referendum on secession from Yugoslavia, and Szopienice was rabble-rousing the Serb population against the move.

'The referendum was set for the end of February, and it was decided to send Jane Badell with a news crew to cover the event.'

'How was Badell chosen for this? Not coincidence, surely,' said K.

'Certainly not,' C smiled slyly. 'We have a certain, er, *influence* with "Auntie Beeb". We made sure that Badell was dispatched to Sarajevo with a film crew supplied by us.'

'Us?'

'Six,' C replied. 'With a little support from our friends at Caesar, and the SAS.' C yawned, stretched, and looked at his watch before continuing. 'The whole world now knows that the mission ended in tragedy, although not many know that it was anything but a ghastly accident that several members of the film crew were killed.'

'What really happened?

'The plan was that after the SAS apprehended the target, Badell would make her way back to Sarajevo, where a real BBC film crew would replace our people and continue to report on the siege. Unfortunately, the Serbs got wind of what Badell's team were really up to and took them prisoner. The SAS team were sent back in on a rescue mission, but only Jane and the cameraman made it out. The other four were all killed – or presumed so – until . . .'

'Until?'

'Until Curlew turned up, out of the blue, at our Embassy in Athens a month later,' Eagle put in. It was the first time he had spoken since C had started telling the story.

'Curlew?'

'That's the code-name of the officer that we were talking about at the beginning.'

'How did she get to Athens?' K asked.

'She claims she escaped from her captors by jumping forty feet from a bridge into the River Drina' Eagle explained. 'She says she was sheltered by a Muslim family in a village downriver from Višegrad. At about the same time, the UN negotiated with the Republika Srpska leadership to evacuate a few coach-loads of Muslim civilians from the countryside around Višegrad. Curlew says she borrowed some clothes from one of the Bosnian women and got herself aboard one of the coaches. The coach took them to a refugee camp in Macedonia. Curlew somehow managed to slip away and got to our consulate in Skopje, who arranged her onward travel to Athens.'

'Claims?' K repeated. 'There's a hint of suspicion in that word.'

Eagle sighed and frowned. 'Badell and the cameraman escaped with the help of an SAS detachment. Another experienced MI6 officer was killed in the attempt. Curlew and her Caesar teammate, Tern, were rookies, wet-behind–the-ears young adventuresses who, in retrospect should not have been on that mission at all. How could she have escaped and evaded recapture alone? It has been suggested that she might have been turned in Sarajevo, and betrayed the mission to the general or one of his aides.'

'What evidence do you have to support that?' K asked.

'She had an affair with the target,' Eagle replied.

'Oh, be fair, Neil,' said C. 'That was her job, after all.'

'What are you saying?' K asked, perplexed.

'Curlew and Tern were there to set a honey-trap,' Eagle replied. 'Their mission was to establish a relationship with the target and lure him into a trap.'

K grimaced with distaste. 'How old were these girls?'

Eagle shrugged. 'What difference does it make? That is what they trained for. They knew what they were getting into.'

K shook her head. 'You seem to be basing your assumption of her guilt on the fact she survived. If you follow that line, why not accuse Jane Badell or the cameraman? What about the others? Have their bodies been recovered?'

'No.'

'Okay, so let's say, for argument's sake, that it was the other one, er, Tern – that was the traitor . . . Why are their code-names all bird species, anyway?' She held up a hand.

'Don't bother answering that. But if she were the mole, she may be alive and well in, where was it – Višegrad.'

'Amanda has a point, Neil,' C conceded. 'Whatever the truth, it seems your Curlew had quite an adventure. When did she get home?'

'Towards the end of July,' Eagle replied. 'She was debriefed at our establishment in Buckinghamshire.'

'Did she say anything that might have made you suspect she was the traitor?' K asked.

'She said she believed they were betrayed by someone in Sarajevo,' Eagle replied.

'Did she say who?'

'Not really,' Eagle replied. 'Her story was that the team, in lieu of any intelligence regarding their target, decided to, er, consolidate their cover story. In short, they went on the prowl for News.' He emphasised the word by using the first and second fingers of each hand to mime quotation marks. 'She says that they happened across the nefarious dealings of some senior officers of the United Nations peace-keeping force.'

'Go on?'

'She says that it was only when they reported this back to their superiors that intelligence on the general's whereabouts suddenly came to light. Her argument is that for three months, no one was able to say where the target was, but the day after discovering some juicy info about senior UNPROFOR officers, up he pops. Curlew said she was suspicious about the timing. She alleges that they were sent away because of what they found out.'

'You can understand her feeling that way,' K suggested. 'It does seem a little, um, convenient for certain people?'

'Curlew was, I'm given to understand, very convincing,' said Eagle. 'Enquiries were made to the US through our CIA contacts and to the UN high command about her allegations.'

'And what was the result?'

'They came back and said it was all a load of tosh, quite frankly. There was nothing to back up her story.'

'What happened then?'

'Curlew was something of an emotional wreck. We thought it best for everyone concerned if she were rested. We offered her home-leave for a while. If nothing else, it would keep her out of the way whilst we conducted more enquiries. She said she couldn't face sitting at home day after day with nothing to do except dwell on the deaths of her friends, so we agreed to find her a desk job. Problem was her home is on the Wirral and we don't have offices up in that part of the country, so we asked for her to be seconded to you for a few months.'

K looked up sharply. 'To Five?'

'Yes. She's been working in Admin Branch in Liverpool for the past month or so.'

'But now you think you should have kept her under tighter control, I imagine,' K suggested.

'Yes, with hindsight, perhaps we should not have given her the benefit of the doubt.'

'What do you plan to do now?' asked K. 'Do you need our help to track her down?'

'Yes and no,' Eagle replied. 'She's in one of your safe houses with another of my officers and one of your Protection Branch people.'

'So you caught her after all,' said K.

'Not quite,' Eagle admitted. 'After escaping from my team she turned up ten miles away and called into Central Support. One of my officers was in the area for another matter, with one of yours as a minder. Support arranged for them to pick her up. And that's where we are.'

'So you want me to hand her over. Is that what this meeting is all about?'

'Yes. That and the need to gloss over yesterday's events, especially the incident on the Wirral.'

'Gloss over?' K repeated incredulously. 'Three people are dead, Neil, one of them a world famous TV reporter, and two innocent pensioners! How do you *gloss over* that?'

'Four, actually,' said Eagle, referring to his dead officer, 'but, yes, I see what you mean.'

'What do you intend to do with this girl if you get her?'

'Question her, of course. She has a lot of explaining to do. Things are not looking very good as far as she is concerned.'

'You're convinced she's your traitor?'

'Either that or she's got a screw loose,' Eagle opined.

'Actually, it seems Jane Badell was very impressed with your girl,' C commented. 'I heard she acquitted herself admirably in Bosnia. Proved herself to be very resourceful.'

'As is demonstrated by her apparent escape from her captors,' K added. 'And tonight she escaped from your goons and melted away into the night, avoiding them and the police and only rocked up when she chose to do so by phoning in to Central Support ten miles from the scene!'

C could not contain a wry smile. 'That does show considerable resourcefulness!'

'If she were your traitor,' suggested K, 'would it not seem rather strange that, having gone to all that trouble to escape, she would phone up and turn herself in?'

Eagle shrugged. 'Double bluff, perhaps? What I don't understand is why she killed her parents?'

'I don't know,' said K. 'None of it makes sense. If she was working for the Serb nationalists – or anyone else, for that matter, don't you think she would have called *them* for assistance rather than place herself back in the hands of the Security Service? No, it doesn't wash. I think she resisted your people because she thought they were someone else.'

'Serbs you mean?' C suggested.

'Maybe,' replied K, 'but if you believe her tale of goings on in Sarajevo, it might have been any number of agencies trying to tie up loose ends. The poor girl must have believed they were there to harm her. She must have been terrified! She might even have shot her parents to save them from a far worse fate.' She stood and paced up and down for a few moments. 'Why hasn't that story come out?' K asked, turning on her heel to face the two men once more. 'Why didn't Badell break the Sarajevo story when she got back to London?'

'Sir Vivian told her it was not conducive to her health,' C replied. 'He told her to keep that little gem under her hat – if she knew what was good for her.'

'And much good it did her,' K mused. 'What was it all about, this scandal?'

C shrugged eloquently. 'I, for one, don't know. It was hushed up at such high level, even I was excluded.'

'But not your predecessor,' K observed.'

'Yes, and he is dead,' Eagle remarked bluntly.

'But you know, Neil,' said K. It was more a statement than a question.

'Yes,' Eagle confirmed, 'and I've been told, in no uncertain terms, never to reveal even the allegations to anyone.'

'They must be true, then,' C muttered mischievously.

'Look,' said Eagle, 'we still have the issue of what to do about tonight's events.'

'Why should we do anything?' asked C.

'Has there not already been enough damage done as a result of the Bosnian balls-up?' said Eagle, looking at C. 'Including your predecessor getting the chop. Do we really want the newspapers examining our poo and dragging us further into the mire?'

'Let's get back to the question of the young woman,' K interjected.

'I want her brought in and questioned,' said Eagle.

'Will she get a fair hearing?' asked K. 'You seem to have convinced yourself already that she's guilty.'

'Yes,' C agreed. 'Why not hand her over to Six? We'll soon get the truth out of her.'

Eagle nodded. 'Good idea. There might be all sorts of repercussions if she came back to Caesar. She killed one of our own, after all.'

'She's already on secondment to Five,' K asserted. 'We'll keep her. We'll question her about tonight and about Sarajevo . . .'

'You can't do that,' Eagle interrupted. 'I strongly advise you not to delve into anything to do with Sarajevo.'

'Whyever not?' K demanded.

A Desire for Vengeance

'Because, Amanda, what they discovered there is so sensitive it could cause an international incident, a diplomatic nightmare. The credibility of the United Nations Protection Force would be jeopardised. No, you must not go there! '

'What could possibly be so damaging?' asked K. She looked at C but got no support there. 'Okay,' she conceded. We will concentrate only on events that happened after her capture. If she satisfies me that she is reliable, we'll put her to work in a different part of the country.'

'She'll need a new identity,' suggested Eagle.

'And what if she doesn't pass muster?' asked C.

'Then we three must meet again and decide what to do with her,' K replied. The two men nodded their concurrence. Then K grimaced. 'We still have three very public murders to explain. How do we play the events of yesterday publicly? We have to act quickly,' she added, 'before the 'papers come out.' She looked at her watch. 'Bother! It's already too late for first editions.'

'Well,' said Eagle, 'I've already taken the liberty of pulling some strings with the Cheshire Police and of having certain, er, assumptions about our little Curlew planted in the minds of the paparazzi.' He explained further.

'That will work, as far as it goes,' said K, 'but with a little modification, we can kill two birds with one stone.'

C looked at K and grinned. 'Was that pun intended, Amanda?'

Chapter 4

'God, Sandy! You look like shit!'

Sandy had not slept at all well. The events of the past six months crowded her mind. Feelings of guilt at her own survival tortured her. What could she have done differently? Could she – should she – have done anything differently? Were the deaths her fault? If not her fault, then who was to blame? When, out of sheer exhaustion, she did eventually fall asleep, the nightmares began. She had woken suddenly with the feeling that the bed was tipping over, her fingers clawing at the bed-sheet to save herself from falling. The feeling passed and Sandy lay on her back, bathed in sweat, her heart thumping. Desperate for more sleep but afraid of the horrors that sleep would bring, she dragged herself out of bed and stumbled into the kitchen looking drawn and haggard, the skin around her eyes red and puffy.

The safe house was a scruffy, two bedroom flat in a tower block on a council estate in a rundown part of Liverpool. The journey from Wallasey, via the Kingsway Tunnel, in a dented and rusty Ford Capri, had taken about thirty minutes. The driver was Adrian, a Scottish MI5 Protection Branch officer who, after the initial brief introductions, had said nothing, asked nothing.

'That's precisely how I feel,' Sandy replied to Maggie's greeting. She poured water from the kettle into a mug with coffee granules and opened the fridge.

'There's no milk,' said Maggie.

Sandy pouted and took a seat facing her friend across the table. 'So what's a nice Cheltenham girl like you doing in a dump like this?'

Tall and athletic with frizzy strawberry-blonde hair, Maggie was product of Cheltenham Ladies College and Oxford University, where she gained a BA in mathematics, and represented the university in track and field events. She had been on the same Caesar training intake as Sandy and they had been great friends throughout the six-month course.

Maggie sipped her coffee and marvelled at her friend's resilience, making small talk despite the way she must be feeling. Perhaps that was Sandy's defence mechanism.

'I'm giving evidence in the Provo trial,' Maggie replied and, to her astonishment, Sandy even managed a little smile, although it did not reach her eyes.

'Ah, so you're the "Mysterious *Femme Fatale*", as *The Sun* puts it; giving evidence behind the screen.'

Maggie put the mug down on the table and tightened the band holding her ponytail, drawing her reddish-blonde hair back from her forehead, emphasising her strong, angular facial features. Sandy thought she looked like a character in an ancient Greek frieze. She remembered the day the instructor gave them their code-names. Sandy was designated Curlew and Maggie Petrel. Caroline, another friend and fellow trainee, had laughed and said that Maggie should be Flamingo because she was a long legged bird with red plumage.

'Yep, that's me, Maggie replied. 'After you and the others went off on your mission to foreign climes, I started screwing Martin May, the son of Danny May – second-in-command of the Liverpool cell.' She paused and Sandy nodded understanding. Screwing gangsters, terrorists and other unsavoury pond-life was part of the job description.

'So how did you infiltrate?' she asked.

Maggie laughed and slipped into a strong Ulster accent. 'He thought I was a slapper from 'Derry working on the Belfast to Liverpool ferry.' Maggie dropped the accent and continued, 'I passed on details of the bombing run they were planning in Liverpool city centre. Special Branch intercepted the delivery team on the way in and the rest of the cell was picked up in coordinated raids.'

'So you've been living here during the trial?'

'Yes, three weeks, now, with the lovely Adrian. He doesn't say much but he fucks like a rabbit. It passes the otherwise dull evenings,' she said with a wink. 'Anyway, once my part is over I'll go down to London and Adrian will have to revert to self-abuse. How about you? I bumped into Jeanette at Park House before coming up here. She told us you had a bad time.'

'She shouldn't have,' said Sandy; 'she should know better than to gossip about operations, particularly that one.'

'Of course,' Maggie shrugged and smiled conspiratorially, 'but you know how we girls like to talk. When did you get back?'

'Six weeks ago. They decided to take me off ops for a while. I've been seconded to MI5 in Liverpool, working for Admin Branch.'

'That's a bit tame, isn't it?'

'I've had all the excitement I need for a while,' Sandy said miserably. 'Did Jeanette tell you about Caroline?'

Maggie frowned. 'Yes. It's terrible, but these things happen. Ours is a dangerous calling. We're like soldiers in wartime; we have to expect casualties.'

'It's such a waste.' The tears finally began to roll down Sandy's cheeks. 'Such a bloody waste!' She dabbed her eyes with a tissue and looked at Maggie. 'The bastards were going to slit our throats!'

Maggie covered Sandy's hand with her own. 'I know you and Caroline were close. I was sorry to hear she'd been . . .'

'Close!' cried Sandy as if the word was somehow derogatory. Then, riding out the storm of emotion that raged through her, she continued more quietly. 'Yes, we were. We became very close friends in Sarajevo – very close.' Sandy's voice tailed off as memories of recent events forced their way once more to the fore. Her face crumpled and her body shook with grief. 'I lost my best friend, and now my dad and stepmother are dead, too. It's all my fault! How am I going to explain all this to my sister?'

Maggie walked around the table and hugged her, resting her cheek on Sandy's head and uttering soothing words that had no discernible effect. Just then, the front door opened and banged shut. Adrian breezed into the kitchen carrying a Co-op carrier bag.

'Hullo, girls,' he said cheerfully, and then caught the atmosphere. Adrian was in his thirties, ten years or so older than the two women. He was a tad shorter than Maggie, with a pale complexion and short ginger hair. He had a deep, cultured voice in which only the over-emphasised vowel sounds betrayed a hint of an Edinburgh accent. He went on hesitantly, 'Er, I've just been out to get some milk and stuff, and a paper.' He threw the latter onto the table and added, 'You're front page news!'

Sandy shrugged Maggie away and wiped at her tears with her fingers. Two photographs dominated the front page, one of Jane Badell and one of Sandy. It was her Graduation picture. In it she was wearing a cloak and a mortarboard and holding up a degree scroll for the camera.

"BRITAIN UNDER THE GUN", the headline shouted. A front-page editorial comment decried the increasing availability of Eastern European firearms in the country since the break-up of the Soviet Union and the Warsaw Pact. It then went on to summarise the two shooting incidents at opposite ends of the country, which it described as unrelated. Following the link, Sandy turned the page and there, accompanied by another photo of herself as a gangly sixteen-year-old with plaited blonde hair reaching past her shoulder blades, sitting astride Piper, her skewbald pony, was a short piece about her parents' deaths. She read the article with mounting disbelief.

DOUBLE SHOOTING TRAGEDY
Daughter sought as parents killed

Cheshire Police are seeking the daughter of a wealthy retired couple found dead in their home on The Wirral last night. Sandra Annette Harris, 24, (pictured) is missing, following the double shooting in the exclusive 'Composers' estate in Amberley. Charles Harris, 68, a retired Lieutenant Colonel of the Royal Engineers, and his wife, Grace, 63, were found shot dead in their £300,000 detached house in Elgar Drive last night. Neighbours called the police after they heard screams coming from the house and shots being fired. A police spokesman said they are treating the case as a domestic incident and are anxious to contact the couple's daughter in connection with the shootings. They described the missing woman as 5' 8" and slim, with blonde hair and blue eyes. The spokesman said that the murder weapon has so far not been recovered and that Miss Harris may still have it in her possession. Members of the public are urged not to approach her but should immediately call 999 if they think they have seen her.

Neighbours described her as "remarkably intelligent" and "very pretty". One, who asked not to be identified, said, "Sandra is a beautiful girl and academically brilliant. She went to Cambridge University and got a double-First in Physics and Electronic Engineering." The neighbour added that since returning recently from Ethiopia, where she was working as a volunteer for a famine relief charity, she had become "reclusive and unapproachable" whereas before, she was "friendly and outgoing". Police have so far refused to comment on the suggestion that she may have spent time in a mental hospital.

Sandy was outraged. 'My God! They think I did it. They think I killed my parents! And where did this crap about being in a mental hospital come from?'

Maggie grabbed the paper from Sandy and quickly read through. Adrian, who, clearly, had already read the article, offered an explanation.

'That's obviously disinformation,' he said. 'I reckon someone planted that part of the story. Now, why? That's the interesting question.'

Maggie looked up from the newspaper. 'It looks like they are trying to set Sandy up as a deranged murderer.'

'Obviously,' agreed Adrian, 'but the question remains. Why?'

'We've got to contact the police,' said Sandy, her voice ragged and desperate. 'We need to clear this up; tell them about the connection with Jane Badell's murder. They need to get after the real killers.'

'The TV reporter?' Maggie shook her head in confusion and turned back to the front page. 'What connection does she have with you?'

'Did Jeanette not tell you?' Sandy asked. 'She was our cover in Bosnia. We were members of her film crew.'

'So you think the attack on you and her murder are connected?'

'Isn't it obvious?'

'What is pretty bloody obvious is that someone doesn't want the connection to be discovered,' said Adrian.

'Yes, but who and why?' asked Sandy.

Maggie posed another question. 'How did these people get your home address?'

Sandy looked quizzically at Maggie then she nodded thoughtfully.

'You're saying that there's a mole in Caesar, or in MI5,' said Sandy. 'It's obvious the operation in Bosnia was betrayed but . . .'

'In Bosnia you were working for MI6 not MI5,' Maggie reminded her. 'The mole has to be in Caesar.'

'Sorry, but who's Caesar?' Adrian asked, puzzled. Maggie and Sandy exchanged glances.

'Caesar provides deep-cover, long-term surveillance operatives to work with Five and Six,' Maggie explained, choosing her words very carefully.

'I thought you both worked for MI5. So, why haven't I heard of this Caesar?'

Maggie began to answer but Sandy cut her off. 'I think we've said too much already.'

'What's with all the secrecy?' Adrian demanded. 'Are we not all on the same side here?'

'It's just that Caesar is under the radar.' Maggie said, and placed a placating hand on Sandy's arm when she tried to prevent her speaking. 'It doesn't appear on any department's budget. Its very existence is secret. Whilst the Government has now finally admitted the existence of MI5, Caesar is still hidden and totally deniable, as are its operatives.' She watched Adrian's eyes as his mind worked on what he had just been told.

'Ahhh! You don't just do surveillance do you? That's what "A" Branch does. What are we talking about here, assassinations? Wet operations, right?'

Maggie was quick to correct him. 'No, no, no. You're barking up the wrong tree. We do long term undercover work . . .' She stopped speaking as Sandy snorted and descended into a fit of giggles. Her whole body shook with hysterical laughter. Maggie and Adrian glanced at one another and then with concern at Sandy. Sandy saw the expressions on their faces and with a supreme effort, controlled her hysterics long enough to explain.

'Yes, Sherlock,' she said, wiping tears from her eyes, 'we specialise in wet operations, alright, but not in the way you mean.' Once again, Sandy shook with paroxysms of laughter at the look of bemusement on Adrian's face. Gradually, however, the hysterical laughter became a high-pitched wail, a primal sound that sent shivers down the spines of both Maggie and Adrian.

'Shit,' said Maggie. 'She's lost it. We've got to get her some help. Call Support. Get a medic in here. I'll take her to her room.'

Chapter 5

Sandy awoke confused and disorientated, and in total darkness. She thought, at first, that she had not opened her eyes; that they were gummed shut by some sticky residue that had built up as she slept. The thought triggered a distant memory from when she was a very young child. Unable to open her eyes the infant Sandy had cried out in panic. Her sister, Samantha, five years her senior, had come to her aid, wiping Sandy's eyelids with a licked thumb until she could blink them open. Sticky eyelids were not the cause this time because Sandy could feel herself blinking. Nervously, she turned her head from side to side but not a glimmer of light showed anywhere within her field of vision. Combined with an oppressive silence, in which she could hear nothing but her own breathing and the thumping of her heart, this fuelled the terrifying thought that somehow, while unconscious, she might have been presumed dead, and was now lying in her coffin awaiting – what? Burial? Cremation?

Oh, God!

She was lying flat on her back, covered up to her chest by a lightweight blanket. Her arms were resting by her sides outside the cover. Moving her left arm seemed only to confirm her fear. She lay within inches of a solid surface on that side. Timidly, she raised a hand upwards, fearful that she would find another barrier close to her face, but the arm flailed in empty space. The same was true to her right.

Thank God, I'm not in my grave, but where am I? Still in the flat? Why is it so dark?

'Is there anyone there?' she asked, softly into the darkness. Her voice echoed back from the walls of a room devoid of soft furnishings that might deaden the sound. Wracking her brain, she tried to recall the sequence of events before falling asleep. She could remember sitting at the table in the kitchen of the flat with Maggie and the Scots guy - what was his name? Adrian. After that, it was hazy. There was something there, an image, a memory, just out of reach. The more she tried to capture it, the more distant it became. After a moment, she gave up and concentrated on her current circumstances.

Sandy placed her hands beneath the blanket and examined her body. There was no pain, no numbness. Everything felt normal. No limbs were missing, no bandages and no restraints. She was wearing a thin cotton nightdress, which reached to her thighs – and nothing else. She wondered where the nightdress had come from. It did not belong to her; she had not worn one since leaving home for university. *God, that was five years ago!* Since then she had usually slept naked, or in a tee shirt and knickers, at most.

Suddenly, with a jolt, the dreadful events at her parents' house came back to her, and she squeezed her eyes shut to control the sudden rush of emotion. With an effort, she forced herself to concentrate on the here and now, and her thoughts returned to the nightdress. It was not rucked up, so whoever put her here must have placed her very carefully before covering her with the blanket. It was evident, by the very decorous nature of her position that she could not have been tossing and turning in her sleep, so her sleep, and her awakening, had to have been controlled by someone, and that someone had obviously used drugs for the purpose.

The bedroom! After the kitchen, she was with Maggie in the bedroom. The paramedics came; only they were not paramedics. They had wanted to give her an injection. "To calm her down," they had said, but Sandy had not believed them, had fought them, but they had overpowered her and the needle went in. The worst of it was that Maggie had helped hold her down while they did it. Maggie had betrayed her! *Oh Maggie!*

Angrily, she threw off the blanket and sat up, half expecting to hit her head on something above, but there was no jarring impact, and she swung her legs around to sit on the edge of the bed. Her feet rested on a hard, cold tiled floor. The nightdress hung oddly around her shoulders, and feeling behind with one hand, she realised that it was actually a surgical gown that she was wearing, the back laced together with tapes, tied in bows.

Gingerly, she stood and felt her way to the end of the bed, and then along the wall. Within a few steps, she had reached a corner and turned along the new wall. Two steps further and her bare foot collided with something that went skittering across the tiles away from her. She moved forward again, more cautiously, until her toe touched the object again. She bent down and felt it with her hands. It was an empty plastic bucket. *So much for the en suite*, she thought grimly. Thankful that she currently had no need to use that facility, she continued her exploration of the room.

On the third wall, her hands discovered a steel door. No handle on the inside, and no discernible hinges but it was definitely a door. A square-shaped recess was positioned at about head height – probably a peephole, and whatever space lay beyond the door, be it another room or a corridor, it was also in darkness. That, or there was a shutter of some kind on the far side of the door preventing the leakage of light into the room. *Not a room – a cell!*

Suddenly, the light came on; a harsh, bright light that overwhelmed her fully dilated pupils, dazzling her and disorientating her once more. Sandy yelled in surprise and threw her hands up to shield her eyes. Blindly stepping into the middle of the room, her thigh collided painfully with some immovable object. Cursing, she felt her way back to the bed and sat down, her eyes gradually adjusting to the light.

The cell was about ten feet long by eight wide. There were no windows; the four walls and the floor were all covered in white ceramic tiles. Even the steel door, set in the middle of one of the shorter walls, was painted white. The light was recessed into a white ceiling, behind a steel grill, and its glare reflected from all the white surfaces, hurting her eyes.

The bed on which she sat was, in fact, a six-foot by two-foot, white-enamelled metal shelf, attached to the wall two feet above the floor, with legs on the two outer corners. The bedding consisted of a thin canvas mattress covered with a white under-sheet, on top of which were one polyester pillow and the lightweight blanket, which was light grey in colour, providing the only point of relief from the unremitting bright white glare.

Apart from the bed, the only other furniture in the room comprised two chairs set facing each other across a small square table (against which she had hurt her thigh, a few moments earlier). The seats and backrests of the chairs were constructed of latticed white metal, and the table was a simple white metal surface supported by a central pedestal. It was bolted to the floor, as were the chairs. This room, she thought grimly, existed for one purpose – interrogation.

She looked around for her clothes, but whoever had put the surgical gown on her must have taken them away. Memories of the cruel abuse she suffered at the hands of her previous captors, just three months earlier, came flooding back, and it took a supreme effort of will to quash the feeling of terror that threatened to consume her.

A metallic clanking sound had Sandy whirling to face the door. A man entered the room and closed the door behind him with a solid clunk. He was in his mid-to-late forties, of slim build and easily six feet tall, perhaps taller. His hairline was receding from the temples, leaving a peninsular of light-brown hair above the middle of his forehead. He wore a dark grey suit, a white shirt and a plain red silk tie, and when he crossed the room to the table, he held his head up and his back straight, exuding a distinctly military bearing.

'Please sit down, Miss Harris.' His voice was higher than she might have expected, and softer. He spoke gently, politely, inviting rather than ordering her to sit. He waited until Sandy had sat down before he did so. Sandy had a vision of them sitting in a restaurant together, both nervous on a first date. She waited until he opened his mouth to speak and then got in first.

'Where am I?' she asked. Her voice was even, betraying neither anger nor fear, although she felt both, especially the latter. The timing was good; she had caught the man had been off-guard.

'All in good time,' He replied, after a brief hesitation.

'Am I a prisoner?'

'No.'

'Can I leave then?'

'Not yet.' He had recovered his composure.

'When?'

'Soon,' he replied. 'Once you have answered my questions.'

How should she play this? Should she deny who she was, what she was, or stonewall every question? She decided immediately that there was no point in playing the innocent party. She had been snatched from an MI5 safe house. There was no possible way that she could talk her way out of this. They knew exactly who she was.

'I can't answer your questions,' Sandy said, 'I don't know who you are.'

'I'm David,' he said.

Sandy raised her eyebrows, waiting for him to elaborate. He did not.

'Would you please confirm your full name?' he asked politely.

Here we go, thought Sandy. In training, the recruits had attended a counter-interrogation course. Sandy recognised the interrogator's opening gambit. Start with something safe, something she was allowed to answer. Even prisoners of war were supposed to give their name, rank and serial number. Her training had taught her not to enter into any sort of dialogue. If this man was any good at his job, and she had no reason to suppose otherwise, then before long she would be unintentionally tripping out answers to more crucial questions.

'Sandra Annette Harris,' she replied tonelessly.

He smiled. It was a nice smile, a friendly smile. 'It's a pleasure to meet you, Miss Harris. Do you mind if I call you Sandra?'

Sandy shrugged her shoulders but said nothing.

'How old are you, Sandra?'

'I'm sorry, I cannot answer that question.' After giving that answer, the training interrogator would have screamed in her face, *'What do you mean, you can't answer? Are you fucking stupid or something? Don't you know how fucking old you are?'*

David did not react that way. He just seemed disappointed.

'All right, I know how to play that game. I'm not your enemy. You don't need to do the name, rank and serial number routine with me.'

Sandy remained silent.

'All right,' said David, taking out a sheet of A4 paper, 'Let me tell you what I already know. You are Sandra Annette Harris of thirty-five Elgar Drive, Amberley, Wirral, Cheshire. You were born on the Nineteenth of January 1968. Your real mother died when you were nine and your father, then a major with the Royal Engineers, remarried three years later. From the age of eleven, you attended Bramsfield College and left in 1986 with three A-levels in Physics, Maths and Biology, all at grade A-plus.' He looked up and smiled. 'Impressive!' He resumed reading from the sheet of paper.

'You went up to Cambridge, where, despite sleeping with half the male students,' he paused and looked at her with raised eyebrows, 'and at least two lecturers, you managed to gain a double First in Physics and Electronic Engineering.' He paused and looked at Sandy as if for confirmation but she stared back at him, expressionless. David continued.

'Before leaving Bramsfield, however, you had some success in athletics, winning medals for swimming, and running. The pinnacle of your athletic prowess, however, was, at the age of sixteen, winning a gold medal in the Girls Pentathlon event in the National Junior Championships.' David looked up from his notes. 'Pentathlon. Remind me, what events make up the modern Pentathlon?'

Sandy remained silent and stared at a point on the wall behind her interrogator, a foot above his head.

'Well, I'll remind *you*,' he continued after a short pause. 'Fencing, swimming, horse riding, running and,' he paused for effect, 'pistol shooting.'

Sandy remained silent.

'So you're good with a pistol,' David mused and then delivered what he thought would be his killer stroke. 'What did it feel like to shoot your own parents?'

Sandy remained silent but her eyes glistened with tears as she glared at him with an expression of utter hatred.

'Well?'

Sandy's lips curled in disgust as she forced herself to answer through the lump in her throat. 'I'm sorry, I cannot answer that question.'

David frowned. Clearly, he had hoped for more reaction than that.

'Very well,' he said. 'Let's move on. We know that you are a member of the Covert Surveillance Resource Service,' he said, looking into her eyes again. 'How were you recruited?'

'I'm sorry, I cannot answer that question.'

'It was at Cambridge, was it not?'

'I'm sorry, I cannot answer that question.'

'Earlier this year you were involved in a mission in Bosnia. What were the objectives of that mission?'

'I'm sorry, I cannot answer that question.'

'Who was responsible for the assassination of Jane Badell?'

'I'm sorry, I cannot answer that question.'

'You do know Jane Badell, though don't you?'

'I'm sorry, I cannot answer that question.'

'How long have you known her?'

'I'm sorry, I cannot answer that question.'

'Were you involved in her murder?'

'No!' Damn! I slipped up there.

He smiled briefly at her mistake. 'Who did kill her?'

Sandy gave no response.

'When was the last time you spoke to her?'

'I'm sorry, I cannot answer that question.'

David sighed. 'Okay, let's go back to last Friday,' he said, speaking gently in what he hoped was a friendly, encouraging tone. 'Tell me what happened at your house.'

Sandy shrugged but did not reply.

'Did you get on with your parents?'

'I'm sorry, I cannot answer that question.'

'What was your relationship like with your stepmother?'

'I'm sorry, I cannot answer that question.'

'Did you and your parents argue?'

'I'm sorry, I cannot answer that question.'

'When was the last time you spoke to her?'

'I'm sorry, I cannot answer that question.'

'They can be pretty infuriating, parents, can't they?' he said. 'I used to have all sorts rows with mine, my father, particularly. We almost ended up having a fist-fight on more than one occasion when I was a teenager.'

Sandy did not believe him. She knew that he was trying to establish empathy. It was a basic interrogation technique.

'It must have been a terrible row, for you to have been driven to kill them,' he continued. 'What triggered it?'

She remained silent. Who was he and who did he work for? If he was the police he would have said so – and there would be a tape recorder and another officer, probably female, in here with him. Why was he asking questions without identifying himself properly? He must be with one of the intelligence services, but which one? He was certainly not Bosnian or a Serb. Israeli, perhaps, but she could think of no reason why MOSSAD be interested in her. He was unlikely to be from either the Russian or Eastern European intelligence services or one of the Arab nations. If he was from British Intelligence, why didn't he say so? Who was he?

Where did you get the gun?'

No response.

Suddenly, he banged the table with the flat of his hand and stood up, leaning threateningly toward her. 'Look, you had better start answering my questions or it will be the worse for you!'

Sandy blinked but her face remained impassive. If his intention was to shock or intimidate her, he was to be disappointed. She could no longer see her chosen spot on the wall because his body prevented her from doing so. She chose a button on his suit jacket and stared at that instead.

David sat down again and for several seconds he stared into her eyes. She refused to meet his gaze and focussed on his left ear. She could sense that he was getting more and more frustrated and for a moment, wondered if he was going to lose control and hit her. Then he appeared to snap out of it.

'Look,' he said menacingly, 'you have one last opportunity to talk to me, to answer my questions. I've been extremely patient with you up until now, but if you don't start cooperating with me, then things are going to get a whole lot nastier. I'm going to leave you alone for a while so you can think about it. When I come back you'd better be prepared to talk.' He stared her straight in the eyes, but she continued to stare into the middle distance. It was almost as if she were in some sort of trance. 'DO YOU UNDERSTAND?'

Her eyelids fluttered in reaction to his raised voice but she showed no other reaction. Without saying another word, David stood up and rapped on the door. Sandy remained seated, following him only with her eyes. He stared fixedly at the door until, after what seemed an age, it opened. Then, without another word, he left the room. The door closed behind him with a clang.

'Round one to me,' she said softly to herself.

She stood up and went to sit on the bed. Whoever these people were, they knew everything there was to know about her. So what were they after? Well, she could guess, but she had been given strict instructions after her debriefing never to reveal that secret – on pain of the ultimate sanction. If that was what they were after, she wondered how long she could resist before telling all. Whoever was holding her would have all the techniques and devices available to them, from crude beatings and electric shocks to sleep deprivation and exposure to white noise. There were also all manner of mind-bending drugs. She decided she would hold out for as long as possible.

Her instinct told her that the longer she resisted, the longer she might stay alive.

The thought of torture made her feel physically sick, but there was no point in fretting. She had no control over her fate right now. She would have to cross each bridge as she came to it; deal with each event as it arose.

She suddenly realised how hungry and thirsty she was. She had had nothing to drink since the coffee with Maggie at the safe house, and nothing to eat for a good twelve hours before that. How long ago was that? How long had she been here? She had no idea.

***

'I can't get a damn thing out of her, Amanda' David reported to K. 'I can't get her to open up about anything – even the deaths of her parents. Can't you tell me what you're looking for, specifically?'

'We need to ascertain what happened at her parents' house,' Amanda Gillette replied. 'What drove her to respond the way she did? Why did she shoot her parents? Was she involved in the killing of Jane Badell, or its planning?'

'But she is not responding . . .'

'Then make her damn well respond, David,' Amanda said irritably. 'I need to understand what she's been involved in and what drove her to react the way she did when people from her own organisation came to see her.'

'But surely, this is a police matter,' David argued, not for the first time. He had raised this point when first instructed to conduct the interview.

'David, I've already told you. There are circumstances surrounding this case that we cannot allow to get into the public domain. The police cannot be a party to this.'

'Yes, you said that, but you didn't explain why.'

'Because, if it turns out that she is *involved* in this, we may need to take, er, precipitous action.'

'You mean you'd kill her?'

'If that's what it takes to wrap this up without causing an international incident, then, yes, I'm afraid that might be necessary.'

'It might help if I can tell her who I work for. At the moment she's acting like a prisoner of war, and I can understand why. She has no idea where she is, or who is interrogating her. She's clearly been trained to resist interrogation under such circumstances.'

'If you tell her you're MI5, what do you think it would achieve?'

'Well . . .'

'I personally think that if she knew who was interviewing her she would clam up even more. Right now, she doesn't know how far you are prepared to go. If she knows you're from Five she will feel more secure. Secure in the knowledge that she won't be tortured.'

'So I can't use the thumbscrews, then?' David said bitterly.

'Don't be facetious, David. Do whatever you have to in order to break her and get her talking.'

'Like what?'

'I don't know. Strip her. Put her in stress positions. Goodness, David, you've done the courses.'

'I would need two or three people to use those techniques.'

'Impossible. There is no one available with the suitable clearance for what she might reveal. I'm not sure even *we* have that! You certainly can't allow the uniformed security staff to overhear anything she might say.'

'Okay, Amanda,' David acquiesced reluctantly, 'There is something we can try.'

'What?'

'The room is set up with the new "Monsoon" system. It's not been used in anger before, but . . .'

'Why not give it a try?' Amanda agreed.

'It might just be the thing to break her spirit. Leave it with me.' David turned to leave the Director General's office.

'Oh and David,' Amanda called after him as he was about to shut the door. 'Please try to hurry up. I've got some very senior people breathing down my neck.'

***

With no way of measuring the passage of time, Sandy estimated that about an hour had passed before David re-entered the room. He had regained his air of dignity and aloof politeness. He sat in the same chair as before and, with a nod of his head, indicated for her to resume her place. She remained on the edge of the bed, defying him.

'Are you prepared to start cooperating?' he asked, with an edge to his voice.

Sandy looked away.

'Sandra,' he said in an almost pleading tone, 'I need you to help me. I have to know what happened at your house the other night. Please help me so I can help you.

A Desire for Vengeance

"The other night" confirmed it was no longer Saturday. It could be Sunday, or perhaps Monday; any later than that and he probably would have said "Last Friday".

'I'm sorry; I cannot answer your questions.'

David shook his head and left the room without another word. Sandy noticed the expression of sorrow on his face and it struck fear into her heart.

Seconds after the door closed, freezing water sprayed into the room from nozzles set into the ceiling at each corner. Sandy was instantly drenched, and she cowered on the floor, hands shielding her head as water cascaded over and around her. A noise intruded into her consciousness, over and above the hissing sound of the water spraying at high-pressure from the nozzles, and it was several moments before she realised she was screaming. With an effort, she clamped her jaws shut.

After a few seconds, she scrambled into the space under the bed and shivered as puddles spread out until the whole floor was covered in a pool of freezing water. Then the jets stopped and in the silence that followed, the only sound she could hear was the chattering of her teeth.

Sandy clambered up onto the bunk, but of course, all the bedding was drenched. She dragged them off the bed and paddled through inch-deep water to the table, where she spread them out as best she could over the furniture in a vain attempt to let them drip-dry. The wet gown clung to her body, chilling her even more, so she took it off and sat naked on the bed while she wrung it out as best she could with her hands, before slipping it back on again. The instant she had finished the water jets started again and she was drenched once more.

The process was repeated over and over again for several hours. The water would spray all around the room for a minute or two and then stop, only to start again at intervals varying from a minute to an hour or more. Even if Sandy had been able to measure the passage of time, she would still have had no way of predicting when the next deluge would occur. The only advantage was that, whether or not it was suitable for human consumption, she had water in abundance to drink; she simply caught some in her cupped hands and drank. So, cold and hungry she may be, but at least she was no longer thirsty.

Somehow, the water level on the floor never rose above an inch or two and in the longer intervals between each deluge, it drained away completely, leaving the tiled floor wet and slippery. Sandy surmised that there must be drains set into the edges of floor, but she felt too miserable and lethargic to search for them. She gave up attempting to avoid the irregular soakings, and sat on the bed, trying to control her shivering, as the water cascaded repeatedly around her. During this time, David returned twice to ask her if she was ready to cooperate. On both occasions, he was to be disappointed.

In the midst of one of the longer dry intervals, an idea occurred to her. She twisted the blanket into a rope, which she then wrapped around the central pedestal supporting the table. Folding the twisted material upon itself, and tightening it with all the strength she could muster, she wrung the water out onto the floor, twisting the blanket tighter and tighter until the flow reduced to no more than a drip. Then, wrapping the blanket around her shoulders, she repeated the process with the sheet, which took far less time and effort.

The physical effort involved in wringing the water out of the bedcovers warmed her body and, when she wrapped the sheet around her, on top of the blanket, she found that, even though both were still damp, they provided enough insulation to conserve her body heat. She guessed that there must be a camera watching her, but whoever was monitoring it must have been asleep because it was not until several minutes later that the next deluge was unleashed upon her. Both sheet and blanket were made of some kind of synthetic fibre, and by holding them tight over her head and around her body, the surface tension of the material was enough to repel much of the water. Mentally, she gave the finger to whoever was watching via the invisible camera. Sandy's little victory was short-lived, however. Moments later the door opened and two burly female guards entered the room.

'Give me that bedding,' ordered the first.

Sandy backed into the corner furthest from the door as the two women advanced on her.

'Give it to me,' the guard repeated, more forcefully. Sandy shook her head and maintained a tight grip on the coverings across her chest.

The second guard suddenly reached out, grabbed a handful of material and pulled Sandy forward. The first guard was then able to get behind her and locked an arm around Sandy's throat. Sandy immediately flexed her knees and threw herself backwards, slamming the back of her head into the guard's nose. The guard screamed in pain and doubled over holding both hands to her face. Immediately, Sandy lunged forward, cannoning into the second woman, who had not yet released her grip on the blanket. The guard flew backwards over the table and ended up sprawled across one of the chairs. Sandy bolted for the open door.

She reached the corridor and turned right. Two large men were approaching fast. She turned to flee the other way and saw a third, just yards away and closing quickly. She backed against a wall just as the first man reached her. With her arms encumbered by the bed covers, Sandy lashed out with her foot. She caught the man on the knee and he went down with a grunt of pain. A second later, the other two were upon her. She tried to struggle but one caught her in a bear hug while the other grabbed her legs. She wriggled and squirmed as they carried her back into the cell and dumped her floor. Meanwhile, the third man limped in and helped the woman with the broken nose out of the cell while the second female guard helped the two men wrench the bed-covers away from Sandy. Then, while Sandy was still trying to get up, they quickly backed out of the door and slammed it shut behind them. Sandy wept with frustration and anger. Then the water jets started again.

After a while, during one of the lulls, as Sandy lay shivering on the bunk, curled into a ball, trying to conserve body-heat, the door opened and David walked in. He did not sit down, but stood near the door, looking down at Sandy, trying not to notice that the gown clinging to her body was soaking wet and completely transparent.

'I can keep this up all night,' he said, mildly, 'Can you?'

Sandy looked at him with hatred and defiance in her eyes. He was not going to break her that easily.

'Do your fucking worst!' she said through gritted teeth.

David's mouth smiled, but his eyes told a different story. She could see compassion there and it surprised and unsettled her. What *was* this all about?

'There really is no need for this, you know,' David said. 'All you have to do is answer a few simple questions.'

Sandy was shivering so hard that David could barely understand her reply.

'I c-c-c-c-cannot answer your q-q-questions.'

'That is a pity,' David said, and shuddered theatrically, folding his arms and gripping his shoulders as if feeling the cold despite wearing his nice, warm, charcoal–grey wool suit. 'It's a bit cold in here, don't you think? Look, I have it within my power to give you dry clothes, fresh bedding and something hot to eat and drink. All you have to do is give *me* something.' He watched his prisoner's eyes, fervently hoping that she would say, *What do you want me to tell you?* He was to be disappointed.

'Go to hell!' she said clenching her jaws to prevent her teeth chattering.

David clicked his tongue in frustration and left the room. The door closed and immediately water began to spray into the room again.

Sandy endured the repeated drenching, the debilitating cold and the hunger, knowing all the time she had but to shout out that she would cooperate and she would be dry and warm and fed.

Then what? What would they do to her once she had given them what they wanted?

The light never went out. She could not tell whether it was morning, noon or night. From time to time, she would exercise to try to keep warm – sit-ups, press-ups, running on the spot, but she was soon exhausted from lack of food, and slumped down once again on the bunk.

Eventually, she stopped shivering; stopped feeling cold; in fact, she felt quite warm. Her mind told her that all she needed to do now was to settle down on the bed and go to sleep. Just sleep and everything would be okay.

There were two cameras set inside the glass of the central light fitting. One was focussed directly on the bunk and the other had a wide-angle lens that showed the whole cell with a fish-eye distortion. In a control room further down the corridor, David stood watching the monitors with a combination of annoyance and deep admiration of Sandy's courage and determination. He wondered if he could have held out this long.

David noticed that the prisoner was once again trying to sleep and, with a feeling of self-loathing, he ordered the fountains turned on again. On every previous occasion she had sat bolt upright and pressed her back against the wall, hugging her knees and keeping her head lowered to her chest. This time she did not even flinch as the icy water hit her body.

'Oh my God,' said David, his voice hoarse with urgency. 'I think she's gone into hypothermia. Get her out of there!'

He continued to watch the monitor as the water stopped and the door burst open. Two female guards splashed into the room, grabbed the unconscious young woman under the armpits, pulled her off the bunk and manoeuvred her through the doorway, her heels dragging through the water on the flooded floor. David could see every detail of that perfect body through the thin, sodden material, and he despised himself for noticing.

As soon as the women were out of camera shot, David ran out of the control room and down the corridor to a second interview room that had been prepared as a recovery room in anticipation of such an emergency. The room was already hot from a bank of infrared heaters arranged in a circle around the chair on which Sandy sat slumped, prevented from falling only by one of the guards holding her upright. David's mouth went dry as the other guard dragged Sandy's gown off over her head before wrapping a thick towel around the inert body. She then proceeded vigorously to rub Sandy's upper arms through the towel.

After a few minutes, the lolling head jerked and her eyes opened. At first, she seemed unable to focus. Her eyes scanned around the room as if searching for something. They found David and like a pair of guns in the turret of a battleship laying onto their target, they steadied on his. Then they glinted as if the guns had been fired. The salvo was not of high-explosive projectiles but the target received a direct hit, a telepathic message that said, 'I won!' David's heart sank and he gave the order to bring up the reserves.

Sandy's brief feeling of victory faded to despair when she saw a man wearing a white coat rolling a trolley into the room. Set on the trolley were a heart monitor, a selection of needles and a number of small, sinister glass vials. Sandy knew that she could not fight the drugs that would breach her mental defences and might well destroy her mind.

David leaned forward until his face filled her vision.

'You know what's coming next, don't you?' he said, hoping the gravity of his tone and the hopelessness of her situation would persuade her to submit to his questioning.
'This is your last chance to tell me what I want to know, voluntarily.' He could see the fear in Sandy's eyes. Her head moved almost imperceptibly. To his astonishment, it was a shake, not a nod.

Chapter 6

Located under a double-fronted sports shop near Chester's brooding medieval cathedral, The Popped Cork was Edwin Brighting's favourite after-work watering hole. Descending the narrow staircase from street-level was like travelling back in time, leaving behind the sights and sounds of the twentieth century to enter a softly lit cellar with exposed brick walls, a stone-flagged floor and a low, beamed ceiling.

Leather sofas and low tables stood in intimate nooks, some of which contained shelves full of reproduction antique books. Low wattage bulbs, designed to resemble candles, both in appearance and in the flickering light that they produced, glowed from wrought-iron replicas of Victorian gas lamps dotted around the walls. All combined to produce an atmosphere of intimacy and old world charm that the pleasant odours of leather, polished wood and a slight below-ground mustiness only served to enhance. Light Jazz/blues music played softly over loudspeakers hidden in dark recesses, adding to the ambience. Edwin looked around. He nodded to one or two familiar faces among the early evening regulars and entered the bar area through a crypt-like arch of artificially aged bricks.

Brighting cut an impressive figure. He was six-foot-two inches tall, with a leonine mane of silver hair brushed back from his creased forehead where thick grey eyebrows nestled above his eyes like giant caterpillars. His cheeks and nose were florid from the frequent indulgence of the fruits of Bacchus, evidence supported by his expansive waistline, which was also testament to his love of good food.

A Desire for Vengeance

The bar area was empty of customers, save for one young female who was perched decorously on one of three high wooden bar stools that were placed in front of the dark oak bar, behind which old wine casks adorned the wall, their visible ends stencilled with some of the great names of classic viniculture.

'No one around?' Edwin asked casually, his voice gravelly, the diction precise.

The young woman gave a slight start and looked up from the Filofax that she had been studying with such intensity that she had been apparently unaware of his presence.

'Sorry,' she replied, placing one elegant hand to her chest as if checking her heartbeat, 'I didn't hear you come in. You made me jump.'

Edwin was rendered momentarily speechless. The woman was perhaps in her mid-twenties; she had voluminous auburn hair that cascaded around her shoulders and reached halfway down her back, shimmering dusky-red in the light from behind the bar like a sunset to delight the proverbial shepherd. She wore a high-necked, figure-hugging, pale-blue woollen sweater and a beige, mid-length, cotton skirt, stretched tightly across a pair of firm, shapely thighs. It was, however, her face that took Edwin's breath away. She had dark, sultry eyes under narrow, dark eyebrows, and full lips that were a delicate shade of rose pink. Her skin was as pale and smooth as fine silk, stretched over the frame of high cheekbones and a well-defined jaw-line that tapered to a slightly pointed, triangular chin. This had to be the most beautiful creature he had ever set eyes upon.

'I, er, I'm sorry, my dear,' Edwin stammered, 'I didn't mean to startle you. I just wondered where... Oh, there you are, John,' interrupting his own flow, he addressed the young man who, at that moment, appeared behind the bar from a back room.

'Afternoon, Eddie,' the barman replied cheerfully. 'Claret?'

'Yes, thank you, a large glass. And er . . .' Edwin looked questioningly at the young woman. She smiled back at him, a big, radiant smile, showing perfect white teeth. Her eyes twinkled with amusement.

'Are you offering to buy me a drink?'

Eddie's florid cheeks reddened further with embarrassment, afraid that she might think he was trying to pick her up. Despite still having a keen eye for a pretty girl, even Eddie would have to admit that at nearly sixty years of age, he was far too late in life to court this beauty. 'It's the least I could do after startling you like that,' he said. Then it occurred to him that a girl like this might very well have a young man in tow, perhaps a very jealous young man, who might take exception to an old codger like Eddie Brighting chatting up his girlfriend.

'I would never accept a drink from a strange man in a bar,' she said haughtily. Then she laughed and thrust out her hand.

'How do you do? I'm Kathy Taylor.'

Eddie was taken slightly aback by the sudden gesture, but took her hand in his. It was cool and dry with long fingers tipped with nail polish that matched the shade of her lips. He had a sudden urge to stoop and kiss it, but he dismissed the idea as absurd. 'Edwin Brighting,' he said. 'Please call me Eddie.'

'Pleased to meet you, Eddie,' Kathy smiled and slid her hand unhurriedly from his grip. 'Now that we've been formally introduced, and as my friend is still not here,' she added, looking meaningfully at her wristwatch, 'I would be delighted to join you for a drink. Small Sauvignon Blanc, please,' she added to the barman. As he went to pour the wine, Kathy looked back at the man standing beside her. 'Aren't you going to sit down and keep me company, Eddie?' she invited, glancing at an empty barstool.

'It'd be my pleasure,' Eddie replied with a courtly bow of his head. He was very conscious of the young woman's appraising scrutiny as he removed his topcoat and draped it across one of the two empty bar stools. Underneath, he was wearing a bespoke-tailored blue pinstriped business suit that, despite the generous cut, did little to conceal his considerable paunch. A white shirt and a blue bow tie, with white polka dots, completed his attire.

'There,' he said as he sat on the third barstool. 'That's better.' He raised his glass to Kathy and said, 'Well, here's to new friends,' hoping that it sounded neither crass nor forward. To his relief Kathy gave him a dazzling smile.

'To new friends,' she repeated and sipped her white wine as Eddie quaffed a mouthful of red from his glass.

'Speaking of friends,' Eddie ventured after savouring the first drop of claret, 'I wonder what's happened to yours? Is he very late?'

'She,' Kathy corrected him, glancing again at her watch. 'Yes, it's six-thirty already. She was supposed to be here at half-five.'

'Oh dear. Has she far to come? Does she work around here?'

'No, she's an old college friend. I haven't seen her for several years. She lives out at a place called Saltney?' She finished with a rising inflection as if asking for confirmation of the name.

'Oh, yes, I know it. What do you do, Kathy? Do you work locally?'

'Oh, I'm unemployed at the moment, but I'm a legal secretary. I used to work for a practice down South – London, but I left to move back up North. I'm from Manchester originally.' She paused briefly before adding, 'but I love Chester. It's such a lovely city. I want to live here. All I've got to do is find a job.'

Eddie rubbed his chin. 'Legal secretary, you say? Well, it so happens that I'm in that profession myself...' He broke off because Kathy had just turned those big, dark eyes on him, clearly reading more into his comment than he had intended to convey. 'I'm a solicitor,' he continued. 'I'm the senior partner in a small practice just around the corner.'

'Don't suppose you have any vacancies?' She suggested hopefully.

'Unfortunately not,' Eddie said with genuine regret because this lovely girl would be a welcome addition to his staff. 'However, I do have a lot of contacts in the profession. I'll put the word about for you. Do you have a phone number so I can contact you?' As he was speaking, Eddie noticed the changes in Kathy's expression. At first, she looked a little disappointed, then more hopeful but now there was something else in her eyes – she seemed suddenly wary. Was she suspicious of his motive?

'I can't really give you a phone number,' she said. 'I've just moved into a little bedsit. It has a communal phone in the hall, but it's not working. Everyone goes to the local phone box.'

'Well,' Eddie said with a hint of frustration, 'how can I get in touch if anyone's interested?'

'I suppose we could meet here,' she suggested. Then she laughed and shook her head.

'What's so amusing?' Eddie asked, a smile playing over his lips because her laughter was infectious.

'I was about to say....' She giggled and raised the tips of her fingers to her mouth as if to subdue it. 'I was about to ask if you come here often,' she finally managed to finish the sentence.

'Actually,' Eddie admitted, 'I'm here most nights. I have a couple of glasses after work and then I toddle off down to the station to catch the train home where my good lady wife will have dinner on the table for eight.'

'Well,' said Kathy, 'that sounds very civilised. Myself? I'll be picking up a Chinese takeaway on the way home.'

'Look,' said Eddie, draining his glass. He could not help noticing that Kathy had barely touched hers. 'Give me a few days and I'll meet you in here, say this time next week?'

Kathy flashed her dazzling smile again. 'Thank you, Eddie. You're very kind. It's lucky for me I bumped into you this evening.'

Chapter 7

When Sandy awoke, she was back in the cell. Only now, it was warm and dry. The bedding was fresh and she was wearing a clean, dry gown. On the table, over which she had faced her interrogator, stood a tray filled with sandwiches, Danish pastries and a jug of orange juice. There was also a steel flask of hot coffee. She was ravenously hungry and, sensing that some diabolical mind-game might be in progress, she was determined to shovel as much food as possible into her mouth before the goons came in to take it away from her. She had barely wolfed down the first few mouthfuls of a cheese sandwich and was pouring coffee into a plastic mug, when, as if to confirm her suspicions, the door opened and a female guard entered. Sandy whirled to face the door, prepared to defend her breakfast like a lioness faced with a hyena trying to rob her of her kill.

The guard was a big woman, tall and broad shouldered. She wore a white, open neck shirt and navy-blue trousers. She recognised the feral look in Sandy's eyes and watched her warily as she placed something on the floor before backing out of the room. As she closed the door, she said, 'Bang on the door when you're ready.'

It was only after the door had closed that Sandy realised that what the guard had left behind was Marks and Spencer carrier bag. Intrigued, and still holding the rest of the sandwich, Sandy got up and looked in the bag. It contained a set of clothes. She took another bite and then emptied the contents of the bag out onto the bed. There was a pair of blue denim jeans, a white, V-necked, short-sleeved top, a white cotton bra, pale-blue knickers, white trainers with pink piping on the uppers, and white trainer-socks. All the items still bore the labels that showed they were brand new and everything was the right size. Briefly, Sandy wondered what had happened to the clothes that she had been wearing when she they brought her here. She shrugged. It hardly mattered now.

She pulled on the knickers and jeans, then, turning her back to the door, swiftly removed the gown and put on the bra and top. The legs of the jeans were a few inches too long so she rolled them up before putting on the socks and trainers.

She sat for a few minutes trying to understand the significance of the food and clothes, and concluded that she must have told David everything under the influence of the drugs. They had no more use for her now and she wondered what would be her fate. Steeling herself, she got up and banged her fist on the door.

For a quarter of an hour, nothing happened, and then David entered the room again, but this time, he left the door open. They sat, as before, facing each other across the table. Sandy's eyes kept glancing nervously toward the doorway. She half-expected someone to appear in the doorway and shoot her. Was David tempting her to try once more to escape? If so, why? David seemed oblivious to her concerns.

'Is that better?' he asked mildly, and then added, with a ghost of a smile, 'And if you say, "I'm sorry, I can't answer that question," I think I'll scream!'

Sandy looked at him blankly. Was that supposed to be a joke?

David's eyes fixed on hers and waited. Clearly, he was expecting an answer. She did not want to speak so she acquiesced with a slight nod of the head. He smiled again then suddenly got up, making her flinch.

'I'll be back in a minute,' he said and left the room. 'Wait there,' he added, closing the door. 'Don't go away.'

Despite herself, Sandy shook her head and smiled at the remark. He was trying to be nice to her. Why? Then she remembered how she had read compassion in his eyes, saw how much he hated what he was doing to her. Who was he? Who did he work for? What did they want from her and what, under the influence of the drugs, did they get?

***

'Are you sure of this?' Eagle challenged. 'She's been trained to resist interrogation, even under amobarbital drugs.'

Eagle was once more in Amanda's office. As before, he was seated upon one of the two sofas. Amanda sat behind her desk and regarded him coolly.

'And my people are trained to spot disinformation in the subject's responses,' Amanda countered.

'If you are right, do you know what this means?'

'If we are right then your survivor has been, what's that phrase, economical with the truth!'

'To what end?'

'To cover his own *rear*-end, clearly,' Amanda said. 'Perhaps we should bring him in here and ask him?'

'Unfortunately, that will not be possible. There is another ongoing activity in which he is involved.'

'But if we are right, he surely needs investigation.'

'Perhaps, but not right now,' Eagle replied assertively, drawing a line under the discussion. 'I will deal with him in my own way and in the time of my choosing. However, I must express my gratitude that you have brought this to my attention.'

'So,' Amanda said pointedly, 'What do we do with young Miss Harris?'

***

Sometime later, the door to Sandy's cell opened and David reappeared. 'Come with me,' he said, beckoning with his head. 'There's someone I want you to meet.'

Sandy was apprehensive. Strangely, this room had become a kind of haven. Perversely, she felt safe here. She feared what might happen were she to leave it. Nervously, she followed David into a bland corridor with walls of whitewashed brick, lit by harsh florescent strip-lights suspended from a bland, whitewashed ceiling. At the end of the corridor was a lift. David pressed a button and the door opened instantly. Filled with apprehension, Sandy followed him inside. Moments later the lift door opened onto a different world. Here were carpets on the floor and reproduction Monet's and Van Gough's on the walls. A Swiss-cheese plant spread its large, shiny green leaves above a small coffee table next to a drinks-vending machine as big as the wardrobe in Sandy's bedroom at home. David led Sandy along another corridor and then opened a door, beckoning her to enter before him. She took a deep breath. Whatever the next stage was, it started here.

'Come in, Curlew.' The speaker was a smartly dressed, middle-aged, slightly overweight, balding man who looked familiar to Sandy. He was sitting on a red sofa under a portrait of the Queen. She recognised the man as the one who had made the welcome speech at the Caesar training centre. He was Eagle, the Director General. There was a woman in the room as well. Tall and very slim, she had short grey hair and steel-blue eyes set in a strong, angular face. Sandy recognised her as Amanda Gillette, the head of MI5, whose picture, bizarrely for a chief spook, had been plastered all over the newspapers at the time of her appointment the previous year.

'Please come in, Sandra,' said K kindly. 'Please take a seat over there.' She indicated a second sofa, which stood at right angles to the one on which Eagle was sitting.

Sandy noticed that David had followed her into the room and was standing near the door, effectively cutting off her escape. Puzzled, Sandy sat down and waited for whatever revelation was coming next. It was Eagle that broke the short silence.

'You can relax, now, Curlew, it's all over.'

Sandy bridled, all nerves banished by a sudden anger. 'What's over? Why the hell was I held and interrogated over the past however-many days?'

'It was necessary, I'm afraid,' Eagle said, nodding his head sympathetically.

'Excuse me,' said Sandy, through gritted teeth, 'but you are aware, I take it, that my parents were murdered the night before I was dragged in here, and that I've been repeatedly accused of killing them?'

'Yes, we are aware of that,' Eagle replied. 'We had to be sure.'

Sandy was shocked beyond belief. 'Sure of what? You didn't seriously think me capable of shooting my own parents?'

'We didn't know . . .' he paused as if unsure of his words. 'We didn't know what had happened.'

'I'll tell you what bloody happened,' said Sandy hotly, rising to her feet. 'My home was invaded by armed men. They shot my parents and tried to kill me. I resisted but was outnumbered. I had to escape. Can you even imagine what that feels like? These bastards murdered my parents. I had no way of protecting them.'

'Yes, I understand . . .'

'No, you don't! And why all the cloak and dagger stuff during the interrogation? If I'd known who was asking the questions we would have got it sorted out straight away! As it was, I was afraid to answer a single question because I had no idea where I was!'

'It was important that we did it that way.'

'Important to who?' Sandy shouted.

'To national security,' K interjected. She spoke softly, trying to ease the tension. 'We had to be sure whose side you were on.'

Sandy turned on her. 'Do you want to know who killed my parents?' Without waiting for an answer, she added, 'It was probably the same people that were responsible for the shooting of Jane Badell in London.'

'We know that, now,' K lied evenly. 'We believe both attacks were committed by Serbian agents. We have known for some time that there was a KOS cell in London but we never suspected they would pull something like this. You can rest assured that we will stop at nothing until we hunt them down, now.'

Sandy nodded, grimly. The explanation fitted with her own theory. 'Why did they have to kill my parents?' she said.

'They could have taken me anywhere. On the doorstep, as I left for work, at the train station, anywhere.'

Eagle looked away uncomfortably and K looked at her sympathetically.

'I expect they were concerned that you might have told your parents the truth about "ethnic cleansing" and the rape-camps and, in particular, the names of some of the senior people involved.'

It occurred to Sandy that those details were sufficiently in the public domain to make such action pointless. The Prime Minister, John Major, had referred to the atrocities at a news conference in Barcelona only the previous month. Revenge, on the other hand, might be a factor.

'The newspaper said that the police think I did it,' she said.

'Yes, we know,' K replied.

'I presume that you have put them straight during the time that I've been stewing in your dungeon?'

'No, we haven't,' said Eagle.

Sandy was outraged. 'Why not, for God's sake? If the police think I did it they won't be hunting for the real killers!'

'The police would be powerless against them,' said K. 'They're bound to be Embassy officials, and will claim diplomatic immunity.' Better that MI5 and Caesar deal with them.'

Sandy nodded. It made sense. 'Then I want to be on the team,' She said.

Eagle shook his head. 'No, you're too close; too involved. You know how important it is to remain emotionally detached during that sort of mission.'

'But I might be of use. The information I have could be of help, even if I'm not on the hit team. I speak Serbo-Croat...'

'No,' Eagle said flatly, 'you will have no involvement. You will have to trust us to do the job.'

Sandy wanted to argue, but she knew he was right; there was no point in pursuing it. Nevertheless, she was still upset and puzzled about the interrogation.

'I still don't understand why you needed to keep me in the dark about who was interrogating me,' she said.

'I thought we had,' said Eagle uncomfortably. 'It was in the interests of national security. I can't go any further than that, I'm afraid.'

'Firstly, you needed to disappear off the ground while the hue and cry was at its height,' K added. 'Secondly, we had to see how you would hold up under pressure. If David couldn't break you after what you had just been through, no one ever would.'

'And you have acquitted yourself very well,' said Eagle emolliently. 'You have proved yourself to be a valuable resource and a credit to the Service.'

Sandy stood again and strode toward K's desk. Out of the corner of her eye, she saw David stiffen, as if preparing to rush to his Director General's defence.

'And you two have proved yourself to be a pair of heartless bastards!' Sandy snarled, swivelling her head to take in both Directors General. 'How dare you treat my grief with such contempt? Apart from anything else, you've given the bastards time to cover their tracks!'

David struggled not to laugh at the astonished looks on the faces of the two service chiefs in the face of the verbal onslaught from this extraordinary young woman.

'I think you've probably said enough for now, Curlew,' said Eagle sharply. 'Whatever you may think, we acted as we did for the best of reasons.'

Sandy remained silent, speechless with anger and bewilderment.

'There's something else,' Eagle said and Sandy noticed that he sounded nervous. 'As far as everyone outside this room is concerned, you are no longer alive.' He took a newspaper cutting from the inside pocket of his jacket and handed it to Sandy. 'This article is from yesterday's *Liverpool Echo*.'

Sandy took the cutting with shaking hands and noted the date, Tuesday, September 8, 1992. So today was Wednesday – four days since her abduction from the safe house in Liverpool. She read the article twice before she could take it in.

BODY IN RIVER THOUGHT TO BE MISSING WOMAN
The body of a young woman found in the Mersey estuary yesterday afternoon is thought to be that of Sandra Harris (pictured right), the daughter of retired Lt-Colonel Charles Harris, 68, late of the Royal Engineers, and his wife, Grace, 63, both of whom were found shot dead in their Wirral home last Friday evening. The body is thought to have been in the water for several days and has been badly disfigured, probably by the propellers of one of the many large ships sailing in and out of the Mersey. A Cheshire Police source said that the body is yet to be formally identified but they are "quietly confident" that it is that of the missing woman. A spokeswoman said that police are not seeking anyone else in connection with the deaths.

Sandy handed the cutting back to Eagle. 'But that means I could never see my sister again. Nor my aunt and uncle, my cousins, my friends from school and Uni,' Sandy said quietly. She looked numb, and David's heart went out to her. 'What if I don't agree to this?' Sandy continued, moderating her tone to avoid sounding hysterical. 'What if I resign from the Service, here and now, and give myself up to the police?'

'That would not be a wise move,' Eagle responded with an edge to his voice. 'All the evidence suggests that you killed your parents and then yourself.'

'No,' Sandy asserted. 'There must be a mountain of forensics to disprove that theory.' She held up an elegant, tapered forefinger. 'One: My bedroom carpet is covered in the blood of the X-Ray I shot with my bow.' She flicked up a second finger. 'Two: There are bullet holes from at least two different weapons in the walls inside and outside my bedroom, and the door itself will show clear evidence of a fire-fight through it. 'Three: I'm pretty sure I wounded a second X-Ray through the door. There must be some trace of his blood on the walls or carpet.' Four: My reappearance from the grave will prove that it wasn't me in the river.' Belligerently, she looked around the room, challenging the other three people present to disprove her arguments.

'The people sent to kill you know that you escaped from the house,' said Eagle. 'Right now the only evidence available to them is that you died in the Mersey. The trail stops there; it goes cold. Only the people in this room and the Director General of MI6 are aware that you are still alive. Once your new identity is established, only Mrs Gillette and Mr Richardson, there,' he indicated David standing beside the door, 'will know who you are. Even I won't know.' When Sandy looked at him quizzically, he continued, 'Clearly, you will no longer be working for Caesar. Your secondment to MI5 will be made permanent, as from now.'

Sandy sat back down on the sofa, the whole gamut of emotions playing across her face. After a minute or two's reflection, she spoke in a quiet voice, barely audible to David.

'Who was she, anyway, the poor cow in the river?'

'She was a prostitute and a drug addict who died of an overdose.' Eagle replied. 'A good trade, I think, a heroin junkie for a real life heroine.' He looked quite pleased with himself.

Sandy sneered at the clumsy compliment. 'How was she any different to me?' she asked. 'We were both prepared to use our bodies as a tool.'

'The difference,' said K, 'is that you did what you had to do for the good of your country.'

Sandy shook her head sadly. 'There's no difference.' She paused for a few seconds then asked, 'Okay, so what do you want me to do?'

'David will explain it all to you, later,' K replied. 'Once you've had a little time to get used to . . .' she hesitated, 'the situation.' Just in time, she had stopped herself from saying *being dead*. Then she stood, walked around the desk, and, in a jaunty, upbeat tone said, 'Welcome to the Security Service!' She smiled broadly and extended her hand for Sandy to shake. Sandy ignored it.

'There's just one more thing you should know,' Sandy said.

'What's that?' Sandy's new boss asked, still unsure what to do with her rejected hand.

'How much do you know about what happened to me when I was held by the Serb militia in Višegrad?'

'Eagle has told me everything,' K replied, glancing reproachfully at Eagle, 'but I guarantee that we won't be putting you at risk in that way.'

David wondered what they were talking about. Sandy's response, when it came, shocked him to the core.

'I'm pregnant,' said Sandy, her eyes downcast. 'I've missed my last two periods. I don't know who the father is; it could be any one of thirty or forty men.'

Chapter 8

Sandy sat at the kitchen table and re-read the paragraph yet again. Each time she got to the bottom of the page she would realise that she had not taken in a single word, let alone the contextual significance, and would try again. After the third or fourth attempt, she put down the novel with a sigh and picked up the coffee mug. It was empty. She glanced at the clock on the wall. It was just ten-thirty. How many mugs of coffee had she drunk in the three hours since getting out of bed?

For two days, she had languished in this safe house in Balham, South London, reading well-thumbed and dog-eared trashy novels left behind by previous occupants, or playing Monopoly, Scrabble or chess with the Protection Branch officers who had been guarding her around the clock. Like their colleague, Adrian, in Liverpool, Anna and Simon seemed very circumspect, unwilling to interact with their charge except at the most superficial level. Sandy wondered whether it was a personality trait of such people or a job requirement. *Keep a professional distance. Don't get personally involved with the principal.* Sandy was that principal, known to her protectors (or were they her gaolers?) as 'Greta'. Why Greta, she had no idea. That was how David had introduced her, and she and they had unquestioningly gone along with it.

Sandy wished she could go out for a run, or to the gym or even shopping (not, by any means, her favourite pastime), anything to escape from this pokey little Victorian mid-terrace hovel. Well, perhaps hovel was a bit unfair. It was small, but it was clean and tidy. However, it had become a prison, and she longed for a change of surroundings, if only for a short while. In her frustration, she banged her fist on the table, and exhaled forcefully, an extended, throaty growl, like a caged wild animal.

'You all right, Greta?' Anna's voice startled Sandy and she spun round to face the doorway.

Anna was roughly the same age as Sandy. Petite in build and fresh-faced, with brown eyes and long brown hair tied back in a ponytail, she looked more like a teenager who should be listening to Nirvana, than a dedicated professional, packing a pistol on her hip and prepared to put herself between her principal and a bullet.

Sandy forced a smile. 'Yes, I'm fine, thanks, Anna. I'm just going stir-crazy in this place. How long do you think they're going to keep me cooped up here?'

Anna smiled in return and shrugged. 'Dunno. Perhaps you can ask Mr Richardson. We just heard on the comms he's on his way to see you. Should be here in half-an-hour.' With that, Anna returned to the living room where she had been playing cards with Simon. Sandy stood up and headed for the jug of filter-coffee on its hotplate.

For some unfathomable reason, Sandy stood up when David entered the kitchen. Like a schoolgirl before the menacing headmaster, she felt nervous in his presence. It was almost as if he had the power of life and death over her. Perhaps he did.

'How are you?' His tone was friendly and accompanied by a disarming smile. 'Are they looking after you?' He stood facing her, the rectangular pine table a physical barrier between them.

'Yes, I'm fine,' she replied. 'A bit fed-up with being cooped up here. Also, I haven't got any clothes, except the ones I'm standing up in, not even a change of underwear. I'm having to wash my smalls out each night and put the same ones back on in the morning.' Not wishing to have David think she was whinging, she added, 'but apart from that, everything's fine.'

'Good, good,' David said expansively. 'Ask Anna to go out and buy you some clothes. Tell her she can send me the bill and I'll sign off the expense. Now, let's sit down and have a chat. Any coffee going?'

Sandy poured them both some coffee and sat on one of the four pine chairs set around the table. David sat on another at right angles rather than face her across the table. That, he thought, would be too reminiscent of the interrogation room. After they had taken their first sips in unison and in silence, Sandy spoke up.

'I'm a bit worried about those two.' Sandy spoke quietly so that the subjects of her concern, who were in the room next door, would not hear. 'Surely, if they read the newspapers they must know who I am. There has been no attempt to disguise my appearance, and my picture has been splashed over the newspapers and the TV news for days!'

'I shouldn't worry about that,' David reassured her. 'Protection people are noted for their discretion. They guard all sorts – Russian defectors, visiting diplomats, errant Security Service officers . . .'

'Oh, is that what I'm pigeon-holed as?' Sandy cut in with a hint of bitterness, 'an errant Security Service officer?'

David looked at her closely for a few seconds before answering. 'You are classified as someone in extreme danger from foreign agents,' he said, then hesitated before adding, 'and possibly, from yourself.'

'Or someone likely to spill the beans to the police, or the *News of the World*, perhaps?'

'Sandy, I have total faith in you. I know you wouldn't do that.'

'But does K?' Sandy asked. 'Does she trust me?'

'Well,' he replied with a smirk, 'you did suggest that you might resign from the Service and go to the police.'

If David had intended the tone of his response to put Sandy at ease, it failed. Instead, she reacted angrily.

'For God's sake! I had just been told that I was officially a deranged murderer, officially dead and that I would never see my sister or friends again! Don't you think I was entitled to be a bit upset?'

David became serious. 'How do you feel about that now?'

'How do you *think* I feel?' She sat back in her chair and looked away briefly before leaning forward again. Her eyes glistened with tears. 'I feel devastated. My parents are dead. My sister, my aunt and uncle and cousins, they all think I did it. And I can never see them again; can never explain to them what happened.'

'No,' agreed David gently, 'you can't. To do so would put your life – and theirs at risk. As hard as it is, you have to let go. You have to move on.'

'It's not that easy,' said Sandy, her voice choking. 'To know my sister is up there trying to deal with the funerals and probate . . .'

'Is she the executor of the wills?'

'We were supposed to be joint executors.' There was a brief silence and then Sandy said. 'I want to see her.'

'Impossible.'

'It's not impossible,' Sandy insisted. 'Anything is possible. It just has to be handled right.'

'I can't authorise that.' David said, uncomfortably.

'Then who can, K?' Now that she had taken the initiative, Sandy was not about to let it go.

David thought for a few moments before replying. He could see the desperation in Sandy's eyes and it was breaking his heart. He decided to use a delaying tactic.

'I'll talk to the DG,' he said. 'I can't promise anything, but I'll talk to her.'

'Thank you, David,' she said, almost inaudibly.

David sipped his coffee.

'I wanted to talk to you about your new role,' he said as he put the mug on the table. 'I am to head a new section in Counter Espionage, focussing on technology. The world of electronics is on the brink of an explosion. With miniaturisation of components such as microchips and printed circuitry, before long, anyone will be able to buy gadgets currently only available to the intelligence agencies. Mobile phones will be small enough to fit in your pocket, and cameras that store pictures digitally will make developing a roll of film a thing of the past; standard film cameras will soon be obsolete.

'One company,' he continued, 'is floating the idea that, before the decade is out, we'll all be wearing spectacles that will be able to pick up and project TV pictures or newspaper pages onto the lenses. They say these devices could interact with one another in the street, from tens, maybe hundreds of yards away sharing information to form a powerful data processing network, without the participation or even knowledge of the wearers. The implications for the identification and tracking of individuals are quite profound.' David took another sip of coffee before continuing.

'Commercial companies, Government departments and the military are becoming more and more dependent on computers, and if the internet continues to expand at the present rate it will be very difficult to prevent terrorists and spies gaining access to sensitive information. Conceivably, someone in Eastern Europe or China could use the internet to burrow into the computers at say, the Ministry of Defence and ferret out our secrets without having to step outside the boundaries of their own country.'

'It's called hacking,' Sandy said, 'and you're right; it will be a major headache for companies – and governments – to keep ahead of the game. The youngsters coming out of schools and universities today have a far greater knowledge of new technology than your generation ever will. It'll be young graduates that devise the security for these systems and their contemporaries that will try to break into them.'

David frowned at the reminder that he was of a different generation to Sandy. 'Precisely! That's why someone of your age, and with your qualifications, would be ideal to work with us.'

Sandy responded with a rare smile. 'That sounds right up my street.'

David was surprised and pleased that she sounded so enthusiastic. 'Good. How much do you know about computers?'

'Well, there was a computer module on my degree course. I learnt a little of several programming languages, "C", "C-Plus-Plus", "Basic" . . .'

'What about the mainframe programming languages such as COBOL and PL/1?'

'We had a very superficial overview of mainframes and their languages and storage technologies,' Sandy replied. 'My tutor was of the opinion that mainframes had a very limited lifespan and would be replaced by networked distributed systems before the year Two-Thousand.'

'Well,' David began, 'We're going to place you as a graduate trainee with one of the government departments, DHSS, MoD, Home Office, possibly. You'll work on their systems and learn all about mainframes, as well as mid-range systems like Oracle and Sybase.'

'Why? To what end,' she queried, 'particularly mainframe, if it's declining technology?'

'Well,' David replied, 'HMG doesn't quite share your tutor's view on mainframe computers. We're told they will be around for many years to come. In fact, their technology is likely to develop to keep pace with the new competition. Anyway,' he said, 'we digress. We want you to combine the undercover skills that you learned at Caesar with computing skills that you will learn under our sponsorship, so that we can place you as a temporary employee – what the IT industry calls a contractor – into virtually any company or government department in this country, or abroad, if necessary.'

'To do what?'

'To investigate any suspected threats or inadequacies in their security systems; to locate and identify individuals who may be accessing sensitive information and passing on to third parties,' David shrugged, 'whatever and wherever the need arises.'

'What, all on my own?'

A Desire for Vengeance

David laughed. 'No, my dear;' (David did not notice Sandy wince at the patronising endearment). 'There will be a veritable army of people like you, though not many, I fear, with your particular range of skills.'

'So where will we be based, in London?' Sandy asked.

'I will be based in out headquarters at Gower Street,' David replied, 'but you will never set foot anywhere near our offices. You will be acting as an external agent and I will be your handler. Your salary will be paid out of a special fund, disguised as a contract agency, and your name, your new name, will not be recorded anywhere in the Security Service systems.'

'How will we communicate?' Sandy asked. 'How will I receive my assignments? Don't tell me,' she laughed; it was almost a giggle. "This tape will self-destruct in five seconds".'

'Something like that,' David replied with a smile. *God, this girl is gorgeous!*

'What is my new name going to be?'

'That's still being worked on. These things take time. A few weeks and then we'll be able to get you started.' David shifted uncomfortably before changing the subject. 'What are you going to do about the baby?' he asked, bluntly.

Sandy grimaced. She had asked herself that question a thousand times since she found out she was pregnant.

'I think I'm going to keep it.'

'Are you sure about that?' David challenged her. 'It's an important decision.'

'No,' Sandy replied. 'To be honest, I'm not sure, but it isn't the baby's fault that his or her father raped me. Killing it would be punishing the son for the sins of the father, as they say.'

Rape. Sandy had not said as much in K's office but David had assumed that Sandy had not been a willing partner to sex with thirty or forty men. He wondered how she had survived the ordeal. Surely most women would have been destroyed by something like that, mentally if not physically.

'You may think that now,' said David, 'but in the future, every time you look at that baby you'll be reminded of the circumstances of its conception. In time you may come to resent, or even hate it.' He watched as Sandy considered that viewpoint.

'On the other hand, it may just be the only good thing to come out of this whole sorry episode. It's as much a part of me as him. More, in fact. His involvement ended the moment he ejaculated. I'm carrying the baby and nourishing it, and it will be me that brings it up.'

'Do you think you will be able to bear being reminded constantly of . . .' unsure of the best words to use, he hesitated briefly before continuing, 'what happened, as the child grows up? What about when it starts asking questions about its father; what will you say?'

'I don't know!' Sandy suddenly shouted back at him.

David was taken aback by the ferocity of her response. In the living room, the two bodyguards glanced at one another, and Simon pulled a face that made Anna smirk. Meanwhile, Sandy had risen from the table and, with her arms folded across her stomach as if to protect the subject of the discussion, she stared out of the kitchen window. It was a sad excuse for a garden. No grass or flowerbeds, just a patio, with weeds growing through gaps in the pointing, enclosed on three sides by six-foot high fences.

'Look, I know it won't be easy,' Sandy said, turning back to face David and punctuating her words with jerky hand movements, 'but, if I'm not allowed to see my sister, this baby will be the only blood family I have left, someone to love and to care for.'

'You can have another child, born out of a loving relationship,' David said with more passion than was appropriate to his relationship with the much younger woman. 'Terminate this poor creature and draw a line under that terrible experience. Give yourself time to get over...'

'Do you think I'll ever forget what happened to Caroline and me?' Sandy, asked, equally impassioned. 'I'll never forget! And I would probably feel even worse if, after all the deaths associated with that mission and its aftermath, I add one more innocent life to the tally.'

Caroline? David made a mental note. Other than the disclosure in K's office, this was the first piece of information regarding the mission that Sandy had allowed to slip out. Even when drugged, she had stonewalled any questions regarding Bosnia, answering only those questions concerned with the invasion of her home on that otherwise normal Friday evening.

'I think you should consider very carefully before you make a final decision. There's still time; I think the time limit is around six months...'

'Twenty-four weeks, to be precise,' Sandy corrected him pedantically.

'So how far gone are you?'

'Where are we?' Sandy mused. 'Today is the Tenth of September, so about twelve weeks.'

'Okay,' said David. 'You still have time…' he almost said *to come to your senses* 'to make a final decision. Whatever you decide, the Service will support you. You're one of us now.'

'I think I've made my decision,' Sandy said and then nodded her head, firmly. 'Yes, I've made my decision. I'm going to keep the baby.' Then she smiled.

David gaze took in the dazzlingly white, even teeth and the twinkling azure eyes, and his heart performed several somersaults.

***

'So where is she?' The American barked into the phone. He had a deep, booming voice and a nasal New York accent.

'She's gone to ground,' replied the voice at the other end of the line. The accent reminded the American of British movies from the 1930s, when all the characters spoke the Queen's English, wore tweeds and smoked pipes. 'They're setting her up with a new identity.'

'Where?'

'Haven't the foggiest, old chap. That information would be very difficult to obtain.'

'Well, fuckin' *obtain* it, will ya? If she starts spreading what we think she knows it could be harmful to our health, you know what I'm saying?'

'Yes, of course. I have my people working on it. That's the best we can do at the present time.'

'Well make sure they get off their asses and get to it. I still can't believe how your guys coulda screwed up. How fuckin' hard can it be to snatch or waste one skinny girl, for Christ's sake?'

'I quite agree, but we are where we are. We have to make the best of it going forward.'

'Right, well make sure they don't fuck this up a second time,' he said, returning the receiver to the cradle with a crash. He sat back in the luxurious leather swivel chair and looked around the room at the dark wood bookcases filled with ancient leather-bound books, the sombre paintings on the walls and the Axminster carpet. The big old house belonged, not the American, but to the man to whom he had been speaking on the phone, as did the sixteen-year-old single malt Scotch which sat before him on the big desk. He grinned and poured a treble into a heavy crystal tumbler, savouring the smoky, peaty bouquet.

Chapter 9

Sandy looked out of the rain-lashed window at a very different back garden. It was three weeks since the murder of her parents, and the ordeal of the interrogation; two weeks since making the momentous, and, to her mind, irrevocable decision to keep the baby; a fortnight during which she had neither seen nor heard anything from David. Then today, without warning, he had arrived and announced that they were going for a drive. Sandy had been thrilled to escape from the little house in Balham that for two weeks had been her prison. As David drove his black Jaguar XJ6 south along the A23 through Streatham, Thornton Heath and Croydon, Sandy revelled in the sights of the shabby South London streets and their cosmopolitan inhabitants. The journey took about an hour before David stopped the car in the driveway of a compact, red brick detached house in a quiet residential road in Purley, close to the London's border with Surrey.

'What do you think?' David asked. He was standing a few feet behind her.

'Garden needs attention,' she mused distractedly, looking at the unkempt lawn and flowerbeds overgrown with weeds. 'My dad would have enjoyed getting to grips with that lot'

'We'll get someone in to manage that for you. What about the house?'

Sandy turned from the window. 'Seems a bit big for one person,' she said.

'Unless you've changed your mind about having an abortion, there'll soon be two of you,' he countered.

'I haven't changed my mind,' Sandy replied, 'but how am I ever going to cope with a full-time job and a small baby?' The idea of being a mother, of being solely responsible for the welfare of a small child, terrified her. David, however, seemed to have an answer for everything.

'You can get a nanny for the child once your maternity leave is over.'

'Will I be able to afford her wages and the rent on my salary?'

David grinned. He looked ten years younger when he smiled.

'That's the best part. Now you are under the protection programme, it all comes fully paid for. Until recently, this was the home of a defected KGB colonel. It has the highest level of security – steel-reinforced doors with special locks, bulletproof windows with reinforced frames. The main bedroom is a strong room. If you go in there and close the door, no one would be able to breach it. It's even fireproof.' He waved his arms to encompass the whole house. 'The alarm has movement detectors covering everywhere in the house and the garden, and there are two panic buttons, one upstairs and one down. It's linked to the local police station less than two miles away and if it's triggered they will send an armed-response vehicle up here immediately. Since the colonel died it's been used as temporary lodgings for a number of visiting transients, but from today it will be shown as no longer available. It's all yours.'

Sandy felt breathless. She was overwhelmed. Being officially dead, she could not benefit from her late parents' estate. Her sister, Samantha, would get everything. She did not begrudge Samantha the money and property, but Sandy had wondered how she herself would manage.

'How long for?' she asked.

'It will be yours for as long as you remain in the Service,' David replied.

'What's the catch?' Sandy asked, watching David's eyes and body language for a hint of a lie in his reply.

'There's no catch…'

'But…' Sandy prompted when she detected a faint hesitation.

'There is an expectation of your continued, er, discretion regarding events in Bosnia.'

'Ah,' Sandy nodded. So they were buying her silence. 'That's not a problem, David,' Sandy said. 'I have absolutely no intention of raising my head above that particular parapet. The bastards have already tried to kill me three times. I'm certainly not going to give them another chance if I can possibly help it!' She ran her fingers through her blonde hair, ruffling it, making it look untidy but somehow making her even more desirable. 'This has got to change, too.'

'What are you going to do, shave it off?' David asked with a grin.

'I'll grow it a bit longer and dye it, I suppose.'

'Such a shame,' David lamented. 'All over the world brunettes are dyeing their hair blonde and you're going the other way!'

'Can't be helped,' she said with a shrug. 'I have to change my appearance. How do you think I'd look with glasses?'

'Don't forget the false moustache,' he added with a laugh. Sandy laughed along briefly, and then became serious again.

'I'm only twenty-four, David, and soon to be a single mother. How am I supposed to explain being able to afford a house like this?

Pulling out a chair, David sat at the kitchen table and inclined his head toward the chair opposite, reminding Sandy of the interrogation room. Nevertheless, she sat and looked at him, expectantly.

'When your late husband died, he left sufficient provision for you in insurance policies and shares, very generous provision, in fact.'

'Oh, I was married was I?' Sandy smiled, although suddenly, she felt like crying. She patted her tummy. So far, there was no visible evidence of her condition – apart from the morning sickness that thankfully had ceased now. 'He must have died within the last three months, then.'

'Yes, very tragic,' David said with simulated gravity, 'He was aboard that Air India jet that crashed a month ago. He was returning to Delhi after a home visit. He was in the Diplomatic Service, you see.'

'What about his family?'

'He was an only child; parents deceased.'

'No friends?'

'Sandy, we've retrospectively added him to the passenger list but he did not really exist. There will be no grieving relatives to deal with, believe me.'

'I see,' Sandy replied, feeling foolish as the realisation dawned. If she had been taken in by the story, why would anyone else query it? 'What was his name, my poor, dear, departed husband?'

'Edward,' David replied. 'Such a shame, you'd only been married for just over a year.'

Sandy grimaced. 'It's bloody typical! Here I am a widow, and I never even got to wear a wedding dress.' She choked back sudden tears at the unbidden vision of her father walking her down the aisle.

David saw the sudden rush of emotion and headed it off by handing her a large manila envelope.

'This contains everything. Birth certificates, your marriage certificate, Edward's death certificate, the whole history of your life and your relationship with Edward. There's a box of photographs and other paraphernalia in the boot of my car.'

Sandy peered inside the envelope and pulled out a passport.

'Hey, you made me a Libran!' Sandy said on seeing the date-of-birth, 'and four years older!'

'Your legend required that we put a few years on you. University, engagement, wedding, getting pregnant. It all takes time you know.'

'Yes, but that makes me nearly as old as Sam!' Sandy said with mock indignation.

'Who's Sam?' David asked, puzzled by the sudden twist in conversation.

'My sister, Samantha…' Sandy's voice tailed off and she saw David shift in his seat. 'You didn't speak to K, did you?' She spoke mildly but there was bitterness in her tone.

'Er, no. It didn't really come up.' He saw the disappointment in Sandy's eyes and added, 'But I will. The next opportunity I get, I promise.'

Taking David's promise at face value, Sandy's mood brightened again and she returned to the passport.

'It seems I was born in Tunbridge Wells. That's in Kent, isn't it? I've never been there.'

'Well,' said David, 'It's time you went. You might need some memories in case you ever get asked any awkward questions.' He shifted in his seat. 'We could go there for a few days; explore the place.'

Sandy looked up sharply. 'Who's we?'

'You and me, of course,' he said, suddenly looking a little uncomfortable, shifty even.

'You and me,' Sandy repeated. 'Just the two of us. Have you had any thoughts regarding our cover?'

David waved his hand, airily, as if such considerations were of no consequence. 'Man and wife, I suppose.'

Sandy eyed him suspiciously. 'And would you be expecting full conjugal rights during this little honeymoon?'

David recognised the warning note in her voice and back-pedalled. 'No, of course not. That's not what . . .'

Sandy spoke over his protestations of innocence. 'David, I like you. You're a nice guy, but I am not going to sleep with you. My short and inglorious career of whoring for the British Government is over.'

David shook his head. 'Sandy, look, I don't think of you in that way. The married couple cover would explain our remaining together the whole time.'

Sandy still looked dubious and he continued, 'Look, I've become very, er, fond of you these last few weeks, but this is purely business.' He smiled disarmingly and added, 'You could also view it as a little holiday. A change of scenery. It will do you good.'

'And I suppose your wife won't mind you spending the weekend in a hotel with a girl half your age?'

'I'm not married,' David protested. 'Oxford, Sandhurst, Coldstream Guards, Northern Ireland, The Falklands, Northern Ireland again with Army Intelligence, and then MI5. I've never had the bloody time!'

Sandy pursed her lips, and briefly closed her eyes. Then she opened them again and looked frankly at him.

'Look, you already know that my friend and I were captured by the Serb militia in Bosnia.'

'This would be Caroline? You mentioned her last time we spoke.' David raised his eyebrows, inviting her to continue.

'We were held for three days, during which time we were tied up, beaten, had cigarettes stubbed out on our bodies . . .' She paused and gathered her strength, demanding that her body control her voice so it did not quaver as she finished the sentence, '...and repeatedly raped. I'll tell you honestly, David, if any man, ever again, approaches me with an erect penis, I will rip it off with my bare hands and shove it down his throat!'

David winced and involuntarily clenched his knees together. He took a deep breath to compose himself.

'Do you know,' he said, evenly, 'I really believe you would.'

Sandy went silent as the terrible memories came rushing back. David could see the tragedy written all over her face.

'What happened to your friend?' he asked gently.

'She died,' Sandy answered so quietly that her voice barely audible. 'At least, I believe so. They took us to a bridge in the middle of the night. They were going to cut our throats and throw our bodies into the river, just as they were doing with truckloads of Bosniaks every day. Then someone we thought was dead came to our rescue. He was killed and

Caroline and I escaped by jumping into the river. It was a long drop – about forty feet – and the river was flowing fast. I nearly drowned, but was washed up on a beach about five miles downstream. Some local people looked after me and then helped me escape to Macedonia. I never saw Caroline again. I can only assume she drowned.'

'How did you come to get involved in all this?' David asked.

Sandy regarded him cautiously. She had avoided answering his questions about Caesar and Bosnia during the interrogation. Did he expect her to tell him everything now? Was this a trap or was the compassion in his voice genuine?

'I assume you must already know everything,' she replied after a few seconds thought. 'I must have spilled the beans when you drugged me in that cell.'

'We didn't question you under drugs,' David lied. 'We just gave you a sedative.'

It was the strangest interview he had ever conducted. Whilst she had shown no reluctance to answer questions about the night her parents were murdered, when he probed about events in Bosnia, she claimed never to have been there. She had said she would not even be able to point to it on a map. When he asked a question about Caesar, she started to recite Shakespeare's *Julius Caesar* in its entirety. Once she had started, he could not get her to stop. He tried in vain for two hours. Eventually, she simply drifted off to sleep without answering any questions.

'Well, you seemed to know quite a lot anyway,' Sandy said. 'You told me that you knew everything about me. You made a point of saying I was something of a tart at Uni . . .'

'I never said that.'

'All right, but that was the implication. It's true, to a point. I slept around. I had a dozen or so boyfriends over a two-year period. Why the hell not? That's not excessive. If I was a guy no one would have batted an eyelid, but a girl! Shock-horror! That would never do!'

'People have different expectations of men and women,' David said, lamely. 'Perhaps it isn't fair but that's society for you.'

'Well,' said Sandy, 'it was probably my sleeping around that brought me to the attention of the resident Caesar recruiting sergeant. Once he got his hooks into me all was lost.'

'So will you tell me now?'

'Tell you what?'

'About Caesar. About Bosnia. I want to understand what makes you you.'

'No, David, I can't tell you about my past. I want to put all that behind me now. Please don't ask.'

Later, Sandy stood at the door and waved goodbye to David as she watched him drive away. Then she came inside, made some coffee and watched TV until it was time to go to bed.

She felt an odd kind of loneliness and it occurred to her that this would be the first time ever that she had spent the night in a completely empty house. For her entire life, there had always been someone in the next bed, or the next room, or somewhere else within the building, be it home, school, the student accommodation at university, the hotel room where she was held prisoner in Bosnia or the cell in Gower Street. It felt strange to be completely alone in the house, knowing that no one else was going to come in through the front door. It felt kind of scary, even with the reassurance of the security features of the house that David had described earlier, and the knowledge that there was a loaded Glock 9mm semi-automatic in the drawer of the bedside table next to her.

She almost wished she had asked David to stay the night. There were two spare bedrooms in the house, each with two single beds. Of course, there was also the king-size in the master bedroom in which she now tossed and turned, trying unsuccessfully to get to sleep.

With sleep eluding her, it was inevitable that memories of the past year would come flooding into her mind. She thought about the conversation with David and wondered why she was so reluctant to tell him about Caesar, and what she did in Bosnia. Actually, when she thought about it, the answer was as surprising as it was obvious. She did not want to tell David about it because she liked him too much.

***

Sandy had been four months short of her nineteenth birthday when she went up to Cambridge University in the autumn of 1986. Suddenly free of the rigid discipline under which she had lived both at home with her parents and at boarding school, and being the subject of much attention from the bright young men in the student population, Sandy had gone to town. She had her long blonde hair cut short; she started smoking; she began to drink heavily; and she lost, or rather, discarded her virginity. Her first lover was a third-year chemistry student called Glynn; but there was little chemistry between them and so she dumped him and moved on – and on, and on, carelessly leaving a number of broken hearts in her wake.

That was until she met Alan.

Alan was, a post-grad student working for a PhD in history and political science. His irreverent personality appealed to Sandy's rebellious nature, but his politics, as a fervent supporter of the Young Communists, challenged the inbred conservative views that she had inherited from her parents. Sandy and Alan often argued long into the night about the big issues of the day, after which they would be angry and flustered with each other. Then they would make love with savage passion until the dawn. For the first time in her life, Sandy was head-over-heels in love.

After they had been seeing each other for a couple of months, Alan said that he was going to stay for the weekend with his uncle, and invited Sandy along. Alan's uncle proved to be an intelligent and engaging man who, since his wife had passed away a few years earlier, lived alone in a grand house in Suffolk. The three of them spent the whole weekend discussing politics, history and current affairs. Sandy was mentally exhausted by the time they said their goodbyes on Sunday afternoon, but she felt pleased that, at the tender age of twenty-two, she had held her own against Alan's far worldlier relative.

Some weeks later, Sandy went again with Alan to Suffolk, where, to her astonishment, the truth was revealed. Alan's uncle turned out to be nothing of the sort, and Alan's Communist affiliations were exposed as a sham. The older man sold her on a life of excitement and danger, of sacrifice and reward, of service to one's country. The proposal appealed to her sense of adventure and she eagerly agreed to join the secret world of the intelligence service.

Having served its purpose, Alan's relationship with Sandy came to an abrupt end and he started dating a pretty second-year Classics student called Julia. Now it was Sandy's turn to be heartbroken. She had not realised – even when confronted with the choice given her by Alan's "uncle" – that Alan's interest in her had not been personal. Nevertheless, she swallowed her pride and stoically accepted the loss of the first man she had truly loved, the man she thought had loved her. Promising herself that she would never fall in love again, she put heart and soul into her final year and concentrated on her studies.

Soon after she graduated, she informed her parents that she had volunteered to go to Eritrea as part of a Christian Aid famine relief mission. Her parents' natural concerns were soothed after a visit from the operational head of the mission, a charming middle-aged man who won them over so completely that her father bestowed upon him the honour of a tour of the garden. He convinced them that Sandy would be in no danger. Everything was under control. It would be exciting and fulfilling for their daughter to encounter something so very different to everything she had experienced so far. The parents bade farewell to their daughter for a year.

She did not go to Eritrea, however; she went to Park House.

Set in sixty acres of beautiful, landscaped grounds and surrounded by the rolling green hills of the Chilterns, Park House was an imposing, red brick Georgian mansion, which housed the training facility of the Covert Surveillance

Resource Service. The fifteen young women and seven young men in Sandy's intake were all in their early- to mid-twenties. Predominantly of white Anglo-Saxon or Celtic stock, there were a few from more exotic ethnic origins.

The first two weeks comprised induction training, which challenged the recruits' views and beliefs on morality, duty, fidelity, honesty, religious teachings and politics. Several of the group were weeded out during this time, and quietly left the establishment having been reminded of the consequences, under the Official Secrets Act, of disclosing to anyone any information regarding the Service.

During the following months, the recruits learned the arts of conversation, listening and observation. They learned how to detect a lie from involuntary body language, and how to conceal their own. They studied methods of intelligence gathering and surveillance techniques, learning how to infiltrate a group and blend in. They learned how to steal without being caught and they perfected the skills of pickpockets and conjuring magicians.

They developed acting skills that would impress a West End theatre director, so that they could adopt any persona. They practised speaking in accents that would allow them to become invisible within a local population in London, Newcastle, Liverpool or Belfast. The more linguistically able students, Sandy included, took crash-courses in basic Russian and Arabic.

They learned how to shoot with a variety of firearms, and how to maintain them. They learned to fight with knives and other weapons, and they trained in karate, aikido and ju-jitsu. Then they had to learn how not to fight; how to roll with the punches and minimise injuries whilst giving the impression that they were incapable of resistance.

They learned First Aid and trauma management. For some of this training they worked alongside medics in the Accident and Emergency department of a major hospital in the midlands, where they gained practical, hands-on experience.

They practised advanced driving skills, learning how to reverse at high speed and to execute 'J' turns; how to force a car though a roadblock without disabling it; how to take control of the car from the passenger seat if the driver had been disabled or killed.

It was not until three-quarters of the way through their course that the trainees learned that sex would be another weapon in their personal armoury. It came as a shock to some that, in the course of their deep-cover surveillance, it might be necessary to sleep with their targets or those close to them. To Sandy it seemed perfectly logical. If the trainees had one thing in common, it was their relaxed attitude to casual sex. Another common factor was that they were all physically attractive. From that moment, she accepted that sex would no longer be restricted to acts of love or pleasure; it was as much a tool of her trade as a bug or miniature camera, to be used in pursuit of an assignment.

Then, one morning, in late January 1992, Sandy, along with two other trainees, Caroline and Jeanette, all of whom had studied Russian, were taken to a room where a stranger awaited them. Introducing himself as Grebe, he revealed that he was putting together a team for an operation in a foreign city. The objective was to locate the target, a war criminal, and lure him into a position, which would facilitate his capture by a Special Forces unit. Their role, he told them quite openly, was to be the bait. The three young women had glanced at each other with widened eyes, but if any of them felt any misgivings, they showed no sign.

With a few weeks still to run before the end of their training, they were at liberty to decline the mission, but none did. Excitedly, they returned to their rooms, packed their belongings and were driven away from Park House within the hour. There had been no opportunity to say goodbye to the others, and Sandy had wondered if she would ever see any of them again.

Ten months later, alone in a strange house on the southern extremity of Greater London, Sandy lay crying softly in the night. Her life had changed more than she had imagined possible. She was all alone in the world. Everyone who had ever known her believed that she was dead, and probably hated her as the murderer of her own parents. She had a new name, a fabricated life history and an uncertain future caring for a rapist's baby.

Chapter 10

'Well, are you going to carry me over the threshold?' Sandy joked as David opened the door to their room.

David had collected Sandy from the house in Purley at ten o'clock on that Friday morning and they had driven down to Tunbridge Wells via a route that meandered through the Ashdown Forest. Surprised that the overpopulated southeastern corner of England could still possess so much beautiful, unspoilt countryside, the rolling, tree-lined hills and frequent long views across The Weald had lifted Sandy's spirits and made her feel alive again. She had been charmed by the sight of sheep grazing alongside a stretch of road that had cattle grids at each end and by the young roe deer buck with two-point antlers that had bounded across the road fifty yards in front of the car. They stopped for lunch at a quaint, timber-framed seventeenth century coaching inn near Hartfield, and chatted about anything and everything, discovering snippets of detail about each other's lives, strengthening their budding friendship.

They reached their hotel, near the centre of Tunbridge Wells, in the middle of the afternoon and checked in as Mr & Mrs Stephenson. If the receptionist wondered about the age difference between the distinguished-looking middle-aged man and his beautiful young wife, she gave no indication and David declined the offer of a porter to carry the two small weekend cases to the room. The wide, richly carpeted, oak staircase creaked with age as they climbed to the first floor. They followed the signs to their room, which was at the end of a long, dimly lit corridor.

Sandy was not sure whether it was she or David that was the more surprised when they entered the room and saw the big double bed that took up most of the floor space. David was incensed.

'I distinctly asked for a twin-bedded room,' he said angrily, his face florid with embarrassment. He was worried that Sandy might suspect that he had done this deliberately in order to share a bed with her. 'I'm going to call Reception and get us moved,' he added, striding across the room.

'Don't,' said Sandy and David looked round at her, telephone in his hand. She continued, 'We're supposed to be married. It would look pretty strange to complain about having a double bed. Don't worry, we'll manage.'

David looked at her with a bemused expression. 'But after what you said last week . . .'

'You'd better not get an erection,' said Sandy with a menacing scowl. Then the mask slipped and she put her hand to her lips and laughed.

David hesitated briefly and then laughed along with her, marvelling at her ability to retain a sense of humour after everything she had been through in the past six months.

'We can build a little wall down the middle with spare blankets,' Sandy suggested, 'so you can rest assured that I won't ravish you in the middle of the night.'

Having no access to her belongings, which were all at her parents' house, the only clothes Sandy possessed were the things that Anna had bought for her while she was at the safe house in Balham. That was two pairs of jeans, five tee shirts, a fleece jacket and some running kit. There was certainly nothing suitable for eveningwear in the dining room of this rather smart hotel, so, after checking in, they headed for the town centre.

Despite her dislike of shopping – or perhaps because of it, Sandy set to her task with single-minded determination. The first purchase had been that essential item of a lady's wardrobe, the *Little Black Dress*. Then came the equally essential accessories and David tried not to look bored as Sandy pored over clutch bags, scarves and shawls. When she started to try on shoes, he made his excuses and left her to it, saying he also had one or two things he needed to buy.

Later they returned to the hotel, each clutching several carrier bags containing Sandy's purchases. If David had bought anything, there was no sign of it.

'Do I look okay?' Sandy asked once she had finished dressing for dinner.

David was wearing a charcoal grey suit, a white shirt and blue tie with a swirling paisley pattern. He looked up from tying his shoelace and gasped.

Sandy's dress was a sleeveless, figure-hugging, knee-length creation in black taffeta with a high neckline to hide the scars of cigarette burns on her chest and back. To cover her bare shoulders she wore a sheer black chiffon wrap. She had not yet dyed her hair and her natural blonde locks complimented the outfit perfectly. The overall effect took David's breath away.

'You look stunning, absolutely stunning,' he smiled, 'but I think there's something missing.' He stood up and, from the inside pocket of his jacket, produced a slim, black, rectangular box.

'What's this?' Sandy asked as she opened the box. Inside, a chain of intertwined yellow and white gold links nestled on a cushioned, white satin lining, flanked by a pair of earrings made to the same design with two inches of chain forming the drop.

'My God, it's beautiful!' She took the necklace from the box and held it up to the light with trembling fingers. 'Oh, David, you shouldn't have. It must have cost you a fortune!'

Without replying, David took the chain from Sandy and stood behind her, fastening the clasp. Sandy took a couple of steps toward the mirror. The chain was the perfect length, lying against her black fabric of her dress, just below the collarbone.

'Oh, David, it's lovely; thank you,' she said, and reached up to brush his cheek with her lips.

'Glad you like it,' he said, thinking that his heart was going to burst out of his chest.

Sandy slipped her feet into a pair of black strappy shoes with three-inch heels and grabbed a patent leather clutch bag from the bed.

'Let's go eat,' she said, 'I'm famished!'

David was the perfect gentleman. He escorted her protectively down the staircase, as if afraid that she might not be able to manage to walk down the stairs unaided. He opened every door for her and even pulled out her chair in the dining room.

'No one will ever believe we're married if you carry on treating me like a duchess,' Sandy chided him. Then she smiled, conspiratorially, leaned forward and spoke in a stage whisper. 'They probably think I'm your mistress and you've got a battleaxe of a wife somewhere who thinks you're on a golf weekend with your cronies.' David laughed. It was a rather brittle laugh. *Why is he nervous? What is he hiding?* Then, in a flash of intuition, she had the answer.

There was a brief interlude as the waiter arrived with the wine – an outrageously overpriced Chablis that David had decided would complement the *entrées*, his smoked salmon pate and her deep-fried camembert. Sandy would have been just as happy with the house wine – red or white.

'Would Sir like to try the wine?' the waiter asked. His tone of voice was at once both obsequious and superior. Sandy suppressed a snigger as David ostentatiously tested the bouquet and palate before declaring it acceptable. The waiter poured a little into two crystal glasses and placed the bottle in a cooler beside the table.

'Tell me about Caroline,' David invited once they were alone.

Sandy's smile faded. She did not want to think about Caroline, lying cold in a grave somewhere in Bosnia. David's lack of sensitivity in thinking that her murdered friend was a suitable topic of polite conversation angered her.

'No,' she replied sharply, and then after a pause, 'Tell me about your wife.' David looked shocked.

'I told you I wasn't . . .'

'You lied,' said Sandy matter-of-factly and saw her suspicions confirmed in David's expression.

'Yes, you're right,' he admitted, shame-faced. 'We're all but separated, nowadays. We live in the same house, when I'm not away with work, that is, but we have nothing in common. We hardly even speak to one another.'

'Where does she think you are this weekend?' He looked at her and she knew what he was going to say before the words reached his lips.

'On a golf weekend with my cronies,' David echoed her earlier words.

Sandy's anger evaporated and she laughed. 'I knew it!' Then, more seriously, 'Why don't you divorce her?'

'Two children,' David replied. 'Jeremy is seventeen and Sarah, fourteen.' At least he had the grace to look contrite, Sandy thought. 'How did you guess?' David asked, avoiding eye contact.

Sandy raised her wine glass to her lips and regarded him over the rim. She knew that she had to lighten the mood again or ruin the evening.

'I can read minds,' she intoned theatrically, before adding in a simulated shocked tone, 'and what I'm reading now is X-certificate!'

David frowned with embarrassment. 'I'm sorry,' he said, 'you must despise me.'

'Oh not at all,' she replied lightly. 'All that fidelity crap doesn't wash with me. It doesn't matter to me whether you're married or not.' Sandy looked closely at his face, where the battle of his emotions and desires were plain to see. 'Does that shock you?' she asked and then shrugged as she added, 'They knocked all sense of morality out of us at Park House.

'Park House?' he queried, bemused.

'Caesar's training centre,' she whispered. 'I shouldn't have said anything. Forget I mentioned it.'

'I've forgotten already,' David replied.

The plates from the first course had long since been taken away, along with the empty Chablis bottle, which had been replaced by a bottle of velvety St Emilion claret.

'When you were in Sarajevo, did you ever come across a man named Andre Devereux?' David asked, unnecessarily touching his napkin to his lips.

Sandy remembered the man only too well, but why was David venturing into her past again? What was he after? Was it just mild curiosity or was there a darker motive? The wine had already loosened her tongue enough to mention Park House. Dare she continue answering questions? She might inadvertently give away something important. She thought about the latest question and decided it was safe to answer – but not too easily. She made a show of beetling her brow as if trying to concentrate.

'The name rings a bell, but I can't place it,' she lied.

'He was with the UN Protection Force, a lieutenant-colonel in the Belgian army.'

'Oh yes,' she said, 'I remember him now. Devereux, yes, that's right. We interviewed him, or rather Jane did. Gave him a really hard time about how UNPROFOR were doing nothing to stop the Serb army from shelling the city. How the hell could I have forgotten him?'

They lapsed into silence as the waiter brought their main course. David had ordered sirloin steak, rare, with French-fries; Sandy had opted for a slow-roasted shank of lamb with a baked potato dressed with sour cream.

'You interviewed him?' David asked when the waiter had gone.

'Yes,' Sandy explained, looking left and right to ensure they were not overheard. 'I was a sound engineer in Jane Badell's film crew.'

'Oh I see.' David took a sip of wine and lowered his glass to the table. 'Any other contact with him, at all, that you remember?' He waited patiently for her answer as the waiter set down a platter of seasonal vegetables on the table between them.

Sandy stared into the middle distance while pretending to search her memory. She did not like where this was going. David's interest had to be more than just polite conversation. Why was he homing in on Devereux? Was he aware of the odious activities of the detestable Belgian colonel? She decided to hit the ball back into his court.

'No,' she replied eventually, slowly shaking her head. 'I'm sure, now you've jogged my memory, I would have remembered if we'd seen him again. Why do you ask? Do you know him?'

There was a slight pause, as if David was now unsure whether to disclose certain information. Then, seeming to come to a decision, he replied, 'Yes, he was my counterpart in the Intelligence Corps of the Belgian Army. I met him a few times.'

'Tell me about your golf,' Sandy challenged before David could ask again about Bosnia. 'What's your handicap?'

David laughed. 'My handicap? My handicap is that I can't hit the bloody ball in a straight line!'

They finished the meal with coffee and cognac before returning to their room. Sandy went into the en suite bathroom to get ready for bed and emerged wearing running-shorts and a strappy vest-top. She saw David's eyes flicker briefly to her chest before averting his eyes. She had seen in the mirror that the shadows of her nipples were visible through the material. She smiled inwardly. He was a man; it was natural for him to sneak a glance. She sat at the dressing table and began to remove her make-up while David took his turn in the bathroom.

Sandy waited until he had closed the door behind him, then she got up and crept across the room. Listening carefully, and keeping one eye on the bathroom door, she opened the door of the wardrobe. Inside, on a hanger, was the jacket that David had been wearing in the restaurant. Quickly, she patted it down and felt something like a cigarette case in the breast pocket. Glancing again at the bathroom door, she quickly removed the object and inspected it. It was a digital recording device. Her intuition was spot-on. There was an ulterior motive to this weekend, after all, and it was not sex. She slipped the device back into the pocket and returned to the dressing table.

Several minutes later, the bathroom door opened and she turned to see David in the doorway. He was wearing a tee shirt and boxer shorts and carrying his suit trousers over his arm.

'It seems that neither of us possesses any proper sleepwear,' he said with an engagingly shy smile. Then he opened the wardrobe door and Sandy's heart raced. Had she left any clue that she had searched his jacket? She watched out of the corner of her eye as he turned to face her. In his arms were several folded blankets that would form their modesty wall in the double bed. Sandy turned to face him and came to a decision.

'When I was a child I had my own pony,' she began. She ignored David's quizzical look and continued, 'The first time I fell off, my father made me get back on again straight away. He said that if I put it off, I would always be too afraid to get on a horse again.' She saw David's confusion but he remained silent, clearly wondering where all this was leading. 'The thing is, David,' she said decisively, 'if I am ever going to have sexual relations with a man again, I'm going to have to start somewhere, and it might as well be here, and it might as well be now, and it might as well be with you.'

David was thunderstruck. 'Do I not get a say in this momentous decision?' he asked, sounding just a little peeved.

'No,' she replied, peeling off her top, and shimmying toward him, 'you don't.'

David looked uncertain as Sandy stood toe-to-toe waiting for him to kiss her or put his arms around her. When he failed to take the initiative, she moved her lower body against him and put her arms around his waist. Her hands found their way under his tee shirt and caressed his back. He had little choice now but to put his arms around her. His fingers traced a line down Sandy's spine, making her shiver, and she tilted her face up toward his for him to kiss her, which he did, unhurriedly, gently, oh so gently, clearly savouring every nanosecond of the experience.

Sandy stepped backwards, drawing him with her. When she felt the backs of her legs touch the bed she allowed herself to fall backwards. David let her go and stood looking down at her. She lay on her back, her arms above her head as if in surrender. He stared hungrily at her body for a moment then slipped his tee shirt off. Downy golden hairs covered his chest, so fine were they that from a distance, it would look smooth. His boxer shorts did nothing to conceal his arousal and Sandy forced herself to reach out and touch him. Then she sat up and pulled the boxers down to his ankles. He stepped out of them then leaned forward to grasp the waistband of Sandy's running shorts; she lay back and lifted her hips. Slowly, he pulled the shorts down across her long, shapely legs, the silky material caressing the smooth skin.

He first kissed the soles of her feet and then his lips worked their way along her legs, kissing each ankle in turn; then each calf; then her inner thighs. Sandy stopped him there and moved more fully onto the bed, laying her head on the pillow. She lay back and looked at the ceiling as David smothered her body with kisses, evidently trying to leave no square millimetre of flesh untouched by his lips. Meanwhile his hands explored her thighs, her stomach and her breasts.

Suddenly he stopped. He remained motionless for several seconds before rolling over and lying on his back beside her. She watched with disbelief as his erstwhile proud and rampant member shrank and contracted until it resembled a fat, pink garden slug. His face was a mask of sadness and something else... disgust? Incredibly, he looked close to tears.

Having decided that seducing David was necessary to counter whatever devious game he was playing, she was somewhat disconcerted by his sudden loss of interest in her. Had she done something wrong?

'What's the matter?' Sandy asked. Her genuine confusion and concern caused her voice to sound harsher than she intended. She softened the effect by placing a cool hand on his burning cheek.

At first, she thought David was going to answer, but then he shook his head and turned his back to her. He sat on the edge of the bed and stared at the floor. Sandy rose to her knees and put her arms around him, stroking the soft ginger hairs on his chest. His back felt hot against her breasts.

'David, what's the matter?'

'I'm behaving like an animal,' he said dejectedly. 'After what you've been through...' he choked up and could not finish the sentence.

'Hey, come on, David,' She said, tightening her arms around his torso. She craned her head, attempting unsuccessfully to look into his eyes. 'Don't be silly. I started this. You're not a rapist. You're not forcing yourself on me.'

'When I see those marks on your body,' David said, turning his head away again, 'I can't help but remember what those bastards did to you.'

'That's in the past, now,' Sandy said, wishing it were true, but knowing it never would be. The doctor that had examined her on her return from Bosnia told her the physical scars of the cigarette burns would take years to fade completely. The mental ones, she feared, never would. Nevertheless, she sought to comfort David.

'My father used to say, "What's done is done and can't be undone." Then he would make me write down on a piece of paper whatever it was that needed to be put behind me. Then I would screw up the paper and throw it in the bin. It was a sort of symbolic cleansing. I've done that with . . . with what happened to me.'

As she spoke, Sandy allowed her hand to drop from his chest, her fingers tracing lightly down to his abdomen before retreating to his chest. Then she repeated the manoeuvre, again and again, each time reaching slightly lower. David seemed not to notice, and when her fingers reached their objective, there was little response.

'Even so...' David muttered, again failing to finish his sentence.

Sandy hated to see him in such a state. All subterfuge forgotten, she yearned to restore his confidence and self-esteem, and there was only one remedy guaranteed to work. If only she could persuade him to cooperate. She put her hands on his shoulders and pulled him gently backwards. He resisted at first, but she persevered and David allowed her to pull him down until he was lying on his back, staring up at her lovely face. He closed his eyes and she kissed his forehead, then she kissed the tip of his nose and then his lips before moving down to his chest, where her lips brushed lightly across his pectoral muscles and her tongue flicked across his right nipple.

Sandy's breasts were now within reach of his lips and he was unable to resist kissing them as they passed by, moving inexorably southwards. They were following a line pioneered by her lips as they traced across his stomach – and lower still. By the time the lips passed his navel, the object of the exercise had risen to meet her. David gasped with pleasure as her mouth enveloped him and with his hands on her hips, he guided her lower body closer until the circle was completed and he could return the compliment.

While David concentrated on his efforts to pleasure Sandy, she applied every trick she had learned at Park House to bring him to climax as quickly as possible. David, however, had other ideas, and they were soon caught up in a tangle of limbs as he flipped her over and turned his body so that they both had their heads on the pillows.

Sandy fought down a sudden wave of panic and steeled herself for the inevitable. She reached down with her hand to guide him. Then, out of politeness and the desire to reward David for his gallant efforts, she turned in an Oscar-winning performance to convince him that she was experiencing the most Earth-shattering orgasm of all time.

Before long, David lost the battle to restrain himself. His breathing became ragged, sucking in air and expelling noisily. His hips jerked spasmodically and then at last he lay by her side, spent and shaking with exertion. David enfolded her in his arms, whispering sweet endearments into her ear and Sandy let out a sigh of contentment that was not entirely feigned.

They rounded another corner and the bridge came into view. It was the middle of the night but the bridge stood out clearly, illuminated in all its majesty by the quarter moon shining among a myriad of brilliant stars in a black velvet sky. The car in front halted in the middle of the bridge and theirs stopped a few feet behind.

Sandy looked at Caroline. She was slumped awkwardly on the rear seat beside her. Caroline returned the look and Sandy could see her own terror reflected in her friend's eyes. Like Sandy, Caroline was naked and had her hands bound behind her back. Like Sandy, cuts, bruises and cigarette burns covered her face and body. Both women were exhausted, no longer capable of offering any kind of resistance.

The two men in the front seats got out of the car and dragged the two young women from the backseat. Neither had the strength to resist as the men frogmarched them to the few steps leading up to the stone bench known as the Sofa. They stood in the chill night air, trembling with exhaustion and fear.

Another four men got out of the leading car. Like the two that flanked Sandy and Caroline, they wore scruffy, dirty, ill-matched paramilitary uniforms. Sandy watched as one of the four men detached himself from the group and approached them alone. She saw his grim expression and a look of cold determination in his eyes. Her eyes fell on the large combat knife that he carried low in his right hand, as if trying to conceal it. Then Caroline saw who it was and cried out his name.

Suddenly, as if by a prearranged signal, Sandy felt herself being propelled towards parapet on the downstream side and forced to lie across the cold, grey stone, bent forward with her head above the rushing green water forty feet below. She glanced to her right and saw Caroline beside her in the same position. Then her executioner put a knee in Sandy's back and took a handful of her hair, forcing her head back, stretching her throat ready for the killing stroke.

'Sandy, Sandy! Wake up!'

Sandy opened her eyes. She was bathed in sweat and her heart was racing. She stared up at David's face above her. It took several seconds for her to calm herself, and all the while David was talking in a gentle, soothing voice, softly stroking her sweat-dampened hair.

'I'm okay now,' she said shakily.

'You were having a nightmare.'

'Tell me about it!' Sandy replied, her body still trembling with the memory.

'Do you want to tell *me* about it?' David invited.

'No,' Sandy replied flatly. She lay looking up at David's face, barely visible in the darkness even though it was so close she could feel his breath on her cheek. It triggered another memory and she shuddered. For a moment, she felt as if she was going to be sick. Then the feeling passed and she craved the comfort of human contact.

'David, make love to me,' she said, reaching for him under the covers. He responded instantly to her touch. 'Make love to me. Make the bad dream go away.'

Chapter 11

'And finally, oh Lord, we ask you to comfort our sister and brother, Samantha and Stephen, as they endeavour to come to terms with the terrible tragedy that has befallen them.' He paused for effect before continuing, 'In the name of the Lord Jesus Christ, Amen'

'Amen.' The murmured response from a larger-than-usual congregation filled the nave and aisles with a susurrant hum, a soft wave of sound that was at once both awe-inspiring and comforting.

The Reverend William Bulford counted to ten before raising his right hand in benediction and delivering his final utterance of the service. 'Peace be with you.'

Each member of the congregation extended a hand to their near neighbours in the pew in front, those behind and those alongside, in fact, anyone within reach of a handshake, and repeated the sentiment.

'Peace be with you.'

'Peace be with you.'

Kathy Taylor reached into the pew in front and took the hand of a blonde woman, a few years older than herself, wearing a black, knee-length, round-necked dress under an unbuttoned black topcoat and a black pillbox hat with a black lace veil over her eyes. 'Peace be with you,' Kathy uttered with a friendly smile.

'And with you,' the woman replied, but her smile was tight and short-lived, and her red-rimmed and sunken eyes betrayed an inner turmoil held in control only by the strength of her faith. She released Kathy's hand and reached out to an elderly, grey haired lady who was standing beside Kathy.

Immediately, Kathy's vacant hand was taken by a man standing beside the blonde in black. He had collar length, dark curly hair and wore a charcoal grey suit with a crisp white shirt and a thin, plain black tie.

'Peace be with you,' he intoned, retaining Kathy's hand an instant longer than necessary, his dark eyes locking with hers.

'Peace be with you,' Kathy replied. Her mouth twitched in a half-smile before she gently retrieved her hand from his and looked for another soul with whom to exchange the fleeting contact.

After a few minutes, the congregation began to edge their way toward the arched oak doors at the western end of the nave, by which time the Reverend Bulford endeavoured to shake hands with every worshipper before allowing them to escape into the grey autumn morning beyond. Deliberately hanging back, Kathy noticed that a small band of worshippers had filtered through a door off the north aisle, level with the transept. Among them was the mourning couple that had been in the row in front of her.

Kathy toured the church, marvelling at the stained-glass windows, reading the tributes etched on brass plaques commemorating local heroes and dignitaries, and finally stopped by a hexagonal stone font, each of its six sides carved with religious symbols.

'Fifteenth Century,' a resonant voice said from close alongside. Kathy looked up into the cheery, round, red-cheeked, bearded face of the Vicar. His eyes briefly swept over her, taking in the extraordinary beauty of her face, even though it was devoid of make-up, and her elaborately plaited auburn hair.

'It's wonderful,' Kathy gushed. 'How old is the church?'

'There was a Christian church here before the Conquest,' Reverend Bulford replied proudly. 'The first was built of wood, and burned down. It was rebuilt and burned down again, several times.' He swept one arm around to encompass the nave, transept and south aisle. 'The present building dates from the twelfth century, though; which explains its solid construction. It was as much a refuge from marauding Welshman as a place of worship.'

Kathy smiled, recognising from his accent that the clergyman's origins were clearly from the other side of that border, which lay only a short distance from this spot. 'Well, I must be going now,' she said suddenly, 'I mustn't delay you. I think you have some people waiting for you in the vestry?' She inclined her head to indicate the door through which she had observed the small group pass, minutes earlier. 'Thank you for such a lovely service,' she finished, enthusiastically.

'Well, thank you for coming,' he replied, smiling warmly. 'I don't believe I've seen you here before. I hope we'll see you again?'

'Oh, I'm sure,' she beamed. 'I'm new to the area and I'd like to get to know more people. I always think joining a nice community church is the best way to meet new people, don't you?'

'Indeed,' he replied, still smiling. 'Look, why don't you join us for coffee? I could introduce you to some of our stalwarts.'

Kathy inclined her head. 'That would be very nice, but...' she glanced at her wristwatch.

'Oh, well, perhaps another time?'

'Actually,' she replied. 'I do have time. Thank you. I'd love to join you.'

'Splendid!' cried the vicar with an even broader smile. 'This way.' He took her elbow and guided her to the arched doorway in the north aisle.

Inside, twenty or so people, proportionately more women than men, and mostly of pensionable age, stood talking in groups of two, three or four. The exception was the black-clad blonde whose hand Kathy had shaken earlier. She was standing apart from the general crowd, staring at a silver spade inside a wall-mounted glass case. Her husband, Kathy noted, stood at a table in the corner, spooning instant coffee granules into two cups before filling them with hot water from an urn. Despite his promise of introductions, the Rev. Bulford had been besieged by three elderly ladies the moment he stepped through the vestry door, and Kathy smiled away his unspoken apology, made eloquent by eyes that signalled his helplessness in the face of the onslaught. Kathy approached the blonde who continued to study the spade as if it held the secrets of the universe.

'Hello,' Kathy said, and the woman turned to face her. 'I'm Kathy, Kathy Taylor.'

The woman smiled her tragic smile again. She seemed flustered, unsure what to do or what to say. Clearly, she had been expecting her husband to break through the invisible cordon that, by turning her back to the room, she had woven around herself. Instead she was confronted by this stranger. After a moment's hesitation, her good manners overcame her discomfort. 'Samantha McNamara,' she replied. 'A pleasure to meet you. We haven't seen you here before, have we?'

'Oh, you're Samantha!' said Kathy excitedly, and when the blonde looked at her quizzically, she added swiftly, 'We work for the same company. I've just started at Brighting and Blount, this week.'

Samantha looked even more confused. 'You work at Brighting's? Doing what?'

'I'm a secretary. Look, I'm terribly sorry. I heard about your loss...' Kathy became aware of another person in close proximity and paused.

'Who is this?' The husband had returned, with a cup and saucer in each hand. Minutes before, he had shaken hands with Kathy. *Peace be with you*, he had said, but now Kathy detected suspicion, hostility, even.

Samantha looked up at the man 'This is Kathy,' she said. 'She's just started working at Brighting and Blount.' Even as she spoke the words, her voice registered surprise at their content. 'Kathy,' she added, 'this is my husband, Stephen.'

Stephen handed one of the cups to his wife. 'Oh, er, pleased to meet you,' he said, and shook Kathy's hand, formally. This time he released it immediately, almost as if afraid of catching something. 'What brings you here?'

'Oh, I have a flat nearby. This is my nearest church. Mr Brighting told me that you also worship here.'

'Did he?' Stephen's suspicion was still evident. 'So why have you only just decided to come here?' he asked directly.

'I just moved in a couple of weeks ago,' Kathy replied, allowing a little irritation to show in her voice at this presumptuous interrogation.'

'Stephen!' Samantha said suddenly. 'Leave the poor girl alone, will you?' She turned to Kathy. 'I'm sorry, Kathy, Stephen is just being protective. We've been bothered a lot by reporters and photographers since....' She left the sentence hanging then turned on Stephen again. 'Stephen, why don't you let Kathy have that coffee and go and get yourself another?'

Stephen hesitated a moment then noticed Kathy's eyes. They seemed to burn deep into his soul. Now it was his turn to become flustered.

'It's white with no sugar,' he said extending his hand toward her. The cup rattled slightly in the saucer, and Stephen realised his hand was shaking. Kathy took the proffered saucer in long, elegant fingers and the rattling stopped.

'That's just as I like it,' she smiled.

Stephen returned the smile briefly then turned and made his way once more to the urn. Kathy sipped the coffee and turned back to face Samantha, but Samantha spoke before Kathy could form any words.

'What did you say you're doing at Brighting's?'

'I'm working as the receptionist-cum-secretary,' Kathy replied. 'I'm standing in for a Mrs Mason?' She finished the sentence with a rising inflection as if requesting confirmation of the name.

'Why?' Samantha asked. 'What's happened to Mrs Mason?'

'Oh, have you not heard?' Kathy replied, looking directly into Samantha's pale blue eyes. 'She had an accident, a week ago last Thursday. She's in hospital.'

'Oh my goodness!' said Samantha, her hand rising to her lips. 'What happened to her?'

'She got run over by a van, apparently,' Kathy replied. 'It didn't stop, either. Drove straight off, leaving her injured on the pavement.'

Chapter 12

'Goodnight, David,' said Sandy. 'It's been a wonderful weekend. Thank you.' She reached out to touch his cheek tenderly and David had to clear his throat before he could respond.

'I wish I didn't have to leave you here.' He turned his head to kiss the palm of her hand. 'In fact, I wish we could remain together in this house for the rest of our lives.'

'We've been through this, David,' Sandy said resolutely. 'We both know an affair would put intolerable pressure on our working relationship.' David looked miserable and she felt sorry for him, but the last thing she wanted was to enter into the type of relationship in which he thought he had the right to jump on her whenever he felt like it.

'Oh, Sandy,' David said, putting his arms around her and drawing her to him. 'We could be so perfect together.'

'Down, boy!' she laughed, trying to diffuse the situation with levity. 'You need to be careful at your age. You'll wear yourself out!'

David laughed. 'There's plenty of life in the old man yet, I can assure you!' Then he sighed and added, 'I wish I had a magic wand that I could wave and make everyone and everything else disappear...'

'Don't look now,' Sandy laughed, placing both hands on his chest and pushing him away, 'but I think you've got one in your pocket!'

David laughed good-naturedly, despite his frustration and disappointment.

'Go on, get out of here,' Sandy said, kissing his cheek. 'Go back to your cave, Merlin, and take your magic wand with you.'

Sandy watched David reverse the car out of the driveway. Then she closed the front door and went to sit in the kitchen. Two coffee mugs remained on the table and she stared at them disconsolately before switching on the kettle to make another for herself. Staring at the steam rising from the coffee cup she replayed the weekend's events in her mind.

David had taken her by surprise by his mention of Colonel Devereux at dinner on Friday evening. He had dropped it into the conversation when he thought that she would be at her most vulnerable, relaxed in pleasant and safe surroundings, a couple of drinks inside her. It would have been easy to slip up, and the consequences of making such a mistake she dare not imagine.

That conversation had altered the whole course of the weekend. Had it not been for that, she would not have seduced him; would not have felt the need to change the nature of the relationship they had formed over the past few weeks. Remembering David's shocked expression when she first made her move, she smiled. He had been hesitant the first time, but after that, there was no stopping him.

It was as if a dam had burst. Friday night, Saturday morning (twice before breakfast), Saturday evening – before and after dinner – and finally, most of Sunday morning. He could not get enough of her, and she had certainly kept him happy!

As a result, they had spent far more time in the hotel room than intended, and consequently, they had seen far less of the town where she was supposed to have grown up. Crucially, they did take a look at the house she was supposed to have lived in. It was a Georgian town house in the Mount Sion district, backing onto an area of open land known as The Grove. They had also promenaded through The Pantiles and hiked the two miles out to High Rocks. All in all, it had been, on the face of it, quite a pleasant weekend.

But why, why, why had David mentioned Devereux?

Sandy found the tale about them being contemporaries in military intelligence hard to believe. That was too much of a coincidence. There had to be another reason. David had asked questions about Caesar and about Bosnia. How much did he know already and what would he do if she told him the whole truth? She discounted his claim that they had not questioned her after drugging her. Why would they pass up that opportunity? They had to have tried. The question was how much had she told them?

So why did he bring up the subject of Devereux? What did he know of that individual's nefarious activities in Sarajevo? If he already knew, why ask her; if he didn't then what prompted the question? What was interesting was that he gave up asking questions about Bosnia after she fended off the question about Devereux. Why?

At the end of her debriefing after her return from Bosnia, they had warned Sandy never to reveal or even discuss what the team had discovered in Sarajevo. She understood why. If the disreputable behaviour of certain UNPROFOR officers were to become public knowledge, the fallout could seriously damage several governments on both sides of the Atlantic. It would also undermine the moral authority of UNPROFOR to carry out its duties within that war-torn country.

Sandy's superiors had assured her that action to bring an end to the scandal was already underway – but how likely was that? More likely, they were simply telling her what she wanted to hear. Clearly, the evidence gathered by Jane's team would be of benefit to UK intelligence. It would provide heaven-sent opportunities for the coercion and influence of some quite important people for years to come. Sandy had no doubt that if it were in the interests of the British and/or American governments to allow it to continue, those considerations would take precedence over the wellbeing of those unfortunates who, through no fault of their own, were caught in its web. Sandy hated the thought, but what could she do about it on her own?

***

David did not know whether to laugh or cry. It was K's idea that he should get closer to Sandy to get her to lower her defences. He was to use whatever means necessary to get her to open up about what happened in Bosnia, generally, and particularly what Badell's team had discovered in Sarajevo. K did not trust the conspiracy of silence that she suspected existed between the Director General of the Covert Surveillance Resource Service and his counterpart in the Secret Intelligence Service, and she wanted David to find out what they were covering up.

From the beginning, David had mixed feelings about his assignment. Sandy was a very desirable young woman. Obviously damaged, clearly troubled, but possessed of a resilience that bordered on superhuman. With every encounter, his admiration for her had grown, and so had his affection. This caused him considerable anguish, because despite what he had told Sandy at dinner about the state of his marriage, he still loved his wife, Fiona. The last thing he wanted was to hurt her or his children.

Certainly, there had been times when he had been tempted to stray. He was tall, slim, well spoken and possessed of a certain urbane charm. Many women found him attractive, and some had made their interest abundantly clear. Being away from home on a regular basis, sometimes for long periods of time, temptation often coincided with opportunity without fear of detection. Nevertheless, David had always resisted.

For a start, one-night-stands were not in his nature. He would never have dreamed of entering into a physical relationship with any woman for whom he did not have a strong emotional attachment. There had been times when he found himself in the early stages of what might develop into such a relationship. However, he could never reconcile the fulfilment of his immediate desire with the emotional turmoil that would undoubtedly prevail when the inevitable choice had to be made. Therefore, sometimes with a regret that almost broke his heart, he remained faithful to his wife and family.

Consequently, it was with some degree of relief to David that Sandy had so comprehensively rejected his somewhat hesitant initial advance. Their trip to Tunbridge Wells could therefore go ahead without the added complications that sex would bring. Until Sandy changed her mind.

Friday had been magical from the start. It was a lovely early autumn day with the sun shining in a blue sky dotted with white cumulus clouds. The leaves on the trees were turning, painting the hillsides of the North Downs and

Ashdown Forest with gold and russet brown. Sandy had been as excited as a child on holiday. Apparently leaving the more morose elements of her personality behind, she chatted animatedly and pointed out the sights as they drove through the leafy lanes. The longer David spent with her, the more smitten he became.

By the time they went down to dinner, David was reluctant to spoil the mood by quizzing her about things she clearly did not want to discuss. K had briefed him on what she knew of the Bosnian mission and its consequences, but there remained the great mystery of what had occurred in Sarajevo. He had little idea how to broach the subject subtly but he had to try because K would want to hear Sandy's answers on the digital recording device that she had given him for the purpose.

His initial attempt to get her to talk about Bosnia had failed when she angrily dismissed his question about Caroline. When he tried to think of another opening, he recalled an interview that he had watched on television. The interviewer had been Jane Badell and the interviewee a man that he had met five years previously at a seminar for NATO military intelligence officers, one Lt Col. Andre Devereux of the Belgian Army, now attached to UNPROFOR in Sarajevo.

After Sandy had skilfully turned the conversation onto a different track for the second time, David thought it best to back off and try again later in the weekend. He allowed himself to enjoy the rest of the evening in the company of a beautiful and intelligent young woman whose charms he found more and more difficult to resist as time went by. No one could have been more surprised than he when Sandy suddenly announced her intention to sleep with him. He almost refused, as much from shock as anything else. Then he remembered his instructions. *Whatever is necessary,* the DG had said.

It did not take much effort to kiss and caress the beautiful young woman who was so desperate for some affection. That was until an image of Fiona kissing him goodbye caused a pang of guilt that cooled his ardour like a cold shower. He hadn't really told her he would be playing golf. He didn't even own a set of golf clubs. He had told her, quite truthfully, that the trip was work-related. That was, of course, as much as he told her – as much as Fiona would expect him to tell her. She knew the secret nature of his work and never questioned his absences, which were now, thankfully, far less frequent than when he was an army officer.

Blaming his sudden impotence on the scars of the cigarette burns that covered Sandy's upper body had seemed a good way to draw a line under the episode, but Sandy had shown such understanding, such compassion such tenderness and such *skill* that he was totally unable to resist. He was like a tiger being mauled by the tethered goat, and he found he quite liked the feeling.

After that he could not stop kissing her and touching her at every opportunity, and she appeared to reciprocate his desire. She seemed as reluctant as he to do anything other than make love.

Unable to prevent himself, he had, like a callow and inexperienced youth, professed his love for her. He convinced himself that he wanted to leave behind all the cares and worries of the Service, and the mortgage, and his wife and children, and run away with his new love to a desert island where they could live the rest of their lives in uninterrupted coital bliss.

Now it was with a sense of failure and guilt that he was driving back home to Ealing. Tonight, he would have to play the dutiful husband and father. Tomorrow, he would have to face his boss and explain why, despite spending a large sum of taxpayers' money on hotel and travel expenses, he had found out nothing about Bosnia and Sarajevo. He decided not to claim for the necklace and earrings that he had bought Sandy. He wanted those to be a gift from him alone.

***

Sandy sipped her coffee and her thoughts returned to David. She almost regretted not allowing him to stay a bit longer. It had been cathartic to have someone to cuddle up to once more, even if the actual sexual act did leave her feeling physically sick.

She shrugged and pursed her lips. He had to go home to his wife eventually. Delaying it for another hour or so would not have helped at all. She wondered if he would make love to his wife when he got home. The thought was just idle curiosity. Sandy felt no jealousy. She did not own David, did not want to own him. Nevertheless, she might borrow him from time to time when the need arose. She smiled at the thought and went to sit in the living room.

The television news was on and, as usual, the war in Bosnia dominated the first ten minutes. One segment centred on the continuing siege by the Serb army of the Muslim enclave of Žepa. Sandy watched the reporter deliver his summary to camera while in the background a field gun fired a shell over the hill into the unseen town beyond.

Chapter 13

'The retired couple murdered in their home at Amberley on The Wirral last month, and the daughter suspected of shooting them, were today buried together in a private service at St. Mary's church, close to the family home. Lieutenant Colonel Charles Harris, formerly of the Royal Engineers, and his wife, Grace were found shot to death in their home last month. The body of their daughter, Sandra was recovered from the River Mersey several days later.' As the newsreader spoke, the television pictures showed a cortege of three black hearses pull up in the parking area outside the small, stone-built church.

'Before the service,' the voice continued, 'the couple's surviving daughter, Samantha McNamara and her husband, Stephen, made a brief statement to reporters.'

Sitting forward on the sofa, tissue already dabbing at moist eyes, Sandy fell to her knees and across the carpet to the television as Samantha and her husband appeared on screen with several microphones vying for position in front of them. In the background, Sandy could see her father's sister, Aunt Celia with her husband, Uncle Raymond and their children, Abigail and James, now adults with their own partners alongside them, and Anthony who was sixteen or seventeen.

As usual, Samantha's attire was perfect for the occasion. She was wearing a plain black topcoat with a large velvet collar and oversized buttons, a black pillbox hat with a satin lace veil that did little to obscure her pale-blue eyes, and her long blonde hair had been wound into a bun. Sandy's fingers caressed her sister's face on the screen as Stephen began to speak.

'We are here today to celebrate the lives of our loved ones and to deliver their souls into the care of Jesus Christ, our Saviour,' he said sonorously. 'They are making that final journey together, as they themselves would have wished.' He paused and then continued, 'We do not know what evil possessed our dear sister on that dreadful night...'

'I'm not your dear sister,' Sandy railed at her despised brother-in-law; 'I'm Sam's! You're loving this, aren't you, you attention-seeking, sanctimonious prick!'

Stephen was a "born-again" Christian who delighted in sharing with anyone who would listen, his joy at having accepted Jesus Christ as his Saviour. In Sandy's opinion, Stephen had sucked Samantha into his mean-spirited, joyless existence, in which almost every normal human activity was somehow an offence against God. Stephen was a control-freak who used his puritanical beliefs to bend others, particularly Samantha, to his will. He had changed Sam from being a happy, fun-loving – if slightly self-obsessed – person into a shadow of her former self; always deferring to him; never challenging his pronouncements.

'...to do the things she did; to take the lives of those closest to her; and then, in her torment, to go on to take her own precious young life.' Another pause, *for dramatic effect,* Sandy sneered inwardly. 'But we have found it in our hearts to forgive her and we pray that Our Lord, Jesus Christ will give her the comfort in Heaven that her troubled soul was unable to find here on Earth.'

Samantha stood by her husband's side, with moist eyes and a tight smile, nodding assent to his words. As he finished his statement Samantha leaned toward the microphones and said, in a clear voice, 'Thank you; and now we would all very much appreciate it you would please allow us to say goodbye to my sister and my parents in peace and privacy. Thank you.' Then she took her husband's arm and they returned to take their place at the head of the procession.

'Meanwhile,' the newsreader said off-camera, 'a large crowd of onlookers and well-wishers gathered outside the church, but police had to intervene when some people in the crowd started to shout abusive comments.'

The images showed the three coffins being unloaded and settled upon the shoulders of the pallbearers. The third hearse displayed a yellow and lilac flower tribute forming the word "SANDY" in the side window, and as the coffin was unloaded, a male voice from the crowd could clearly be heard shouting, 'Murderer! Rot in hell!' Other voices were calling out. The words were indistinct but their animosity was clear from the tone.

Sandy recoiled from the television screen as if physically struck. She fetched up with her back resting against the sofa, her hand covering her open mouth in shock. She fumbled around for the remote control, pointed it at the TV as if it were a weapon, and pressed the off-button so hard it was as if she was trying to drive a nail through a piece of wood with her finger. The images on the television screen were instantly cut-off and she sat looking at the blank screen for several seconds, her mind in turmoil. Then she buried her head in her hands and sobbed.

Distraught as she was at unexpectedly watching the funeral of her parents through the impersonal medium of television, separated from the event by time and distance, the realisation that she had attracted such vilification was more than she could bear. She shuddered to think that the people calling out those vile comments may have known her, may have been her own friends or those of her parents. It was more likely that they were strangers, come from miles away to enjoy the spectacle and to bay like ghoulish spectators at an eighteenth century public hanging.

For the thousandth time since she learned of her official death and her official culpability for the murders, and despite the pronouncement of forgiveness by "Saint" Stephen, Sandy wondered what those closest to her, especially her sister, really felt about her now. It was heartbreaking that she could not put the record straight, at least with Sam, if no one else. Oh, how she longed to see Sam again, if not regularly then at least for one last time. She had badgered David again, but he had told her that the Director General had refused point-blank.

'Absolutely not,' she had said, according to David, 'No way!'

Memories of birthdays and Christmases, weddings and christenings came rushing back and the images crowded Sandy's tormented mind. The last such occasion was Samantha and Stephen's wedding, when a seventeen-year-old Sandy was chief bridesmaid. She grimaced at the memory of the flowing rose-pink satin dress with its lace-edged neckline that she had been compelled to wear. Sandy had at that time hated to wear pink, especially pink dresses, for the expectation of femininity that wearing such things engendered. She had actually accused Sam of choosing pink specifically to upset her, and had sworn that she would never wear anything so grotesque. Sam, of course, had been terribly offended and Sandy's teenage sulk might have marred her sister's big day had her father not given her a stern talking-to. It had all seemed so important at the time; so trivial now.

Sandy poured herself a large scotch and sat in the silent living room. She was afraid to switch the television back on and she felt too depressed to read, or even turn on the radio. The house crowded in on her until she thought she would suffocate. She raised the glass to her lips again only to find it was empty, and padded on bare feet to the sideboard to pour another.

'Can I speak to David Richardson, please?' Sandy said into the telephone.

Although David had visited her at the house twice in the ten days since their weekend in Tunbridge Wells, there had been no resumption of their brief but intense sexual relationship. The madness of that weekend, it seemed, was not to be repeated.

'Who's calling, please?' Sandy wondered whether the voice belonged to his wife or his daughter.

'This is Greta Morgan at the office.' Sandy replied, trying to sound brisk and businesslike – and, for some reason, slightly Welsh. Remembering how she had coined the nickname "Merlin" for David after the joke about his magic wand, she had come up with the surname Morgan after Morgan le Fay, the evil half-sister of King Arthur, a sorceress to rival the wizard, Merlin.

'Okay, wait one moment, please, I'll call him,' the voice responded, and then in the background, away from the receiver. 'David, someone called Greta Morgan, from work, for you.' There was a brief wait and then the voice spoke again, but in the muffled and disembodied way that told

Sandy that David's wife was covering the receiver with her hand as she spoke to her husband. 'I hope this doesn't mean you'll have to go rushing off,' she said, 'I'm just about to serve supper.' Then there was the sound of the receiver changing hands and she heard David's voice.

'David Richardson speaking, who is this again, please?'

'It's me, Greta.'

'Oh, er, hello, this is unexpected.' Sandy could hear guilt, concern and apprehension, bordering on panic in his voice.

'I know I shouldn't call you at home but I need to see you.'

'Why, what's up?' He was making no attempt to lower his voice; in fact, he was speaking unnaturally loudly. His wife must be standing beside him, trying to gauge whether or not their supper together was about to be ruined. By raising his voice David was demonstrating to her that this was business, nothing clandestine; not his mistress committing the unforgivable sin of calling him at home.

I'm not his bloody mistress. He is supposed to be looking after me! 'Did you see the news on the telly?' She asked, trying but failing to make her voice sound normal.

'Yes,' David replied guardedly, but still affecting an unconcerned air, 'I did.'

'Their funeral was held today.' Sandy's voice choked on the words.

'Yes, I saw that.' His voice was crisp, businesslike, as if they were discussing a memo that had been circulated around the office.

'Did you know? Ahead of time I mean.'

'No, I didn't.' He replied. 'If I had known I would have warned you beforehand.' He was speaking normally now. Perhaps his wife was no longer hovering nearby.

'David, I can't be alone tonight. I need you here with me.' The pleading tone in her own voice disgusted her and she wished now that she had not called. He had given her his home number for dire emergencies. This did not really count.

'I'm sorry, Greta, I can't manage that now. It'll have to wait until morning.' Perhaps his wife was still within earshot, after all.

Sandy felt her disappointment threaten to overwhelm her. She felt worthless and ashamed. *Why am I demeaning myself in this way?*

'I understand,' she said, trying again to make her voice sound normal. 'I expect I'll have resolved the problem another way by then. Goodnight, David.'

'Wait! What do you mean?'

'Goodnight,' she said again and hung up.

David rang back seconds later, his voice hushed and anxious.

'Sandy, what did you mean, "resolve it another way"? You're not planning to do something stupid, are you?'

So that was it, more guilt.

'Don't worry, I'm not planning to top myself,' she said flatly. 'I might go out to a pub. Who knows, I might even get laid, if I'm lucky.'

'Oh, Sandy, for God's sake,' despite the whispering, she could hear the agony in his voice. She knew he wanted nothing more than to be with her tonight, but he was trapped – trapped in his little prison of domesticity. 'Don't do anything foolish, anything you might regret.'

Sandy laughed bitterly. 'A bit late for that, I think. Go on, go back and enjoy your supper. I'm fine.'

'Sandy, please don't be like that. I would come if I could. It's, well, it's difficult.'

David, it's fine, I'm fine,' Sandy said, trying to sound bright and cheery. 'Don't worry. I was just feeling a bit sorry for myself. I'm okay now.'

'Well, if you're sure…'

The bastard sounds relieved! 'Yes, I'm sure. I'm absolutely sure.'

'What are you going to do now, tonight?'

'I think I might go for a run. That will make me feel better…'

'But it's dark out. It might not…'

'I think I can take care of myself, David, don't you?'

'Are you on the phone again?' said his wife in the background.

Poor David; he's been caught. Some spook!

'Yes, Greta,' David's voice was businesslike again. 'I think that should do it. Okay? I've got to go now.'

'Yes, fine, Merlin,' Sandy answered. 'Just don't expect me to polish your wand for you – ever again!'

David heard the dialling tone buzz in his ear. 'Yes, okay, Greta, that's fine. Call me back if you need anything else.'

'Supper's on the table,' said Fiona. 'Is this likely to go on all night?'

'No,' David replied, thoughtfully, 'I don't think so.'

Sandy put down the phone and looked out of the living room window. It was dark outside and the wet pavements reflected the light from the street lamps. A car drove past, illuminated the drizzling rain in its headlights. It looked like smoke. Sandy sighed and looked again at her empty glass. She was tempted to refill it with yet another scotch but she resisted. She had already sunk three large ones, neat, no water, no ice. She knew that if she had another she would not stop until she had finished the bottle. It was now eight o'clock and the evening seemed to be dragging out interminably. She considered going out for a walk, for a run, or to a pub. She thought about the scotch bottle again, and then went into the kitchen and made coffee instead. She switched on the television and half-watched a programme about gardening, which unfortunately sparked memories of her father. The programme that followed was a current affairs documentary about the economic crisis caused when the Pound was forced out of the European Exchange Rate Mechanism, a few weeks earlier.

Nine o'clock came; the News was starting on BBC1. She could not bear to see the funeral again so she switched to BBC2. There was an arts programme about to start, but Sandy was not into art. ITV: a police drama. Channel 4 was the last hope; it was showing a sitcom about a TV station. At this point Sandy realised that no matter what was showing on television, she needed physical release and finally decided that she would go for a run after all.

After dressing in a blue Adidas track suit and spending ten minutes warming and stretching her muscles and tendons, Sandy, piled her hair up under a black baseball cap, sporting an "NYC" logo, and ventured out into the chilly autumn air. *At least it's stopped raining!*

She locked the door behind her, secured the keys inside the zipped pocket of the tracksuit top and glanced at her watch before starting off. The time was 9:45.

Chapter 14

Sandy's daily five-mile run included Riddlesdown, more than a hundred acres of steeply sloping grassland, bordered by wooded areas, to the south of Purley. It was criss-crossed by uneven earth pathways where the tips of flint rocks broke the surface like oceanic icebergs. Crucially, the area was unlit, making the prospect of tripping or turning an ankle in the dark very real indeed. Sandy decided instead to explore the still unfamiliar, but adequately lit, suburban streets in the vicinity of her new home.

At first, she felt her pace to be lumpy and unbalanced, partly because of the alcohol she had consumed earlier and partly because of the pistol strapped in its special holster against her right calf, its bulk hidden by the loose-fitting tracksuit trousers. After five minutes or so, however, Sandy began to feel more comfortable. She settled into a steady pace of seven minutes per mile and her breathing began to adopt its familiar working rhythm. Automatically, she adjusted her stride in response to the gradients, leaning forward onto her toes when attacking the inclines and lengthening her stride, striking with her heels, on the downhill stretches. On and on she ran, meandering through the dark, deserted streets, the soles of her running shoes slapping on pavements still wet from the earlier rain.

Twenty minutes into her planned forty-five minute run, after completing a steep hill-climb, and now on a flat stretch of pavement, Sandy adopted a steady recovery pace, taking deep, controlled breaths, allowing the oxygen to rejuvenate tired muscles. Endorphin, the body's natural painkiller, released into her bloodstream by the pituitary gland at the base of the skull, was coursing through her veins, triggering a slight light-headedness – the runner's high. The despair brought on by the funerals had receded, as had the hurt she had felt at David's rejection. She was feeling, if not happy, then at least content and, lost in her own thoughts, and had long since stopped concentrating on what was going on around her.

'Watcha, darlin', where are you off to, then?'

The sudden awareness that a car had drawn level, and was keeping pace with her, startled her and she castigated herself for her lack of attention. If that had been an assassin, she would have been dead before even being aware of the danger. Once the initial fright had passed, Sandy glanced sideways at the car. The driver had his window open as he called out to her. Without slackening her pace, she shouted a response.

'I'm running for the bus.'

'You've missed it, love. Ain't anuver one 'til tomorrer. Wanna lift?'

'No, I'm doing just fine, thanks.'

'Ohh, aren't we posh!' He replied, attempting to caricature her accent, before adding in his rougher tones, 'Yeah, you look pretty good to me too! Fancy a bit of rough?'

'Hah! You'll be lucky!' She replied good-naturedly, and then became slightly alarmed when the car swerved over to her side of the road and continued to pace her, driving close to the kerb on the wrong side of the road, not that there was any other traffic around at that moment to notice.

'Yeah? Wot's yer name, then?' The driver asked, his arm hanging out of the window as if trying to touch the road surface with his fingertips.

Sandy groaned inwardly. She could do without this. She had expected the car to speed off once they had exchanged a little banter, but this guy thought his luck was in.

'Forget it, sunshine. I'm not interested.' Another glance told her there were two men in the car, both early-to-mid-twenties. The car, a dark Volkswagen Golf, was right alongside her, and she angled away to the inside of the pavement, increasing the distance between them.

'Come on, darlin',' the driver said, 'don't be like that.'

'Gimme a break, guys,' Sandy said, irritated now. 'Go and bother someone else will you?'

'Ooooooh!' the passenger sneered loudly, 'Gettin' a bit stroppy, ain't she!'

Just ahead, there was a side turning on the right, and a car parked at the kerbside just beyond. The pest in the Golf would have to swing around the parked car to maintain his position alongside her. She slowed her pace fractionally just as he accelerated around the parked car and pulled into the kerb on the far side, waiting for Sandy to catch up. With a small smile of satisfaction, Sandy turned into the side road and stepped up the pace down the hill. She hoped that, having been outmanoeuvred, the men would take the hint and give up, but to her dismay, she heard a squeal of tyres, as the driver put the car into an aggressive three-point-turn, followed shortly afterwards by the sound of the engine approaching from behind.

Sandy had hoped to see a footpath between the houses, but there was nothing except a service road that led to some garages. She could see no point in going down there. The Golf could easily follow and she would be trapped. She ran on past. Sandy was now on the left-hand pavement, so it was the passenger who called out of the window as they drew level.

'That wasn't very friendly, was it?' He said, and Sandy thought that the tone had a slight undertone of menace. She ignored him and carried on running, hoping that they would get bored and drive off.

Sandy had no fear that she was in any real danger. She had no doubt that she could defend herself against the men if they tried to molest her. Despite being four months pregnant, the bump was barely visible and she was in superb physical condition. She was an expert in several martial arts and if all else failed she had the Glock strapped to her leg; it could be in her hands in less than two seconds. Using the gun would be the last resort, though. The sight of the weapon might frighten these two idiots away, but there could be serious repercussions if the police should get to hear of a gun-toting female runner pounding the pavements of Purley. Indeed, she should take all possible steps to avoid any kind of violent encounter. As the instructors always said, the best way to get out of a fight is not to get into one in the first place!

Up ahead was another side turning, this time on the left, and, Sandy intended to make another sudden turn once the Golf was committed to go straight on. She was a matter of yards from the turn when the Golf suddenly accelerated around the corner and, with a screech of tyres, stopped directly in her path. Changing her plan, Sandy skirted behind the car and continued along the same road. With an angry revving of the engine and more squeals from the spinning tyres, the Golf reversed out and drove past her. It screeched to a halt again at the kerbside, twenty yards ahead. Sandy ran past, not turning her head but watching the men from the corner of her eye. They were looking straight ahead, apparently taking no notice of her, but once she had passed them by they did the same again. This time, Sandy had had enough of their games. As she drew level with the car, she approached and spoke to the men through the open passenger-side window.

'Look, guys, this has gone far enough,' she panted. 'Give it a rest will you, please?'

The passenger, a skinny individual with a mop of brown hair and a black bomber-jacket zipped to the throat, stared at her insolently.

'D'ya wanna suck my dick?' He said, straight-faced. Then he laughed and the car sped away another twenty yards before pulling in and waiting for her again.

Sandy shook her head in impotent anger. She considered turning around a running the other way, but she knew they would follow her again. They would continue their little game of cat-and-mouse until they got bored or became bold enough to try physically to accost her.

Just let the bastards try!

Thirty yards in front of the Golf, at the top of a short, steep incline, was a junction with a main road, and directly opposite another residential road climbed steeply uphill. Sandy started jogging slowly toward her tormentors, but at the last moment, just before reaching the rear of the waiting car, she sprinted across the road to the pavement on the other side and up the slope to the junction, where she turned right and ran along the main road. The Golf could not follow immediately because of the number of vehicles approaching from both directions, but after Sandy had run fifty yards, they caught up with her again and slowed to match her pace. She glanced over her shoulder and saw that another car had come up behind the Golf. The driver was flashing his lights at the slow moving vehicle, wanting to get past.

Sandy had been waiting for this moment. She turned and ran back in the other direction, crossed the road behind the second car and sprinted up the hill, leaving behind an altercation played out on car horns and insults shouted through open windows.

In her haste, Sandy had taken the hill too fast and her breath quickly became ragged. Despite the burning sensation in her tortured lungs and tired legs, she forced herself to maintain the pace. She was nearly at the top of the hill before she heard that now familiar engine note again. It had taken a while for them to turn around but she knew without looking that it was the Golf climbing the hill behind her. She cursed under her breath.

Damn, I thought they'd given up!

She reached the end of the road and looked both ways. To the right the road descended for a long way in a straight line; to the left there was another junction a hundred yards away. With the Golf getting closer and closer, she turned left, sprinting toward the junction. She reached it just as the Golf turned the corner behind her. She looked in both directions; to her right, another two-hundred yards away there was a line of trees bordering the downs. She turned right and ran as fast as her tired legs would carry her.

Smart, detached houses lined the road on both sides, but it did not occur to her to knock on one of the doors to seek help. This was a personal conflict. These morons had challenged Sandy by their actions, and Sandy had to beat them at their own game by her own efforts. She had never expected anyone else to fight her battles for her and she was not going to start now.

The road turned left before reaching the trees. Straight on was a thirty-yard long tarmac track leading to a gate, which prevented unauthorised vehicles from venturing onto the downs. Beyond the gate, the track continued through the woods. Once there, Sandy knew she could easily give the two yobs the slip.

Bordered on both sides by tall hedges, the track was just wide enough for a one vehicle to negotiate. Sandy was halfway along the track when she heard the Golf close behind her. She threw herself into the hedge on the left to avoid being hit as it overtook her, but the side-mirror caught her right arm, causing her to stumble against the hedge and fall to the ground.

Chapter 15

The car stopped a few yards further on and the two men got out. They reached her before she could rise, and dragged her to her feet.

'Right, you stuck-up cow, do as you're told and you won't get 'urt!' the driver threatened. A shaven-headed bruiser with a geometric tattoo on his bull neck, he was a few inches taller than Sandy with the broad chest and muscular arms of a manual worker, and the rotund stomach of a regular beer-drinker. He held her by the arm with one hand. The other held the blade of a pocketknife less than an inch from her right eye. The weedy passenger hesitantly held her other arm, more for effect than any practical purpose.

At that moment, a cold rage descended over Sandy. Even when fighting the intruders at her parents' house, her body had not reached the level of physical preparedness for action that it did now. Suddenly, she was back in the clutches of the Serb militia in Višegrad, and the abuse she had suffered at their hands came flooding back to her. She knew that these louts were the same species of animal as they, and had the same intentions. They might even decide to kill her after having their fun, just to prevent her identifying them. Their very existence was a stain on humanity.

Sandy knew she could probably disarm and disable the bigger man and make short work of the other, but she did not attempt to do so. Pretending to be too exhausted and weak to offer any resistance, she took the opportunity to breathe deeply. The oxygen and adrenalin coursed through her bloodstream, refuelling her muscles ready for fight or flight.

However, this time there was to be no flight.

The big man started to force Sandy along the track toward the gate and the seclusion of the woods beyond. The smaller man maintained his hesitant grip on her other arm.

'Please don't hurt me!' Sandy cried. She sounded weak and frightened.

'I fink you're gonna enjoy this,' the driver said as if he were bestowing a favour upon her.

If only he knew how true that statement to be, Sandy thought. The vision of this toad pawing and slobbering over her body made her skin crawl. Continuing to feign weakness, she made a small mewing sound but allowed him to push her toward the trees. Nevertheless, Sandy wanted to make sure that this brute was in no doubt that she was an unwilling participant in his plans, so she gave him one last chance to relent.

'No,' she begged. 'Let me go, please let me go!'

'Ho,' he replied, scornfully, 'too late for that, you little prick-teaser. You're gonna get what's comin' to yer!'

They entered the woods and he slowed the pace, almost feeling his way along the path between the trees until their eyes began to adjust to the darkness. The weedy one had dropped behind, and Sandy had the impression that he was an unwilling accomplice to what was about to happen. However, unless he had the decency, and the *cajones*, to intervene, she would show him little mercy when the time came.

A few moments later, the bigger man pushed Sandy off the track and they stumbled for fifty paces through wet leaves and over fallen branches, eventually stopping in a small clearing. The fences bordering the back gardens of the nearest houses were only twenty or thirty yards away, but the houses themselves were twice that distance, their inhabitants cloaked by their protective curtains, ignorant of the drama being played out beyond their garden fences.

'This'll do,' he said, still holding her in his firm grip. Trembling, Sandy struggled ineffectually, continuing to feign weakness and fear.

Finally, the smaller man found the courage to speak up. 'Look, Jonno,' he said, nervously, 'I'm not sure about this.'

'Wot, you bottlin' it now?' The driver sneered, 'No mate, I'm not stopping now. This little tart's got me well wound up. She's gonna get my dick up both ends!' The second man lapsed into uncertain silence and Jonno turned his attention back to his captive.

'Right, let's have a look what we've got 'ere.' In his excited state, Jonno's breathing was as ragged as Sandy's had been when she reached the top of the hill. He ripped off her baseball cap and threw it to the ground. He grinned as her blonde hair cascaded around her shoulders. He licked his lips as he took hold of the zip of her tracksuit top and started to pull it down. Sandy raised her hand and slapped his hand away.

'Stop it, please. I don't want you to do this!'

'Shut the fuck up!' He snarled into her face and threatened her again with the knife. Sandy could smell stale cigarettes and alcohol on his breath. He had clearly been drinking but he was not drunk.

'Oi, bottler, grab 'er arms for me.' Jonno ordered his meeker accomplice.

'I dunno…'

'Do it!'

The other man took hold of Sandy's arms, his fingers digging into the crooks of her elbows while Jonno pulled the zip to the bottom and the jacket fell open.

'Smells a bit sweaty,' he remarked, grinning. His voice was hoarse with his mounting excitement. He closed the knife and put it in his pocket. Now he had both hands free to lift the sweat-dampened tee shirt. He pulled it and wedged it above her breasts. Then he hooked both thumbs under the bottom edge of her sports-bra and began to push it up. He was off-guard, now, concentrating on exposing her body, drooling with anticipation. Sandy sensed it was time to act.

In one movement, she thrust her right knee into Jonno's groin and threw her head back against the nose of the man holding her from behind. Jonno gasped and staggered away. Doubled-over and with both hands between his legs, he sank to his knees. His accomplice cried out and released his grip on Sandy's arms. Turning, she saw that he was bending forward with his face in his hands. She drove her heel into his temple and he dropped to the ground as if pole-axed.

Jonno, meanwhile, had started to stand, but he was off-balance and vulnerable. Sandy skipped in close and landed a blow on his nose with the heel of her right hand. He cried out and fell to the ground, while she stepped back, giving him time to get to his feet again. She noted with satisfaction the blood trickling from his nostrils. She wanted to humiliate and hurt him just as he had planned to humiliate her. She laughed at his plight.

'Feeling alright Jonno?' she sneered.

'You fucking bitch. I'm gonna rip your fucking head off for that,' he snarled angrily, his shoulders hunched and his chin thrust forward aggressively.

Sandy noticed that her tee shirt was still wedged under her armpits, exposing her bra. 'I take it you're finished with my tits for the time being, Jonno?' She taunted him, pulling the shirt back down.

'You cocky little cow!' Jonno replied, shaking his head. 'You ain't 'arf gonna suffer for that!'

'Come on then,' Sandy replied, smiling. Her feet were braced shoulder-width apart, her knees slightly bent. Her arms were loose and low to her front, fists lightly clenched as she waited for him to come at her.

To Sandy's surprise, he made no attempt to pull out the knife again; he just lunged forward with his arms spread wide as if to prevent her dodging away from him., Sandy, however, had no intention of trying to elude him. She advanced her left foot and swept her left arm upwards across her body, deflecting his right hand. Then she stepped forward with her right foot and jabbed her right fist into his diaphragm. Her momentum put her body-weight behind the blow. It connected with the force of a sledgehammer and Jonno doubled at the waist, expelling his breath in a grunt of pain. Sandy followed up with a kick to his head and he fell to the ground once more. Sandy watched him roll onto his side, trying to regain his breath. She felt elated but calm; she had all the time in the world.

Or did she? Sensing a movement behind her, Sandy bent her knees and pivoted on the balls of her feet, simultaneously sweeping her left arm up to protect her head. Jonno's accomplice had recovered more quickly than expected. He had picked up a fallen branch, four-feet long and as almost as thick as his wrist, and was swinging it at her head. Her forearm took the full force of the blow. Fortunately, the branch was rotten and snapped in two with the impact, but it still sent a wave of pain through her arm and shoulder.

Before she could recover, Jonno was on her and locked his arm around her throat. She twisted and elbowed him high in the stomach, hearing the breath explode out of him once again, but his grip did not falter. Meanwhile, the second man started somewhat nervously to step forward.

Ignoring the constriction in her throat, Sandy used Jonno's body as a springboard to launch a double-footed kick at the torso of the second man. He flew backwards and lay on the ground, groaning and struggling for breath. The momentum of the strike also caused Jonno to overbalance ,but he maintained the lock on her throat and pulled her down with him as he fell to the ground.

Sandy struggled in his grip. From that position, she was unable to land any significant blows. Then their twisting and struggling presented an opportunity. She grabbed his scrotum through the fabric of his jeans, squeezing and twisting as hard as she could. Jonno screamed like a girl and sought to extricate himself from the source of his pain, but Sandy held on, crushing his testicles in a vice-like grip. Jonno's hold on Sandy's throat weakened, but he landed a heavy open-handed blow on the side of her head. She saw stars, but was able to roll off him. Panting with adrenalin and exertion, she got on her hands and knees and shook her head to clear it.

Jonno lay on his side, his knees drawn up and his hands between his legs as he struggled to overcome the agony that she had inflicted upon him. Shaking, Sandy stood unsteadily on her feet and delivered two vicious kicks to his kidneys. Jonno yelled in pain and gasped for breath, rolling on his back and then doubling forward again trying to find a position that minimised the pain in both back and groin.

Sandy heard a rustling sound behind her and turned to face the threat. The second man had once more regained his feet. He saw Jonno writhing on the ground, and Sandy standing over him like a victorious Amazon and his nerve broke. He turned and ran back toward the road.

'Oh, no you don't!' Sandy went after him like a lioness after a fleeing zebra. She closed the distance quickly and seconds later, rugby-tackled her quarry, bringing him crashing to the ground.

He curled into a defensive ball, crying out for mercy, but Sandy was beyond mercy. Straddling his hips, she reached around his head and forced her hand against his upper lip. Using the strength of her thighs, she raised her body and leaned back. The middle joint of her forefinger dug into the soft underside of his nose, causing excruciating pain. He screamed, but the only way to relieve the pain was to allow her to steer him onto his back. As he turned, Sandy lifted her body slightly to maintain her position over his hips. At the same time, she unzipped the leg of her tracksuit trousers, drew the Glock and rammed the muzzle into his cheek.

'Get up, you snivelling piece of shit,' she snarled, 'Get up!'

'No! Oh, shit! Don't… I've got a kid.'

'Then you'd better do as I say. Get up!' With that, Sandy stood and, while pointing the gun at his head, she grabbed a handful of his jacket and dragged him to his feet.

'Let's go and see how your mate's doing, shall we?'

Sandy tucked the pistol close to her body and keeping her elbow locked, held the back of his jacket collar in her left hand as she frog-marched him back to where she had left Jonno.

'What's your name?' She demanded.

'Steve.'

'Well, Steve, what do you think your kid's reaction would be to finding out daddy's a rapist, eh? And what about your wife or girlfriend, what would she say.'

'Look, I didn't wanna do this. It was Jonno's idea…'

'But you went along with it, didn't you, you bastard! You held me while he was trying to strip me. You could have said no! Would you have held my legs open too? I bet you would have wanted your turn as well, right?'

Before the miserable Steve could answer, they had reached the spot where Jonno still lay doubled in pain on the ground. The vapour of his expelled breath was visible as clouds of condensation in the cold damp air and the acrid smell of his vomit assaulted the nostrils. He heard them approach and when he looked up, Sandy could see that he was finished.

'Fuck, I thought you'd gone,' he said, his voice rasping. 'Look, you win, okay? You beat me. Now just fuck off and leave me alone.' He collapsed onto his face with his hands in his groin and retched again.

Sandy gave Steve a hefty shove. He stumbled forward toward his friend.

'Jonno, she's got a gun!' Steve said, his voice cracking with fear.

Jonno rolled up to a kneeling position and looked incredulously at the gun pointing at his head.

'Who are you?' he demanded, 'Are you the Filth?'

Sandy grimaced. 'No, Jonno, I'm not the police. Actually, from your point of view, I'm far worse, as you are about to discover.'

'What are you going on about?'

'Think of me as an avenging angel for all the women that have been assaulted and abused by scum like you.'

'Oh, for fuck's sake,' he groaned wearily.

'Stand up.' She ordered.

Jonno rose unsteadily to his feet, his eyes fixed on the muzzle of the Glock.

'Steve, go and stand next to him.'

'Wot you gonna do?' Steve whimpered.

'Just do it.'

When Steve still hesitated, she pointed the gun at his head, warily watching Jonno for any movement. Injured he may be, but Jonno was still the greater threat. Steve finally obeyed and the two men stood side-by-side.

'Good,' she said. 'Now Strip!' She waved the muzzle of the pistol back and forth. 'Both of you; get your kit off.'

'What? Don't be stupid,' Jonno said.

'I mean it. Take your clothes off.' She tensed as Jonno took a step forward.

'You won't use that. It's probably not even real... Shit!' A round buried itself into the ground next to his foot and he leapt backward.

Sandy cursed as the spent cartridge case spun off to land amongst the debris on the ground a few feet to her right. Even in daylight, it would be difficult to retrieve; in darkness, it would be impossible. Her reckless discharge of the weapon had left irrefutable forensic evidence of her presence at the scene of... Of what? What was she going to do to these men? She had yet to decide.

Meanwhile Steve had started hurriedly to unzip his bomber-jacket.

'Come on, Jonno,' Sandy taunted, forcing herself to ignore her mistake, 'you seemed keen enough to get it out a few minutes ago. Now let me see what I'm missing.'

Jonno reluctantly began to undress and two small piles of clothes began to grow around the two men. Eventually, they both stood facing her, wearing nothing but their socks and underwear.

'Those too,' she said with a wicked grin. The feeling of turning the tables and having total power over these bastards was almost orgasmic. 'Good, that's better. Now put your hands on your heads.' The two naked men obeyed. 'Good grief, Jonno,' Sandy laughed, 'is that all you've got? Blimey, I wouldn't bother if I were you!'

'Fuckin' bitch.'

'Now, now; mind your manners. Right, turn around and walk until I tell you to stop.' Neither man moved, other than to glance nervously at each other before fixating once more on the gun. 'Do it now, boys, please.'

Reluctantly, they turned and walked away. Sandy followed until she stood amongst the discarded clothes.

'Okay, stop there,' she called when they were five yards away, the pale skin of their bodies dimly visible in the darkness. 'Kneel down!'

Jonno muttered something that she did not hear, and Steve whimpered again. He was close to tears and she could hear his teeth chattering from where she stood, though whether from fear or the cold she neither knew nor cared.

Sandy squatted and quickly searched through the discarded clothes. She found the key to the Golf on a ring that also held some house keys; she found two wallets, containing, between them, around sixty pounds; there was some loose change in the pockets of both men's trousers and another set of house keys in Steve's pocket. As she finished searching each garment, she rolled it into a ball and threw it away from her, each in a different direction. By the time she had finished, the men's clothes and footwear were scattered all around.

She opened Jonno's wallet, took out his driving licence and, using a small torch attached to her key ring, read the details.

'Do you know what, Jonno?' Sandy said after a silence that had dragged out for several minutes. 'If I had asked you your name and you'd answered "John Smith" I wouldn't have believed you.'

'Yeah, I've 'ad that 'appen wiv the Old Bill too,' he answered sulkily.

'I'm sure. Now, what am I going to do with you two?'

'Just let us go,' Steve begged; 'we've learned our lesson.'

'I think I believe that of you, Steve, but Jonno there, I don't think he has; have you, Jonno?'

'Yeah, whatever you say. We won't do it again.'

'I get the impression, Mr John Smith,' Sandy said, walking toward them, 'that this isn't your first time! Would I be right?'

'What? No, honest. I ain't dun nuffin' like this before!'

'I don't believe you. Right, both of you, put your hands on the ground and stick your arses in the air.'

'What? What the fuck...?' Jonno flinched and gasped aloud as Sandy drove the barrel of the Glock into his ribs.

'Come on,' Sandy ordered, 'straight arms; straight legs; feet apart, further! Come on, spread them! That's better. Good. Now hold it there.'

Sandy counted the seconds. Less than a minute later, Steve's legs were quivering and Jonno started complaining.

'Jesus! I can't stay like this for long.'

'Sure you can! Now, Jonno, what am I going to do with you?' Sandy said, almost conversationally, but as she spoke, she placed the muzzle of the Glock against his scrotum, making him flinch and gasp. 'I'm undecided,' she continued, 'whether to blow your bollocks off or put a bullet in your head.' Jonno whimpered and his knees buckled but Sandy raised the barrel, jamming the foresight into his perineum. Jonno sucked the breath between his teeth and straightened his legs again. Sandy could see that his limbs were quivering with the strain of the stress position. Steve was in an even worse condition. She doubted that his arms could support even his slight weight for more than a few more seconds.

'Steve,' she said, 'I want you to lie flat, face-down, with your hands behind your head. Now!' she barked, suddenly, and he dropped, with a sigh of relief only to groan as twigs and bracken pierced and scratched his bare skin.

'What about me?' Jonno asked, hopefully.

No, Jonno. You stay where you are.'

'Fuck, man, what's wrong wiv you?' Jonno's attempt at bravado failed and the words came out as a whine. Sandy ignored the question and kept the muzzle pressed against Jonno's scrotum.

'What were you going to do to me, Jonno?'

Jonno did not answer.

'What was it? Oh, yes. "She's going to get my dick up both ends". That's right isn't it?'

'Look, I'm sorry, yeah?'

'You will be,' she said ominously and, before Jonno could respond, Sandy pushed the gun roughly between his buttocks, grinding the unyielding muzzle into his anus, twisting it from side to side so that the foresight gouged lumps of skin out of the soft tissue. Jonno screamed in pain, his knees buckled and his left arm came back in a reflexive sweep but Sandy intercepted it and doubled it behind his back. Jonno fell forward onto his face and, bracing her body against his wild convulsions, Sandy continued to push and twist the muzzle, now an inch inside his rectum and tearing at this most sensitive of places.

'How's that Jonno?' Sandy panted with the effort of holding her position as Jonno's body bucked and squirmed. 'Are you enjoying being fucked, you bastard? No? Now there's a surprise!'

'Stop! Stop!' Jonno screamed, crying with pain, humiliation and fear. Sandy twisted one more time and he broke, beating the ground with his one free hand and crying openly. 'Please stop! That's enough! Stop it! Please stop!'

None too gently, Sandy removed the gun and took two paces back, watching Jonno rolling on the ground in agony, and crying openly.

'You are a piece of scum, Jonno,' Sandy said contemptuously. 'Your continued existence on this planet is an abomination. My every instinct tells me to do the world a favour and put a bullet in what passes for a brain inside that cue ball of a head of yours. And I'll tell you what, Jonno, if it wasn't for the fact that I would also have to kill Steve, if I shot you, I would not bloody hesitate. Do you understand?'

Jonno made a whining noise that she took as affirmation.

'I want you to remember how that felt next time you get the urge to force yourself on another woman,' Sandy said with the passion of one who had been on the receiving end of such treatment. Then she looked at the gun with distaste.

'Come here, Steve,' she ordered sharply and when Steve started to rise to his feet, she added, 'No, stay on your knees. Now, face me. Good boy. Now, open wide. Stop snivelling; just open your mouth. That's right, now suck it, come on suck it nice and clean. I don't want any of Jonno's blood and shit on my nice new gun.'

Steve obediently kept his lips around the muzzle and she moved it back and forth. Jonno was lying curled up in a tight foetal position, still crying like a four-year-old with a grazed knee.

'Oh, Jonno,' Sandy said in a conversational tone, 'as we are now such intimate friends, would you mind awfully if I borrowed your car to get me home? I found the keys in your pocket.'

'No,' he gasped, trying to regain control of his breathing. 'Take the fuckin' thing. Just go away and leave us alone.'

Sandy looked down at the man kneeling at her feet. He was still dutifully keeping his lips around the gun, despite gagging at the taste of his friend's body fluids. 'Okay, Steve, you can stop now. Now, both of you lie face down and don't move until you hear the car drive away. Do you understand?'

'Yeah, okay,' said Jonno.

'Yes,' agreed Steve, 'we won't move.'

'Good. Now, I don't want to hear any tales of the police or your mates looking for me. Do I make myself clear? You've pissed me off once and got away lightly. Piss me off again and I will find you and I will kill you.' Then she added, 'I have your driving licence, you see, Jonno. I know where you live. Do you understand?'

'Yeah, okay, okay!'

'Yes,' added Steve.

'Do you believe me?'

'Yeah, I fuckin' believe yer!'

'Please, we'll do whatever you say.'

'Good, then I'll bid you gentlemen goodnight. Remember; don't move until you hear me drive off.' She walked swiftly but silently away, taking with her not only the keys but the two wallets and the pocketknife as well.

Chapter 16

Sandy pulled up in a quiet road half-a-mile from her house and stared blankly ahead. The elation brought on by the action in the woods, and the punishment that she had meted out to the two would-be rapists had worn off and she began to feel depressed again.

She thought about the gun and the way she had used it to intimidate the two men. Sure, they deserved it, but she had to a certain extent lost control. She should never have drawn the weapon. She should certainly never have fired it, not in those circumstances. She realised that, to a degree, she had led the men on. She could have stopped them earlier, but she had allowed them to continue just so that she could exact revenge for offences perpetrated by other men at a different time in another country. For a time she had wanted so badly to kill Jonno and she silently thanked whatever passed for God in her mind that she had possessed enough self-control to prevent herself from doing so.

That she had the capacity to take the life of another human being without compunction and without remorse was beyond doubt. She had proved that more than once in the past few months. In fact, the first time, when she and Caroline had saved the rest of the team from capture by a Serb death squad, had left her not just elated but also feeling the first flutter of sexual arousal. Surely, that was a reaction to the adrenalin and the danger – and the triumph of victory over superior numbers, rather than the killing itself. Otherwise, she would seriously have to question her mental state.

Sandy had intended to dump the car here and make her way home on foot, but now she had acquired a useful piece of kit she was reluctant to part with it. She sat in the car and stared ahead at the sodium street lamps with their warm, amber glow, the detached houses on both sides of the road with neat front gardens, well-trimmed privet hedges and smart cars in the driveways. There was something familiar about them. Then she realised what it was. It reminded her of home. She was feeling homesick, and she was desperate to see Samantha again, if only to put the record straight.

K's words, as related by David, came back to haunt her. *Absolutely not. No way!* Then she remembered how David had failed her this evening. Despite being responsible for her well-being, he had ignored her cry for help. True, she may have been behaving like a pathetic teenager, but he owed her some degree of consideration, a modicum of compassion, especially after sleeping with her and professing his love for her. Some love! He would rather have supper with the wife he claimed no longer to love than spend another night of passion with Sandy in her hour of need. In fact, *love* was not really an accurate description of David's feelings for her. Oh, the desire was there; it was obvious in every move he made, every look with those hazel eyes, but it was probably just lust.

Lust!

Sandy had long since accepted that lust rather than love was the emotion that she provoked in men – and not just men. Even Caroline, the beautiful, insatiable, bi-sexual, Caroline, who had tried so many times to seduce Sandy, and had succeeded on a few occasions, was motivated not by love but by lust. In retrospect, and despite her denials to Caroline and to herself, Sandy had to admit that she had not regretted those occasions when she had surrendered to her friend's advances. Did that make her a lesbian? Caroline was the only woman to whom she had ever been attracted. It was Caroline the person that she had loved. She would have felt the same about her if she had possessed a penis instead of breasts. In fact, Sandy wished that Caroline had been a man; then there would never have been any doubt about her feelings. It was too late now. Caroline was gone and Sandy had never revealed her feelings. She sniffed and shook her head to forestall a tear. She knew that was something she would regret for the rest of her life.

What else might she regret for the rest of her life? Not seeing Sam, that's what! Not telling Sam what really happened that dreadful night when their parents died. Not receiving forgiveness, or absolution, or whatever it was that *Believers* like Sam bestowed upon misguided, unenlightened souls like Sandy.

Absolutely not. No way!

Well, sod David and sod Amanda bloody Gillette! Sandy, or whatever her name was supposed to be now, was going to take her destiny in her own hands. She patted the steering wheel as if it were a dog's head. Now she had the means with which she could accomplish her goal.

Starting the engine, Sandy and embarked on a joyride around the area, building a map in her head of shops, pubs and railway stations, and the road network that connected them. After thirty minutes, she returned to her house and parked the car in the garage.

***

'You have?' Sandy sounded excited. 'Great, what colour is it?'

'Petrol Blue,' the voice on the phone replied.

At last!

'That's fantastic,' Sandy squealed excitedly. 'My favourite colour!' She glanced around for the umpteenth time; there was still no-one waiting to use the telephone box that she had occupied for the past forty minutes. She had deliberately chosen one in a quiet side street, three miles from home, on the other side of the steep-sided valley that carried the A22 trunk road from London to the south coast town of Eastbourne, and doggedly worked her way through her list of car dealers, and more than two pounds-worth of coins.

'One thing,' she added; 'Can you tell me the Reg. number?'

'Reg. number?' the dealer asked suspiciously, 'What do need that for? You haven't even seen the car yet.'

'Well, promise not to tell anyone, but my boyfriend is in the police and he can check on the computer to make sure it's not stolen or a write-off or anything like that. He's not supposed to, of course but he'll do it for me.'

'Look, Miss, I can assure you...'

'Please?' The dealer relented and she jotted down the number on the notepad. 'Thanks. I'll call you back to arrange a time for a test drive. Cheers!'

'Bugger!' Sandy swore aloud.

She had walked back via the town centre where she had bought a DIY number-plate kit from a motor accessories shop, along with a few other items to change the appearance of her new acquisition. Then she saw David's Jaguar XJ6 parked in the driveway. It was imperative that David did not see what she had bought otherwise she would have some awkward questions to answer.

As she got closer, Sandy could see that David's car was empty and realised that he must be waiting for her inside the house. That made hiding her purchases all the easier. Before walking up to the front door, she surreptitiously slipped the bags under the side-gate leading to the back garden.

'Where the bloody hell have you been?' David demanded as she came through the front door.

'What the bloody hell are you doing in here?' She countered angrily. 'I was under the impression that this was my house now. How dare you waltz in here uninvited?'

Taken aback by her aggressive response, David replied falteringly, 'I, er, didn't think you would mind me waiting inside. I've been here over an hour. Where have you been?'

'I've been for a walk,' Sandy said, throwing herself onto the sofa, affecting a sulk. 'I had to get out of here for a while.'

'What's the matter with you?' He asked, barely concealing his irritation at her attitude. He had been worried about her when he found she was missing but now his anger was growing.

'What's the matter with me?' She repeated, allowing her voice to rise. 'I needed you last night, David. I begged you to come but you couldn't be bothered…'

'It wasn't that I couldn't be bothered,' David protested. 'It was difficult. You shouldn't have called me at home. What was my wife supposed to think?'

'It was difficult for me, too. I was upset and I needed a friend; and you let me down!' Sandy knew how unreasonable she was being. Good. The more unreasonable the better!

'Piss off, I don't want you here!'

'Don't take that tone with me, Sandy! I'm still your boss and . . .'

'Oh, you're my boss, are you? She interrupted. 'I thought you were also my friend. I needed you last night and you weren't here.'

David edged closer. 'Let me make it up to you now,' he murmured, already fully aroused in anticipation of the joy of making up.

Sandy pushed him away and leapt to her feet.

'You must be bloody joking! If you think you can treat me like some little trollop, grateful for a knobbing when it suits you, then you can think again.' She watched David's face redden, though whether through embarrassment or anger was difficult to say.

'I didn't mean it like that, Sandy . . .' he tailed off and looked searchingly at her. 'What happened to your face?'

Sandy self-consciously brushed a hand across the scratches from the previous night's confrontation.

'It's nothing,' she said, 'I ran into an overhanging tree in the dark when I was out running last night.'

David stood and took a closer look. 'There's quite a nasty bruise too,' he said. He reached out to touch her face and then retreated in shocked surprise when Sandy slapped his hand away.

'Leave me alone!' She shouted. 'It's nothing. And you're not going to get around me by offering to kiss it better!'

David cracked his most engaging smile. 'Come on, Sandy, come here and let Uncle David have a look.' He could not have adopted a tone, or form of words more certain to inflame Sandy's temper if he had tried.

'Get out!' she shouted. 'Get out, you patronising bastard, and leave me alone! And if you want to see me – about work matters,' she added with emphasis, 'then call me and let me know when you are coming. Otherwise don't bother!'

Sandy slammed the door behind the departing David and then burst into tears.

Later that afternoon, Sandy went out to the garage and fitted the new registration plates to the Golf. Now, if a suspicious police officer should call in to check, he would find the number belonged to a Blue Volkswagen Golf GTi, and, crucially, one that had not been reported stolen. The fact that the number was still showing as registered to a car-dealer in Crawley could easily be explained by the assumption of laxity in their administrative procedures.

Next, she had to remove some of the other identifying features, such as the giant speakers on the rear shelf, whose vibrations on full volume threatened to shake the car to bits. Finally, there were the stickers.

Jonno had decorated the windows with stickers variously proclaiming his undying support of Crystal Palace Football Club, that his "Other car is a Porsche" and that "Scaffolders Do It with Big Erections". These had to go to prevent anyone recognising the car when she was driving around the local area. The residue they left would be covered with "Baby on Board", "No Hand Signals - Driver Applying Make-Up" and "Don't Get Too Close, I Hardly Know You".

Eventually, Sandy was satisfied with her handiwork and began to work out the next part of the plan.

Chapter 17

'We look forward to receiving your response to our client's concerns at the earliest opportunity. Yours etcetera, Samantha McNamara.'

Samantha set the Dictaphone down on the desk, took a powder compact from her handbag and used the small mirror in the lid to check the condition of her pink lipstick and pale-blue eye shadow. Her eyes looked tired and her face pale and drawn, which was only to be expected after the stress and lack of sleep of the past couple of months. More out of habit than necessity, she applied a little more powder to her cheeks and nose, then, satisfied with her appearance she closed the lid and replaced the compact in her handbag.

Samantha was the youngest and the only female solicitor among the five that worked in the Brighting and Blount legal practice. She got the debt cases, the traffic offences and the benefits fraudsters, while the juicier divorce and criminal cases went to her older, more experienced and male colleagues. Nevertheless, she seemed to fit in well and the others were not overly patronising toward her.

She glanced at her watch. It was already time for the next appointment, after which there were another two before lunch. It was as though her clients were on a conveyer belt today, but she was glad to be busy. Glad that she had no time to brood. Today was an anniversary of sorts; it was the first Friday in November; nine weeks to the day since her sister had gone murderously insane, brutally murdered their parents, and then committed suicide. What had possessed Sandy to do these things, no one could fathom, except perhaps to speculate that some dreadful experience, during her year in Africa, had unbalanced her mind.

Following the tragedy, Eddie Brighting, the senior partner, had granted Samantha an indefinite period of compassionate leave. He advised her to get plenty of rest and to take as much time as she needed before coming back to work. Far from resting, however, Samantha had kept remarkably busy, coping with enquiries and solicitudes from friends and family, dealing with the police family-liaison officer and beginning the lengthy probate process. When the bodies had finally been released after the inquest – which had returned verdicts of unlawful killing and suicide – Samantha had set about arranging the funeral service and the subsequent cremation of the bodies. A few days later, the ashes were interred in the burial ground adjacent to the church and Samantha planted an Elizabeth Harkness rose nearby.

Afterwards, Samantha had been at a loss, having nothing to do all day except to grieve, and to dwell on the unimaginable suffering that her loved ones must have endured before they died. The sudden and unexpected appearance of Death in such close personal proximity prompted Samantha to question her satisfaction with her own life. Should she be confronted unexpectedly with her own demise tomorrow, would she feel that she had done everything with her life that she would have wanted? The answer to that had to be a resounding "No". It seemed to Samantha, that, at the relatively young age of twenty-nine, life had already passed her by. Not for her the pubs and clubs and rock-concerts of her contemporaries, nor did she crave the self-indulgent pursuits of retail-therapy and health spas. When she was not at work, her husband's needs and drivers dominated Samantha's life. Somehow, she had allowed herself to transition smoothly from a life dominated by her nit-picking and overbearing stepmother to one dominated by her increasingly self-righteous and overbearing husband.

Their natural mother had succumbed to breast cancer when Samantha was just nine-years-old and Sandy barely four. Concerned that his young daughters needed a mother, their father had remarried only three years later to the glamorous, but pretentious, social-climbing snob, Grace. Grace had very specific views about how her young charges should behave and this brought her into continual conflict with the obstinate and independent-minded Sandy.

Sandy's refusal to remain within the behavioural boundaries that their stepmother considered appropriate for a young lady, and her unyielding defiance in response to the consequential admonishments and punishments, had been a constant source of wonder to the polite, obedient, timid Samantha.

Although five years Sandy's senior, Samantha had always lived in her younger sister's shadow. From the time she could walk and talk, Sandy, had been adventurous, inquisitive and boisterous, frequently getting into the sort of scrapes that one might expect from a boy rather than the supposedly genteel younger daughter of Lieutenant Colonel Charles Harris.

Whereas Samantha played with dolls, prams and tea sets, the tomboyish Sandy preferred toy guns and cars. Rather than paint, or make jewellery out of beads and string, Sandy played with daddy's old Meccano set that she had found during clandestine expeditions to the attic. By the age of nine, much to her stepmother's disapproval, Sandy had successfully lobbied for a chemistry set. Expelled for indiscipline from the ballet lessons that Grace insisted were necessary for her stepdaughters' development into elegant young ladies, Sandy persuaded her father to let her join a Judo club.

When Sandy was eleven, she became a boarder at Bramsfield College, in the Yorkshire Dales, where Samantha was, at that time, in the Lower Sixth. True to form, and in contrast to Samantha, Sandy excelled in every sport and physical activity, whilst paying scant attention to her academic studies. Gallingly, to the diligently studious Samantha, this negligence seemed to have little effect on her sister's exam results, and she rarely failed to achieve top marks, particularly in the sciences. Their time together at the school overlapped for two years before Samantha left to study Law at Durham University.

It was as Sandy was approaching her sixteenth birthday, that Samantha first noticed that her skinny, gawky, disproportionately limbed sister had emerged from her chrysalis to become the most beautiful of butterflies. A little envious of her sister's beauty, Samantha had found it infuriating that Sandy made every effort to play down her blossoming womanhood, eschewing make-up and any feminine apparel in favour of jeans, tee shirts and trainers. To their stepmother's annoyance, she would often tie back her long blonde hair in a tight ponytail or hide it under the baseball cap, which was her habitual headgear.

Unlike Sandy, who from a young age had regarded Christianity – and every other religion – as superstitious nonsense, Samantha had always believed in the existence of God and the resurrection of Jesus Christ. She continued to attend church on Sundays, even at Durham, and it was there that she met Stephen, a lecturer in mathematics at the university, and a lay preacher. At first, Samantha had found his dedication and devotion inspiring. However, as the years passed, he had become increasingly pious, sanctimonious and unctuous until, it seemed to Samantha, that nearly every conversation between them ended with a sermon. So domineering and controlling was her husband that Samantha was unable to make even the simplest of decisions, domestic or personal, without first obtaining his consent. She was afraid even to visit the hairdresser or buy new clothes without first consulting him. It was only in the past few weeks that Samantha had allowed herself to consider how much she resented the situation.

Since she had burst into her life, six weeks ago, Kathy had challenged Samantha to assert her independence. Kathy helped her to see that, throughout her marriage to Stephen, she had taken the line of least resistance and over the years, allowed him to take control of every aspect of her life. The one exception was her professional career, which was definitely outside his sphere of influence. She was a qualified professional, respected in her own right by clients and colleagues alike. Samantha did not allow herself to be intimidated by criminals, police or magistrates, Kathy had said, so why did she allow herself to be cowed by her husband?

Nine years his junior, Samantha earned more than Stephen did as head of the mathematics department at a sixth-form college in Chester. Moreover, with her sister's death, she was the sole beneficiary of her parents' substantial estate. She could be completely financially independent, if she so chose. So why should she not have an equal say in the decisions surrounding their domestic and social lives? At last, Samantha was coming to the realisation that she did not have to be dependent upon her husband like some Victorian housewife. In the days following the funeral, she decided that things were going to change.

Her first act of independence was to visit the hairdresser and have her long blonde hair cut and layered in the style favoured by the Princess of Wales. Inevitably, Stephen had criticised her choice of style, not least because he disapproved of the Princess, whom he considered shallow, self-centred and disloyal to her husband. Samantha took no notice. Stephen was going to have to get used to the idea that his wife would never again be so – subservient!

Samantha's next independent decision, in defiance of Stephen's strongly expressed opinion, was to return to work, which she had, almost three weeks before, on the Monday following the funerals.

In contrast to her sister's indifference to her appearance, Samantha had always taken pains with clothes and cosmetics to enhance what she considered to be her inferior looks. Even more so of late, because, in the seven years that she had been married, Samantha's once willowy figure had become rather matronly. Nevertheless, she contrived to mitigate this by ensuring that she was always perfectly turned out, whatever the occasion. From elegant ball-gowns or cocktail dresses at social functions, to sober and demure outfits for church, to Hunter wellington boots and Barbour waxed jackets in the great outdoors, Samantha's couture invariably exuded sheer, understated class. As might be expected, she paid equal attention to her business attire. Today she was wearing a hip-slimming, navy-blue wool skirt-suit over a light-cream blouse, set off with a diamond brooch and a single-strand necklace of cultured pearls with earrings to match.

A soft knock on the office door brought Samantha back to the present, and she realised that her mind had been wandering.

'Come in,' she called, brightly. The last thing she wanted was for her colleagues to be walking on eggshells around her, so she did her best to make her voice sound bright and cheerful. The door opened and Kathy stood in the doorway. She wore a grey skirt and open-necked white blouse, with her lush tresses of rich auburn hair secured in a neat bun.

'Mrs Sanderson is here, Mrs McNamara.'

Samantha rose to her feet to greet her client. She was an elderly lady with dull-grey hair bunched beneath a black, narrow-brimmed hat. She was wearing a shabby, three-quarter-length, grey wool overcoat, a scarf that obscured the lower part of her face, opaque, flesh-coloured stockings and well-worn lace-up black brogues. As she hobbled into the room, leaning heavily on wooden walking stick, tipped with a rubber ferrule, she stared fixedly at the floor through large, brown-tinted spectacles.

The offices of Brighting and Blount were located on two floors above three shops in Frodsham Street, in the centre of Chester. There was no lift, and the staircase leading up from street level to the first floor reception area was steep and narrow. Samantha wondered how this poor old soul had managed to climb it unaided.

'Please, let me help you,' Samantha offered, walking around the desk to lend a guiding hand, and immediately felt her nose wrinkling at a faint but pungent odour that made

Samantha think of a tomcat peeing in a lavender bush. The old lady settled onto the green leather seat of Samantha's mahogany visitor's chair and expelled a heavy sigh of relief. Samantha returned to her place on the other side of the desk.

'How can I help you, Mrs Sanderson?'

'I wanted to show you this, luv,' Mrs Sanderson replied. She had a high, tremulous voice and a pronounced Merseyside accent. With a gloved hand, she withdrew an envelope from her beige canvas shopping bag and handed it to Samantha. Then she sat hunched forward, both hands resting on the handle of her walking stick waiting for Samantha to read the contents.

Samantha blinked at the document. It was a final demand from British Telecom to Mrs Enid Sanderson for a relatively small sum of money.

'Mrs Sanderson,' Samantha said gently, as if breaking bad news, 'the amount owing here is less than our fee to write a letter to them. Have you tried going to the Citizens' Advice Bureau? They should be able to help you at no cost to yourself.'

'Perhaps you should look at the second page,' the old lady suggested mildly.

The second page contained a handwritten note, and Samantha paled visibly as she recognised handwriting as familiar as her own. Her eyes widened with shock and one hand flew to her mouth.

'The thing is, luv,' said Mrs Sanderson, forestalling any comment from Samantha, as the latter looked up, sharply, 'I'm sure I've already paid it. I've tried telling them, but they won't take any notice. And they keep sending me those letters. Each one is ruder and more threatening than the last.'

The effort that it took for Samantha to keep her emotions under control was clearly visible, and it was several seconds before she was able to answer, and only then after clearing her throat several times.

'Let me make a few enquiries, Mrs, er, Sanderson,' said Samantha. 'Perhaps I might be able to help you after all. How can I contact you to let you know the outcome?'

'I think you'll find my contact details at the bottom of the page, luv,' Sandy replied, still using the voice she had practised for hours over the past few days since deciding on her disguise. She watched anxiously as her sister reread the note, this time all the way to the end, and then looked up again, the emotions visibly boiling inside her. Once again, Sandy took the initiative.

'Now,' she said, with a small smile of encouragement, 'would you be a luv, and help me down the stairs? They are very steep and I'm quite shaky on my pins, you know. I should hate to fall down on my way out.'

'I can't believe it's really you!' Samantha gushed, fighting back tears. Having declined Kathy's offer to take over the task of helping the elderly client down the steep staircase, Samantha had attempted to embrace her sister as soon as they were alone in the stairwell, but Sandy had fended her off, brusquely. Now the two sisters faced each other, a few feet apart, fiercely resisting the urge to enter into physical contact.

'Leave at one-fifteen, on the dot,' Sandy whispered hoarsely. Leaning on her sister's arm, she remained in character, as step by step they descended to street level. 'Blue Golf. Don't, for God's sake, say anything to anyone. Anyone,' she repeated, resisting the temptation to say *especially that prat of a husband of yours.* Instead, she said, 'Don't even tell your secretary or your boss that you won't be coming back today.'

'I can't do that, Sandy,' Samantha protested in a hushed voice. 'I've got two appointments this afternoon. I've got to let them know.'

'Seriously, Sam; it's vitally important. On Monday, you can tell them you had an emotional breakdown during your lunch break and had to go home. They'll be full of sympathy, believe me.'

Samantha nodded reluctantly but said nothing. She looked as if that emotional breakdown might start a little prematurely.

'Keep it together, Sam,' Sandy pleaded and then, ignoring the shocked look on her elder sister's face, she added, 'Our lives may depend on it.'

Mrs Sanderson hobbled along Frodsham Street to the bus stand and took a bus to the railway station where she boarded the train bound for Birkenhead. As expected from her dry runs over the previous two days, the train had few passengers at this time of day, and Sandy was able to remain unobserved as she shed Mrs Sanderson's hat, coat, tights and shoes. Underneath, she was wearing a grey fleece top and skin-tight black Lycra leggings. Inside the shopping bag was a small brown leather shoulder bag, a pair of flat pumps, a baseball cap and a large Marks and Spencer carrier bag into which she crammed Mrs Sanderson's coat, shoes and accessories. It was a much younger woman who, with her hair piled up under the baseball cap and carrying the bulging carrier bag, left the train at Hooton, two stops to the north of Chester. She put the carrier bag in the boot of the Golf and drove back to the city centre.

Despite her many visits to the city over the years, Sandy's knowledge of Chester's topography was rather superficial. Therefore, in preparation for today's rendezvous with her sister, she had spent many hours studying a street map of the city until she could have drawn much of it from memory. She had planned the whole exercise in meticulous detail, but things rarely turn out exactly as expected. It's impossible to plan for every eventuality. Sometimes, it is necessary to be flexible, to adapt to a changing situation on the ground. It had been that way in Bosnia – with disastrous results, and now it seemed that similarly malevolent forces were at work in Chester.

When she recognised the secretary who welcomed Mrs Sanderson into the reception area at the top of the stairs, Sandy thought she might faint. It took every ounce of nerve and self-discipline to keep calm and continue to act her part. Had she been recognised, life might suddenly have become very dangerous, and potentially, very short. Her first thought had been to abandon the plan, but she could hardly have turned and run from the office at that stage.

She could have simply withheld the second page from her sister and, after having received the advice that it was not economically viable to use a solicitor to contest the debt, she could have left the building with Samantha none the wiser. However, once she was in Sam's office, within touching distance of her sister, Sandy could not help but continue. She had to tell Sam the truth about that night.

The Final Demand that Sandy had handed to Samantha, was genuine. She had found it after trawling through dustbins in an alleyway behind a row of houses in a run-down district of the city. The letter gave credence to Sandy's desire to consult a solicitor, and a genuine name and address with which to make the appointment. She had no idea what the real Enid Sanderson looked like, but it was very unlikely that anyone in Sam's office would either.

Originally, Sandy's main concern had been the uncertainty of Sam's reaction to the hand-written second page. The first paragraph warned Samantha that the office might be bugged, so to say nothing other than what she might say to a confused elderly lady worried about a final demand from the telephone company. The note went on to explain that she, Sandy, was not responsible for the murder of their parents, and that Sandy herself had been the target of the killers. Her disappearance had been forced upon her against her will and it had taken two months before she had been able to find a way to make contact. Finally, it gave detailed instructions regarding the rendezvous that Sandy had planned, explaining that the precautions were necessary in case Samantha was under surveillance. When she had written the note, Sandy had thought it only a very remote possibility. Now she knew it for a fact.

Sandy looked again at her watch. In another ten minutes, before driving to the rendezvous point, she would perform the extra task that she had hastily added to her original plan. She still had the option of driving away, of not meeting with Sam, but that would leave her sister confused and angry. She might even go to the authorities to report that her younger sister was still alive. No, it was too late, now. The chance to abandon the plan had gone. Sandy had to continue, but now she was going to have to be even more cautious. She looked at her watch for the tenth time in half-as-many minutes and decided, finally, that now was the time. She got out of the car and crossed the street to enter a red public telephone box.

Chapter 18

Samantha pulled on her beige topcoat and left her office, closing the door behind her. Sandy had said to leave at one-fifteen "on the dot". Samantha was not sure of the reason, but she complied with the instruction. Sitting at her desk in the outer office, Kathy looked up, surprised to see Samantha dressed for the outdoors.

'Off out?' She enquired with a smile. 'I thought you weren't going.' Samantha had said as much half-an-hour ago when Kathy had asked if she wanted to spend lunchtime shopping together.

'I need some fresh air,' Samantha replied, adding unnecessarily, 'Need to clear my head.'

'I'll come with you,' Kathy said, making to rise from the desk.

'No!' Samantha replied too sharply. Then, not wishing to offend Kathy, she sought to soften the message, adding, 'No, I just want to be on my own, today. You know . . .'

'Of course, Sam,' Kathy replied with a concerned smile. 'Whatever you think is best.'

Samantha was relieved and returned the smile. 'You're a good friend, Kathy. Thank you for being so understanding.'

'I only want what's best for you,' Kathy replied, remaining in her seat. However, as soon as the door to the staircase closed behind Samantha, Kathy headed for the stand where her outdoor coat was hanging.

It was at that very moment that the phone rang. She could hear Samantha's heels on the stairs and decided to ignore the damn thing. As she reached for her coat, Martin Blount's door opened. He looked from the phone to Kathy and raised his eyebrows. Guiltily, she retraced her steps across the room and picked up the receiver.

Samantha crossed Frodsham Street and entered the short cul-de-sac leading to the car park behind the shops and to a flight of stone steps that led to the walkway on top of the city walls. When she reached the top, she glanced briefly at the brooding mass of the twelfth century cathedral and turned left, passing the cathedral's detached campanile, which she had always thought looked more like a windmill without a sail than a bell tower. A few minutes later, she climbed the steps up to the top of the Eastgate and passed under the wrought-iron frame that held the famous clock commemorating Queen Victoria's Diamond Jubilee.

Although it was not actually raining, it was a dank November day with a chilly breeze and there were very few people walking on the walls. Samantha wondered if any of them were following her. With some effort, she resisted the urge to look over her shoulder. Sandy's note had stressed how doing so might alert any tail that she was not out for a lunchtime stroll. Sandy had also instructed her to walk at a normal, unhurried pace, but as she passed the curiously misspelt Marlbororough Arms, on the street below, Samantha realised that she had been striding out purposefully. Deliberately, she slowed her pace and after passing through Newgate and Wolfgate, she actually stopped, making a show of admiring the Roman Garden adjacent to the wall. Further on, the walkway turned west, running parallel with the River Dee, which was separated from the city wall by an esplanade called The Groves.

Nervous from the start, Samantha was physically shaking as she neared the rendezvous. She paused once more and watched a pleasure boat, the *Lady Diana*, pulling away from the jetty and nosing into the river. Casually, she glanced to her left. A thickset, youngish man in a denim jacket had also stopped to watch the *Lady Diana* depart but showed no obvious interest in Samantha. She took a deep breath and quickly descended the flight of stone steps leading from the walkway down to the esplanade.

From where she had parked the car, Sandy could see the bottom of the fight of steps in her side mirror. She looked again at her watch and muttered to herself. Sam should have been here by now. Sandy was tempted to leave the car and climb up to the walkway to look for her, but she resisted the temptation. It would increase the risk of her being seen by anyone tailing her sister.

Suddenly, Sandy's heart beat faster. In the mirror, she could see that Samantha had appeared at the bottom of the steps and was walking briskly toward the Golf. Sandy started the engine and furtively glanced all around. There were several other people in the vicinity, any one of whom could have been vectored here by radio in advance of Samantha's arrival. Sandy studied each of them, but none showed any obvious signs of alarm or even interest as Samantha climbed quickly into the car. The door had barely closed before Sandy pulled away fast.

'Hold on, Sandy,' Sam protested, 'I haven't got my seat-belt on yet!'

'Hurry up, then. We can't hang about,' Sandy replied sharply.

***

The young man in the denim jacket had reached the esplanade. He appeared suddenly to sneeze into his hand. In fact, he used the movement to conceal the fact that he was speaking into a radio microphone concealed inside the sleeve of his jacket.

'Shanks One – Spider.'

'Spider receiving. Go ahead, Shanks One.'

'Sapphire gone mobile in Blue Golf GTI. Leaving The Groves and heading up toward Pepper Street.'

'Spider – Shanks One. Received. Any index?'

'Foxtrot Four-Five-Seven Lima Golf Whisky.'

'Received. ID on driver?'

'Negative. No visual,' he said, turning and running back up the steps. As he ran, he could hear through his earpiece the operation commander ordering the support vehicles to fan out in an attempt to locate the new target. On reaching the top of the stairs, the young man turned right and sprinted along the walkway back to Wolfgate, startling people strolling along the wall-walk as he passed by. If he hurried, he might just spot the car as it emerged into Pepper Street, but he was disappointed. Whether it had turned left or right at the top of the road leading up from the esplanade, it was gone by the time he reached the point at which he could see the street.

***

'I simply can't believe this is happening,' Samantha cried. Tears formed in her eyes and her lower lip trembled as she spoke. 'I thought you were dead.'

221

'You were meant to,' Sandy answered as she drove west along Pepper Street. She realised how harsh that sounded and added hastily, 'It wasn't my idea. In fact, as I said in the note, I had no choice in the matter. Did you destroy that, by the way?'

'The note? No, it's in my handbag. Why? Who made you do that?' Samantha asked, perplexed. 'What are you mixed up in, Sandy? Please, you have to tell me what's going on. What happened that night at home? Where have you been all this time? Who was that woman we cremated in your place?'

'All in good time. I'm taking you somewhere safe where we can talk; then I'll explain everything.' Well as much as I dare, anyway, she thought, and then aloud, 'Okay?'

Samantha lapsed into silence. Sandy glanced in the rear-view mirror, mentally keeping a tally of the vehicles following them. The two immediately behind had carried straight on when she turned into Lower Bridge Street but three others still followed. It was unlikely that any of those were tailing them, not impossible, but unlikely that they could have been in just the right place at just the right time. What she was looking for was another vehicle joining their little convoy.

'I like your hair,' said Sandy, as if everything was completely normal. 'You should have had that done years ago.'

Resentful at her sister's brisk manner and refusal to answer her questions, Samantha pointedly ignored Sandy's compliment. 'Where are we going?'

'Handbridge first,' Sandy answered, evenly, 'then, when I'm sure we not being followed, I'll take you to where I'm staying.'

Samantha looked sharply at her sister. 'Why would anyone be following us?'

'It's just to be on the safe side,' Sandy replied distractedly. She checked the rear-view mirror again and made a mental note that a red Ford Escort or Orion had attached itself to the back of the line of cars behind the Golf.

The traffic light at the northern end of the narrow Old Dee Bridge was against them, and Sandy waited, impatiently tapping her fingers on the steering wheel, while a number of cars and vans crossed the bridge toward them. Were any of those cars surveillance vehicles? Just in case, Sandy turned her head away as they passed by. The light turned green and Sandy pulled away. She forced herself to drive normally. If anyone was following, she wanted to lull them into a false sense of security, not have them fired up and alert.

'Where are you staying?'

'At a pub on the Warrington road,' Sandy replied, taking the road through the centre of Handbridge and continuing south, past the college.

'You're going in the wrong direction,' Samantha said. 'Do you want me to direct you?'

'Sam, I know the way, for Christ's sake! I have to be sure that we're not being tailed.' Sandy replied testily. She took a left turn and then a right onto a road that ran parallel to the main road that they had just left.

'There's no need to blaspheme, Sandy,' Samantha grumbled automatically, 'and stop being so melodramatic! Who on Earth is going to be following us?'

'I'm not sure, but whoever it is, they're driving a red Ford Orion.' At the last turn, Sandy had seen that the vehicle was a saloon, not a hatchback.

'What?'

'It's been following us since the bridge.'

'Sandy, what are you talking about? Stop acting as if we're in some sort of spy film!'

'We've made a couple of spurious turns,' said Sandy, 'the last being a manoeuvre that made no sense unless you planned to visit someone down here.'

'Perhaps he lives here,' Sam shrugged, puzzled by her sister's erratic behaviour and now becoming slightly concerned at her state of mind.

'Let's see, shall we?' Sandy turned left at the end of the road and then immediately left again. In the mirror, she saw the Orion drive straight on, not following them into the second left. Her sister was watching in the nearside door mirror.

'See?' Samantha said smugly, 'you were worrying about nothing.'

Sandy pursed her lips and wrinkled her nose. She was not convinced. 'Possibly; I hope you're right.'

Sandy continued taking left turns until they reached the main road again, where she again turned left, heading south, as before. Then, at the next junction, they saw the Orion waiting to join the main road.

'He must have guessed we would double-back, and did a U-Turn to head us off,' Sandy mused aloud. She eased off the accelerator to allow him space to pull out in front, but the driver seemed in no hurry and failed to take the opportunity, instead waiting until the Golf, and a few other cars following had passed before tagging along behind.

'He's back with us,' Sandy said quietly, watching the rear-view mirror, 'He's four cars back.'

Samantha remained silent for a moment then shook her head, asking again, 'Why would anyone be following us?'

Out of the corner of her eye, Sandy could see her sister's agitation. 'Don't worry,' Sandy said more calmly than she felt, 'When the time comes, we'll lose them.' Sandy took another left, and again, the Orion followed them round at a discrete distance. No other cars were between them, now.

'Look out!'

At Samantha's urgent warning, Sandy dragged her eyes from the rear-view mirror and braked sharply. A rusty and battered white van was reversing into a tight space between two cars parked at the kerbside. The road was narrow with cars parked on both sides, leaving room for just one vehicle in the middle. With insufficient space to pass the van, Sandy had to wait. She glanced in the mirror again as the Orion came to a halt behind. Then, to her dismay, the front passenger door opened and a man got out.

'Shit!'

'Sandy, don't swear like that!' Samantha admonished her. 'Really! I don't like what you've become, lately.'

'Oh, shut up, Sam! You're beginning to sound just like Grace,' Sandy snapped, watching in the side mirror.

'Mother hated you calling her by her Christian name,' said Sam.

'I could never call her "mum",' Sandy replied. 'I never felt she was a mum to us. She was more like a governess.'

She was speaking distractedly as she watched the Orion's passenger. He passed between two parked cars onto the footpath on the driver's side of the road and sauntered towards them with his hands in his coat pockets. Sandy's right hand grasped the Glock in her fleece pocket. The van was still blocking the road ahead and the Orion was preventing her from reversing out.

'She did her best, you know, but you never gave her a chance. You could have met her halfway.'

'Sam,' Sandy said, affecting an unconcerned air, like an airline pilot warning his passengers that they may soon encounter some mild turbulence, 'if I say "get down" I want you to slide into the foot-well and make yourself as small as possible. Do you understand?'

'What are you talking about?'

'Just do as I say. Take your seat belt off now. Don't make a song-and-dance about it. Just be ready.'

'Sandy, you're scaring me,' said Samantha nervously. 'What's going on?' Then she saw the pistol in Sandy's hand and her eyes widened in alarm. 'Sandy, what in God's name…?'

Sandy gripped the weapon between her thighs, muzzle down. 'Just be ready.' In the door mirror, she could see the man was approaching with exaggerated nonchalance. She noted with satisfaction that Samantha had obediently released the safety belt and was letting it slide off her shoulder. 'This guy just wants to see who it is taking you for a lunchtime joyride. Hopefully, it's nothing more than that, but I have to be prepared.'

'What guy?' Samantha looked around but could see nothing suspicious about the man strolling along the footpath. 'I think you're being paranoid,' she concluded. 'Why have you got a gun? What are you mixed up in, Sandy?' She was shaking and her voice was becoming shrill with tension.

'Later!' Sandy barked, making her sister flinch. 'I don't have time for this now.'

The van had manoeuvred further into the space and Sandy judged that there was just enough room for her to squeeze the Golf through, but the van was already starting to move out again for yet another try. Biting her lip to keep her nerves under control, Sandy sounded the horn and moved the Golf forward through the gap before the van could close it off again. The nearside door mirror banged against the van's front wing but then swung back into place undamaged. Out of the corner of her eye, Sandy saw the driver gesticulate crudely at her impatience.

The van continued to roll forward, effectively trapping the Orion once more. Sandy had been concerned that the van might have been part of the surveillance team, and deliberately blocking their escape. Now that her fear had proved unfounded, Sandy grinned with elation as a shocked Samantha fastened her seat belt again.

'The Orion's caught behind the van,' Sandy explained, 'and he knows he'll lose us. But he won't be the only one. They should have at least another two, probably more vehicles, all in touch by radio, and paralleling our route. If we're lucky, it might be too early for them to have got into position. If not, there'll be another car, or worse, a motor-bike, that will pick us up at the next junction.' Sandy turned right into a wider road and noticed a light blue Volvo estate pull away from the kerbside to tuck in behind them.

'Yep, blue Volvo estate behind us now,' muttered Sandy almost to herself. 'No, don't look round,' she added sharply when Sam made to turn in her seat.

They were approaching another junction with a busy main road, and Sandy approached it slowly, timing her arrival carefully. She flicked the indicator stalk up to show that she intended to turn right and stopped behind the broken white line at the junction to wait for a bus that was approaching from the right.

'Sandy…' said Samantha, 'will you please tell me what's happening?'

'Hold on to your hat!' Sandy shouted exuberantly and floored the accelerator.

Samantha screamed at roughly the same pitch as the squealing tyres as Sandy threw the Golf to the left in front of the bus and accelerated away. The bus driver slammed on the brakes and rolled to a halt across the junction, effectively blocking the Volvo's exit. Sam screamed for a second time when Sandy dropped a gear, accelerated hard and pulled onto the wrong side of the road to overtake two cars, causing another, which was heading toward them, to brake and swerve sharply. Horns blared from every direction, but Sandy ignored them. Checking the mirror again, she noted that the bus had now started to move forward and was hiding them from the view of the occupants of the Volvo, which was caught up behind and probably looking for an opportunity to get past. Sandy followed the road around a sharp left-hand bend then spun the wheel right to turn into a side-road at the apex, almost putting the Golf up on two wheels in the process.

'Sandy,' Sam screamed, 'for God's sake! Slow down. You'll get us both killed!'

Sandy laughed with exhilaration and, with her hand on the horn, sped past a car that had started to emerge from a side turning, earning yet another angry hoot in reply. She took the time to glance at her sister, who was holding on to the inner door handle with her left hand and the edge of her seat with her right.

'Don't look so worried,' Sandy said with a grin. 'It's all under control. I'm starting to enjoy myself!'

'Well I'm bloody not!' said Samantha, tight lipped, and glared at Sandy in fear and anger.

'Sam!' said Sandy, pretending to be shocked. 'Now who's blaspheming? What would Saint Stephen say?'

'Actually,' Samantha replied in a brittle voice, 'under the circumstances, I think he might forgive me.' She tightened her grip again as Sandy took another sharp right turn at the end of the street. Then, unexpectedly caught up in the madness of the adventure, she started to laugh. Sandy joined in and soon they were both chortling like schoolgirls.

Confident that she had shaken off her pursuers, Sandy slowed the Golf to a sedate pace and drove back to the main road.

'You do realise that you're taking us back to Handbridge?' Sam said, her voice edged with concern.

'Yes, hopefully, I've convinced them that we're heading south. Now we'll skirt round to the north-east. Then we can talk in my room.'

Chapter 19

'Spider from Mobile One,' said the dark-haired, female driver of the Volvo.

'Spider receiving. Go ahead, Mobile One.'

'Lost them! Traffic's too dense to catch up without drawing lots of attention.'

'Spider – Mobile One. Received. Spider to all mobiles! Eyes peeled. Let's pick 'em up again.'

David Richardson looked at the loudspeaker as if he could see through it to the part of the city where Sandy had just given the surveillance team the slip. He had to assume it was Sandy driving the Golf. Who else could it be?

David was sitting alongside the operation controller, call-sign Spider. They were in a van with British Telecom markings parked near to the Brighting and Blount offices where Samantha worked. For the past ten days, they had been watching the comings and goings, and monitoring telephone calls to and from the office, while bogus technicians pretended to rewire a junction box. Three other vehicles waited nearby, ready to tail Sapphire, should she leave the office by car or taxi. When she travelled on foot, members of the surveillance team followed her. Still others kept watch on her home and her husband, designated Topaz. As a matter of course, a tap was placed on their telephone, and on the second day, quite illegally, members of the team had entered the house a few minutes after Sapphire and Topaz had left for work to ensure that Sandy was not taking refuge inside. Whilst they were inside, they planted bugs in the living room, kitchen and main bedroom and left the house, leaving no trace of the burglary.

This morning's crop of visitors to the offices of Brighting and Blount included the postman, two businessmen, a slovenly-looking woman in her twenties, accompanied by a thickset man in a shell-suit with gold chains around his neck and wrist, and an elderly lady whose clothes had clearly seen better days. Audio surveillance from bugs in Samantha's office and the reception area confirmed the bona fides of each of them. There had been an uncomfortable moment when the old lady reappeared and gave the van a hard stare. She had been the one having some trouble with British Telecom and David half-expected her to come over and give the bogus engineers a piece of her mind. To his relief, however, after a few seconds, she turned and slowly made her way down to the bus stop.

David had last seen Sandy at the house in Purley ten days before. She had welcomed him cordially on that bright but chilly Wednesday afternoon, even apologised for her unreasonable behaviour during their argument, the week before. There had been an awkward few minutes, during which they treated one another warily, but then they began to regain that friendly, easy rapport that had developed between them since Sandy had joined David's section. Despite the restored warmth between them, and the almost unbearable desire that he felt for her, David had resisted the primal urge to throw Sandy over his shoulder, caveman-like, carry her up the stairs to the bedroom and make passionate love to her. He smirked self-consciously. Fantasy apart, he accepted that if there were to be any resumption of the intimacy that they had enjoyed in Tunbridge Wells, it would be up to Sandy to make the first move – as indeed she had on that occasion.

Enjoyed? David examined the word in his head. He had certainly enjoyed the encounter with Sandy, but had she? Had she truly wanted him to help her to overcome a fear of sexual relations that were a result of her brutal treatment at the hands of her captors in that foreign land several months before? If that had been her motivation, then her dedication to her rehabilitation had been remarkable. He had lost count of just how many times had they made love during that weekend. Just thinking about it caused a reaction that made it necessary for him shift his position as he sat waiting, hoping, that the surveillance team would pick up the trail again.

The radio remained silent.

Perhaps she had simply been using her training in the sexual arts to manipulate him. If that was the case, then he had to admit that she had undoubtedly succeeded. He was infatuated with the woman, and would do anything for her; give her anything; forgive her anything. Well, almost.

On the morning that he had last seen her, Sandy had given no indication that she would soon go missing, so when he had tried several times during the weekend to call her, and she had failed to pick up, David had started to worry. His concern increased when, on the Monday morning, she failed to turn up for her first day as a trainee computer programmer at the Ministry of Defence. Now very worried, David had driven to the house, arriving at around midday.

Despite her inexplicable fury at David's letting himself into the house on the day of their quarrel, Sandy had not demanded the return of his key. Nevertheless, because of that uncomfortable episode, it was with some trepidation that he used it to gain access on that Monday.

Unsure whether he was more afraid of finding her lying dead in the house or of again feeling the force of her anger at his intrusion, David somewhat gingerly explored the ground floor. He found a note on the kitchen table in which Sandy explained that she was in need of a holiday and had decided to go away for a few days to the seaside. She finished by promising that she would call him when she got back. The note was undated and there were no newspapers or mail (apart from some junk mail and advertising flyers) lying around, so it was impossible to ascertain how long she had been gone.

Despite the reference to the seaside, David guessed immediately where she was really going, and knowing how dangerous that might be to Sandy, to her sister and to the Service, he felt he had little choice but to share his concerns with the Director General.

As expected, Amanda Gillette had been furious that Sandy had disobeyed a direct order, and she instructed David to mount a surveillance operation centred on Sandy's sister, in the expectation that Sandy would make contact with her. This he had done with the help of A4 (surveillance) branch in Manchester. Now, at the end of the second week of fruitless endeavour, which had tied up twenty highly experienced officers, the operation was about to be cancelled, on the assumption that their target had probably gone to Blackpool, Brighton or Bournemouth after all.

Then everything changed. On what was, potentially, the last routine foot-tail of Sapphire, at lunchtime, the officer reported losing contact when the target unexpectedly rendezvoused with a car, which then drove off at speed. The three vehicles assigned to the operation, caught out of position by Samantha's use of the walkway on the city walls, and the frustrations of the city's labyrinthine traffic system, set out to search for the suspect vehicle.

Having found the Golf as it waited for the light on the Old Dee Bridge, it soon became obvious to the surveillance team that the driver was using counter-surveillance measures, and they radioed for instructions on whether to try to remain covert or to move in to intercept. David instructed them to intercept, but before they could act, the Golf shook off the Volvo and disappeared into thin air.

'Spider from Mobile Three,' said a disembodied voice over the loudspeaker. Mobile Three was a motorcyclist.

'Spider receiving. Go ahead, Mobile Three.'

'Have eyeball on target vehicle. Heading south on Eaton Road, south of Handbridge.'

David punched the air. 'Yes!'

'Mobile Three from Spider. Received. All mobiles from Spider, converge on Eaton Road.'

'Spider from Mobile Three. Target vehicle is turning east on A-Five-Five. Repeat: east on A-Five-Five.'

***

Kathy looked at the clock. Sam should have been back by now. This had been the first time since Samantha's return from compassionate leave that she had declined Kathy's company at lunchtime and gone out alone. Normally, they would walk past the cathedral to the main shopping streets or browse through the Grosvenor shopping centre. On a nice day, they might stroll along the city walls. Some days they would go to a cafe and have some lunch, but never to a pub or wine bar because Samantha rarely, if ever, drank alcohol, and certainly not at lunchtime.

Since the initial contact at the church, Kathy had swiftly wormed her way into Samantha's life and had become her new best friend. It was easy to form an attachment to Samantha. Kathy had simply to wear the same type of clothes, read the same kind of books (or at least pretend to have done so) and adopt similar views on current affairs. Samantha was pleased to have someone with whom she could discuss anything from make-up and hairstyles to the recent tragedy in her life – and Kathy was a good listener. So close had they become that Kathy had no doubt that Sam would tell her if her sister were to get in touch – in strictest confidence, of course.

So what was different about today? Samantha's sudden departure was out of character and Kathy would have followed her but for the phone call. It was Sam's elderly client asking if she had dropped one of her gloves in the office. Kathy checked Sam's office and the stairwell but the glove was nowhere to be found. She tried to explain this to Mrs Sanderson but the old dear would simply not hang up, insisting on telling Kathy her recent life history, leading up to the loss of the glove. By the time Kathy had finally managed to get rid of her, she had lost all hope of tailing Samantha, so she sat down and waited impatiently for her return. That was more than an hour ago. Now it was 2:30 and with still no sign of Samantha, Kathy began to get seriously worried.

Checking Samantha's diary, Kathy could find nothing to suggest that she had an off-site appointment, so she slipped out of the office and went to her car, which was in the car park behind the office. From the glove box, she took out a small device with a three-inch-square monochrome screen, plugged it into the cigarette lighter and switched on the tracking screen. A blip appeared showing that Samantha, or at least the powder compact in her handbag, was stationary, eight kilometres, or five miles, to the northeast of the city centre. This was especially puzzling because Samantha's black BMW Touring was in the car park next to Kathy's Metro.

Perplexed, Kathy went back up to the office, sat at her desk and thought for a few minutes before reaching a decision. Moments later, she knocked on Eddie Brighting's door.

'Eddie,' she said in a weak, shaky voice, 'I'm terribly sorry, but I have the most awful migraine. Would you mind if I went home? Audrey can cover for me.' To add to the dramatic effect, she held her fingers to her temples.

Eddie looked up from the contract he was reviewing. 'Oh, my dear girl, yes, of course you must. Are you okay to drive? Do you want me to get someone to take you home?'

'No, thanks. That won't be necessary. I'll be fine.' She forced a pained smile. 'Oh, by the way, Sam's not back from lunch yet and she has a client due at Three.'

Eddie was surprised. 'Not back? Where's she gone?'

'I don't know. I wasn't feeling well, so she went out without me today. I do hope she's alright.'

'Indeed! We've had enough tragedies in this practice lately to last a lifetime.'

Chapter 20

'This is it,' said Sandy, ushering Sam into the unprepossessing bedroom, with its threadbare carpet and tired décor and furnishings, 'a real home-from-home.' She saw her sister's expression and realised it was a poor choice of words.

'I'm sorry Sam,' she said blinking back tears, 'I'm so, so sorry!' Then they fell into each other's arms, sobbing with grief for their parents, and with the joy of their reunion.

When they broke the embrace, Sam took off her coat and laid it on the double bed while Sandy went into the en suite bathroom, returning seconds later with two cheap glass tumblers. Then, while her sister was repairing her make-up in the dressing table mirror, Sandy reached into a bedside cabinet and pulled out a half-empty bottle of scotch. She splashed a generous measure into each tumbler and handed one to Sam.

'I don't usually drink spirits,' Sam said, accepting the proffered glass with a tight smile, 'but today, I think I'll make an exception.' She took a sip and grimaced. 'Ugh! I need some water with it.' She said, heading for the bathroom. When she returned, she noticed that Sandy had already emptied her glass and was pouring another.

Sam sat on the edge of the bed, which creaked alarmingly, and looked at Sandy as if for the first time. Her younger sister was wearing a grey fleece, zipped to the neck, and black Lycra leggings that would look very unflattering on most women, but most women did not have Sandy's legs. On her feet were white Reebok trainers with pink piping. The Nike baseball cap was lying on the bed and Sandy's straggly hair hung loose.

'You look awful,' said Sam bluntly. 'You're hair's grey and your skin looks like it needs a good moisturiser.'

Sandy smiled, showing perfect white teeth, and her blue eyes twinkled. 'All part of the old lady disguise,' she replied, using the weak, croaky voice of Mrs Sanderson. Then returning to her normal voice, 'The grey came from a can of spray-on dye that I bought from a fancy dress shop, and I mixed some with face powder to make my skin look grey and mottled. It'll all wash off – I hope!'

'Where did you get that coat?' Sam asked, 'It smelt awful!'

Sandy had been expecting her sister to ask about the shootings, not her dress sense. Perhaps Sam was working up the courage to ask the hard questions. Sandy shrugged as she answered.

'I trawled round lots of charity shops in... where I'm staying. The smell was a mixture of ammonia, the perfume that Gran used to wear and my own urine.'

'Ugh, that's disgusting,' said Sam, wrinkling her nose. 'Why?'

'It was a ploy to avoid being scrutinised too closely. People avoid someone who doesn't smell very nice. They certainly wouldn't want to get too close to them!'

Sam took a sip of her watered-down whisky and again grimaced at the taste. Then she finally broached the subject that Sandy had been dreading.

'What happened *that night* – at home?'

Sandy drained her Scotch and poured another, her third, Sam noted. She waved the bottle in Sam's direction. Sam shook her head and Sandy placed the bottle on the bedside table. She stood facing her sister.

'Three armed men came to the house at around nine-fifteen in the evening. Dad opened the door and they forced their way inside. Grace came to see what was happening and two of the men pushed both of them into the living room.'

Sam remained composed but attentive and nodded for Sandy to continue. Sandy sat down on an upright chair next to the scratched mahogany dressing table.

'The third seemed unsure whether to come upstairs or go into the kitchen,' she continued.

'Where were you?'

'I was at the top of the stairs, hiding behind the banisters. I had been in my room when I heard the doorbell. I tried to warn Dad not to open the door.'

'Why? Why did you want to stop Daddy opening the door? Did you know what was going to happen?'

Sandy lost control of her emotions and her face crumpled. 'I guessed,' she cried, tears streaming down her face. 'It was almost a premonition. I just knew.' Sam made no effort to comfort her, and remained seated on the bed as she fired the next question.

'How could you have known? You must know who they were. You said in your note that they were after you. Why? What had you done?'

'I had seen on the News that Jane Badell had been shot. I guessed they would come after me next.'

'Jane Badell, the reporter? What had you to do with her?' Sam trawled her memory. 'There was something in the newspapers about that in the past few days...' Then she remembered. 'They're saying that she was assassinated by Serbian agents.'

Weeping openly and fishing in her shoulder bag for a tissue, Sandy nodded in confirmation. She had not intended to disclose the connection with Jane's murder, but by not preparing beforehand what she would say, she had allowed a crucial piece of information to leak out. It only served to reinforce the lessons learned in counter-interrogation training. Only this was not supposed to be an interrogation; this was supposedly a difficult conversation between two sisters, who had always been close, concerning the tragic deaths of their father and stepmother. Sandy knew that she had to regain control and steer away from her own part in the Bosnian operation. As these thoughts ran through Sandy's mind, Sam continued to speak, articulating the details she could remember from the newspapers and television bulletins.

'They've just expelled, er, eight, I think it was, so-called diplomats from the Yugoslavian Embassy, saying they were responsible for the murder. How were you connected with that?'

Sandy was amazed at how controlled her sister was under the circumstances. She was hearing a distressing tale about the night her parents were murdered, and she was questioning Sandy in the most detached way, almost as if she were cross-examining a witness in a courtroom. Sandy struggled to regain her own composure and, to a point, succeeded.

'When I left Cambridge, I didn't go to Ethiopia,' Sandy began, and then immediately raised a hand to forestall Sam's interruption. 'In short, I'm working for the Security Service.' It was not a lie but neither was it the whole truth. She had left out the fact that originally she had worked for the Covert Surveillance Resource Service.

'Security Service?' Sam repeated. 'What, MI5? Are you saying that you're some sort of secret agent?'

'Yes,' Sandy answered simply. 'So when you asked in the car why I was acting as if we were in a spy film, you weren't far wrong.'

Sam's eyes widened with surprise. 'Oh my goodness!' She held her palms together as if praying, fingertips touching her lips. 'Did Daddy know?'

'No.'

'That's a pity. He would have approved.'

'Grace wouldn't!'

'No,' Sam agreed. 'Mother always blamed Daddy for you turning out the way you did.'

Sandy bridled at the remark. 'What's that supposed to mean?'

'Well, look at you,' Sam replied with an expressive wave of her hand. 'You drink like a fish, you swear like one of Daddy's sergeant-majors, you drive like a maniac, and you're carrying a gun. Hardly the genteel young lady our stepmother hoped you would turn out to be. Daddy always treated you more like a son than a daughter,' Sam continued, as Sandy sat speechless and open-mouthed. 'He and mother argued like cat and dog when he let you join his shooting club. But,' she added, smiling at a fond memory, 'she was proud of you when you won the Pentathlon. She told everyone, the ladies at the W.I. – even the neighbours.'

'She never once told me that she was proud of me!' Sandy said, her vision once more blurring with tears.

Sandy's relationship with her stepmother had always been difficult. No matter what the subject of discussion, unconsciously and unintentionally each would find just the right tone of voice or choice of words to inflame the other. The most trivial discussion would often end in a screaming match. For Sandy to discover, too late, that she had ever inspired anything other than anger or contempt in her stepmother was a bittersweet sensation.

'So, what happened?' Sam returned to the point of the conversation, 'With the reporter, I mean? Why would the Yugoslavians want to kill you?'

'I can't tell you much,' Sandy replied. 'It's all super-secret. You must promise me now that you'll never repeat anything that I'm telling you, not to anyone, not even – especially not Stephen. You mustn't even tell him that I've been in touch with you.'

'Why not Stephen, *especially*?' Sam was ever irritated by Sandy's obvious, but unexplained dislike of her husband.

'Because he's the sort of idiot that would tell everyone he knew. You know what a self-centred, attention-seeking prat he is. You have to promise me. Swear on Jesus's name. I know that means more to you than it would to me, so if you say that now, I'll know I can trust you.'

Sam's jaw dropped. What Sandy was saying was an astonishingly accurate reflection of what she had been thinking earlier, but she could never admit it. She defended her husband loyally.

'You're wrong about Stephen, but alright.' She took a deep breath and intoned, 'I swear by the Lord Jesus Christ, our Saviour, that I will never tell anyone that I've seen you. Now, tell me!'

Sandy took another swallow of scotch and ignored her sister's disapproving look. Then she began.

'Jane Badell and her film crew were in Sarajevo reporting on the referendum to decide whether Bosnia should secede from the Yugoslav Federation. While they were there, the civil war broke out and... well you probably saw the broadcasts.'

'Yes, of course,' Sam confirmed. 'I suppose they could be taken as anti-Serbian because they focussed on the hardships of the people of Sarajevo as the Serbian army surrounded and bombarded the city.'

'Exactly,' said Sandy. 'The Serb leaders were furious at what they considered to be biased reporting.'

'Didn't several members of the team get killed?' Sam asked, remembering the news stories.

Sandy swallowed hard to prevent her emotions from showing. She could not tell Sam that she had been there and that the people who died were her friends.

'Yes, that's true,' she answered in what she hoped was a detached manner. 'They went outside the city into the countryside and found evidence of genocide. The Serb nationalists were – are still – attempting to wipe out the Muslim population in the area that they call *Republika Srpska*.'

'I know; there have been lots of news reports about that. Isn't that why the United Nations force is there, to prevent that sort of thing?'

Sandy swallowed again. She could not divulge what she knew about UNPROFOR's impotence in Bosnia. Nor could she disclose that the real object of Jane's mission was the capture of the war criminal Brigadier-General Antonije Szopienice.

'Well,' she said, 'According to Jane, the film crew was captured by a Serb militia unit and held prisoner for several days. Badell's team had seen too much of what was going on and the militia commander decided to make them disappear. They planned to murder them and dispose of them amongst the bodies of the Muslims that they had massacred. Jane Badell and her cameraman were rescued by a Special Forces team sent in to find them, but the others were killed.' Sandy paused again before emphasising, 'This is all classified "Top Secret". Nothing of what I've just told you is in the public domain. As far as the world is concerned, the deaths of the people in Jane's team were a tragic accident.'

'Why?' Sam asked, 'Why would anyone want to keep that secret – anyone other than the Serbians, of course?'

'Our Government didn't want to admit they were running an illegal military operation on foreign sovereign soil and the Serb leadership doesn't want the world to know what their supporters are doing.'

'Extraordinary,' Sam remarked. 'So how did you get involved?'

'I was part of the team that debriefed the survivors,' Sandy lied smoothly. 'I got very close to Jane; spent a lot of time with her, drawing information, assimilating evidence. That was my job.'

'I see,' Sam said. 'So when the Yugoslavian agents decided to silence her, they felt they had to get rid of you too.'

Sandy suppressed a crafty smile. Sam had swallowed the story, even to the point of working out the ending for herself. That was good. It meant that Jane and her team's MI6 status remained a secret and secondly, it saved Sandy from answering embarrassing questions about her own role in the doomed operation.

'Yes,' she confirmed. 'That about sums it up.'

Sam stood up and paced the room. Sandy waited patiently for the next question.

'Alright,' Sam stopped pacing and began to recap, tapping the knuckles of one hand into the palm of the other. 'So you were at the top of the stairs, having seen Mother and Daddy forced into the living room. What happened next?'

'The third man came up the stairs. He didn't see me as I had crept back into my bedroom. I was afraid of what they would do to me and to Grace and Dad so I looked around for a weapon. I found my old archery kit under my bed. I had literally just strung the bow and nocked an arrow on the string when the third man burst into my room, pointing his gun at me. I put an arrow through his throat. Then I took his gun and tried to work out the best way to rescue Grace and Dad, but I was too late. I heard Grace scream and then the shots . . .' Sandy choked on the last word and started to cry. Sam broke down as well, and the sisters hugged each other for support. Eventually, Sandy sniffed and cleared her throat.

'Then the first two men came out of the living room into the hall. I shot at them and they fired back. I had to retreat back upstairs again. I hid in my room and barricaded the bedroom door with my bed.' Sandy paused in case Sam wanted to ask a question but her sister remained silent.

'They tried to batter down the door,' Sandy continued, 'and fired shots through the panelling. I realised that I couldn't stay there so I jumped out of the bedroom window and escaped through the neighbours' gardens.'

'You said you heard shots,' Sam said, 'but you couldn't have – couldn't know that Mother and Daddy were . . . dead.'

'It was all very quiet, downstairs. Then I heard two shots and Grace started screaming. There were two more shots and the screaming stopped immediately, cut off like . . .'

Sam held up her hands as if to blot out the image. 'Alright, alright. For God's sake, don't tell me any more!'

'I couldn't do anything to help them, Sam, I tried to help them. I tried, but I just couldn't save them!'

'Wait. Wait a minute.' Sam started pacing again. 'None of this makes sense. I've been to the house. There is simply no evidence of anyone battering your door down; just two large bloodstains on the floorboards in the living room where the carpet has been removed...' The final few words were lost as Sam finally cracked. She sank to her knees, buried her face in her hands and sobbed uncontrollably. Sandy went to her sister, put her arm around her shoulders and pulled her close. Tears were running down Sandy's cheeks as well, dampening Samantha's hair.

'How long before they let you inside?' Sandy asked.

'Not until after the funerals. They said it was a crime scene. They spent weeks gathering evidence. When we finally got inside, they'd taken away the carpets from the living room, the stairs and landing and . . .' she tailed off as if the significance of what she was about to say had only just occurred to her.

'My bedroom,' Sandy finished for her. 'Someone, presumably the Security Service, must have cleaned the house, repaired the damage and removed any evidence of what really happened,' said Sandy.

'Why? Why would they do that?'

'Well, I guess they didn't want to admit that one of their own officers was attacked in her own home. Can you imagine the press getting wind of that? I would never be able to work in the intelligence field again!'

Sam was horrified. 'So you agreed to this?'

'Actually, no,' Sandy answered truthfully. 'I knew nothing about it. Not until afterwards. They held me in protective custody for several days. I didn't even know who was holding me. I was terrified!'

Sam looked askance at her sister. 'What do you mean? Who was holding you?'

'It was actually my own people – MI5.'

'Why did they conceal who they were?'

'At first they suspected that I had actually done it. They thought I'd killed Grace and Dad. So they interrogated me. Anyway, MI6 intelligence about the plot eventually came to light and they worked out a way to keep it under wraps.'

'By making you the scapegoat?'

'By the time I was let out of chokey, the deal had all been sewn up. The dead girl had been mutilated and "discovered" in the Mersey. The first I knew of it was being shown an article in the Liverpool Echo about my own death.'

'My God!' said Sam reproachfully. 'So you just accepted it?'

'No,' Sandy replied, again truthfully. 'At first I refused to go along with it; but eventually they persuaded me that it was for the best. I'm to be given a new identity and will work in another part of the country.'

'And meanwhile the real murderers are allowed to leave the country unpunished!' Sam said angrily. 'That just isn't right.'

'No, it isn't. But it's international law, isn't it?'

Sam grimaced. 'That's true. Foreign diplomats can't be prosecuted without the express permission of their own government.'

'My boss promised me that they would eliminate these people, not just deport them,' Sandy said. 'Now I feel betrayed. I feel like going after them myself.'

'An eye for an eye?' said Sam, shaking her head. 'No, you mustn't even think of it.'

'What would you do, forgive them? Turn the other cheek?'

'I think I need to seek guidance on that,' Sam answered, honestly, 'It won't be easy, that's for sure.'

'Seek guidance from whom, Saint Stephen?' Sandy asked bitterly. To her surprise, her sister smiled.

'Perhaps a higher authority even than Stephen. It's strange,' she added, 'but somehow, I feel better about the whole thing now. Knowing that you weren't responsible; not directly, anyway.'

'I don't think I'll ever understand you,' said Sandy, shaking her head. 'I know for sure I'll never forgive them! In fact, if I ever get the chance, I will kill the bastards that murdered our parents!'

Sam pursed her lips. A thought had just occurred to her. 'From what you said, faking your death was merely for the benefit of the newspapers. Surely the people that tried to kill you must know that you're still alive.'

Sandy shrugged. 'I expect they do, but now they have no way of finding me.'

'Except through me,' Sam reminded her. 'Is that why we were followed?'

'I'm afraid it looks that way,' Sandy replied. 'I didn't really expect them to be keeping you under surveillance. Perhaps I should have foreseen that, but I was so desperate to see you....' Sandy swallowed before continuing. 'I suppose they've been watching you in case I turn up again. I'm sorry Sam, but I may have put your life in danger now.' Sandy slumped on the bed and looked disconsolately at the floor.

Sam sat on the bed and placed an arm around Sandy's shoulders. 'Clearly the Yugoslavians that were deported weren't the only ones. There are others still out there trying to find you.' Before Sandy could reply Sam spoke again, so quietly that Sandy was not sure she heard correctly. 'They shouldn't have even been there!'

'What do you mean? Shouldn't have been where?'

'Mother and Daddy. They should have been out. It was Friday evening. They always play– *played* Bridge on Friday evenings. Why didn't they go to the Collins's house to play Bridge that night?'

Sandy shook her head. She had not made the connection. It was the missing part of the puzzle. That was why the killers came to the house that night. That was why they came so late. Her parents were supposed to have gone out to play Bridge! Unconsciously, she ran her fingers through her hair, and tugged at it. If only their father had not followed his usual routine of putting the car away in the garage, the X-Rays would have known that Sandy was not alone. What then? Would they have postponed the attack until the next day? Would her parents still be alive? If that were the case, it was highly likely that she herself would not be. So that was it, a trade-off. In taking the lives of Sandy's parents, the X-Rays unwittingly gave their primary target the opportunity to escape. Suddenly, Sandy felt hot, as if the room were closing in on her. She unzipped her fleece and dropped it onto the bed.

'I had completely forgotten that,' she said at last, shaking her head. 'Grace had a bit of a headache and didn't feel like going. Dad was quite annoyed. God! I had completely forgotten.' She looked guiltily at Sam, who for once ignored the blasphemy.

Sam stood shakily and approached the window, with its heavy red-and-cream striped curtains drawn back, leaving the thick net-curtains to maintain the room's privacy while still admitting light, albeit fading fast as the November afternoon drew on. She stopped as Sandy took hold of her arm.

'Don't go near the window,' Sandy warned. Sam turned to face her and saw fear in her sister's eyes.

'Do you think they'll come after us here?'

'I don't know. I hope we gave them the slip.' Sandy pulled the curtains closed and they sat down together on the bed in silence once more.

'Who was the girl they found in the Mersey?' Sam asked after a few minutes. 'They said it was you.'

'Apparently, she was a prostitute and drug addict. She died of an overdose,' Sandy replied.

'I had to identify the body,' said Sam, grimacing, 'but there was nothing recognisable about her; the face had been completely destroyed. The police said she must have been hit by a ship's propellers.'

'The poor girl! So how did you identify her as me?' Sandy asked.

'She was wearing your clothes, your earrings and the watch that Mother and Daddy gave you for your Eighteenth.

Later they said dental records and DNA confirmed it was you.'

Sandy nodded, understanding at last what had happened to the clothes she had been wearing that night. She had not been wearing her watch or jewellery, so they must have taken those items from the house afterwards. She stood up and headed for the scotch bottle.

'Don't drink any more of that stuff,' Sam pleaded.

Sandy was standing sideways on to her sister with the bottle in one hand and the glass in the other. She turned her head to respond and saw Sam's eyes widen with surprise.

'Sandy, you're putting on weight!' said Sam, adding jokingly, 'You're not pregnant, are you?' Sandy cursed her own carelessness. If this was to be the last time that she would see her sister, she did not want to make it harder by letting Sam know that there was a baby on the way. However, her brief hesitation was evidence enough for Sam. 'You are!' she said excitedly. 'You're pregnant, aren't you?'

Realising that the game was up, Sandy nodded and grinned self-consciously. 'Nearly five months gone, now,' she said, unintentionally pushing the bump out a little more.

'My goodness!' Sam's hand flew to her mouth. Then she looked more closely, appraisingly. 'Are you sure? You're not showing much for five months. Who's the father?'

'No one you know,' Sandy answered evasively. She had tears in her eyes but she could not stop smiling. 'You're going to be an auntie!' It was a strange feeling; Sandy could not believe how happy she felt. She felt almost proud to be pregnant. It was almost as if she *wanted* to be a mother, was actually looking forward to it! Why? What was all that about? Sam, on the other hand, looked surprised, shocked even.

'Is he still around, the father? Are there wedding bells in the air?' There was more than a hint of sarcasm in Sam's voice.

'No,' Sandy replied, concealing her irritation at her sister's tone. 'It was someone in...' just in time, she stopped herself saying Bosnia. 'A guy I met in London. He doesn't know about the baby.'

'Are you keeping it?' Sam asked, her voice sounded strange – choked, but with a whimsical undertone.

'Yes, I am,' Sandy replied, matter-of-factly.

'I could be more than just an auntie,' Sam said hopefully, the words gushing out in an uncontrolled flow. 'Stephen and I have been trying for years to have a baby, but... Well, we could take the baby and raise it as our own. You don't want to be saddled with a child, do you? You've never been the motherly type.'

'You and Stephen?' Sandy snorted. 'Sam, if you think I would let a child of mine be exposed to that... that... arsehole husband of yours, you must be mad!'

'Sandy! How can you say such a thing? What has Stephen ever done to make you despise him so? I know you're scornful of his religious views...'

'It's got *fuck all* to do with religion, or politics, or anything like that!'

'Then what?' Sam grabbed Sandy's hand and pleaded. 'Tell me! What is it with you and Stephen? Is it because of what... *happened* between the two of you?'

Sandy wrinkled her nose and pursed her lips. 'What do you mean?'

'Look,' said Sam, 'there's no need to be coy. He told me all about it.'

'He *told* you?'

'Yes, but he's forgiven you. So have I. You don't have to worry…'

'You've forgiven me? *He's* forgiven me? Are we talking about the same thing here?' Sandy could feel her temper rising. 'What did he tell you?'

Sam shrugged and held her hands out as if in supplication. 'Look you were young and headstrong – always looking for adventure…'

'What did he say?' Sandy demanded, gripping her sister's wrists so hard that Sam winced with pain.

'I'm talking about that Sunday he came home early from church. As usual, I stayed for the after-service coffee morning, but he felt unwell and left to come home. You were staying over for the weekend, as you often did when you came home from Cambridge. You used to spend half your life in bed in those days,' Sam added. 'Anyway, he said he came up to the guest room to see if you were awake.'

'Well, so far, I don't dispute his story,' Sandy said. 'What then?'

Sam swallowed and looked away. 'He said you exposed your body to him and tried to seduce him. He said he resisted you, and that you and he argued. After that he did not want you in the house because he thought you were sent by the Devil to tempt him.'

'What bollocks!' Sandy spat. 'It was he that tried it on with me!'

'Oh, Sandy!'

'No, Sam, you listen to me! He burst in, and started ranting about it being time for me to get out of bed. He said I was a lazy, good-for-nothing slut. I was shocked – and a little frightened, but I said okay, and I would get out of bed once he left the room. But he insisted on staying, *he said*, to make sure I really got up. The thing is I was naked under the duvet. I always slept naked in those days, and he knew it, because I had mentioned it the night before. You might remember the conversation. It was after dinner, and I said it to wind him up. You remember how much I used to like winding him up? That's why I used to tell all those sex and drugs and rock 'n' roll stories about Uni – all those three-in-a-bed tales and boasting about the wild orgies. It was all bollocks; it never happened. Sure I slept with my boyfriends; everyone did; but nothing like I used to kid him about.'

Sam's voice was cold. 'So he refused to leave the room in the hope of seeing you naked. Is that what you're saying?'

'Yes, but it was a standoff. I wouldn't get out of bed, and he wouldn't leave the room. After a minute or two, he started pulling at the duvet, trying to pull it off me. I held on really tight, trying to keep myself covered, but he was like a madman! I kept yelling at him to leave me alone. Anyway, eventually he won. I let the quilt go suddenly and he flew backwards. I held a pillow in front of me and tried to get past him to the bathroom, but he jumped up and started wrestling me for the pillow. His hands were everywhere – touching me. He tried to tickle me with one hand while pulling at the pillow with the other, and all the time he was alternating between ranting and laughing like a lunatic. Eventually, I fell against the bed and fell onto the floor. Now he had the pillow and I was completely naked. I curled up into a ball on the floor so he couldn't see anything.'

'What did he do then?' Sam's voice was a whisper and tears were running down her cheeks.

'He stood over me, calling me a whore and a hussy. He said I was shameless and evil and I would burn in hell. After a while he stormed out of the room.'

'Then what?'

'I washed and dressed, and waited until I heard you come back. Then I came downstairs.'

'You never said anything to me about it. Why? Why didn't you say anything?'

'I was too embarrassed. I didn't know what to do. We all had lunch, as if nothing had happened, and then I went home to see Grace and Dad before getting the train back to Cambridge. That was the last time ever that I visited you at your house.'

'I don't know what to say. What you're telling me is the exact opposite of what Stephen told me.'

'And you believe him? You believe that I would come on to Stephen?' Sandy asked scathingly, 'Really?'

Sam opened her mouth to answer, but stopped as the room telephone rang. Sandy looked at it, but made no move to answer it. Sam looked from the phone to Sandy and back again.

'Aren't you going to answer it?' She asked, perplexed because no one ever leaves a ringing telephone unanswered.

'Nobody knows I'm here,' Sandy said, nervously. 'Who would be ringing me?'

The telephone continued to ring.

'Oh, don't be ridiculous!' said Sam, moving toward the phone.

Sandy leapt bodily onto her sister and they both tumbled to the floor.

'What on Earth are you doing?' Sam demanded. 'Have you gone completely mad?' She struggled to free herself from her sister's grip but Sandy was too strong. The phone stopped ringing, ushering in a brooding silence.

'It could be a trap,' Sandy whispered. 'A sniper lines up through the window, on a point three feet above the phone. When it's answered, he fires. He's almost certain to get a kill, even if he can't physically see the target.'

'Surely, he wouldn't be able to see through those net curtains,' Sam argued.

'He would know the aiming point.'

'But...'

'It's real, Sam. They killed Grace and Dad. They tried to kill me. We were tailed after I picked you up . . .'

The telephone started to ring again.

'What are you going to do?' Sam asked tremulously, fear and bewilderment etched on her face.

Chapter 21

Standing forty feet back from the old Chester to Warrington trunk road, and surrounded by open countryside, the Waterloo Inn was the quintessential English country pub. A white-rendered, two-storey, rectangular building, it was topped by a jumble of grey-tiled roofs, all of which varied in pitch and height.

Originally called the Plough, the building dated from the time of George III and had been extended many times over the following two hundred years, swallowing up several structures that had once been outbuildings. At some point in its history, a flat-topped portico, supported by two concrete pillars, topped with neo-Regency scrollwork, had been added to give the main entrance an air of grandeur. That grandeur was now sadly faded, with tired rendering and woodwork both in need of renovation. The wide forecourt, which once welcomed teams of horses pulling the mail coach, was now a car park with room for about thirty cars, but currently held a mere half-a-dozen, all clustered in the spaces nearest the portico. One of these was a blue Golf GTi

'Sorry, sir. No answer from Room One.'

'Try again, please,' David requested politely. His voice may have sounded calm, but David was anything but. Angry, concerned, betrayed – any number of adjectives, singly or combined, would better describe his feelings.

Sitting in his car with a Nokia mobile phone pressed to his ear, David drummed his fingers on the steering wheel impatiently as he waited for the connection to be made. The mobile phone was state of the art, the most up to date technology, but it was the size of a house brick and the analogue signal hissed in his ear.

Brrr, brrr. The electronic warble in David's ear told him that the phone was ringing.

Unobserved, the motorcyclist, Mobile Three, had tailed the Golf all the way to this location. He then kept watch until the other two vehicles arrived. By the time David had joined them, they had somehow managed to find out which room the two women were in. It was still not certain that the second woman was Sandy, David thought bitterly. This could still turn out to be a wild goose chase.

Brrr, brrr.

The building stood in forlorn isolation. Its nearest neighbour was a cottage two hundred yards away. The windows of the bedrooms at the front of the building had an unobstructed view of the car park and the road, which was virtually straight for half-a-mile either side, so any vehicles stopping in the vicinity would be easy to spot. On the other hand, there did not seem to be an escape route. If she could not get to her car, she would have to run across the fields behind the pub to the nearest cover, a copse at least two hundred yards distant.

The surveillance team waited in their vehicles a few hundred yards either side of the pub. If the target were to leave, one of them would be in position to intercept. David had pulled up behind the Volvo on the Chester side near to the cottage, and this was where he waited, less than patiently, for the phone to be answered.

Brrr, brrr. The phone started the fourth ring.

'Hello?' David's heart missed a beat. Her voice was quiet and strained over the crackly analogue signal. She sounded nervous, afraid.

'Hello, Morgan,' he said, keeping his voice even. 'This is Merlin.' The use of the Arthurian pseudonyms appealed to his sense of irony.

'Oh, it's you!' The relief in her voice was clear. Prepared for a torrent of invective, David's heart soared at the thought that Sandy was actually pleased to hear from him. Then, *sotto voce*, away from the phone, he heard her say, 'It's my boss at MI5.'

David thought Sandy's breathing sounded strange. He was not to know that she had leopard-crawled to the bedside table, and was lying on the floor alongside the bed as she answered the telephone. Feeling foolish on hearing David's voice, she had clambered up off the floor and was now perched on the edge of the bed.

'Are you alright?' he asked.

'Yes, I'm fine. 'How did you find me? I thought I'd given them the slip.'

'We're not bloody amateurs, you know!' he replied testily.

'Look, I understand that you're angry. I'm sorry I disappeared...'

'You have absolutely no idea how much trouble you've caused, young lady,' David interrupted harshly. He had not intended to sound quite so paternal, but relief at finding her safe had fuelled his anger. 'You've got some explaining to do! But first, I want you back in London.'

'Actually,' Sandy replied stubbornly, 'now I'm here, I'd like to spend some more time with my sister.'

'Listen, you idiot,' David thundered, 'if it was anyone other than me that found you, you'd be spending bloody Eternity with her.'

'Okay, I'll start back this afternoon. Will you come and see me at the house tomorrow?'

'No, you won't *start back* at all!' David realised that his authoritative tone would be upsetting to Sandy, but he wanted her to know he was angry. It wasn't just that she had disobeyed orders; she had betrayed his trust. 'I'm outside the pub now. The only reason I'm phoning rather than knocking on the door is because I don't want my bloody head blown off!'

'Ah! I suppose you'd better come up then,' Sandy replied, adding, 'I should warn you, I still have my sister with me.'

'Yes,' David answered, tightly, 'I'm quite aware of that, thank you.'

David heard another voice in the background saying, 'He can't force you to go. MI5 don't have powers of arrest.'

'Leave it, Sam,' Sandy answered, away from the phone; 'What they're allowed to do, legally, and what they do in practice are very different things.' The other voice protested, but Sandy quelled it again. 'Forget it Sam. Just do whatever they ask of you. And remember your promise not to breathe a word to anyone.'

'Morgan!' David shouted down the phone to get her attention.

'Yes, I'm here.' Hurt; compliant; contrite.

'I'll give you five minutes; then I'll be knocking on your door.'

'Okay.'

Sandy replaced the receiver and turned to her sister. 'I've got so much to say, and no time to say anything.'

'Will they let us meet again?'

Sandy shook her head, 'No. They expressly forbade me to contact you at all. You were supposed to believe I was dead, but I simply couldn't let you go through life thinking that I had killed our parents.'

Sam nodded. 'I understand. I don't know if the separation will be harder, knowing you're still alive out there.'

'I'll have a new identity, too,' Sandy added. 'Sandra Harris is officially dead, of course.'

'What's your new name?'

'I can't tell you,' Sandy replied, her eyes sparkling with yet more suppressed tears. What was it, lately? She seemed to cry at the slightest thing, nowadays, whereas before she had been as hard as nails. Before what? Before pregnancy. Perhaps her hormones were to blame. Suddenly she had an idea. 'Quick,' she said, 'tell me the name of someone from school. Someone you're no longer in touch with.'

Sam shook her head in confusion, her mind blank. 'I can't think, er...'

'What about Andrea Nelson?' Sandy suggested, remembering a particularly unpleasant girl in Sam's year, the leader of a gang of bullies who made life a misery for many of the other students, Sam included.

'What are you thinking?'

Sandy smiled craftily as she explained.

'Yes,' replied Sam, doubtfully, 'I think I understand.' Then she started as someone knocked on the door.

'Damn! I suppose that means our time's up,' Sandy said. Reluctantly, she turned and walked slowly to the door. There was no peephole, so even though she knew who she was expecting to be on the other side, she opened it cautiously, standing to one side, her cocked pistol concealed behind her back, ready for instant action.

David strode into the room. 'Good afternoon, ladies,' he said briskly. He managed to look distinguished despite being casually dressed in a black quilted bomber jacket, unzipped to reveal a harlequin patterned rugby top over beige slacks and rugged hiking shoes. 'You must be Mrs McNamara,' he said with a tight smile. 'Pleased to meet you, at last. I've heard so much about you.'

Sam stared back defiantly. 'I wish I could say the same! What sort of mess have you got my sister into?'

'Sam, please!' Sandy protested. 'It's none of David's doing. He's shown me nothing but kindness and support.' She added the last part as much to emolliate David as to calm her sister. David glanced significantly at the Glock in Sandy's right hand. She made the weapon safe and put it on the dressing table.

'I just don't want to lose you again,' Sam replied, eyes flitting between Sandy and the stranger, gauging, from their body language, what, if any, threat his presence posed to their future.

'Sam, just do as they say,' Sandy said earnestly. 'It's for the best, *remember?*' Sandy placed heavy emphasis on the last word to remind her sister that she would find a way to stay in touch.

'I'm assuming,' said David, 'that Sandy has impressed upon you the importance of maintaining absolute secrecy about her continued survival?'

'Yes, she has.'

'You realise how much danger she, you and your husband would be in if the wrong people were to find out?'

'Is that a threat?' Sam raised her chin, defiantly.

'Sam!' Sandy protested, shocked at her sister's accusatory tone.

'No, of course not, Mrs McNamara,' David replied, his expression deadly serious; 'Not from us at least, but from whoever it was that made the attempt on Sandy's life in the first place.'

'The Yugoslavian agents,' said Sam, confirming, to David's dismay, that she knew more than she should, 'but I don't understand why they would want to kill her – or me. What could they achieve?'

'I told Sam about my debriefing Jane Badell after her return from Bosnia,' Sandy cut in before David could respond to Sam's indiscretion, perhaps with a different story to the one she had told. 'I explained that she was an eye-witness to war-crimes, and that I was probably targeted because of what she had disclosed to me.'

'I see,' David replied, thankful that Sandy had invented a credible cover story. He had been afraid that she would tell her sister the whole sorry tale. Damn! He didn't even know the whole story himself. 'Sandy has told you rather more than she should have,' David told Sam. 'This whole affair is top secret, and it is vital that the details do not leak out.'

'I've promised my sister,' Sam replied, 'in Jesus Christ's name, that I will not disclose anything I've heard from her today to anyone else;' she shot a glance at Sandy. 'Not even to my own husband.'

David looked from Sandy to her sister and back again. Then, withdrawing some sheets of paper and a pen from his jacket pocket, he handed them to Samantha. 'Mrs McNamara, I'm afraid I'm going to have to ask you to sign the Official Secrets Act. The information you have become party to is a matter of national security.'

Samantha shrugged her shoulders and, without hesitation, signed her name. The paper made no difference. She had promised that she would never disclose to another soul anything that she had heard in this room.

'Now,' said David, taking possession of the signed document, 'I really need to discuss matters with Sandy in private. There is someone waiting for you downstairs in the bar. She will drive you back to your office, or if you prefer, to your home.'

Samantha exchanged glances with Sandy. 'Could we have a few minutes alone to say goodbye?' she asked.

David sighed with barely concealed irritation but he saw Sandy's desperate expression and acquiesced. 'Yes, of course. I'll wait outside the door.' He turned to leave, and as he closed the door behind him, he added, 'Not too long, please, Sandy.'

Chapter 22

Sandy waited alone while David escorted Samantha to the bar to hand her over to the A4 officer who would drive her back to the city centre. When he returned, his stern expression reminded her of her father when she had been particularly naughty as a child. It was a blend of sadness and reluctant severity. Sandy steeled herself. There were things she had to say to David; things she needed him to understand. Before then, however, she had to make sure he was not wired for sound, as he had been in the hotel in Tunbridge Wells.

'I know I deserve a bollocking,' Sandy said quietly, dejectedly, her blue eyes glistening as they looked into David's, 'but I really need a hug first.'

David stopped in his tracks, his anger dissolving instantly to vapour. Sandy's heartfelt request, like that of a condemned prisoner asking for a last cigarette, had taken the wind of indignation out of his sails. He shrugged his shoulders and reached out to enfold her in his arms. Sandy stepped into his embrace and rested her head on his shoulder. His hands stroked her back through the thin cotton of her tee shirt.

'I'm sorry,' she said, 'I know I shouldn't have disobeyed orders but...'

'Oh, just be quiet,' he said hoarsely, and Sandy could tell from his voice that he was already sexually aroused. Poor David; this was almost too easy.

Disguised as a caress, her hands flew nimbly over his jacket, checking the pockets for anything untoward. She could identify his wallet, keys, a spectacle case and the bulky mobile phone, but not the digital recording device with which he had attempted to entrap her in the hotel dining room in Tunbridge Wells. She then slipped one hand inside his jacket and around his waist, brushing the handle of a pistol in its holster hooked onto to his belt in the small of his back, before tracing her fingers up his spine. Meanwhile she used her other hand to explore his chest and stomach, but she failed to detect any sign of wires or microphones. If there was anything to find, it would be below the waistband of his trousers, but it was too early in the proceedings to venture there. Yet.

David's arms gripped tighter, squeezing her protectively. She felt him kiss the top of her head before resting his cheek on it. It felt good; it felt comforting. She felt secure, even loved, and as she waited for David's next move, Sandy had to remind herself that there was a purpose to this charade. She wondered how he would progress from here. Would he stoop to kiss her lips? Would one of his hands head south to stroke her bottom? Perhaps he would start by groping a breast. On the other hand, he might just throw her onto the bed and start ripping her clothes off.

To her confusion, nothing happened. Despite the full-on contact that she had initiated, David seemed content merely to hold her in his arms and nuzzle the top of her head. Sandy did not know that David was resisting his almost overwhelming desire for her, suppressing his baser instincts out of respect for her most recently expressed wish regarding their relationship.

Oh, come on, for Christ's sake! What's wrong with him? Surely, he can't have turned gay in the past couple of weeks!

The impasse lasted for a minute or two before Sandy realised that she would once again have to take the initiative. Reluctantly, because she was enjoying the sensation of being in his warm embrace, she turned within the circle of his arms and pushed back against him. Now his arms were folded across her chest, and, whether by accident or design, his right hand covered her left breast and his fingers instinctively kneaded the soft flesh.

At last! Now we're getting somewhere! She faked a small moan of appreciation and moved her bottom across his lower body, feeling, with satisfaction, the hardness that confirmed her earlier assumption. The recording device was in his right trouser pocket.

'Your breasts are getting bigger,' David murmured, kissing her neck just below the right ear.

Grandma, what big breasts you have!

It was true that she had gone from a 'B' to a 'C' cup in the past month but boy, did he need to work on his seduction technique! Sandy reached her hand behind to excite him even more. That was the catalyst. Immediately, his hand found its way under her tee shirt and inside her bra. She felt the nipple stiffening and growing in response, heralding her own arousal, but there was no time for that now.

Turning to face David once more, Sandy reached up and kissed him wetly on the mouth, parting her lips to admit his probing tongue while at the same time pushing his jacket off his shoulders. He released his hold on her while he struggled out of it. Then she wrenched the shirt up over his chest, just as his hands found the hem of her tee shirt and began to pull it up. Both garments hit the floor simultaneously and Sandy began feverishly to unfasten David's belt, while he fumbled with the fastening of her bra-strap. Both were breathing heavily: David with unbridled excitement; Sandy with well-practised role-play.

Suddenly, Sandy squealed with surprise as David scooped her up in his arms and dropped her onto the bed. He pulled off her trainers then yanked at the waistband of her leggings. They got stuck as he tried to pull them over her feet and she kicked her legs to shrug them off, leaving her wearing nothing but white trainer-socks and black bikini briefs. Sandy leaned forward to take off her socks, leaving David nothing to do except to strip out of the last of his clothes. Naked, he began to reach for her again, but she dodged him, slipped off the bed and ran for the bathroom.

'Where are you going?' David grabbed her around the waist, but she twisted away from him.

'I need the bathroom,' she panted, and she heard him groan in frustration.

David flopped back on the bed, eagerly awaiting Sandy's return, but his anticipation turned to bewilderment when he heard the bath taps running.

'David?' He heard her call and padded across the worn carpet to the open door.

If the bedroom was seedy and run-down, the bathroom was worse. It looked as if it had not been decorated since the 1970s. Once-white tiles, many of which were now cracked or chipped, covered the lower half of the walls, the grouting stained with patches of mildew. Above the tiles, the walls were painted in a pastel green emulsion that had been touched up in several areas in an unsuccessful attempt to disguise where the paint had peeled away. On the floor were geometrically patterned, vinyl floor tiles which were badly trimmed, leaving ragged edges and uneven gaps around the "avocado-green" sanitary ware.

Sandy was standing in the middle of the room, a white bath towel wrapped around her body, covering her from chest to knee. She saw David's obvious distaste at her choice of accommodation and shrugged.

'It's all I could afford. I had to pay cash to stop you tracing me through credit card transactions.

'Sensible,' he replied, inclining his head. 'What's all this about?'

'Close the door,' she said abruptly. David obeyed unthinkingly and turned back to face her. 'How much can I trust you?' she asked quietly, her words almost lost in the sound of the water from two taps gushing noisily into the bath.

'More than I can trust you, evidently,' he answered with a mischievous half-smile.

'Ouch!' Sandy replied, stung by his repost. 'Look, I'm sorry about the subterfuge,' she said, handing him a towel to cover himself, 'but I had to be sure you weren't recording our conversation.'

David wrapped the towel around his waist. 'Why would I do that?' he asked innocently, but guilt was written all over his face.

Sandy sat on the edge of the bath. 'Well, you did in Tunbridge Wells,' she said without any trace of bitterness.

'You knew about that?' David replied, obviously surprised at having been found out.

'Of course,' Sandy smirked and, echoing David's earlier words, added, 'I'm not a bloody amateur, you know!'

David raised his eyes to the ceiling. 'Touché! Look, I'm sorry about that, but I was told to ask you about Bosnia,' he explained quietly. 'K suspected that Eagle and C were keeping something from her. She wanted to know what it was.'

David sat beside Sandy on the edge of the bath, sitting close, their hips touching. He wished his erection would subside, but despite his feeling foolish for having allowed Sandy to manipulate him, it remained stubbornly at attention, an obvious bulge in the front of the towel. Sandy looked down with amusement.

'Old Mr Happy doesn't give up easily,' she laughed, giving the subject of discussion a playful squeeze and David gasped with surprise. 'Come on, surely you must have tried when I was sedated after the interrogation,' Sandy added, suddenly serious again.

David seemed reluctant to answer. Sandy lifted his right arm and placed it around her shoulder. Then she rested her head on his chest. Her hand began to stroke the fine hairs on his chest with her fingertips and David's breath caught in his throat. Automatically, his fingers gently caressed her upper-arm.

'No,' he replied, thickly. 'We didn't do anything of the sort.'

'David,' Sandy crooned. 'Tell me the truth for once.'

'Sandy . . .'

'David, you and I shouldn't have secrets from one another. You said you loved me. Didn't you mean it?'

'Sandy, I . . .'

'Please David, let's trust one another. It's you and me against all these other bastards. I don't trust a single one of them – except you.'

'I'm sorry, I've forgotten the question,' David laughed.

'Did you question me about Bosnia when I was drugged?'

'Yes,' he finally admitted.

'What did I tell you?'

'You didn't tell us anything. You denied ever being there. You said you couldn't even point it out in an atlas.'

'Anything else?'

'Like what?'

'What else did you ask me?'

'Nothing.'

'I don't believe you. I bet you asked details about Caesar.'

A thought struck David and he turned and grasped Sandy's shoulders. 'Were you conscious? Were you faking it?'

'No,' Sandy replied.

'Then how . . .'

Sandy shrugged. 'Just a guess,' she said. 'What did I tell you?'

David laughed and squeezed her with his arm. 'You recited *Julius Caesar* – the whole bloody play. You talked for two hours. We couldn't make you stop. Then you fell asleep. What?'

Sandy was rocking with laughter.

'What's funny?' asked David. He was also laughing because Sandy's humour was infectious.

'Our counter-interrogation methods include self-hypnosis, a deep seated subconscious trigger to detect hostile questioning and respond with some rubbish.'

'You think Shakespeare is rubbish?'

Sandy laughed again. 'No, of course not, but my answer to your question was hardly what you wanted to hear, was it?' She became serious again and slipped from under his arm. 'David, in Tunbridge Wells, why did you ask me about Colonel Devereux?'

David attempted to put his arm around Sandy's shoulder again but she stopped him and moved a little further away from him. 'Tell me about Devereux,' Sandy persisted.

David shrugged his shoulders. 'What about him?'

'Why did you ask me about him?'

'Because I couldn't think of any other way to bring Sarajevo into the conversation,' he replied truthfully.

'You weren't prompted or briefed to talk about him?'

'No, I told you. I knew him slightly; I met him at a conference. Why is it so important?'

Sandy thought about that answer for a moment. Eventually she asked, 'How much do you know about the mission?'

'Very little,' he replied, 'and most of that is what you've told me about going under cover as a TV news film crew, and what happened to you and your friend Caroline.'

'What else?'

'I know you were sent to try to locate a war criminal, and that the operation went pear-shaped. That's it.'

Sandy looked again at the level of the bath water. 'I ran the taps to drown out our conversation,' she said, 'but it seems a shame to waste it. I'm dying to have a bath. I feel all hot and sticky. Do you mind?'

'Er, no,' David said standing up. 'I'll wait outside.'

'Don't be silly,' Sandy laughed and dropped the towel; 'you've seen it all before.' She still wore the black bikini briefs and David watched hungrily as she slipped them off and stepped into the bath, sinking down until only her head and knees were above the surface. She had no bubble bath or salts to add so the water was completely clear. David sat on the side of the bath trying not to stare at her naked body. Not for the first time he was struck by how perfect Sandy's skin would be if not for the cruel disfigurement of the cigarette burns around her breasts and stomach. Oblivious to his thoughts, Sandy closed her eyes and began to tell her story.

'It was designated Operation *Cevapi*. We were sent to Sarajevo at the end of February to locate the target, a Colonel in the Yugoslavian Army, the "JNA". He was responsible for the massacre of over a hundred civilians in a small town in Croatia, and of two SIS officers when they tried to intervene. Our cover, as you said, was that we were a TV news crew reporting on the referendum on Bosnian secession from Yugoslavia.

'Some Bosnian Serbs, particularly those from Sarajevo, were in favour of secession, but there were many Serbs who were opposing not just secession but the referendum itself. They had held their own plebiscite a few months before and had overwhelmingly voted against secession, which, to be fair, should have killed the issue stone dead. The Yugoslav Constitution demanded that a majority of each of the ethnic groups in any of the republics that made up the country had to agree to secession in order to make it binding.

'There are three main groups in Bosnia,' she continued, 'Muslims, also called Bosniaks, are the largest, followed by ethnic Serbs and, lastly, a much smaller population of Croats. The groups are divided religiously too. The Bosniaks are Muslims, obviously, then the Serbs are Eastern Orthodox Christians, like the Greeks, and the Croats are Roman Catholics.

'But the Muslim-dominated Bosnian government ignored the Serb plebiscite and declared a simple majority vote would be sufficient to give them a mandate for secession. They were encouraged by the success of Slovenia, which had won independence the year before, in an almost bloodless ten-day revolution. Significantly, and perhaps naively, they ignored the carnage that was still going on in Croatia, and decided to press ahead anyway. Our target, and other allies of the President of Serbia, Slobodan Milosevic, demanded that Bosnian Serbs boycott the referendum so that its result could be declared null and void.'

'Surely,' David said, 'rather than boycott the referendum, they could simply have voted against secession?'

'No, you see, to the militant Serbs opposed to secession, it was obvious that the Bosniaks, being the largest group, would win the vote, so, many Serbs boycotted the referendum in protest. By so doing, they could hope to have the referendum declared null and void. Some went further and started to try to intimidate people not to vote. On the first day of the referendum, Serb militants started putting up roadblocks. We were stopped several times by masked gunmen barricading the roads, demanding to see identification.'

'What did the Bosnian government do about it?'

'When the fighting started, the militants were pushed out of the centre and west of the city and took up positions in the north and east. As I said before, not all Serbs were against secession. The majority of people in Sarajevo wanted to continue living in harmony with each other as they had done for decades since the Second World War under Tito. The day after the referendum there was a peace march by thousands of people, including Muslims, Serbs and Croats; But the demonstration was fired on, allegedly by Serb gunmen. They even shot at a wedding procession, a day or so later, killing the groom's father.'

'Christ!' David said, shaking his head.' He waited for Sandy to continue but she had lapsed into silence. He decided to prompt her. 'So did you locate your target?'

'No, not at first. We didn't know whether or not he was still inside the city. Local agents were set to work to try to find him, but without success. It's as if he had disappeared off the face of the Earth.'

'So what happened then?'

'The violence escalated very rapidly. Toward the end of March The JNA tried to occupy the city but the defence force repelled them. The JNA then completely surrounded the city and took control of the airport. Then the UN and the EU put a lot of pressure on Milosevic to pull the JNA out of Bosnia, which he did, eventually. The catch was that many of the JNA soldiers had originated from Bosnia, and they remained in place – with all the weapons and equipment that the JNA had left behind. It was then that they started to pump artillery shells into Sarajevo, destroying the electricity supply, the water supply, public transport, you name it. People in the city tried to go about their daily business – it must have been a bit like it was in the Blitz in London and other cities in the Second World War.' Sandy paused, remembering a broken doll lying in the gutter, its once white dress grimy and splattered with blood. On another occasion there was a running shoe lying in the middle of the road with the owner's foot still inside.

'The Serb besieging the city also had snipers shooting at civilians,' she continued. 'Certain streets and junctions became death traps – the locals called them "Snipers' Alleys". People would sprint across to avoid getting shot. People got shot queuing for water, or bread. Street cleaners were employed to recover the bodies and they got shot in the process. People ended up dreading sunny days because that's when the snipers could operate. It was much safer if it was raining or foggy.'

'My God,' said David softly, 'It must have been terrifying.'

'Yes, I suppose it was at first, but then you sort of get used to it. You've been under fire; you know what it's like.' Sandy paused as another memory clouded her thoughts. 'Anyway,' she continued, 'we went out onto the streets, filming the destruction, interviewing people…'

'So you'd given up trying to locate the target?'

'We hadn't given up. It's just that no Intel came in about him. So we just continued acting out our cover story. Anyway, this went on for three months. By this time, conditions in the city were pretty dire. This was before the United Nations Protection Force – UNPROFOR – reopened the airport, so there was no food or humanitarian aid coming in. Even the Red Cross evacuated their personnel from Sarajevo because it was considered too dangerous for them to stay.'

David nodded. 'Yes, I remember being quite shocked at that.'

'Somehow,' Sandy continued, oblivious that David had spoken, 'a bakery was operating without running water and electricity, and people were queuing daily for hand-baked bread. They foraged for wood to heat improvised stoves in their homes for cooking and heating, because the weather was still cold. They queued at natural springs to collect water in whatever receptacles they could carry. The UN soldiers placed steel shipping containers around the spring at the main water company to protect people who were queuing from the snipers.'

'But you did locate him, eventually?' David said when Sandy paused for breath.

'I was just coming to that. After months of not being able to find out where he was, he suddenly and miraculously materialised.'

'Where, in the city?' David prompted.

'No. Listen,' Sandy said. 'Let me tell you the story, because what happened next seemed to be connected with his being found.'

'Apart from feeding me a few snippets,' David said, standing up and stretching to relieve an ache in his back, 'you've steadfastly refused to discuss the details of the operation before. So why are you telling me all this now?'

'Something's changed,' Sandy answered flatly. 'I'll get to it, but you must let me tell it my way. I want you to understand.'

'Understand what? What's changed?' He perched on the side of the bath once more. Sandy sat up, the water dripping from her wet hair and shoulders.

'We were filming on the street, one day toward the end of May, when we were approached by a teenage Bosniak girl. Her name was Emira. She told us that her parents were both dead. Her father was in the defence force and had been killed early on in the fighting. Two weeks later, her mother was killed by shrapnel when a shell exploded near their home. With her elder two brothers on the front line, Emira and her eight-year old sister were taken to an orphanage that had been set up in the basement of the hospital.

A couple of nights later, two men woke her in the middle of the night and forced her to go with them. They took her to a building somewhere near the river. She said that the basement was a large area, divided into cubicles using curtains like those that they have around beds in a hospital. There was a metal framed bed in each cubicle, and each bed had a young girl chained to it. Emira was stripped naked and had one wrist handcuffed to the bed frame. Then, night after night, men would come to use her, one after the other. Some nights she would have to service up to fifteen men!' Sandy's voice choked in the last few words of the sentence; then she added, 'Fifteen men a night! She was fourteen years old, David, fourteen bloody years old!'

David shook his head. 'Oh my God; that's terrible! What happened to her sister?'

'All she knew was that her sister wasn't taken with her. She hoped that she was still safe in the orphanage, but we'll come to that later,' Sandy explained and then continued with the story.

'Emira said that some of the clients, if you can call them that, were Westerners – Westerners who spoke English and French. David, these were United Nations soldiers – some even came to the bar in uniform! They were going down to that basement and raping, yes *raping,* young girls like Emira. They must have known that the girls were under-age, and they must have known that they were not working of their own free will!'

'I find that very hard to believe,' David said sceptically. 'Did you believe her?'

Sandy shook her head. 'None of us wanted to believe it, but she was so credible. But even worse was to come,' Sandy said, her eyes burning into David's.

'Worse? How could it get any worse?'

'Emira said that children younger than her – prepubescent girls and boys – were kept in a side room. As well as a brothel, these bastards were running a service for paedophiles. Emira began to have serious concerns about her eight-year-old sister.'

David shook his head and grimaced in disgust as Sandy continued relentlessly.

'The day before Emira approached us, one of the young boys died. He was maybe three or four years old, she said. God knows what they had done to the poor kid. The boss sent one of his men to dump the body in the ruins of a building nearby that had been destroyed by shellfire. He told the man to take Emira with him to help and she was afraid that he intended to kill her, too. As they approached the ruined building, another shell landed nearby. The blast blew both Emira and the man off their feet, and Emira took the opportunity to escape. She ran away and made her way back to the orphanage in the hospital. She found out that her sister had gone missing several weeks before, soon after Emira was taken, and no one knew where she was.'

'Why did Emira come to you?' David asked. 'Why did she not go to the authorities? Even in a hell-hole such as you describe, there must be some kind of organisation, some authority.'

Sandy drew her knees up to her chin. 'She did go to the police department, but she recognised the officer behind the desk as one of the regulars at the brothel. He saw her waiting in the queue and he recognised her, too. He came out from behind the desk and came toward her. She ran away. He chased her but she gave him the slip. That's when she saw us. She needed to tell her tale to someone and she hoped we would be able to help her.'

'In what way?'

'I don't know,' Sandy shrugged her shoulders and frowned. 'Perhaps she thought if we were to make it public something would get done about it.'

David shrugged and shook his head but said nothing.

'We took her back to the Holiday Inn, where we were staying, along with nearly all the other foreign journalists, and settled her into Jane's room. Then, that evening we went to check out her story.'

'You keep mentioning "we", but how many of you were there in the team?'

'Well, there was Jane, obviously, Helen, an MI6 officer who was the team leader, Lenny, the cameraman, who was actually SAS; he was there to protect us if things got rough; I was the sound engineer; Caroline did make-up, lighting and generally assisted with anything that was needed, and Jeanette, who was a researcher. She was a Caesar officer like Caroline and me. Finally there was Milovan.' David noticed that the pitch of Sandy's voice changed when she mentioned Milovan's name, and guessed that there was some kind of emotional attachment there. 'Milovan was our driver, interpreter and fixer,' Sandy continued. 'He got us into places from which other Western reporters and TV crews were excluded. He was supposed to be one of MI6's local agents, but we all were convinced that he was working for the Bosnian intelligence service.'

'So the likelihood is that he reported your mission back to his controller.'

'Yes, probably, but it was just as much in their interests to get rid of Szopience as it was in ours,' Sandy shrugged. 'Anyway, Milovan knew about the place. It was called Dzenita's and had always been a notorious fleshpot. Strippers, prostitutes, you name it. It was obvious that our white armour-plated Land Rover with BBC markings and Union Jacks all over it would be a little conspicuous, so we used his own rather downbeat old VW Dormobile for the stakeout. Over the next few nights, we filmed people, well, *men*, coming and going. Some were in uniform – soldiers of the defence force and some policemen but there were some others that were obviously Westerners, some of which wore NATO uniforms – United Nations troops! So what the girl, Emira, had said was true. Then we got the shock of our lives.'

'Go on…' David leaned forward, his interest piqued.

'We filmed your friend, Colonel Devereux, one of the most senior officers of the UN forces in Sarajevo, going into a seedy bar that would make most Soho joints look respectable and was, allegedly, a brothel providing underage slaves of both genders to perverts for sex.' Sandy's voice was full of indignation and anger, and David wondered if her own experience at the hands of such people fuelled that anger.

'You're sure it was him?' David queried. 'Could you have been mistaken?'

'No, it was him; no doubt at all,' Sandy replied flatly. 'Worse still, when we showed Emira the film we'd taken, back at the hotel, she identified him as a regular who was in with the Serb gangsters who ran the place. He also used to meet there regularly with another Westerner who spoke good

Serbo-Croatian, but with an English accent. The latter seemed
to be the real boss. The heavies who worked there treated him
with a lot of respect.'

'Did you find out who this other man was?'

'We knew that most foreigners in the city were journalists,
staying at the Holiday Inn. We changed Emira's appearance
and took her to the bar when most of the guests would be
there, but she was unable to identify any of them as the Brit.'

'So what happened next?'

Before answering the question, Sandy said, 'There's some
shampoo in that toiletries bag over there. Pass it over for me,
would you, please?'

David sought out the bottle and handed to Sandy. She slid
down until her head was under the water then came back up.

'Caroline and I reported it to our Caesar team leader,
Grebe, and Helen reported via satellite phone back to MI6 in
London.' She started to massage the shampoo into her wet
hair. The action made her breasts jiggle around appealingly
and David watched, enraptured.

'What happened?'

'Grebe told us it was none of our business. He said we
weren't investigative journalists; we were just a couple of
whores there to help find and entrap the target.' Sandy's eyes
glistened with remembered humiliation.

'Bastard!' David growled. He wanted to find the man and
punch him on the nose.

'He said rather than trying to make trouble for
UNPROFOR officers, we should be trawling the bars and
clubs, picking up young Serbs, screwing them and pumping
them for Intel on Szopienice.'

'The bastard,' David repeated. 'Did you take it any further?'

'No.'

'Why not?'

'Because the very next day, we were told that the target had been located in Pale, a town about ten miles southeast of Sarajevo. Furthermore, arrangements had been made with both sides to allow the BBC film crew through the siege lines and out of Sarajevo.'

'I see. So you think there was a conspiracy to send you out on a wild goose chase to cover up the fact that a senior UNPROFOR officer was engaging in criminal activity in conjunction with this mysterious Englishman.'

Sandy was now sitting with her head bent forward and David was using the shower attachment to rinse the soap from her hair. As the grey dye was washed away, he was surprised to see her hair was now chestnut-brown instead of blonde.

'That's right,' Sandy replied, then added, 'Come on, David, surely you can see how that would make one a teensy bit suspicious?'

'I see what you mean,' said David. He began vigorously to towel-dry her hair. When he had finished, she stood up and raised her arms to allow him to wrap a fresh towel around her.

'I've often wondered what became of Emira after we left. We failed her and her sister and all those other kids.'

'She wasn't your responsibility, Sandy,' said David, shaking his head.

'That's the problem, David. In a city where scores of people are dying and having limbs blown off every day, no one has the fate of couple of dozen orphans as their top priority. She was nobody's responsibility. She had nowhere else to turn and we let her down.'

'Through no fault of your own,' David said, trying to reassure her. 'You did what you could. You reported the matter to your superior, but your mission had to take priority and once you had all been sent out of the city, what more could you do?'

'That's another thing,' Sandy said. 'We weren't all sent out of the city. Jeanette and Grebe remained behind.'

'I understand why Grebe would stay behind,' David said, 'but why Jeanette?'

'Yes,' said Sandy. 'Why indeed?'

David nodded thoughtfully. 'You still haven't explained why you've chosen to tell me all this, now.'

'Everyone who knew about Dzenita's is now dead, except me, and they've tried to get me at least three times. I don't know anything about Lenny, but I expect he's a lot harder to get at if he's on some mission somewhere with his SAS buddies. Anyway, after I got back, I was told never to reveal to anyone – *anyone* – what we discovered in Sarajevo.'

David grimaced. 'So why are you telling me? Why now, after all this time?'

'Jeanette,' Sandy replied, 'codename Lapwing. She knew about the brothel but she's not dead.'

'No?'

'No, she's operating undercover as a legal secretary in my sister's office.'

Chapter 23

It was 3:30 on a dank November Friday afternoon. Heavy clouds crowded together, darkening the sky and ushering in the dusk an hour ahead of its time. A light rain had already begun to splatter the windscreen as Jeanette Williams, code-name: Lapwing, current assignment: legal secretary Kathy Taylor backed her car into a space furthest from the entrance, alongside an overgrown and untidy hedge of blackthorn, ash and elder. She switched off the lights and the engine and settled down for a long wait.

To her surprise, she had been there only a few minutes before two women emerged from the porticoed entrance into the fast-fading light and, with shoulders hunched against the cold wind and drizzle, strode briskly across the wet car park. Jeanette wound down the window a few inches and raised a pair of miniature, low-light binoculars to her eyes. She recognised Samantha McNamara immediately, but the second woman was unknown to her. Shorter than Sam, with long dark hair tied back, it was clear to Jeanette that this was not Sam's missing sister, Curlew. Jeanette watched Sam climb into the passenger seat of a blue Volvo 240 estate while the other woman took the wheel. Neither woman had so much as glanced at the little red Austin Metro.

With the light from the headlamps sweeping across the wet tarmac, the big Volvo reversed from its parking space and joined the road heading back toward Chester city centre.

Jeanette looked at the little monochrome screen clipped to one of the air-vents. The screen showed a flashing white dot moving rapidly outwards across a series of concentric rings, each of which demarcated a hundred metres from the centre. When the dot reached the tenth and outermost ring, the display flashed off and reappeared, each ring now representing a kilometre. The dot continued to recede, but at a tenth of its former speed, resembling a space probe passing the outer planets of the Solar System on its way into deep space.

Jeanette was aware that members of the legal profession sometimes took long liquid lunches, and the older, male solicitors in Brighting and Blount frequently lived up to that image, but in Sam's case, this was, as far as Jeanette was aware, a first. Now she needed to ascertain whether Sam's two hour excursion was business, pleasure – or something more sinister. She decided that first she must identify the car in which Sam had left the pub. If it turned out to belong to an old friend from school or university then Jeanette was probably wasting her time sitting here. If not . . .

She reached into her handbag for the mobile phone, but hesitated before making the call. The analogue signals from mobile phones were notoriously easy to intercept. On the other hand, if she were to leave her position in order to find a payphone she might allow the quarry to escape, if indeed the quarry was there to start with. Jeanette grunted with frustration and indecision. Then, after a few seconds more hesitation, she dialled the number.

'Lapwing,' she said as soon as the call was answered. 'Need a check on a vehicle index.'

'Go ahead.'

She quoted the registration mark of the Volvo and she could hear the operator typing the letters and numbers on a computer terminal keyboard.

'Stand by...' It was about a minute before the answer was relayed to her. 'Registered to a Mr Michael Ithell, in Manchester. Want the address?'

'No,' Jeanette replied. 'Check out if there's a woman living there; late-twenties to mid-thirties; five-six or seven; dark hair. And if there is, does she have any history with Sierra-Mike-One?' Sierra-Mike-One was Samantha McNamara's code-name.

'Will do. Do you want a call back?'

Jeanette planned to reconnoitre the pub and did not want the phone ringing while she was inside because it would draw attention to her. 'No, I'll call you back in a while. Oh, just in case, also check for connection with Sierra-Hotel-One.' With that, Jeanette terminated the call.

Jeanette decided to wait a while before moving, just in case Sierra-Hotel-One, aka Sandy Harris, aka Curlew, should follow the two women out of the pub, but after ten minutes, she decided that was not going to be. So, *if the mountain would not come to Mohammed...*

Stuffing her luxuriant auburn hair under a woollen hat, and donning a pair of spectacles with oversize square-framed, plain-glass lenses, Jeanette buttoned her heavy outdoor coat and walked briskly to the main entrance. The entrance opened into a small reception area with oak panelling on the walls, a dark oak counter, and an oak staircase leading up to the bedrooms. On the wall behind the counter was a board with six numbered hooks, four of which had a key hanging from them. To each key was attached a long wooden key fob, on which the room number was stencilled in gold paint. Two keys were missing, the ones to rooms One and Four. A scruffy middle-aged man looked up at Jeannette from behind the counter. She ignored the scrutiny and ambled through a doorway to her left, which led into a bar. No one challenged her or paid her any attention as she wandered through the bar as if looking for someone that she had arranged to meet. She turned right into another bar that was set out like a restaurant, and which overlooked a garden at the back. She continued round to the right into a third bar, with a dartboard and pool table, eventually ending up back at the main entrance, having circumnavigated the ground floor. There had been no sign of Curlew, but Jeanette hardly expected her to be sitting alone hunched over a glass of Chardonnay. It was more likely that she had booked into a room, and certainly not in her own name.

The reception desk was unmanned when Jeanette returned, and she took the opportunity to steal a glance at the register. As suggested by the missing keys, only two of the six rooms were so far occupied on this Friday afternoon. Room One was registered to a Mrs Jackson of Tenby, South Wales, and Room Four to a Mr & Mrs Watson, from Northampton.

Climbing the stairs to the first floor, Jeanette had intended to listen outside the door of each room, but a tall, bespectacled man was sitting on a faded leather Chesterfield on the landing reading *What Car* magazine. He looked up as Jeanette reached the top of the stairs and thinking quickly, she asked him if he had seen a dark haired man in a blue jacket come up the stairs. The man smiled and shook his head. Jeanette thanked him then turned and went back down to Reception, where the scruffy middle-aged man was using the telephone. He looked at her quizzically as she descended the stairs but said nothing, and Jeanette left the building. She returned to her car, memorising the registration plates of the other cars as she passed. Back in the seclusion of her car, she jotted the registration numbers down in a notepad and then dialled the phone again.

'Lapwing,' she said. 'I have some more registration plates for you to check out.'

'Go ahead,' the disembodied voice invited, and Jeanette read out the numbers.

'Any joy yet on the owners of the Volvo?'

'Nothing showing up. We'll have to dig deeper. It'll take a bit of time.'

'Okay,' she replied, 'Call me back when you have some info on the reg. numbers.' Fortunately, the porticoed entrance was the only way in or out, other than the garden, which, at this time of year, would not be in use. Consequently, she had no need to leave her car again for a while, so the phone ringing would not be a problem.

Reluctant to be accused of crying "wolf", Jeanette hesitated to call in the rest of the team until she was certain that it was indeed Curlew that Sam had been meeting. Her suspicions were reinforced by the presence of the bespectacled man, who could have been waiting on the sofa for his wife to return from the ladies room. On the other hand, he could have been clandestinely guarding the corridor. It was so frustrating – not knowing, not having any proof, one way or the other.

It was possible that Sam had not been meeting her sister after all, Jeanette thought, recalling the slim, attractive, dark-haired woman that had left the pub with her. What if the ostensibly straight-laced Sam had been conducting a secret assignation with a lesbian lover? Who knew what hidden depths lay inside that uptight, butter-wouldn't-melt exterior?

Jeanette smiled at the salacious thought but she knew it would not be the case. She had grown to know Sam quite well over the past few weeks. As entertaining as the mental imagery might be, she had to admit it was fanciful in the extreme. The woman was more likely to be a client or an old friend.

It was ten minutes before Jeanette's phone rang, during which time a man and a woman had emerged from the pub, climbed into a Ford Escort and driven away. For a moment, Jeanette had been quite excited because the woman was fair-haired, but, on closer inspection, she was clearly too short, too dumpy and too old to be Curlew.

'Yes?' she said, picking up the call.

'One of those numbers is showing as listed,' the voice said, repeating the number of the Jaguar XJ6 that was still in the car park. 'The others belong to locals, except the Golf, which is registered to a Volkswagen dealer in Sussex, and a Ford Escort from Northampton.'

'Understood,' she replied, terminating the call without a further word. *Listed* meant that the Jaguar belonged to a member of the Royal Family or a senior Government figure. It might also indicate that it was being used in an undercover police operation – or perhaps it belonged to a member of the Security Service. That settled it for Jeanette. Why would the sort of person that would use a car with such a number plate be in an obscure, run-down country pub at the same time as a junior solicitor like Samantha McNamara? Was it possible that someone had arranged a reunion with Sam's supposedly deceased sister?

'Reports of her death,' Jeanette muttered aloud, paraphrasing Mark Twain, 'have been greatly exaggerated.'

She dialled another number.

Chapter 24

It was just after six o' clock in the evening, and fully dark by the time Samantha McNamara arrived home at the 1930's semi-detached, red brick property that she shared with her husband, Stephen. Parking her BMW on the drive behind Stephen's Vauxhall Cavalier, she followed the crazy-paved pathway to the front door and let herself in.

'Samantha, is that you?' Stephen's voice filtered into the hall from the living room. She took a deep breath in an attempt to slow her suddenly racing heartbeat.

'Yes, it's me, darling,' she called, hoping her voice would not betray her emotions or the fact that she had been drinking.

Unable to face going back to work after the shock of meeting her resurrected sister, Sam had asked Angela, the MI5 officer, to drop her off at a wine bar, a short distance from work. During the following hour and a half, she had sunk two large glasses of Chardonnay while pondering the day's events. As she closed the front door, it occurred to her that she must have been well over the alcohol limit for the drive home. She stood at the doorway to the living room. Stephen was sitting in his favourite armchair, The *Guardian* newspaper resting on his lap.

'Where have you been?' he asked. 'I've been worried about you.'

'Why?' asked Sam, 'I'm not that late.'

'I called the office, this afternoon,' Stephen replied. 'I was told you hadn't returned after lunch. Where have you been?' There was an edge to his voice that Samantha did not like.

'Oh? What did you call for?' she asked off-handedly. Slipping off her coat, she started to walk back out to the hall to hang it up.

'Don't walk away when I'm talking to you,' Stephen said angrily, rising from his seat. 'Where have you been all afternoon?'

A few inches taller than his wife, Stephen was thirty-eight years old, with collar-length wiry black hair, showing the first tinges of grey at the temples. He was still wearing his work attire – tailored charcoal grey trousers and a blue shirt, which was now open at the neck, with his red and gold, diamond patterned tie at half-mast.

'I'm not *walking away*, as you put it,' Sam protested, her own anger rising. 'I'm going to hang my coat up. What's the matter with you?'

'What's the matter with me?' Stephen demanded, running a hand through his hair, 'What's got into you, more like? Where have you been all afternoon? Who have you been with?'

'How dare you interrogate me?' replied Sam angrily.

'Have you been seeing another man?' Stephen shouted, grasping Sam's elbows and shaking her.

'Don't be ridiculous! Why would you think that that of me?'

'Don't lie to me!' he roared. 'This is all that Kathy's doing, isn't it? You've changed since she came on the scene.'

'Well, I haven't exactly noticed you trying to avoid her,' Sam retaliated.

'What are you talking about?'

'You're all over her when she's here, sniffing around her like a dog with a bitch on heat.'

'You're being ridiculous! Kathy's your friend, one of the nicer ones. I like her, that's true, but to suggest . . .'

'Don't give me that! I can see it clearly. Given half a chance, you would be jumping on her. It's only because I'm always here when she is that you haven't made a pass at her.'

'How can you stand there and say something like that?' Stephen demanded, the decibel levels growing by the second. 'How can you possibly accuse me of infidelity? You're saying these things to assuage your own guilt. Isn't that the truth?'

'No, it bloody well is not! I've done nothing wrong and yet, with no cause whatsoever, you accuse me of deceiving you!'

They were now standing almost toe-to-toe now, there faces inches apart and Stephen's nose wrinkled. 'You've been drinking!'

Sam recoiled as flecks of his spittle landed on her face. 'I just had a small glass of wine,' she lied, taking a step back. Sam knew she had to elaborate further, but made herself speak calmly in an attempt to diffuse what had quickly become a screaming match. 'I bumped into, er, someone I used to know, unexpectedly.'

'There, you admit it! You were with another man weren't you?'

Sam shook her head. 'No. That's not true. It was a woman I was with.'

'I don't believe you!' Stephen looked as if he was going to turn away but suddenly, with an anguished howl, he turned back and slapped her hard on the cheek. It was completely unexpected and Sam was unprepared. She cried out in shock and pain, reeling backwards, colliding with the living room door. Having struck her once, Stephen followed with another openhanded slap to her face, then another and another.

'No, no! Stop! Stop! Stop!' Sam cried. She dropped to her knees, holding her arms up to ward off the blows that kept raining down on her head and face. She curled into a ball and lay on the carpet sobbing and he stopped hitting her.

'You whore!' He screamed at her. 'You disgusting whore! I should throw you, naked, into the street!'

'It isn't true,' Sam screamed at him. Even in her anguish and confusion, she recognised the scene that Sandy had described from that Sunday morning five years before. 'I met up with an old school friend, a woman, not a man. God, Stephen,' she cried, 'what in Heaven's name has got into you?'

'I don't believe you,' Stephen shouted. 'You have been seeing another man behind my back, haven't you?'

'No, I have not!' She screamed back, cowering as he raised his hand again, but no blows landed. 'I told you, I met up with an old school-friend I haven't seen in years. We spent the afternoon together.'

'Who is this friend?' Stephen demanded, 'What's her name?'

'Andrea,' Samantha replied without hesitation, thankful that the conversation with Sandy had planted the name in her mind.

'So why haven't you mentioned this Andrea before?' Stephen was still shouting, and Sam was worried that the neighbours could hear what was going on.

'I told you I haven't seen her for a long time.' Using the wall for support, Sam started to rise shakily to her feet. She withdrew her hand from her face, checking for blood; there was none but she expected that she would have some bruises to show for the encounter.

'You're lying!' Stephen shouted and hit her again, this time with a closed fist.

Sam's head whipped back and crashed into the wall. The world exploded in a blinding light and she sank to the floor.

Chapter 25

'What's that noise?' Sandy asked. She could hear an odd little melody. A repeating sequence of five notes, which sounded as if it was being played on an electronic xylophone, each repetition offset by one note; then the whole sequence was repeated.

After drying off in the bathroom, Sandy and David had wrapped themselves modestly in their towels and lain together on the bed discussing the possible reasons for Lapwing's presence in Samantha's office. It did not take much time before they had exhausted all the possible reasons, sinister and benign, and then they lapsed into silence.

As they lay side-by-side, their hands were touching and David absent-mindedly covered Sandy's hand with his own, squeezing gently. That gesture transmitted his feelings for her more than words ever could.

No matter what she did, Sandy reflected, David was always there for her. He was always on her side, always protective. Even when she disobeyed orders and contacted Samantha, he was more concerned with her wellbeing than matters of discipline. Then there was his reaction to her tricking him out of his clothes to separate him from his recording device. How many other men would have accepted that with such equanimity and good humour? Where most men might have given vent to their frustration with displays of anger or petulance, David had graciously accepted the situation and forgiven her. He then listened patiently to her story about what the team had discovered in Sarajevo and shared her concerns about the ongoing implications.

She wanted to please him, to thank him; to reward him for his patience and forbearance, and there was only one way to do that, she decided. She had laid her head on his chest and stroked his thigh. She had smiled as she watched the front of the towel change shape and then she left the rest to David.

Now they were lying in post-coital contentment. David's fingertips explored the ridges of her spine as she lay, once again, with her head on his chest, one arm flung across his midriff and a leg draped across his thighs. She was still unable gain any pleasure from the act itself – sex was something to get out of the way as quickly as possible – but she liked lying here like this. She liked David – a lot, and it was obvious that he was genuinely fond of her. The age difference was unimportant – or maybe it was important. Perhaps it was his maturity that appealed to her. He could almost be a father figure.

No, she decided. After what had just passed between them, that was a bad analogy.

'That's my mobile phone,' David replied, struggling to extricate himself from Sandy's clutches. 'Richardson,' David barked into the handset when he finally found it amongst the discarded clothes scattered across the floor.

***

Samantha had not fully lost consciousness, but she felt groggy and her head was pounding. She was vaguely aware of a door slamming somewhere in the distance, then the revving of a car engine, and she knew that Stephen had taken her BMW. He had probably driven to the church to ask for God's forgiveness for what he had just done, and she was thankful that he had not waited around to ask for hers.

Using the wall for support, Sam dragged herself slowly to her feet and staggered into the cloakroom, where she examined her face in the mirror. She was surprised not to look as bad as she felt. That final punch had broken the skin on the point of her left cheekbone, leaving an abrasion the size of a penny, which, rather than bleeding, was weeping clear fluid. Her eyes looked puffy and dark, but that was probably from crying, and a trickle of blood, now dried, traced a line from her left nostril around the side of her mouth to her chin. Not yet visible were the bruises that would develop over the next few hours on the parts of her face that made her wince when she touched them.

Stephen had never hit her before, well, not like this. Usually he would shout and berate her with verbal abuse. Occasionally he would resort to the odd slap on the arm or a push, but never before had he hit her face. He would never have dared while her father was alive. Was this a warning sign for the future? How much further might he go?

As a lawyer, she had studied enough domestic violence cases to know once it starts it can only get worse. No matter how much the abuser apologises and promises never to do it again. No matter that the abused party often takes responsibility for the inexcusable behaviour of the abuser, once it starts it never stops.

Sam was not going to allow herself to get into that situation. She had played the meek wife for long enough, and far from inheriting the Earth she had sacrificed her self-confidence and self-respect on the altar of her husband's narcissism. She decided, there and then, that she that she would leave Stephen. Right now, tonight, and for good. However, if she was going to leave him, she must do it now, before he returned, full, not of remorse, but of self-serving excuses that would place the blame for his actions squarely at her door.

Now was the time to go, but to where? She thought of her parents' house. It was up for sale but not yet sold. She could stay there for a while, but surely, that would be the first place Stephen would come looking for her – and come looking for her he would, of that she had no doubt.

Where could she go for a few days until she could decide what to do with the rest of her life? Where could she hide so that Stephen could not find her until she decided it was time to confront him? The answer, when it came, was so obvious it made her wonder why it had not been her first thought. It would be the perfect sanctuary. Stephen would not even dream of looking for her there.

It suddenly occurred to Sam that this was what she had wanted for some time, but had not the courage to admit – even to herself. She nodded at her reflection; even saw the slight curl of her lips as they twisted into a grim smile. She bathed her face with warm water, and when she climbed the stairs to the bedroom, where she would fill a suitcase with enough clothes to last a few weeks, she had a spring in her step.

***

Startled by a sudden knock on the bedroom door, Sandy glanced anxiously at David. They were both now fully dressed and David was preparing to leave. The call on his mobile phone that had disturbed their contented slumber had forced an immediate change of plan.

David nodded to Sandy and flattened himself against the wall adjacent to the door, his Walther PPK in hand. Sandy held the Glock behind her back, and prepared to open the door.

'Who is it?' She called, standing to one side so as not to be in line of fire should someone put a bullet though the panelling.

'Landlord;' came the reply.

Remaining to one side of the door, Sandy opened it enough to see that it was indeed the man who had checked her in a few days before. He was scruffy in appearance, with at least two days stubble on his face. His lank brown hair looked as if it had not seen a brush or comb in days; he wore a creased blue cotton shirt with the top three buttons undone, revealing a grimy vest, and brown corduroy trousers that looked as though he had slept in them. His breath reeked of stale cigarettes. Sandy wondered why she had ever thought it "cool" to smoke. She smiled politely.

'Yes?'

'Sorry to bother you, Missus Jackson,' he began, his eyes not meeting her hers, 'but, er, if the gentleman is planning to stay the night, you'll have to pay extra.' He shuffled his feet and added, 'We charge per head, y'see, not for the room.'

David concealed his weapon and stepped into view.

'That won't be necessary,' Sandy replied, suppressing a laugh. 'We've been having a business meeting and my associate is just leaving. I'm sorry if we gave you the wrong impression.' She smiled pleasantly at the manager who smiled in return, a shifty, knowing smile that made Sandy's skin crawl.

'Of course, missus, sir,' he said, nodding to David, 'My mistake. Sorry to bother you.' He nodded tersely, then turned on his heel and strode down the corridor. He heard the door close behind him, and muttered, 'Dunno what business you're in, but I ought to charge commission.' He had an obscene thought and chuckled to himself, 'or corkage!'

***

Jeanette watched the casually dressed, tall, slim man get into the Jaguar with the listed registration and drive away. The light was too poor to be sure whether or not he was the man she had seen on the sofa on the landing, earlier, and decided it did not matter. He was the spook or undercover cop or whatever, and he had gone, but where to and for how long? If only she had some back-up. One of them could have followed him while the other maintained watch on the pub.

For the hundredth time, Jeanette checked her watch and wondered why it was taking so long for the rest of the team to arrive; it was two hours since she had made the call. True, the others had been scattered around the other likely places that their target might turn up – the family home, the churchyard where the ashes of her parents were interred, the home of one of her old university friends. That friend had been one of only two that had shown up as in any way special to the young Sandra Harris. The other, a young man called Alan, seemed to have disappeared from the face of the Earth.

Jeanette was still musing when she became aware that a van had pulled up close alongside her car and doused its lights. *At last!*

'Okay, what have you got?' asked the operation leader in an accent that reflected his origins in the West Midlands. When Jeanette had finished summarising her observations, he looked around at the four people in the van. 'Okay, call-signs for this op. Designations for this operation are,' he pointed a finger at Jeanette. 'Pluto;' the finger moved to the man beside her. 'Saturn;' the finger moved on. 'Mercury. Paul,' he said, referring to the driver, who was watching the front of the pub from the cab as the others sat in the back. 'Paul is Jupiter and I'm Neptune.

'The orders are not, repeat, not to eliminate her. Our orders are to snatch her and take her to Crane for interrogation. He wants to know what she knows and who she's told.' He flicked his head as if to clear a lock of hair from his face, but it was just a mannerism; his hair was fully contained within the black ski-cap he wore.

'How are we going to take her?' Jeanette asked, and withered under the team leader's flat stare. Clearly, he had neither forgotten nor forgiven her previous foul-up.

'First we need to confirm what room she's in,' Neptune said, 'assuming she is actually staying there.'

'I think she's in Room One, the corner room on the first floor,' Jeanette reported and explained her reasons.

'Okay,' Neptune said, 'Pluto and Saturn go and book in for the night. Try to play the star-crossed lovers, married, but not to each other. Later,' he continued, 'Jupiter will go in with a photo of the target and play the private detective, checking on a client's errant wife,' Neptune said, then with a wink, added, 'he's the only one who looks shady enough.'

'She might have minders with her,' Saturn chipped in.

'True,' agreed Neptune, 'That's something else we need to try and find out.'

'There was someone,' Jeanette explained, but he left a while ago. It's possible there could be others.'

'Taxi entering the car park,' Jupiter reported tonelessly. It must have been the twentieth car to pull in since the team had arrived forty-five minutes earlier. 'Busy tonight!'

'They've got live music on tonight…' Jeanette said to explain the sudden influx of customers. Then, when Jupiter observed that the occupant was a single female, she stretched across the front seat to look. 'Shit! That's Samantha McNamara, Curlew's sister! And she's got a suitcase.'

'Looks pretty heavy too,' added Jupiter. 'Either she's planning on staying a while or…'

'Or she's bringing some of Curlew's belongings,' Jeanette finished the sentence.

'Ace!' said Jupiter, getting out of the van, 'I'll tail her and see which room she goes to.'

There was no one in Reception when Jupiter sauntered in. The McNamara woman was starting up the staircase, but she suddenly looked round and straight him. He noticed the marks on her face and wondered what had happened to her.

'D'ya want 'and with that, luv?' He offered, with a convincing Lancashire accent. 'Looks 'eavy, does that.'

'Oh, would you?' Sam accepted the offer with gratitude.

'Sure, no problem!' Jupiter picked up the case and they walked up the stairs together.

'Just here,' Sam said as they reached the door of Room One, 'Thank you.'

'No problem,' he repeated and walked quickly back to the staircase where he waited out of sight, listening.

***

'Who is it?' Sandy called in response to the knock on the door. At the same time, she raised the Glock in a two-handed grip.

'It's me, Sam.'

Shit!

'Sam what are you doing here?' She said, hurrying to open the door. 'My God, what happened to your face?'

Sam pushed past her and dropped the suitcase on the floor with a thump. 'I've left Stephen,' she announced dramatically. 'I'm not going back to him.'

If she had expected a sympathetic response from her sister, she was to be disappointed.

'Are you mad?' Sandy replied testily. 'You can't stay here!'

'What?' Stunned by Sandy's response, Sam tried to explain. 'He beat me up! Look at my face! We argued and he accused me of having an affair; and I accused him of fancying my secretary; and he beat me up.' All of this came out in a garbled, tearful rush and Sandy took in only half of it.

Taking a cursory look at her sister's face, Sandy offered less sympathy than Sam was expecting. 'Oh, it's not that bad.' Then she added, 'Look, you can't stay here. It's not safe. You have to go.'

'Sandy…' Sam wailed. 'Help me! I can't go back to him, not tonight.' Then she noticed the gun in Sandy's hand and the way her attention was drawn to the door, the window, anywhere but her distressed sister. Suddenly she realised that something had changed. 'Sandy, where's your boss?' Somehow, when he was here everything felt under control. Now he was gone and the normally self-assured Sandy was acting like a frightened rabbit.

'He's not here,' said Sandy. 'Look, something's going down here, and I don't want you around if it kicks off. Go home. Or, if you've really come to your senses about that prick of husband of yours, then go to a different hotel. You can't stay here another minute.' She saw the bereft look on her beloved sister's face and looked away to hide the tears that sprang to her eyes.

Chapter 26

The driver's door opened and Jupiter climbed back into the van.

'Confirmed,' he said. 'Room One; the corner one on the first floor, just as Pluto said. The sister's in there with her now.'

'So now what?' Jeanette asked.

'Now, we carry on with the plan,' Neptune replied. 'You and Saturn will book in and go to your room. I'll go in with Mercury ...'

'Are we a couple too, ducky?' Mercury teased, pouting his lips.

'No,' Neptune replied, forcing a grin. He resented any reference to his sexual preferences, even if in jest. 'We're rufty-tufty footballers just back from training, going for a few pints and to listen to the band. After a while, we'll filter out and slip upstairs to join the love-birds in their room. Meanwhile, Jupiter stays here as lookout, communicating with me via shortwave.' He held up an earpiece disguised as a hearing aid.

'How long do we wait?' Saturn asked.

'We can't act before midnight,' Neptune replied after a moment's thought.

'What if Samantha's not out by then?' Jeanette asked.

'If she's not gone by the time we go in, we'll have to take them both.' Neptune replied coldly.

'That could be dangerous,' said Jeanette. 'She's a lawyer, a stalwart of the local church; she does charity stuff. If she disappears, questions will be asked. It will be all over the papers and TV.'

'In that case she won't disappear,' Neptune replied coldly. 'She'll have a nasty accident on the way home.'

'Assuming the Tangos are in the room,' asked Jupiter, 'how do we get in?'

Neptune reached into one of three holdalls on the floor of the van and held up a gas canister. It was about the size of a household fire extinguisher. 'This contains GBS-2, a derivative of Sarin. We pump this into the room under the door. Then, thirty seconds later, we can go in. We'll need gas-masks and gloves, which we've got in the kit bags, '

'Sarin?' Jeanette repeated. 'That's going to kill them within seconds, isn't it?'

'Proper Sarin would,' Neptune replied, 'but this is a weakened compound. We have a few minutes to administer the antidote, Atropine.' He held up a small vial containing clear liquid. 'After that, we can keep her subdued while we spirit her out of the building in the small hours.'

'What if the sister is still around?'

'Same with her. Then we stage the accident in some remote spot.'

'What sort of accident?' Saturn asked. 'She doesn't have a car.'

'Good point,' Neptune replied, 'How about stripped, raped and strangled? That should keep the press and the boys in blue happy for weeks!'

'Oh Jesus,' said Jeanette, 'I hope it doesn't come to that!' No sooner were the words out of her mouth than Jeanette regretted uttering them.

'Look,' said Neptune 'I hope you're not going to screw-up again!'

'What do you mean by that?' Jeanette demanded indignantly, but knowing full well where this was leading.

'You had the back of the house. You saw her come out. You had plenty of time to drop her.'

'That's not fair! I told you my gun jammed, bloody Russian piece of shit! By the time I'd cleared it, she'd gone over the fence.'

The leader had accused her of having a lack of moral fibre. She sneered inwardly at the phrase. Perhaps a lack of *immoral fibre* would be more appropriate.

'Yeah, yeah,' the team leader sneered, 'so you said, but you've not proved yourself yet. What if I told you to take out Samantha McNamara, now, tonight?'

'I'd do it,' replied Jeanette, but even she recognised that her assertion lacked conviction. She glared at Neptune, daring him to challenge her resolve.

'Ah well,' he said after a few moments, 'We'll never know. If the sister is going to meet a sticky end, you're bound to get questioned by the plods.' He looked away contemptuously. 'Go on. Take your car and build yourself an alibi somewhere. Make sure you do something outrageous. Get yourself noticed. We'll handle it from here.'

'But...'

'But nothing. Do as you're ordered and piss off!'

Jeanette hesitated for a moment. Her professional pride was injured by her superior's contemptuous and imperious manner, but at the same time, she was relieved not to have to take part in the cold-blooded murder of a woman she had grown to like and respect.

'You're the boss,' she said with as much dignity as she could muster. She let herself out of the rear door of the van and got into her car.

'You were a bit hard on her, weren't you?' Saturn asked after Jeanette had gone. He had been looking forward to whiling away a few hours alone with the beautiful young redhead.

'Not as hard as you'd like to have been,' Jupiter quipped, prompting a round of raucous laughter.

'Bloody woman's a liability,' grumbled Neptune. 'We're better off without her.'

'Still,' said Saturn, climbing out of the van, 'you could have been a bit nicer about it.' He walked through the rain to the entrance to check in alone.

Jeanette was still fuming over her curt dismissal. She replayed the conversation repeatedly in her mind. It was far too late, but only now was she able to think of a suitably cutting riposte that would have exacted some revenge on Neptune for his intemperate attitude.

As instructed, Jeanette was heading toward the city centre where she would establish her alibi. She ran through the options in her mind. She could pick up a man in one of the pubs or wine bars in town; she could speed through the city centre and get pulled over by the police; God, she could run naked through the cathedral grounds; that should get her noticed!

'Shit! Watch out, you idiot!' Distracted by her thoughts, she had been startled when a red Ford Orion pulled out in front of her. Angrily, she beeped the Metro's horn, but the puny sound was poor retribution for such inconsiderate driving. Now, to add insult to injury, he or she was driving too slowly as they approached the traffic lights at the next junction. They were on green but it was almost as if the Orion's driver wanted them to turn to red before they reached them.

'Jesus!' Jeanette raged and beeped the horn again, 'Put your bloody foot down and we'll get through!'

Just as Jeanette feared, the green light disappeared to be replaced by amber, but rather than speed up to get through before the red, or slowing gently to a halt, the Orion's driver suddenly slammed on the brakes, stopping well short of the line. In her impatience, Jeanette had been too close behind, but her reflexes were incredibly fast and she managed to stop the Metro inches from the Orion's rear bumper.

'You bloody idiot!' She shouted impotently. Then another car slammed into the Metro from behind, shunting it forward to collide, after all, with the Orion's rear. 'Oh, for Christ's sake!' she shouted aloud, and climbed out to inspect the damage. The car that had rear-ended the Metro was a big estate car, and its driver was already walking toward her.

'What do you think you're bloody doing?' he yelled at her.

'Me?' Jeanette retaliated. 'You hit me, you prat!' Then everything went dark. Someone had come up behind her and thrust a sack over her head. She gasped with surprise and tried to struggle, but found her arms pinned to her sides. The Orion driver, a tall, bespectacled man, and the driver of the estate car were working together. They were abducting her! She felt a sharp pain in her arm as someone thrust a needle through her clothes into her flesh. Within seconds her knees gave way. Had her abductors not supported her, she would have fallen to the ground. As she lost consciousness, she was vaguely aware of being manhandled into a car. Then everything went black.

***

'BT van entering the car park,' Jupiter intoned.

'Working late, aren't they?' said Mercury.

Neptune moved so he could see across the car park through the grimy windscreen. The British Telecom van was reversing up toward the portico. Then two men got out of the cab and entered the building. The van looked out of place and out of time. Neptune's suspicions were immediately aroused. He opened his mouth to speak, but before he could issue any orders, a black van, with hazard lights flashing and blue lights revolving on top, pulled up just inside the car park entrance, broadside on to them. A group of men wearing black body-armour and helmets, and carrying Heckler and Koch machine-carbines piled out and adopted firing positions. They were all aiming at the van. Overhead a helicopter circled, its rotors clattering rhythmically, its searchlight illuminating the van in brilliant white light.

'Armed police!' The amplified voice seemed to bounce off the sides of the van. 'Throw your weapons out and come out through the driver's door, one at a time.' There was a short pause, before the voice added, 'Do it now!'

Two police cars stopped next to the BT van and the drivers ran into the pub. They began to herd everyone from the two bars at the front to the restaurant area at the rear.

'Any guests upstairs?' One of the officers demanded of the landlord.

'Three rooms,' he replied, looking at the key rack, 'No, two. Rooms One and Three. Room Four's out. Why, what's going on?'

Ignoring the question, the police officer ran for the stairs and was surprised to meet two women and two men descending hurriedly. Between them, they were carrying two suitcases and a holdall.

'What room are you from?' The officer demanded.

'One,' replied the younger of the two women. Even under the stressful circumstances, the policeman registered the fact that she was strikingly beautiful, despite the dishevelled clothing and with her hair stuffed under a baseball cap.

'Put that stuff down and go into the area at the rear of the building,' the officer ordered, continuing up the stairs to round up the occupants of Room Three. He had taken several steps before he realised that the group had not followed his instruction, but were instead heading for the exit.

'Hey, stop!' he shouted, descending the stairs two at a time. You can't go that way. It's dangerous!' He reached them just as they funnelled through the doorway. He grabbed the arm of the younger woman but she shrugged him off forcibly; then one of the men flashed an ID card in his face.

'UK Security Service,' he said. 'Keep out of the way!' By now, the other man had opened the rear doors of the British Telecom van and the two women scrambled inside with their baggage.

'Customs and Excise,' shouted Jupiter, the first out of the van. He was holding a fake ID card in front of him. 'Put down your weapons!'

'Keep your hands above your head!' Three feet in front of him, an officer ignored his protestations and aimed his carbine at Jupiter's head. 'Kneel down,' he shouted.

'Kneel! Kneel!' Another voice came from behind Jupiter. 'On our knees, now! Keep your hands above your head.' Jupiter swore and sank to his knees. He tried again to identify himself as a Customs officer but he was once again shouted down.

'Lie down! Face down. Now!' When Jupiter complied, he added 'Hands behind your back!' Immediately, a third officer appeared and handcuffed him.

'Next one,' the amplified voice shouted. 'Out of the van, now! Keep your hands above your head. Come on. Now! Out of the van!'

'Police! Open the door! Is anyone in there? Open the door. It's the police!'

Saturn ignored the pounding on his door and watched from his window in disbelief. Under the glare of arc lights mounted on the police van, his three comrades climbed out of the van, one by one, were forced to the ground and handcuffed.

Eventually the policeman at the door must have concluded that the guests must be out, after all, and made his way back downstairs. Saturn did not notice at first. He was watching the British Telecom van drive quietly out of the car park. A startled constable made to wave them down but another, more senior officer stayed his hand. They both turned their backs as the van, which presumably contained the target of this evening's operation, turned northeast.

In the back, Sandy clasped her sister's hand and breathed a sigh of relief. The enemy had been wrong-footed and outsmarted once again. How many more times would she get away with it? How long before the luck was on their side, rather than hers?

Chapter 27

Samantha McNamara awoke with a start. At first, she thought she must have dreamed the events of the previous day, but looking around at the unfamiliar room by the wan light filtering around the edges of the drawn curtains, it all came rushing back to her.

Sandy's miraculous reappearance from the grave and the harrowing revelations in the shabby hotel room; her own fight with Stephen and her decision to leave him; the discovery that terrorists were preparing to attack them and the heart-stopping terror of their escape. None of it seemed real – and yet it was all true.

Minutes after escaping from the Waterloo Inn, the bogus BT van had stopped in a dark country lane where she and Sandy had transferred to a big Ford saloon for the remainder of the journey. Forty-five minutes later, they had pulled up outside a two-storey terraced house in the middle of a vast housing estate in Ellesmere Port. Two bodyguards swiftly ushered the sisters inside and showed them to this small bedroom at the back of the house, where they spent the night.

Now, Sandy's bed was empty and the covers in disarray. As she wondered where Sandy had gone, Samantha's nose wrinkled at the delicious smell of toast, triggering a pang of hunger. Taking a dressing gown from her suitcase, she made her way downstairs to find the bodyguards, Petra and Anthony, having breakfast together at the kitchen table, but there was no sign of Sandy.

Petra was in her mid-twenties with collar-length mid-brown hair, brown eyes and a pleasant oval face. An attractive girl who, Sam decided, would look much prettier with the right application of make-up, of which, this morning, she was wearing none. Anthony was in his early thirties, tall with dark curly hair and dark stubble on his rugged face. When he looked up at Sam, with his brown eyes and lopsided smile, it made her heart flutter like the wings of a moth near a lamp.

'Morning, Monica,' he said cheerfully, and Petra echoed the greeting.

Samantha recalled that Sandy had introduced them on their arrival last night as Monica and Greta. What was wrong with using their real names, she was unsure.

'Good morning,' she replied. 'Where's er... Greta?'

Petra swallowed a mouthful of toast and replied, 'Mr Richardson came for her at about what . . .?' She looked at Anthony.

'Two o'clock,' he said.

Sam was suddenly panic stricken. 'Why? What did he want her for? She is coming back, isn't she?'

'Yes, I think so,' replied Anthony. 'Richardson said something about a meeting.'

'A meeting, at two in the morning?' cried Sam. 'Why on Earth would they...?'

'They didn't say,' replied Anthony, then, seeing Sam's distress, he added, 'Come and sit down. I'll make you a cup of tea.'

'They never tell us anything,' Petra shrugged. 'Not unless we need to know, of course.'

As Sam sat down Anthony said, 'Want some toast put in?'

It was late afternoon before Sandy and David returned. Sam had been on edge all day, afraid that Sandy, so recently returned to her, had been snatched away once more. She was sitting with Petra and Anthony in the living room watching some asinine game show on the television when they heard the coded knock. Petra ushered Sam into the kitchen while, with gun in hand, Anthony squinted through the peephole in the solid front door before opening it. Remembering just in time not to blurt out Sandy's real name Sam ran to hug her.

'Where have you been all day?' she asked, winding her arms tightly round her sister's neck. 'I was so worried.'

'Oh, get off me, please,' replied Sandy irritably. 'It's been a long day.' Sam released her and stood back. She looked close to tears. Sandy saw David's disapproving look and relented. 'Sorry. Look, don't mind me. It's just...' She left the sentence hanging.

'What's wrong?' Sam asked. 'You look terribly upset.'

'I'm fine,' Sandy replied in a tone that belied the words. 'I just need a drink.' She headed for the kitchen. There was a bottle of scotch in one of the cupboards.

David put a gentle restraining hand on Sam's arm and she turned to face him. 'Give her a while,' he advised gently. 'She's had a bit of a shock.'

Sam was full of concern. 'Why? What's happened?'

'Look, just leave it will you?' Sandy had appeared in the doorway leading to the kitchen. She had the bottle in her hand and was in the process of unscrewing the top.

'We can't really talk about it,' David explained. 'It's, well, you know . . . '

'What have they done to you?' Sam demanded. Then she turned to David. 'What have you done to her?'

'For Christ's sake,' said Sandy, raising her voice. 'Will you please just leave it!' With an effort, she brought her temper under control and continued more evenly, 'No one has done anything to me. I just discovered something today which upset me, that's all.'

Sam looked from Sandy to David and back again. David smiled wanly and half-heartedly shrugged his shoulders. Sandy disappeared into the kitchen to get a glass. Sam made as if to follow her, only to have David restrain her again.

'Let go of me,' she hissed, shrugging his hand away.

'Okay,' David replied, releasing her and ostentatiously holding his hands clear of her, 'but, please leave your sister alone for a while. She needs some space.'

This little drama was taking place in the living room, and David was very aware of the presence of the bodyguards, even though they were trying very hard to make themselves invisible.

'What, so she can drink herself into a stupor?' Sam demanded. 'Can't you see Sand, I mean, *she's* got a drink problem?' Before David could answer, Sandy reappeared in the doorway. There were tears in her eyes. Then, without speaking, she walked briskly across the room and put her arms around Sam, holding her close. Then she burst into tears. David found himself moved almost to tears himself.

'I'm taking her upstairs,' Sam said in a tone that defied anyone to try to stop her, and, with a protective arm around her sister's shoulder, she led her through the doorway into the hall and up the stairs.

David exchanged glances with Petra and Anthony, who shrugged in unison but did not comment. 'She's been under a lot of pressure, today,' David said. 'She'll be okay in a while. I think I need a drink myself,' he added, moving toward the kitchen. 'Anyone else?'

'No thanks,' Anthony replied.

'A bit early for me,' said Petra.

'Can't you tell me what happened today?' Sam asked again.

Sandy was lying on the bed with one hand on her forehead, as if she had a headache. Her sister was sitting on the edge of the bed, holding her other hand in both of hers.

'No, Sam,' Sandy replied with a tight smile. 'I can't tell you anything about my work. Please stop asking.'

Sam shrugged her shoulders and changed the subject. 'Will you be going out again tomorrow?'

'I don't know,' Sandy replied guardedly. 'Hopefully, we'll get to spend most of the day together.'

'What about the sleeping arrangements for tonight?' Sam asked.

'The same as yesterday, of course,' Sandy had replied. 'You and I will be in here together.'

'What about your boss?'

'David? He'll have one of the beds in the other bedroom, I expect, why?'

'You don't have to keep up the pretence for my benefit. If you two want to spend the night together it's okay with me.'

'No, thank you!' Sandy said, as if shocked by the very idea. 'I'd rather have the time with you.'

'But you are sleeping with him?' Sam pressed the point.

'Am I?' Sandy replied coyly.

'It's pretty obvious,' Sam said. 'It's not you that gave it away, it's him. I can tell just by the way he looks at you, his whole attitude towards you.'

Sandy smiled. 'You should join MI5! We slept together once,' she lied. There was no need to complicate matters, after all. 'I was feeling low and I needed comforting.'

'You don't need to explain to me,' Sam said. 'I'm not our stepmother!'

Sam's lack of concern surprised Sandy. 'I thought you'd disapprove,' she said. 'Carnal sin, and all that.'

Sam pulled a face. 'I don't know what to think anymore,' she replied. There was something in her voice – an emotion that Sandy could not fathom.

'What are you not telling me?' she asked.

Sam did not reply directly. She was thinking about Anthony. She had never been so physically attracted to anyone as she was to him. She fantasised about him. She imagined that stubbly chin nuzzling her throat as his lips kissed her neck; she imagined him tearing the clothes from her body and ...

Shocked by the train of her own thoughts, she shook off the fantasy and said wistfully, 'It's funny; you think your life is settled, that nothing is ever going to change. Then something . . . quite cataclysmic happens, unexpectedly, and your whole life changes forever. She looked at Sandy and her eyes glistened. 'Do you know what I mean?'

Sandy remembered what she had heard a few hours earlier and answered honestly, 'Yes; I know exactly what you mean.'

**

She was falling. She knew she had to stay upright and she knew she had to keep her legs tight together, but her legs were open and she was unable to bring them together. She looked down to see Szopienice lying between her legs, his face contorted as he thrust and ground inside her. Behind him was an endless queue of naked men, each with an erection, all of them awaiting their turn at her.

Suddenly she was tumbling through the air, tumbling out of control. Now she was in the water. It was deep, so deep that the surface seemed impossible to reach. She tried to claw her way up to the surface but her limbs were leaden and would not obey her. Then, suddenly, she was on the surface. Small wavelets kept breaking over her head and the current was bearing her swiftly downstream. She looked around her, searching for something – or someone. Where was Caroline? That was who she had been looking for – Caroline. Then she saw her and shouted her name. Sandy stretched out her arms and Caroline did the same, but they were too far apart to make contact – and the distance between them was increasing. As Caroline drifted further and further away from her, Sandy called out to her again, screamed her name, but Caroline turned away. Then she was gone. Gone forever.

Chapter 28

It was not so much like waking as struggling toward the surface from the darkened depths of a deep pool of viscous liquid. When she did finally break through the barrier into consciousness, she found that she was lying on her back, staring up at a white ceiling. A plastic oxygen mask covered her mouth and nose, and the bedcovers were tucked tightly around her, restricting her movements. The light was so strong that it hurt her eyes, sending a sharp pain lancing through her head and it was several minutes before she could open them enough to focus on her surroundings. At first, she was unable to summon up the strength even to turn her head, but her peripheral vision revealed that blue-and-white check curtains were drawn around her bed, restricting her view of the world to a space ten feet long and six wide. It took a great deal of effort, but eventually she was able to lift her head a little, a movement she immediately regretted because of the pain and nausea it caused. However, the slight movement was sufficient to get a clearer view all around her.

On a metal stand beside the bed was a bag from which a clear liquid dripped regularly, fed into her bloodstream via a cannula in the back of her right hand. She willed the fingers of the hand to move and was strangely relieved to see them respond. For some reason she had had it in her head that she was paralysed.

Wires led from contacts attached to her chest, under the hospital gown, to a machine, just out of view, which monitored her heart rate and produced a reassuringly regular electronic beep. She tried to sit up, but she was unable to move anything other than her arms. The rest of her body seemed to be made of lead, and although she could see the shape of her legs under the pale cream counterpane, she could neither feel them nor move them, causing a resurgence of the fear of that she might be paralysed. Suddenly, the curtains parted and a nurse, wearing a pale-blue uniform and a white apron, entered the cubicle.

'Ah, awake are we, me love?' the nurse asked in a detached, cheerfully professional manner. She had a West-Country accent. Somerset; Dorset; Devon, perhaps. 'How are you feeling?' she asked while wrapping a cuff around the patient's upper arm to check her blood pressure.

'Where am I?' She knew it was a stupid question; obviously, she was in hospital. Perhaps 'Why am I here?' would have been more appropriate, but being in a state of delirium and fatigue, the words came out as an incoherent mumble, so it hardly mattered.

'You've had a bit if an accident,' the nurse said as she inserted a probe into the patient's ear to take her temperature. After some seconds, it bleeped. She removed it and made some notes in ring binder that had been hanging at the foot of the bed. 'It says here your name's Katherine. Should we call you Katherine or do you prefer Kathy?'

'Accident? What accident?' Confused, by the use of her cover name, Jeanette ignored the question.

'Don't you remember, me love?' the nurse asked sympathetically, 'You were brought in by ambulance. Seems a lamppost jumped out in front of your car,' she said smiling at her own witticism. She lifted the oxygen mask away from Jeanette's mouth and nose and used a wet sponge to moisten her lips. Jeanette was grateful because her mouth was so dry.

'Nil by mouth,' the nurse explained. 'Can't give you anything to eat or drink until after you've seen the doctor. I've just got to change your bag then I'll let Sister know you're back with us, alright?'

'Change what bag?' Although her head was still swimming, Jeanette's speech was becoming clearer; the moist sponge had helped.

'Your catheter bag, me love' the nurse explained. 'You've filled it up; needs changing.'

'How seriously injured am I?' Jeanette asked in a small, nervous voice.

'I'm sorry, me love, you'll have to wait for the doctor for that.'

'My head hurts,' said Jeanette, 'and I feel really dizzy.'

'Yes, well you just get some rest, my lovely, and the doctor will come and see you shortly.' With that, the nurse left the cubicle.

Jeanette could hear movement and voices outside the cubicle but the curtains remained closed, preventing her from seeing what was going on around her. Time passed, but she did not know whether it was minutes or hours because she kept slipping in and out of consciousness. At one point a woman poked her head through the curtains and offered Jeanette a cup of tea. She withdrew apologetically when she saw the "Nil by Mouth" sign above her head. Jeanette must have slept for a while because the next thing she knew she was being woken by someone squeezing her hand. She opened her eyes to see a man, not much older than her, perched on the side of the bed. He had tousled, collar-length brown hair and wore a white coat. A stethoscope dangled from his neck.

'Hello, I'm Doctor Matthews,' he said, smiling down at her. 'How are you feeling, Miss Taylor?'

'Confused,' Jeanette replied, her voice muffled by the oxygen mask. Her head had cleared a little but she still felt dazed.

The doctor used a thumb to raise one of Jeanette's eyelids and shone a light into first one then her other eye. 'You have a slight concussion,' he explained. 'You're bound to feel a little woozy for a while.'

'What happened?' Jeanette asked. She could remember nothing of the accident; the last thing she could remember was being in the office, as Sam left to go for a walk. Without her!

'We don't really know,' the doctor replied. 'We know you were found unconscious in your car with a minor head injury. It looks like you hit your forehead on the steering wheel. If you'd been wearing your seat-belt, it wouldn't have happened,' he added reproachfully.

'I... I don't remember,' Jeanette replied. 'I always wear my seat-belt.'

'In itself, the injury shouldn't have been enough to render you unconscious for so long, so we've taken some blood and urine to run some tests. Not diabetic, are you?'

'No,' Jeanette replied vaguely. 'I don't remember the accident at all.' and then the jolt at the traffic lights flashed briefly into her head. 'I remember...' She hesitated.

'Go on,' the doctor prompted.

Jeanette frowned. The doctor's interruption had cut the thread of the fleeting memory, which now vanished like a deer into a thicket. Visible for a second and then gone without a trace. 'How long have I been here?'

'Let's see,' the doctor replied, looking at the notes. 'You were brought into A&E this morning, and were transferred up to the ward at about three am. It's now two-thirty pm, so twelve hours, give or take.'

'Oh my God!' Jeanette cried as a wave of panic enveloped her. 'Why can't I remember?'

The doctor patted her hand. 'Don't worry. It will all come back. Look, I've got to go now. We're a bit short-handed, being Sunday. I'll try to come and see you again later.'

It was only after he had left that it registered. *Sunday*?

Following the doctor's visit, the nurse returned and removed the oxygen mask and catheter, but left the saline drip in place. Then she drew back the curtains surrounding the bed. Jeanette found that she was in a small ward with five other women. At the far end was a wall of windows through which golden autumn afternoon sunlight streamed brightly. Visitors clustered around three of the other patients. Of the other two, one was asleep and the other knitting.

Feeling weak and listless, Jeanette kept slipping between awareness of her surroundings and semi-consciousness. At some stage, an auxiliary nurse brought her a cup of tea and an egg mayonnaise sandwich, which she ate, propped up by several pillows. Afterwards she began to feel better; less confused; less nauseous. Then the young doctor came back.

'Hello,' he said, 'Feeling any better?'

'A bit, thanks,' she replied. 'I still feel really out of it!'

'That's not surprising, really,' the doctor replied. 'We had to keep you under sedation because you were thrashing about and raving when they first brought you up from A&E.'

'Raving?' Jeanette asked, puzzled, 'About what?'

'I don't know for sure,' he shrugged apologetically, 'I wasn't here. Something about a crane apparently.'

A memory intruded into her thoughts; a vague, fleeting memory of a conversation. 'Has anyone been to see me?' she asked. 'Have I had any visitors?'

'No, of course not,' the doctor replied. 'You've been out cold for most of the past twelve hours.'

'It must have been a dream,' Jeanette muttered, shaking her head.

'We couldn't find any details of your next of kin in your handbag,' Dr Mathews continued, 'so we've not been able to contact anyone to let them know you're here. The police went to the address on your driving licence, apparently, but got no answer, and none of the neighbours there had heard of you.' He looked at her meaningfully, clearly intrigued by his beautiful but mysterious patient.

Jeanette brushed the enquiry aside. 'I haven't lived there for long.'

Matthews nodded. 'Is there someone we can phone for you, to let them know where you are?'

Jeanette thought quickly. As the day had worn on, part of her memory had returned. She remembered her lone vigil outside the Waterloo Inn, and the rather uncomfortable conversation with her team leader in the van, but from that point on everything was a blank. So what had happened after she left? Had the team captured Sandy? What about Sam? Jeanette should have been there. She should not have left. She should have stayed close by and observed what had happened, but she had obeyed her superior's orders and left the rest of the team to it. She had failed in her mission. She was supposed to be there when they captured Sandy. Now she had to find a way to get back – before it was too late.

'Yes, please,' Jeanette replied. 'Have you got a pen? I'll tell you the number.'

Once the doctor had gone, Jeanette tried to recall the dream. She remembered seeing Caroline, who seemed to hover in space above her, with a blinding halo around her head. Caroline and a halo? Surely there could be no more incongruous a combination!

'Hello, Nettie,' the apparition had cooed in her coarse East London accent, her hand gently stroking Jeanette's hair. Caroline was the only person to use the nickname Nettie for Jeanette since her grandmother had died. It all seemed so real. No, it could not be real because Caroline was dead. Poor Caroline!

'Kathy, Kathy, you have a visitor. You're mum's here.'

Jeanette lurched back to wakefulness again. How long had she been asleep? She glanced at the window. It was pitch dark outside so it must have been at least a couple of hours. Why was she so *tired*? A young nurse that she had not seen before was gently shaking her hand. She was a plain looking girl with short, light-brown hair and spoke with a Lancastrian accent.

'My mum?'

'Hello, Kathy, dear. Are you all right, darling?'

The over-familiar endearments spoken by a voice she did not recognise shook off the last remnants of sleep, and Jeanette focussed on the source. The woman stood beside her, her face and body language a testament to motherly love and concern for her child. Who the hell was she? Confused and unsure, Jeanette played along but without committing herself.

'What are you doing here?' She asked the strange woman.

'What a question!' she replied in a hurt tone. 'What sort of mother would I be if I didn't come to see my daughter in hospital? I came as soon as I got the message. It's been quite a journey too, I can tell you!'

Jeanette could see the nurse hovering nearby, pretending to read the notes at the foot of the next bed, but obviously listening to the conversation. She appeared to be suspicious about the relationship between the patient and the visitor. Jeanette realised that she had not reacted as a daughter should to her mother. It was as if she did not recognise her – which, of course, was true. Jeanette was unsure how to proceed. Should she reject the woman as a fraud or embrace her as if she truly were her mother? Who was she? Who had sent her? Then, to Jeanette's relief, the woman came to her rescue.

'Look, dear,' she said, 'we've all been so worried about you. We haven't seen or heard from you for so long. Claire said to give you her love.'

Jeanette closed her eyes in relief. "Claire" was the recognition code. She held out her arms and the woman hugged her. The nurse, apparently satisfied, walked away.

'The nurse told me you have only a mild concussion,' the stranger whispered into Jeanette's ear. 'I'm taking you out of here with me. It would be better if you could walk. Are you up to that?'

'Yes,' replied Jeanette. 'I feel fine now, but they want to keep me in for observation for another night.'

'We can't take the risk. You're going to have to discharge yourself.'

'Can I do that?'

'Of course! They can't keep you here against your will. We'll just tell them you want to leave.'

Jeanette thought for a moment. 'They're bound to make a fuss. Is it wise to draw attention to ourselves?'

'I'll say I want to take you home with me and that you'll see our GP at the earliest opportunity.'

'They'll probably ask who that is…'

'Don't worry. I'm prepared for all the questions.'

'Where are we going?'

'We're taking you to Crane. Sierra-Mike-One has disappeared, and there's still no sighting of Sierra-Hotel-One. Crane wants you off the plot now.'

'What! We didn't get her?' Jeanette asked uncomprehendingly. 'When I left, they were all geared up to take her.'

'Crane will explain,' said the woman. She broke physical contact and she sat on the visitor's chair beside Jeanette's bed.'

Jeanette felt uneasy. 'Did I do something wrong?'

'Don't ask me, dear,' the woman replied, quietly. 'I just follow orders. And now you have yours!'

Jeanette tried to hide her nervousness, and nodded her understanding. She hoped that her role in the Curlew affair was not over.

Second-year student nurse Sally Tindall replaced the clinical notes folder and returned to the nurse's station near the entrance to the ward.

'Okay if I pop down to the Friends shop?' she asked Janice, the day shift Sister. 'I need some mints.'

'Yes, okay, Sally, love. Don't be too long though. We've got the notes to write up before shift change-over.'

'Right-oh,' Sally replied, and left the ward.

The Friends kiosk was in the foyer near the main entrance. Sally walked straight past, and out of the building. She crossed the packed car park and approached a blue Volvo estate. When she reached it, she glanced around furtively before slipping into the front passenger seat.

Like everyone else on the ward, Sally had been intrigued by the patient with the super-model looks. Her odd behaviour on her arrival on the ward had been the talk of the nursing staff since Sally came on shift this morning. Her interest was piqued even more when the patient regained consciousness and claimed to have no memory of the past few days. The strangest thing of all, regarding this patient, however, was the interest shown by the woman who now sat in the driver's seat of the Volvo, looking at Sally expectantly.

The woman had first approached Sally early in the shift, as she left the ward to go to the dispensary. Introducing herself as Angela, the woman had claimed to be a reporter for a national Sunday newspaper. She said that the enigmatic patient on Sally's ward was in fact the mistress of someone in the public eye, and that she was very keen to find out anything she could about her accident and her stay in hospital. She offered Sally fifty pounds just to report on any developments.

At first, Sally was reluctant, even though fifty pounds was a lot of money to a student nurse. After all, breaking patient confidentiality could cost Sally her job. When Angela promised that she would never reveal the source of her information and said there would be another fifty in it for her when the patient left hospital, Sally capitulated.

'So, what have you got for me?' Angela asked.

Sally took a deep breath. This was the point of no return. 'Her mother arrived to see her.'

'Describe the mother,' Angela instructed.

'Five-five or five-six; dark hair – almost black, but with a lot of grey.

'What's she wearing?'

'A fawn overcoat, a dress or skirt – not trousers.'

'Good work!' said Angela, patting Sally's knee.

'There's one other thing,' Sally ventured.

'Go on.'

'At first the patient seemed surprised to see her mother. In fact, she didn't even recognise her.'

'Go on.'

'I was hanging around, trying to earwig…'

'You shouldn't have done that,' said Angela mildly. 'I didn't ask you to do that.'

'Sorry.'

'What did you hear?'

'Nothing. They were whispering.'

Angela nodded. The woman was never going to be Lapwing's real mother, especially as the hospital staff knew her by her cover-name. She glanced at Sally. The girl's body language hinted at more to come.

'And?' she prompted.

'I think she realised I was hanging around trying to hear what they were saying, and she suddenly made a show of affection to the woman. I tell you, I'm sure she'd never seen that woman before today!'

This girl's in the wrong job, Angela thought. Aloud, she said, 'You've done really well, Sally.' Keep an eye on things and let me know of any further developments.' She handed Sally five ten-pound notes and repeated, 'You've done very well.'

'Thanks. Oh, one other thing,' Sally began. 'The blood tests showed no alcohol at all but there's a trace of a drug, which they've not yet identified.'

'Interesting,' Angela remarked. She knew what had happened to Lapwing during her missing hours and knew they would find no alcohol. It would be a disappointment if they had found the amobarbital. It was supposed to have cleared the woman's system before any tests could be carried out. She hoped it was not a recreational drug. The last thing MI5 wanted was for Lapwing to be held under suspicion of "Driving under the Influence". They needed her free to lead them to other members of the cell. 'Let me know what shows up.'

'I'd better be getting back,' said Sally, glancing around to make sure there was no one she knew to see her get out of the car. Look, I finish at five-thirty. What happens after that?'

Angela looked at her watch; it was nearly five o'clock, already. Don't you worry about that,' said Angela. That's my problem. Are you on tomorrow?'

'No, it's the end of my four-on. I've got a three day break now; then I come back on nights.'

'That'll be too late. She'll have gone by then. Come and see me with a final update on your way out, and I'll give you your other fifty.'

'Right. See you later then.'

Sally slipped out of the car and hurried across the car park to the main entrance. She hurried through the doors and across to the kiosk to buy the mints that had been her excuse for leaving the ward, but it was closed. Oh well, luckily she had some in her bag, which was in her locker upstairs. She would make a show of eating one and offer them around to the others as well. She turned and walked quickly in the direction of the stairs leading up to the ward – and almost collided with Kathy Taylor and the older woman, who were heading for the exit. Sally was rooted to the spot, unsure what to do. The two women saw that she was staring at them and she realised that she had to say something.

'Are you leaving us, Kathy?' she asked, not attempting to mask her surprise.

'I've discharged myself,' the ex-patient replied.

'Oh, is that wise? I thought they wanted to keep you in for...'

'We've had the lecture, young lady, thank you very much,' said the older woman. 'Now, if you will excuse us, we're in a hurry.'

Sally faltered under the peremptory tone 'Oh, sorry. I just meant...' she let the sentence tail off.   'Well, look after yourself, Kathy,' she added and watched the two women hurry through the exit.

Sally waited just inside the door until they were far enough away for her to follow at a discrete distance. Ducking behind a large Rover saloon, she watched as they climbed into a light-coloured Toyota Corolla, then she ran quickly to where Angela was waiting in the Volvo. She yanked open the passenger door and blurted excitedly, 'They've just left!'

'What? Who?' Angela asked, recovering from her surprise. 'Who's left?'

Sally perched on the passenger seat but left the door open. One foot was inside the car, the other on the ground outside.

'Kathy Taylor's discharged herself. She and the other woman are in that Toyota that's heading for the exit now,' she said, pointing to where the barrier was lifting to let the Toyota out.

Immediately, Angela grabbed a radio microphone.

'Mobile One to Mobile Two,' she said urgently. 'Tango on the move in cream or beige Toyota Corolla. No index. They've just left the car park. Mobile Two, do you have eyeball?'

'Mobile Two to Mobile One,' the radio speaker buzzed with static as the response came back. 'Negative visual. Moving now.'

'How many people in the car?' Angela asked Sally.

'Er, I didn't see…'

'Did either of the women get into the driver's seat?' Angela asked abruptly, cutting over Sally's answer.

'Er, no. Kathy got in the back and her mother – the older woman – got in the front left.'

'This is Mobile One,' Angela said into the microphone. 'Three up, at least. Repeat: at least three occupants in the Toyota.'

'Mobile Two. I have them in sight. 'Mobile One? I have index. Hotel One-Nine-Zero, Juliet Lima Papa. Shadow me in case I have to break contact.'

'Who are you?' Sally asked, wide eyed. 'You're no bloody reporter are you?'

'Never mind,' Angela answered. 'Look, you've been a great help, but I have to go now.' She fished out some notes from her jacket pocket and counted out three twenty's. 'Please forget all about it. Don't tell anyone about me, or the help you've given me. Apart from anything else, you'd probably get the sack. Now get out of the car, quickly. I have to go.'

'I wish I could come with you. Can't I? This is great!'

'No!' Despite the urgency, Angela laughed at Sally's sense of adventure, 'Go on bugger off – and don't tell anyone anything, right?'

Sally tapped the side of her nose. 'Right-oh, Double-O-Seven, your secret's safe with me.' Before closing the door, she asked, 'How do I join up?'

Angela looked at her seriously. This girl could have something. 'You're a bright girl. Figure it out. We're in the phone book nowadays. Now shut the bloody door, will you?'

Chapter 29

Sandy's prediction came true. David had left the sisters alone for the most part, spending his time chatting and playing cards with the bodyguards. Sandy continued to refuse to enter into any discussion about her work, or elaborate on anything that she had done in the previous eighteen months, so the conversation revolved around poignant reminiscences and their respective futures – Sandy's with the baby and Samantha's with or without Stephen. Then there was the question of whether or not they would be able to maintain a relationship with each other.

At one point during the morning, Sam had suddenly asked, 'What was all that about Clermont last night?'

Sandy tensed at the reference but hid her consternation and replied guardedly, 'What do you mean?'

'You had a very restless night, last night. You kept talking in your sleep,' Sam explained. 'You called out a lot of things, mostly unintelligible, but several times you said something like "don't talk about Clermont" or "mustn't talk about Clermont."'

'Did I?' Clermont. Sandy had heard that name for the first time yesterday, but all attempts to expand on its meaning had come to nothing. 'I've no idea what that was all about.'

'I thought you must be having nightmares about old Mrs George,' said Sam with an expression that was half grin and half grimace.'

'Who?'

'Mrs George, head of history at Bramsfield. You remember her, surely?'

'Er, oh yes! We used call her Mrs Dragon,' Sandy said, smiling at the memory of giggling fifteen-year-old girls whispering at the back of the classroom. 'We used to say she survived because St George didn't want to stick his lance in her.'

Sam frowned. 'Trust your lot!'

'What about her, anyway? What was it about Clermont that reminded you of her?'

'You know, the Council of Clermont.'

'What are you talking about?'

'History never was your strong point was it,' Sam teased. 'The Council of Clermont was where Pope Urban the Second launched the First Crusade in ten ninety-five.'

'How on Earth do you remember things like that?'

'I did the Crusades for my History O-Level project. I remember it very well. I found it all jolly exciting.'

Sandy made a face but made no comment. Her mind was busy processing the information. The Crusades were holy wars to recapture the Holy Land, particularly Jerusalem from . . . The Jews? No, Saladin and all that – Muslims. The Muslims captured Jerusalem in . . . whenever.

Suddenly, Sam spoke again, this time putting on a theatrical voice, like a female Laurence Olivier.

'I, or rather the Lord, beseech you to persuade all people of whatever rank, foot-soldiers and knights, poor and rich, to carry aid promptly to those Christians in the Holy Lands and to destroy that vile race and drive them from the lands of our friends.'

'What?'

'The "vile race" being Muslims, of course,' Sam elaborated unnecessarily. 'When they finally got into

Jerusalem, the Crusaders' leader, Tancred, took the Pope at his word and ordered all the inhabitants killed. They massacred thousands of Muslim men, women and children. Not one of Christianity's most edifying episodes!'

Sandy swallowed hard. Suddenly everything had become clear.

At about the same time that Angela was setting off in pursuit of Lapwing, the sisters were once more facing each other across the kitchen table, drinking tea. David and the guards were watching an old war-film on television in the living room. Sam and Sandy could hear the ping....... ping....... of the ASDIC as a Royal Navy Corvette, escorting a trans-Atlantic convoy, hunted a German submarine. Then an authoritative voice said, 'Go round again, Number One!' When the depth charges started exploding again, Sandy quietly closed the door and returned to her seat, facing Sam.

'I don't know whether I want to leave Stephen,' Sam said suddenly, 'Not forever, anyway.'

'You'd be mad to go back to him,' Sandy replied.

'Why?' Sam asked, sipping her tea. To Sandy, she sounded half-hearted, as if she wanted to be convinced.

'Well, apart from him being a complete prat, he hit you.'

Sam put down her cup. 'He's never been as violent as that before,' Sam answered. 'He hasn't been himself since the... Since Mother and Daddy died.'

So frustrated was Sandy by her sister's meekness, she felt like hitting her herself. 'It wasn't just a playful slap, he beat you up! Why are you defending him?'

Sam seemed to steel herself before answering. 'I promised to love, honour and obey him, after all. For better or for worse!'

'And he promised to love, honour and cherish you,' Sandy countered, adding brutally, 'Getting punched in the face isn't my idea of being cherished.'

'Till death do us part,' Sam continued to recall her marriage vows.

'Say the word and I could arrange that,' said Sandy. 'If I wasn't dead I'd go round to your house and kick the crap out of him.

Sam was not amused and gave her sister a severe look. 'Perhaps I should give him another chance. A lot of it's my fault . . .'

'It's not your fault that he hit you!'

'I made him angry. I should have handled him better, tried to calm him down instead of arguing and . . . '

'Standing up for yourself? Why should you always have to give in to him, always let him win?'

'I've been a different person since the funerals. I've asserted my independence.'

'Good for you! It's about time.'

'It was Kathy that helped me – encouraged me to start making my own decisions. She's been the most wonderful friend.'

Sandy bit her tongue. This was no time to tell Sam that her friend, Kathy, was a spy, who had befriended her solely to entrap her sister.

'What's going to happen now?' Sam asked. 'Are these people going to continue coming after you? Am I still in danger? Oh, God! What about Stephen?'

'What about Stephen?'

'He's at home. He's vulnerable. What if they do something to him?'

Sandy pursed her lips and wrinkled her nose, as she always did when she was thinking. *Sod Stephen, the little bastard!*

'I'll have to talk to David about that. We have to find a way to protected you from these people.'

'What about us? Will be able to see each other again?'

'I really don't know,' Sandy replied. 'Things have changed since yesterday. I have no idea how this will all pan out.'

'Oh, Sandy,' Sam said, fighting back tears, 'I don't want to lose you again. You're all I have left.'

Sandy took her sister's hands in her own and looked into her eyes.

'You won't, Sam, I promise. I won't let them keep us apart.'

Then she looked up to see David standing in the doorway. The expression on his face told her that the waiting was over. The next phase of the operation had begun.

Sandy heard her father's voice as clearly as if he were there in the room, and she shivered.

Never make a promise unless you are sure you can keep it.

Chapter 30

'Hello?'

'Stephen, it's me.'

'Samantha? Where are you, darling? Are you alright?'

'Yes (voice cracking), I'm fine. Are you all right? Is everything okay?'

'Everything's fine apart from, well, you know. Where are you?'

'I can't tell you. I just wanted to know you were, you know, all right.'

'Why wouldn't I be? I've been so worried about you. Where are you? Where have you been? It's been two days! I've reported you missing to the police; I've been phoning all your friends; the hospitals. I can't get hold of Kathy. Is she with you?'

'I'm sorry, I should have phoned sooner.' (pause) 'Stephen, I'm not coming home.'

'What? Why? Look, I'm sorry about what happened...'

'What, beating me up, you mean?'

'That's an exaggeration. I didn't beat you up, but I am sorry I hit you. I really don't know what came over me. It won't happen again, I promise'

'You're right; it won't happen again. I'm never going to give you the opportunity.'

'Samantha! What's got into you?'

'I think it's called common sense.'

'Don't be flippant!'

'I'm not. I'm not coming back to you, Stephen.'

'Look, I know I shouldn't...'

'It isn't just what happened the other night. I've been thinking this way for a long time. After Mother and Daddy er, died, I realised that I don't love you. You are self-centred, self-righteous and self-obsessed. I don't want to spend the rest of my life living in your shadow. I want to live a life of my own. For me!'

'There's someone else, isn't there?'

'No, Stephen, there isn't, but there will be, one day. At least I hope so.'

'Look, Samantha, we can't do this over the telephone. We have to sit down and talk it all through. We can work this out.'

'There's nothing to work out, Stephen. I'm going to start divorce proceedings....'

'Citing what?'

'Oh, where do I start? Unreasonable behaviour, assault, mental cruelty...'

'You wouldn't ...'

'Oh yes I would! And, believe me, if you dare to make life difficult, I'll have you arrested for assault and battery.'

'Samantha, listen ...'

'No! My mind is made up. I'm going to leave Brighting's, and I'm going to move down to London.'

'But what about the house?'

'I'll make you a fair settlement...'

'I wasn't talking about money.'

'I am. I don't want a long, drawn out process; I want a clean break from you. When Probate is complete and the estate is settled, we'll divide everything equally. I'm happy for you to keep the house in Chester. I'm keeping the house in

Amberley and I'm going to rent it out. It's perfect for a corporate let, and it will give me an income.'

'You've got it all worked out.'

'Yes. (pause of several seconds) You'll be hearing from my lawyer. Goodbye, Stephen.'

CLICK

'Samantha? Samantha? Sam? Oh God!'

CLICK

Jerry Radford, who had been designated Saturn for the aborted snatch operation on Friday evening, leaned forward and turned the switch. As the slowly spinning reels of magnetic tape ceased revolving, he removed the headphones and placed them on the bench where the tape recorder now sat idle.

'Any joy, Paul?' he asked his partner.

Paul Duncan, formerly Jupiter, switched off the device with which he had traced the calling number. 'Yes, loads of time. Ellesmere Port.'

'Address?'

'It's a phone box in Overpool Road.'

'Let's get over there. I hope the tracker's still working.'

'They might have found it, in which case we'll be wasting our time.'

'Got any better ideas?'

'Nope.'

'Right, let's go then.'

***

'Come on, let's get out of here,' Anthony said, beckoning impatiently. It was dark and the drizzling rain formed misty halos around the streetlamps. The street where the telephone box was located was deserted on this cold, wet Sunday evening, but nearby Overpool Road was busy with traffic.

'Okay, coming,' Sam replied, allowing Anthony to take her elbow and hurry her to the kerbside where Petra sat impatiently behind the wheel of a black Audi Quattro. The moment both passengers had boarded, Petra floored the accelerator.

'You spent a bloody long time on that phone,' Petra grumbled. 'If anyone's monitoring your house phone, they'll have had plenty of time to do a trace.'

'Sorry,' said Sam, 'I had to…'

'We told you to keep it short!' Petra scolded her. 'Anthony, you should have…'

'Look, it's no sweat,' said Anthony. 'The safe house is miles away. Let the buggers waste their time trawling around here. They're never going to find us in a million years.'

Petra exhaled loudly to show her displeasure. 'Let's hope you're right,' she muttered. The damage was done now anyway. She looked in the mirror at Sam who, yet again was touching up her make-up from the powder compact that seemed to be her constant companion – almost a security blanket, Petra thought.

***

As Petra was driving Samantha and Anthony away from the phone box, the Toyota Corolla had just passed the point where the M6 motorway merged onto the M1. The three vehicles of Angela's surveillance team, her Volvo Estate, a black Vauxhall Astra and a Honda motorbike, followed the Corolla at a respectful distance, swapping places regularly to avoid detection.

Tailing the target had been relatively easy because the Corolla driver did not seem to be using any anti-surveillance manoeuvres. Angela was concerned about that, but she had little choice other than to continue with the operation.

'They've got to be heading for London,' said David, breaking the silence of a lull in radio transmissions. To the uninitiated, the coded messages would sound like exchanges between taxi drivers and their despatch controller. Every so often, a keyword had everyone changing to a different frequency to make eavesdropping more difficult.

Sandy was with David in his Jaguar, heading south on the M6, fifty miles behind the surveillance operation. The wet tarmac ahead shone with reflected light from the taillights of the vehicles in front, adding to the glare from the headlights of traffic on the opposite carriageway. Rain and spray covered the windscreen, scorning the efforts of the wipers that scraped monotonously back and forth.

Sandy had been distant and introverted since leaving the safe house. Barely a word had passed between them on the journey. Even now, she was frowning and staring blankly through the windscreen. He wondered what was causing her to be so glum. God knew there were enough trials and tragedies in her recent life from which to choose.

'Are you okay?' he asked, but Sandy did not reply. He tried again. 'Sandy?'

'Eh? Oh, I'm fine,' she answered finally, but so softly that David had to strain to hear her. 'Why do you ask?'

'Oh, I don't know. You've been very quiet ever since we left the safe house. Worried about your sister?'

Sandy sniffed in the darkness, and David wondered if she was crying. 'It's just that I started thinking about Caroline again.'

'Tell me about her? What was she like?' He was hoping she would not change the subject as she had on the other occasions that he had asked.

'She was very beautiful,' said Sandy, staring out of the side window, preventing him from seeing her face.

David grinned. 'Not a patch on you, I bet!'

'Hah! She made me look like one of Cinderella's ugly sisters.' She cuffed a tear from her cheek. 'She had a figure that men fantasise about and most women would kill for. She had jet-black curly hair, soft olive skin and her smile...' Sandy made a noise that was half laugh and half sob. 'When she smiled her whole face lit up, but her most outstanding feature was her eyes. They were brown: big, soft brown eyes that seemed to look right inside you. When she looked at you in a certain way, your heart would miss a beat and you'd go weak at the knees. No one could resist her.'

'Jeanette seemed besotted with her,' David observed. 'In fact, you make it sound as if you were almost tempted yourself.' He meant it as a joke but he did not see Sandy's secret smile.

The radio hissed with static and a voice uttered the codeword to change over the lead vehicle. Silence reasserted its reign for a minute or two and then David said, 'Do you mind if ask you something?'

Sandy turned her head and eyed him suspiciously. 'Depends.'

'About the baby,' he ventured. 'How did you come to get pregnant?'

'Are you kidding? Do you want me to draw you a diagram?'

'I meant: given the type of mission you were on . . .'

'Meaning?'

'You and Caroline were there as bait – a honey-trap, right?'

'I told you that on Friday,' she reminded him sullenly, wishing she had kept that particular aspect of the mission to herself.

David frowned as he tried to formulate the awkward question. 'You must have known there was a slight chance of being, er, being put into a compromising situation. What were you doing to avoid getting pregnant? Were you using any form of contraceptive?'

Sandy bit back a sarcastic retort about asking rapists to wear condoms. 'I was on the pill, but I'd just finished my period the day we left Sarajevo, so I hadn't taken any for a week. I took the first of the new pack that evening.'

She stared out of the front windscreen again, remembering the night that the team stayed in Brigadier-general Szopienice's villa in Pale.

Szopienice and a younger officer, a major named Danislav Ković, had burst into the room that she and Caroline were sharing. They brought with them a bottle of the fiery local plum brandy, but it was clear they wanted more than just share a nightcap. Sandy had wanted to send them packing, but Caroline saw an opportunity to develop the relationship, as indeed was their role. She made a move on the younger man, leaving Sandy no option but to pair with the brigadier-general.

Physically repulsed by the man and everything he stood for, she struggled to act the part of an impressionable, flirtatious young woman turned lascivious and wanton after a few drinks. After nearly two hours of debauchery, the two men bade the women goodnight and left the room. Only then was Sandy able to run into the bathroom.

She said none of this aloud. She could not bring herself to tell David what she had done, could not tell him how degraded she had felt or the depth of her self-loathing in the days that followed.

'Shortly after taking it,' she said, 'I threw-up. Then, what with one thing and another, I never got round to taking any more before we were captured, and well, you know what happened then.'

Although he could see her only out of the corner of his eye, David could tell from her body language that she was crying again.

David had to choke back a sudden unmanly urge to shed a few tears of his own. 'I'm sorry,' was all he could say, and those words were barely audible above a renewed static hiss from the radio.

***

'There's the phone box,' said Paul Duncan, pointing. 'It's empty.'

'Well, of course it's bloody empty,' said Jerry Radford scornfully. 'What d'you expect, that they'd be sitting there waiting for us to come and get them?' He looked out of the window at the surrounding houses. 'No, they'll be nowhere round here. Not unless they're total idiots. What have you got?'

Duncan looked at the tracking screen. It was a duplicate of the one in Lapwing's car. She had stashed it in the glove compartment when she had left the Waterloo Inn to drive back into Chester, and there it remained, undiscovered by anyone involved in the abduction or in staging the accident.

'Nothing,' Duncan replied.

'Told you!' said Radford. 'We'll have to widen the search. 'Effective range is a ten-k radius.'

'Yes, I know. Which way first?'

'We're pointing north; let's go up as far as the river.'

'Fair enough. Let's go.'

Twenty minutes later, they reached the M53 and took the arbitrary decision to circle the town in a clockwise direction. They turned south on the motorway and watched the tracker screen in vain for the hint of a signal. They exited at Little Stanney and turned west, heading for Blackford Cross. They were about halfway between the two when a weak signal showed up on the screen.

'Gotcha,' said Radford. 'Let's follow it in.'

The safe house was near the end of a cul-de-sac where the houses were set around a grassy square with a single oak tree in the middle. Duncan followed the road around the green and drove out again. A few hundred yards on, he turned the car again and returned to stop at the end of a line of cars parked outside a row of terraced houses. From here, they could see the entrance to the cul-de-sac, if not the safe house itself.

'Good choice of bolt hole,' remarked Radford. 'I bet they've noted every car and van within a hundred yards of that place. We won't be able to get any closer than this without being spotted.'

Call it in?' Duncan asked.

'Yep.' We can't take them on our own!'

***

It was shortly before midnight when the Corolla turned into the driveway of a large, detached house in a rural lane in Tadworth, Surrey. Surrounded by a tall fence of iron palings and an even taller hedge of copper beech, the house was hidden from casual observation from the lane, except through the open electric gates, which were already closing behind the Corolla as Angela cruised slowly past with the Volvo's lights extinguished. Now the gates were fully closed and even that view was obscured.

Angela drew up two hundred yards further on. The motorbike and the Astra pulled up nearby and the drivers came to join her in the Volvo. They all agreed that there was no obvious position from which to keep watch on the house. The lane where it was located was narrow and bounded by large properties on both sides. Any vehicle parked here would invoke suspicion immediately and would most likely trigger a police patrol to come sniffing around. Infiltrating the grounds would be a specialist job. The property would almost certainly be protected by CCTV and alarms driven by movement detectors.

Angela took out her mobile phone and dialled the number for London Central.

Chapter 31

The room was exactly as Sandy remembered it. The windowless white walls, white ceiling and floor, and lighting so bright it hurt the eyes. It reminded her of the fear and anger she had felt when incarcerated here for three days, back in September. At least this time she was fully dressed and not being drenched with freezing water spraying out of the nozzles set into the corners of the ceiling. She sat on one of two white metal chairs that faced each other across a square white metal table upon which an empty coffee mug and a plate with a half-eaten bacon roll waited to be cleared away.

After the long drive down from Ellesmere Port and a hurried conference with the team that had tailed the Toyota, David had dropped Sandy off at the security office at three in the morning. Then he had gone home to shower and change. Meanwhile, Sandy had been escorted to the cell where, with the ordeal of her interrogation still fresh in her mind, she had stretched out on the bunk and slept fitfully. At seven-thirty a smiling guard, who said his name was Tony, brought her breakfast. Now it was eight-forty-five, and Sandy looked up resignedly as the door opened and David Richardson breezed in.

'Morning,' he said with his by now familiar disarming smile. '*Déjà vu*?' He was wearing a blue pinstriped suit and crisp white shirt, and Sandy noticed that he was wearing the same tie as the day she first saw him in this very room. By contrast, she was casually dressed in jeans, trainers and pale blue *Fruit of the Loom* sweatshirt.

'Somewhat,' Sandy replied, without returning the smile. 'What happens now?

'Are you going to finish that?' David asked, sitting opposite and eying the discarded bacon roll. When she shook her head, he picked it up and took a bite. 'Haven't had breakfast, yet,' he said, chewing furiously.

'You didn't answer my question,' Sandy said. 'What's happening?'

'The DG will be down soon,' he said before popping the last piece into his mouth.

'I'm in deep shit, aren't I?'

'Yes, I'm afraid so. Actually, I think we both are.'

'What's she going to do to us?'

'Well, we'll just have to wait and see, won't we?' David replied with a wink.

***

Riding the lift to the fifth floor, Amanda Gillette pondered the sketchy details of the hunt for Sandra Harris, as related by David Richardson in two phone calls to her home during the weekend. Being an open line, it had been necessary for him to speak in oblique terms but she understood the gist. The first call was late on Friday evening, during which he told of his success in locating Sandy Harris, but too late to stop her making contact with her sister.

'I finally made contact with our friend today, but, unfortunately, I was a little late and the meeting had started before I got there. Then some people from a rival firm turned up unexpectedly. There was a bit of a scene, I'm afraid, and we left quietly while their attention was elsewhere.'

'So there was no contact at all?'

'No. I'm not sure they knew for certain who was attending the meeting.'

That 'bit of a scene' had succeeded in making the national newspapers on Saturday morning.

ARMED POLICE FOIL CUSTOMS STAKE OUT

Cheshire Police were left red-faced yesterday after an armed response unit pounced on a van containing Customs and Excise officers in the car park of a public house near the city of Chester. The mix-up was due to a failure in communication, a spokesman admitted, but declined to comment any further on the incident, or the case under investigation.

Eyewitness, Andy Fraser, who was in his car in the car park as the drama unfolded, said . . .

The second phone call, on Saturday evening, made Amanda wonder if David had taken leave of his senses.

'We ran into someone from our friend's old firm and had a bit of a chat. We learned all sorts of very interesting details. Stuff we had not been aware of previously. It seems they've been intent on making an acquisition for some time.'

Amanda wondered just how David had managed to coerce the Manchester surveillance branch to assist him in such an audacious and potentially dangerous operation, the political and professional repercussions of which she had yet to discover. She feared that she would not have long to wait.

Amanda entered the outer office and Susan looked up. Susan Butler was Forty-five years old and as round as she was tall. She had been Amanda's secretary since the latter's appointment to Director (Anti-Terrorism) seven years previously.

'Mr Mitchell-Hunter phoned,' she said. 'He says he wants to see you and will be here at about ten o'clock.'

Amanda was not surprised that Eagle should want to see her. In fact, she was more surprised that he was not here already, in person, waiting for her to arrive. Oh well, that gave her some time to find out what in God's name had occurred over the weekend. Declining Susan's offer of coffee, Amanda strode into her office, hung up her coat and reappeared seconds later.

'Susan, I'm going down to the interview suite. I don't want to be disturbed down there, so field my calls. Also, please call Mitchell-Hunter back and tell him not to come here. Tell him I'll see him at Osprey House at eleven.'

***

The door opened and Sandy turned to see a haggard-looking Director General enter the room, followed by Tony, the security guard, who carried a wooden straight-back chair with a wicker seat. He placed the chair down beside the table and backed out of the room. As he closed the door, he caught Sandy's eye and winked. The small gesture, unnoticed by her superiors, raised Sandy's spirits and the corners of her mouth lifted in a wry smile.

'Good morning, Sandra,' said the Director General as she sat down. Sandy was on her right hand, David on her left. 'I hope you slept better than I did?'

'Good morning, Ma'am,' answered Sandy diffidently, reminded of many such interviews with her old headmistress at Bramsfield. 'As well as could be expected in the circumstances.'

'Please don't call me ma'am,' said the Director General. 'It makes me feel old. Nor "K", which I find terribly pretentious. Just call me Amanda, or if you're uncomfortable with that, Mrs Gillette. Okay?'

'Yes, Amanda. Thank you.' Amanda Gillette had just shot up twenty points in Sandy's esteem.

'Right, let's get down to business,' said Amanda. 'What did you think you were doing, running off like that and disobeying a direct order?'

The sudden change in tone made Sandy flinch. 'I'm sorry,' she said dejectedly, 'but I had to see my sister. We have always been close...'

'But you were ordered not to,' Amanda interrupted. 'Why do you think that was?' Sandy remained silent, unable to trust herself to speak aloud for fear of either losing her temper or bursting into tears. Unconsciously, she placed a hand on the bulge in her tummy. She was still not used to it being there. She felt a slight tremor through her hand and wondered if it was a kick from within or her own pulse.

'Well,' Amanda continued when Sandy failed to respond, 'the reasons were twofold. Firstly, to avoid you being spotted by someone who knew you, and who might make public your resurrection from the grave; and secondly, because if the wrong people became aware of your continued existence, your life and that of your sister would be in the gravest danger. You do understand that, don't you?' Amanda leaned forward to add emphasis to her words.

Amanda's tone was beginning to remind Sandy of her stepmother, who always insisted on speaking to her stepdaughter as if she was a great disappointment – always quick to voice her disapproval. As always happened, when Sandy had his type of conversation with her stepmother, she went of the offensive.

'Yes, of course I do, but I went to great lengths not to be recognised, and with some success.'

'The A4 surveillance chaps still spotted you,' David interjected, hoping to avert a more stinging admonishment from Amanda.

'No, actually they didn't,' Sandy argued. 'They followed a car. They had no idea who was in it. If they hadn't already known to look out for me, I would never have been spotted.'

'That's beside the point,' Amanda cut in, but Sandy had not finished.

'Look, I'm sorry, but I walked in and out of Sam's office, right under your people's noses and they didn't spot me.' As her argument developed, so Sandy's self-confidence increased. She held up her hand when Amanda started to speak, and, ignoring the daggered look that the Director General gave her, continued, 'I mean, how corny is that street workman cover? And they were there for more than a week! It doesn't take that long to fix a telephone junction box!' She paused, taking perverse satisfaction from Amanda's scowl and David's shocked expression. 'And, inside,' Sandy continued,

'I came face-to-face with someone I knew from Caesar, without her recognising me, despite being within touching distance. Even my own *sister* didn't recognise me until I identified myself!'

Amanda bit off a retort at Sandy's insolence. That did seem strange, especially given Eagle's acquiescence to Sandy's transfer into MI5. 'Perhaps she was there to protect your sister from the people that attacked you,' she suggested.

Sandy shook her head. 'No, that's not the case. She was there in case I turned up. They were planning to abduct me and probably kill me.'

'What makes you so sure of that?'

'It's pretty clear from what happened later,' David interjected mildly.

Amanda turned to face him. 'You'd better tell me exactly what happened on Friday. I'll be talking to Eagle very shortly and I want to know what went on, the full sequence of events.'

Sandy remained silent while David recounted how an operative had followed Samantha on foot when she went out at lunchtime and that the surveillance officer tailing her had been caught out when she had been driven away in Sandy's car. The mobile units were out of position but soon caught up with the suspect vehicle and began to follow. Spotting the tail, Sandy had used counter-surveillance methods to throw off the first two vehicles but was later picked up by a third, which managed to follow the sisters all the way to the Waterloo Inn.

David then explained how he had gone inside to confront Sandy, and that he had instructed one of the A4 officers, to take Samantha back her place of work in the city centre. Then, leaving out certain details of his time with Sandy that he considered should remain private, he summarised the tale that Sandy had related during their discussion in the bathroom.

Shortly afterwards, he explained, the A4 officer mentioned earlier had called him on his mobile phone to tell him that she had spotted a women in a little red hatchback watching the pub as she and Samantha had left Sandy's hotel.

David had organised a counter operation in which they had used sophisticated electronic surveillance equipment to eavesdrop, first on the woman's mobile calls and later, on the conversations inside the van, which brought her backup team. As soon as he had learned of the scale of the plot, David had enlisted the help of MI5's Manchester office to organise the police armed response unit, and while that chaotic episode was in progress, Sandy and her sister had been spirited away in the van with the British Telecom livery.

'Why did Samantha McNamara return to the pub?' Amanda asked.

'She had a fight with her husband,' Sandy chipped in. 'He hit her and stormed out of the house. She decided to leave him, at least temporarily, and she came back to where I had been staying.'

'It's unlucky that you had not already left,' Amanda replied.

'She couldn't,' said David, 'not with the place under surveillance.'

Amanda nodded. That was understandable. 'What happened next?'

'By now we realised that the woman who was watching the pub was the same one that had been working undercover in Samantha McNamara's office, Sandy's ex-colleague, Jeanette, code-named Lapwing.

There seemed to be quite a lot of animosity between her and her team leader, a chap who called himself Neptune. Then, because Sandy's sister returned, Neptune told Lapwing to make herself scarce and build an alibi, in case the sister had to be killed. She left the scene in her car. We followed and staged a fender-bender at some traffic lights.'

'A what?'

'Fender-bender. It's an American term for a minor traffic accident. When she got out of the car to remonstrate with our driver we bagged her, drugged her and took her away.'

'What in God's name made you do that?' Amanda demanded. 'Abducting an officer of a sister organisation? What *were* you thinking of?'

'That's what they were planning for me,' Sandy interjected. 'Or worse.'

Amanda looked at Sandy for a long moment but said nothing. Sandy held her gaze steadily and David took up the story again.

'We took her to Manchester HQ and interrogated her.'

'Where is she now, this Lapwing?' Amanda asked. 'Where are we holding her?'

'We're not,' David said.

Amanda was shocked. 'Why not? Where is she?'

'She's back with her own side.'

'Are you mad? You abduct her, interrogate her, and then release her? I'll be scraping egg off my face for a long time to come over this!'

David stiffened at K's tone, but whether through indignation or intimidation, Sandy could not be sure. Incensed by Amanda's placing the responsibility solely upon David's shoulders, Sandy leapt to his defence.

'*We,*' she placed heavy emphasis on the pronoun, 'went to great lengths to put her into a state of mind where she would answer our questions without hesitation – and then remember nothing about it afterwards.'

'How did you accomplish that?' Amanda asked.

'Well, basically, she was drugged up to the eyeballs, and I pretended to be Caroline. I put on a black wig and a push-up bra, and mimicked Caroline's accent and mannerisms.'

'Also,' David added, 'we used eye-drops to dilate the subject's pupils, so it hurt her to open her eyes. She could catch only fleeting glimpses of Sandy before she was forced to close her eyes again.'

'Who the devil is Caroline?' Amanda asked, bewildered.

Sandy faltered. A lump had suddenly formed in her throat and she was unable to reply. David answered for her.

'Caroline was Sandy's friend and teammate. She died on the Bosnian mission.'

'Oh,' Amanda said. 'Did this Lapwing girl not know this?'

'Yes,' Sandy replied, 'she knew.'

'Then I'm confused,' Amanda admitted. 'Why impersonate a dead woman, if the subject of the deception knows she's dead?'

'It added to the surrealism,' Sandy explained, 'especially as Jeanette was emotionally involved with Caroline.'

Amanda's eyes narrowed. 'What do you mean by emotionally involved?'

Sandy shrugged. She did not want to go into the details of Caroline's penchant for sexual adventures. *Male, female, animal, vegetable or mineral!* Sandy remembered her semi-jocular summary of Caroline's tastes in a conversation with Lenny during their dash southwards to Višegrad.

'Jeanette – Lapwing – had a crush on Caroline. They were, er, intimate several times in Sarajevo.' Sandy could feel David's eyes on her but she avoided his gaze, convinced she would otherwise reveal the depth of her own feelings for Caroline.

'They were lovers? How could you possibly expect to fool her into thinking that you were someone she knew intimately and that she knew was dead?' Amanda demanded in exasperation.

'We kept her on the very edge of consciousness. She had a spinal anaesthetic, which paralysed her from the waist down. The doctor pumped her full of Sodium Amytal to make her talk, and caffeine to stop her falling asleep. If she remembers anything, it will be so surreal she'll think she dreamed it.'

Amanda was still not wholly convinced. 'But, with Sodium Amytal, anyone could conduct the interview,' Amanda said. 'Why did you feel in necessary to impersonate this dead woman?'

'Drugs like Amytal don't negate one's intelligence,' Sandy said, 'they just remove any inhibitions about speaking. At Park House we were trained – conditioned – to resist all forms of interrogation, including truth drugs.'

'Conditioned?' Amanda noticed Sandy's choice of word. 'How?'

'Self-hypnosis,' Sandy explained. 'If the subject is under hostile interrogation, and he or she reaches a point where resistance is becoming intolerable, a subconscious trigger causes him or her to start reciting nursery rhymes or something.'

Amanda thought for a moment before asking, 'If that's the case, why didn't you start singing *Bah, Bah, Black Sheep* when David was interviewing you?'

'He didn't get to a point where I could no longer resist.' Then she looked at him and winked, adding, 'He still hasn't.'

David shifted uncomfortably in his seat and Amanda coughed to stifle a laugh.

'So how did impersonating Caroline help?' Amanda asked.

'Lapwing thought she was talking to someone she knew and trusted.'

'And was dead,' Amanda added sceptically.

'Caroline's death did come up in the conversation,' David interjected, 'as you will hear from the recording, but the girl was obviously very confused. Had she been given time to think, she may well have queried it.'

'And you think this was the only way – the drugs, the impersonation of a dead woman?' Amanda said. 'Normal interrogation methods would not have worked?'

'No,' Sandy replied, 'for two reasons. One, she would have resisted interrogation, as I explained earlier, and two, we needed her to forget all about it. We hoped that when she recovered she would lead us to the person we know only as Crane.'

I hope you're right,' Amanda said, 'for all our sakes. If you've got this wrong...'

Sandy bridled. 'Look, they went to extraordinary lengths to put tabs on Sam. They nearly killed her secretary just to get Lapwing in place.'

Amanda frowned, before nodding to David. 'Let's hear it then.'

He reached into his pocket, brought out the digital recorder, laid it in the middle of the table and pressed the Play button.

Chapter 32

'Hello, Nettie. What you been up to, then?'

Despite gaining an MA in English Literature and History, Caroline had never really lost the mode of speech from her childhood in London's East End. The letters 'T' and 'H' were optional extras in many words, as was the 'G' in the 'ING' endings. Sometimes they were present, sometimes not; it depended on her the circumstances. In contrast, Jeanette's accent betrayed her middle-class upbringing in leafy Surrey.

'Who's that? I can't see… the light's too bright.' Her voice was dreamy, vague, as if waking from a deep sleep. She was lying on her back on a hospital style bed borrowed from the medical suite. There was a bandage on her forehead and a cannula dripped saline fluid into the back of her hand. A monitor beeped regularly in the background. Behind the bed, where Jeanette could not see him, sat a doctor, monitoring the subject's vital signs on a computer, through which he also controlled the balance of the drugs that he was feeding into her bloodstream through a second cannula in her lower back.

'It's me, Nettie, darlin', Caroline.'

'Caroline? Caro, is that you?' Jeanette became agitated; tried to lift her head from the pillow but was unable to do so. She tried to shield her eyes from the light with one hand, but it was too much effort and the arm flopped back onto the bed.

'Yeah, it's me, Nettie. Never fear, Caro's 'ere.'

'Caroline? Is it really you? They said you were dead.'

'Nah, not me, darlin'. I'm 'ere, ain't I?'

Jeanette tried to move again but she was not able. Her voice grew panicky. 'Caroline, I can't move! What's wrong with me? Why can't I move?'

'You've been in an accident, Nettie,' "Caroline" explained gently. 'You've got to tell me ev'rythin' what's been 'appenin', so someone else can take over if, well, you know, just in case – ' Sandy left the sentence hanging, knowing that the dreadful implication would prey on the mind of the confused and frightened Jeanette.

'Oh God,' Jeanette wailed, 'I'm not dying am I?'

'The doctors are doing their best, Nettie, but we've gotta talk to you; just in case, yeah?'

'Oh Caroline, help me; help me, please!'

'Come on, Nettie, be brave. You've got to be brave for me, darlin'. Tell me everyfing I need to know, yeah?'

'Hold me, Caroline. Please hold me.'

'There. Okay, Nettie, darlin', okay, I'm 'ere now. There, that's better, eh?'

David was standing out of Jeanette's line of sight and Sandy could feel his eyes on her as she held Jeanette in her arms, tenderly, lovingly.

'First of all, Nettie, tell me why Samantha McNamara is under surveillance.'

Sandy knew that the effect of Sodium Amytal, one of the so-called truth drugs, was to make the subject garrulous, unable to resist talking. Unfortunately, however, contrary to their common name, truth drugs did not guarantee that the subject spoke only the truth. The truth would be in there, somewhere – possibly – but it may be mixed up with fantasy, perhaps even a deliberate lie. It was up to the interviewer to separate the wheat from the chaff.

'I'm trying to find out if Curlew has been in touch with her sister,' Jeanette mumbled sleepily.

Sandy made Caroline sound incredulous. 'But Sandy's dead, ain't she? What's her sister been doin', goin' to séances?'

'Not dead. Curlew's not dead. That's why we're looking for her.'

Sandy realised that by referring to her by her code-name rather than using her name, Jeanette was dehumanising her. That did not bode well for Jeanette's intentions toward her.

'What makes you think she's not dead?'

'Crane says she's still alive,' Jeanette replied. 'She's gone into hiding.'

Sandy's first instinct was to ask who Crane was. She had not heard of that code-name before. She could not ask the question outright, however. Such an obvious display of ignorance might trigger suspicion in Jeanette's mind, drugged and confused though it was. Jeanette might realise that this was an interrogation and not a debriefing.

Sandy listed in her head all the people that knew she was still alive. There was David, obviously, and the chiefs of the three security/intelligence services, the two officers from Protection Branch who had guarded her in London and the other two in Ellesmere Port. They may or may not have guessed her real identity. Then there was Maggie and Adrian who had rescued her from the pub in Wallasey and taken her to the safe house in Liverpool. Sandy wondered if they believed that it was her body that had been found in the Mersey, a couple of days after she had been taken away, or if they had worked out that it was all a sham. Any one of those people could have informed this Crane person – whoever he or she was.

'How does Crane know Sandy's alive?' asked Sandy.

'He knows. He just knows.' She sounded as if she were about to fall asleep and the doctor increased the caffeine level in the cocktail of drugs.

Sandy realised that she had reached a dead end and tried an approach from a more oblique angle.

'How long were you in place at Brightin' and Blount's?'

'Six weeks, I think. Yes about six weeks.'

'Okay, good. How'd they get you in?'

'They arranged for the practice secretary to have an accident.'

'Yeah? What sort of accident?'

'Hit and run.'

'Blimey! Is she alright?'

'She was in hospital for weeks! They nearly killed the poor woman.'

'Well, they must've thought it was worf the effort to get you in, eh!' Sandy said, continuing to emphasise Caroline's diction. However, it seemed that Jeanette had stopped listening.

'Stroke my hair, Caroline,' she pleaded, 'like you used to.'

Sandy obliged. 'There you go.' *There you go* – such a typical Caroline phrase. Sandy shook her head to drive away a sudden rush of emotion. 'There. That's nice, init?'

'Mmmm,' Jeanette replied contentedly, but there was still a catch in her voice, like a child recently calmed after crying.

'How did you get the job?'

'What job?'

'The job at Brightin' and Blount,' Sandy prompted, 'the place where Samantha McNamara works.'

'I made contact with Eddie Brighting, the senior partner.'

'Where and when?'

'What?'

Oh for God's sake!

'Tell me about meeting Eddie Brighting.'

'He goes to a wine bar in the city centre after work every night before catching his train home. I made contact about a week after Curlew's disappearance. I let him buy me a drink and chat me up. Told him I was a legal secretary looking for a job. He said he'd ask around some of his contacts for me. I met him there several times, so when the position in his own firm became unexpectedly available...'

'Did you 'ave to screw 'im?' Sandy put a little giggle in her voice as she asked the question, the way Caroline would have. She was holding Jeanette close, with one arm around her shoulders and her cheek on Jeanette's head. Every so often, she stroked Jeanette's cheek, neck or hair; gentle caresses, like those of a lover, which Caroline and Jeanette had been, back in the spring, in Sarajevo.

'No,' Jeanette replied. '...Not necessary... just flirting with him was enough.'

Sandy sniggered, something else Caroline might have done. 'Prob'ly just as well. You prob'ly would've killed the poor old sod! Still, 'e would've died 'appy, wouldn't 'e?'

Jeanette did not respond.

'Have you found any evidence yet that Sandy's made contact with her sister?'

'No,' Jeanette replied. 'They said to stay in place for a few more weeks. They said if she hadn't made contact after three

months, she probably never would. I got really close to Sam,'
Jeanette continued. 'I went to her house a number of times.
There was never any hint that her sister had been in touch.
Sam firmly believes that her sister shot her parents and then
killed herself.'

'How did you begin the friendship with 'er?'

'We knew she and her husband were regular church-goers.
After making contact with Brighting I arranged to bump into
Sam and Stephen at the church.'

'Stephen? Is that Sam's 'usband?' Sandy asked to keep the
flow of words going.

'Yes. He was a bit standoffish at first. He was so
possessive and controlling... I think he resented me taking
Sam's attention away from himself. So I turned on the charm
a bit; paid him some attention; flattered him; flirted with him
a bit. He loved it!'

'Did 'e?'

'God, he's a real creep. He makes my skin crawl.'

'Why, what did he do?' So fascinated was Sandy by this
part of the story that he forgot to use Caroline's voice. David
nudged her with his elbow as if to say, *What are you playing
at? Don't dwell on this!*

Regardless, Jeanette was already answering.

'He's just creepy. He's the sort that undresses you with his
eyes, "accidentally" touches you and pretends he hasn't
noticed. He's sly . . .' she shuddered, '– nasty. I like Sam. I
feel sorry for her having to spend her life with a creep like
him.'

Sandy grimaced. Jeanette had summed up all her own
feelings about Stephen it that one word – *Creep*. It was time
to move on.

'She's nice, Sam,' unbidden, Jeanette continued to ramble. 'I really like her. I hope nothing nasty happens to her.'

'Why would something nasty happen to Sam?'

'It's all this – this cloak and dagger stuff. They're so scared of anyone finding out about Clermont they'll do anything to keep it secret.'

Clermont? Sandy glanced at David but he just shrugged. 'What about Clermont, Nettie?'

'They can't let people find out.'

'Find out what?'

'Can't talk about Clermont,' Jeanette muttered, shaking her head.

'You can tell me, though, can't ya?'

'No!' Jeanette shouted, suddenly agitated. 'I can't talk about it. Shut up! Don't ask questions about . . .'

'Okay, Nettie, luv,' Sandy said, stoking Jeanette's hair. 'Don't worry. We'll forget all about Clermont.'

'Forget about Clermont,' Jeanette repeated dreamily.

'You alright, darlin'?'

Jeanette gave out a light snore.

David made a signal to the doctor and he added a little more caffeine to the mix. Jeanette's eyes opened and she groaned.

'What? What?'

'Nettie, what were you supposed to do if Sandy turned up?' Sandy asked as soon as Jeanette regained consciousness.

'Who? What?'

'Nettie, listen to me. It's Caroline.'

'Caroline?' The voice was soft, dreamy. 'Can't be you. You're dead.'

'Nettie, darlin', it's me. I'm not dead; I'm 'ere, right 'ere.' Sandy stroked Jeanette's hair again. It seemed to calm her.

'They said you were dead. I was so upset. Where've you been?'

'I 'ad to 'ide out for a while, that's all, but I'm back now, ain't I? Tell me what you're supposed to do if Sandy turns up.'

'We have to take her to Crane,' Jeanette answered without hesitation.

'Why?'

'What?'

'Why does Crane want Sandy picked up?'

'Because of Jane Badell.'

Sandy shivered as if someone had just walked over her grave. 'I don't understand. What about Jane and Sandy?'

'Jane Badell was being watched. She met Curlew for afternoon tea at Claridges. They were together for nearly two hours.'

'Why was Caesar keeping watch on Jane?'

'Not Caesar. It was Crane's people.'

So Crane is not a Caesar codename!

'Okay, Nettie. Why was Crane having Jane watched?'

'They discovered that she was planning to go public about Dzenita's place.'

The slave brothel! Jane should have known how damaging that would have been to the UN and the governments of the countries supplying troops to the peacekeeping force. Sandy had been warned off discussing it even with her own colleagues. To threaten or attempt to go public with it was asking for trouble.

'Did Crane have Jane killed to stop 'er talkin' about Dzenita's?'

'Don't know Crane,' Jeanette said contradicting her earlier references. Sandy assumed it was due to the confusion in her mind caused by the drugs.

'Nettie!' Sandy snapped harshly. 'Tell me more about Jane Badell.'

'The surveillance team couldn't hear what they were talking about,' Jeanette continued as if she had not heard. 'When Crane found out about the meeting he wanted them both picked up. He wants to know what they talked about, but, for some reason, they killed Jane, then Curlew escaped when we went to pick her up.'

Sandy thought she had misheard. 'What? What did you say?'

'One team was sent to get Jane in London and our team was sent to pick up Curlew at her parents' house. Bittern told us Eagle wanted her questioned about the meeting with Jane, but Crane wanted to interrogate her first. She was supposed to be in the house alone . . .' Jeanette's voice faded.

'I'm confused, Nettie. Are you saying it was a Caesar team that went to Sandy's house?'

'Bittern was the leader. He chose Caesar people who also work for Crane.'

Sandy suddenly felt faint and she clutched David's arm for support. If what Jeanette had just revealed was true, then the people that murdered her parents, that night, were not Serb extremists or even a CIA hit team, but her own colleagues, at least one of whom, Jeanette, was a close friend. She felt David's fingers grip her forearm in a gesture of support, and she made herself ask the next question.

'Jeanette, are you saying you were there that night m... that Sandy's parents were killed?' Sandy was so shocked that, for the second time, she had failed to maintain Caroline's accent. She hoped that Jeanette, in her drugged state, would not notice. She need not have worried.

'It all started to go wrong when her father opened the door. Then Curlew killed Jackdaw and took his gun. Her parents were killed in the crossfire. Bittern reported that she had shot them deliberately, but that was just to cover himself. He should never have just burst in like that.'

'Curlew barricaded herself in her bedroom,' Jeanette continued, 'and Bittern called for back-up. He told me to cover the back of the house in case she tried to escape that way. It was a big garden with lots of shrubs in the borders and dotted around the lawn. I hid in the shadows. I could hear shots from inside and lots of crashing and banging.'

Jeanette started to cry. 'I could have shot her,' she said through her tears. 'I could have killed her.' She began to hyperventilate and, despite her own emotional turmoil, Sandy gently stroked Jeanette's cheek, all the time cooing reassuringly. After a few seconds, Jeanette calmed and began to speak again, her voice dreamy, as if she were about to fall asleep.

'Then, suddenly, she was hanging out of the window, just hanging there for a second or two. Then she dropped to the ground. I could have killed her,' Jeanette added more aggressively, then concluded lamely, 'but I didn't.'

'What stopped you?' Sandy made Caroline sound puzzled.

'I told Bittern that my gun jammed, but that was a lie. I just couldn't pull the trigger.'

'Why not, Nettie? Why didn't you shoot 'er?'

'Because it was Sandy!' This was the first time since the interview started that Jeanette had used Sandy's name. 'I couldn't kill her any more than I could kill you!'

Sandy hugged Jeanette closer, fighting both to control her emotions and to remain in character.

'Bittern?' Sandy repeated the leader's codename only because she could not think of anything else to say.

'Yes,' Jeanette replied. 'Do you remember? He was one of the firearms instructors at Park House. He was hit in the hand later when Sandy was cornered in her room. She shot at him through the door.'

Sandy remembered the man. He was Martin Gresham, an ex-Royal Marine, slightly taller than Sandy, with a wiry build and floppy fair hair. She remembered him as a petulant and egotistical bully who seemed to take pleasure in demeaning and humiliating the trainees – particularly the females, should they put a foot wrong during his training sessions. He had some effeminate mannerisms, leaving some to conclude that he was gay, although no one knew for sure either way. Caroline had tried to seduce him with the declared intention of trying to make him a nicer person. He had been one of her few failures.

'How many Caesar people work for Crane?'

'I don't know for sure. I only knew about Kestrel before that night.'

Sandy pursed her lips. 'Kestrel?' She did not remember coming across anyone with that codename before.

'Kestrel's the one who contacted me when I got back from Sarajevo.'

'He recruited you?'

'Not really.'

'What then?'

'What?'

'Why did Kestrel contact you when you got back from Sarajevo?'

'Rod told me someone would contact me.'

'Who's Rod?'

'Roddy Ekerich.'

'Ekerich? Do you mean the American journalist in Sarajevo?' Sandy remembered the man – average height, heavy build, black hair and a deep, booming voice. When he spoke in his nasal New York accent, he could be heard from the other side of the dining hall.

'Yes. Grebe ordered me to work with him.'

'When?'

(Silence)

'Nettie, when did Grebe order you to hook Ekerich?'

Jeanette appeared to trying to go to sleep. Her voice was once more dreamy and her speech slurred, as if she were drunk. 'What? No, not hook. Grebe made me liaison officer. Ekerich is CIA. It was in April, soon after the siege started. It was all right at first, but later he started pestering me for sex. I told Grebe. He told me to, and report pillow talk.'

'Charmin'!' This was an astonishing revelation. There had been no hint of this assignment when they were together in Sarajevo. 'What were you and Ekerich working on?'

'Roddy told Grebe that there was a mole in our team passing information to the Serb army and they wanted to catch whoever it was.'

Sandy was shocked. It became obvious on the road to Žepa that someone had betrayed the mission, but this suggested the existence of the traitor was known while they were still in Sarajevo.

'A mole in our team? One of us, you mean?'

'That's what Roddy told Grebe, yes.'

'So what are you saying? You spied on the rest of the team? Spied on us?'

'Yes, I suppose so. I never thought it was you, Caro.'

'So did you find out who was the mole, if there even was one?'

'Yes, I did.'

Sandy went cold. 'Who was it?'

'I didn't find out until after you had been sent out of the city. It was Roddy himself. He was in contact with someone called Marko . . .'

'What sort of information did Roddy pass to Marko?'

There was a protracted silence and then Jeanette started sobbing.

'Nettie? What's up, darlin'?'

Jeanette began to shake her head from side to side, wailing like a soul in torment. The words that she spoke were barely intelligible. 'I didn't know, Caro, I promise I didn't know...'

'Didn't know what, Nettie? Tell me darlin'.'

'He told him about you,' Jeanette wailed. 'The team sent to get Szopienice.'

'Who told who?'

'Roddy warned Marko about the team sent to get Szopienice,' Jeanette sobbed. 'It was Roddy that betrayed the team – but it was my fault for telling him about the obbo on Dzenita's bar. Emira's Englishman was really a Yank. It was Roddy! He was running it. That's why he had to get rid of you. I didn't know! I swear I didn't know. Oh, please believe me. Please forgive me...'

'Oh shit!' Sandy cursed. So that was how Szopienice knew they were coming, but was Ekerich working alone? 'Did you report this to Grebe?'

'No.'

'Why not?'

Silence

'Nettie, why didn't you tell Grebe what Ekerich was doing?'

'He took me there, one day – to Dzenita's. He made me look at the girls lying chained to the beds waiting for their next customer. He told me if I ever betrayed him he'd put me in there until I was used up, then he'd kill me,' Jeanette sobbed. 'I believed him, Caroline! I really believed he would do it and I was so frightened!'

Sandy struggled to control her emotions. 'Why did Grebe keep you behind when the rest of us went to find Szopienice?'

'Roddy told Grebe to hold me back. He wanted to keep me in Sarajevo. I didn't know they planned to kill you all, to make you disappear. Not till afterwards.'

Sandy's mind reeled at Jeanette's words and for a second time David gripped her arm to support her. Jeanette continued babbling through her sobs.

'Not until it was too late.'

Sandy fought back a wave of nausea. 'Nettie, was Grebe involved as well? Did Grebe know what was going on?'

Jeanette continued to sob and wail but did not answer.

'Nettie!' Sandy was shouting now. David laid a hand on her arm to restrain her. 'Did Grebe know what was going on?'

The doctor looked up disapprovingly. 'You have to stop this aggressive questioning. Her heart rate's going through the roof!'

Suddenly, Jeanette stiffened as if she had received an electric shock. Sandy was worried that she may have had a seizure.

'Oh, for Christ's sake!' Jeanette sounded exasperated. Had she suddenly realised she had been duped?'

'What's up?' Sandy asked, wondering what had prompted the sudden exclamation.

'Some idiot's crashed into the back of me,' Jeanette said indignantly; then she passed out.

Sandy looked up at the doctor who shook his head.

'She's had enough. Her heart's racing. Her blood pressure's sky high. I'll have to call a halt now. I'm Sorry.'

Leaving the sleeping Jeanette snoring softly, Sandy walked away from the bed and pulled off the black wig. David followed her until she reached one wall of the small interview room and had to stop. She had her back to him, her forehead resting on the wall. He touched her shoulder to get her attention and she whirled round, eyes blazing and stared at him for several seconds. For a moment David thought she was about to attack him physically, but she broke down in tears, her body wracked with sobs.

'Hold me,' she begged. 'Please just hold me.'

David folded his arms around her. 'I love you, Sandy,' he murmured, without realising that he had spoken. 'I love you more than anything in this world.'

Chapter 33

'She's had enough. Her heart's racing; her blood pressure's sky high. I'll have to call a halt now. I'm Sorry.'

David leaned forward and switched off the recorder so that Amanda would not hear the exchange between himself and Sandy that followed the termination of the interview.

'Just after midnight yesterday,' David said, 'the Manchester people ran her car into a lamppost and bashed her head on the steering wheel. Then they called an ambulance. Prior to that she had been given a long-lasting sedative and would have remained unconscious for several hours.'

'The doctor assured us that she would have no recollection at all of the interview session,' Sandy added.

'A team of A4 officers maintained surveillance on her while she was in hospital,' David continued, 'and late yesterday afternoon, someone came to collect her. They followed them all the way from the hospital to a house in Tadworth, Surrey, arriving late last night.'

Sandy cleared her throat to get Amanda's attention. 'It's clear from what Jeanette said that it wasn't a Serb hit-squad that attacked my house and killed my parents, but a team of Caesar operatives under orders from this Crane character.' Sandy noticed how Amanda's eyes flickered away briefly while she was speaking. She was concealing something.

God! She knew already!

On the day that David had taken Sandy from this very room to the Director General's office, Amanda had said that Serb agents were responsible for the murder of her parents and Jane Badell. Now it looked as if she had known the truth all along and had conspired with Eagle to cover it up. Amanda had lied and Sandy bristled with rage and indignation.

'Her version of events certainly contradicts what Eagle told C and me that same night,' said Amanda.

'He may have simply told you what had been reported to him,' David suggested.

'Or he was party to the lie and decided to cover up a bungled operation,' Sandy countered, adding coldly, 'as, it seems, did you, Amanda.'

David started at Sandy's accusation and the DG glared at her for several seconds before her expression softened.

'Yes, Sandy, Amanda admitted, using the younger woman's nickname for the very first time, 'I was party to the cover-up. We had no idea how you would have reacted to the truth. We couldn't take the risk that you might jeopardise an ongoing operation.'

'What ongoing operation?'

'Eagle didn't say, but I suspect it's something to do with Crane and whoever or whatever Clermont is?'

'I have a theory about Clermont,' said Sandy, and then went on to summarise her conversation with her sister about the Crusades. 'I think they are supporting the Serb nationalists in their ethnic cleansing of Muslims,' she concluded.

'It's rather a tenuous connection,' replied Amanda.

'Maybe,' said David, supporting Sandy, 'but, in the absence of any other ideas, it's worth keeping in mind.'

'Why would someone link an operation to carry out ethnic cleansing in Bosnia with the Crusades?' Amanda suggested. 'The only connection I can see is the Muslim one, but in

Bosnia, the Serb nationalists are also driving out Croats and all other non-Serbs.'

'That's true,' replied Sandy, 'but the majority of non-Serbs in eastern Bosnia are Muslims, and the atrocities carried out against them are far more extreme than against other groups. Forced migrations are one thing, but the Muslims are being routinely massacred or sent to concentration camps and starved. It's nothing short of Genocide.'

'Maybe,' Amanda mused, 'but if you were going to link it to a historical event why not a Bosnian one? There must be any number of possibilities from past conflicts, such as with the Turks.'

'Clermont isn't a Bosnian operation, or even a Serb one,' Sandy insisted. 'It's something to do with the American, Ekerich,' Sandy reminded them, 'who according to Jeanette is CIA.'

Amanda looked at David 'What do you make of the claim that he is colluding with someone outside the city?'

'Marko,' added Sandy, irked that the DG appeared to be excluding her from the question. Perhaps Amanda thought her responses were too emotional, her judgement clouded.

'He could have been passing information to the Serb army via Marko,' opined David. 'Equally, Marko could be a CIA agent inside the Serb camp. We just don't know.'

'Oh come on, David,' Sandy contradicted him. 'Jeanette clearly said Ekerich betrayed Cevapi.'

'That could be just her interpretation,' replied David evenly.

'Well, how do you explain him threatening to prostitute Jeanette if she crossed him?'

'That doesn't prove he was operating against your team,' David argued. 'If he really was the brains behind the brothel, that in itself would be enough for him to want to ensure Jeanette's silence.'

'Okay,' said Amanda. 'So at best he arranged for your team to be sent out of Sarajevo for a while to avoid you kicking up a fuss about the brothel, and at worst, he tried to arrange for your permanent disappearance. Whichever is correct, how does it relate to what's going on now?'

'I think they're still mopping up anyone who knew about the brothel,' said Sandy.

'Jeanette mentioned Ekerich only in context with Sarajevo,' David noted. 'Now we seem to be dealing with Crane.'

'Do we know if Ekerich is still in Sarajevo?' Amanda asked.

'No,' Sandy and David replied in chorus.

'Well, let's find out,' Amanda said, looking at David. He nodded and she went on, 'Do we know who owns the house in Tadworth?'

'Not yet,' David replied. 'We're still waiting to find out from Land Registry and the local council.'

'Couldn't you have got someone out of bed?'

'Possibly, but I wanted to keep a low profile. Keep it run-of-the-mill. Otherwise someone might leak something to the press.'

Amanda nodded tiredly. 'Good thinking. Do we have people watching the house?'

'Yes, but it's difficult. It's a large house, standing in its own grounds in a country lane. There are a few similar sized houses nearby and little passing traffic.' David explained.

'We've had a specialist electronics team conduct an aerial survey of the grounds and they've found that the place is bristling with infra-red movement detectors and CCTV. Also, any vehicle parked in the lane for any length of time would immediately be under suspicion.'

'So what are we doing?'

'We placed a concealed O.P. in woodland overlooking the front gates, but that can't stay in place in daylight, because it looks like the sort of place that people walk their dogs and ride horses. Capitalising on that point, we have four people taking turns to walk two dogs in the area. We also have drive-bys in a selection of vehicles. Between the lot of them, we should be able to monitor comings and goings until we can get something more sophisticated set up.'

That subject exhausted, Amanda turned to Sandy. 'What was all that about your meeting with Jane Badell?'

Sandy frowned and looked the DG in the eye. 'I came across her file when I was working in Admin Branch in Liverpool. It had her address. I wrote to her and we arranged to meet. She didn't know I had survived and returned from Bosnia until she got my letter.'

'Oh, Sandra,' Amanda said, sitting back in her chair and covering her eyes with her hand as if to blot out the image. 'That is an unacceptable breach of procedure. You should know better than to use Service resources for your personal use.'

'Yes, I'm sorry,' Sandy replied, full of remorse. 'None of this would have happened if I hadn't contacted her.'

'Possibly,' said David, 'but we don't really know. They still might have killed Badell.'

'But they probably would not have come after me,' Sandy said miserably, 'and my parents would still be....' The sentence was choked off as she fought back the tears.

'So you met in Claridges,' Amanda prompted. 'Why there?'

Sandy had to swallow hard to clear the lump in her throat before she could answer. 'Jane chose the venue.'

'You were together for two hours,' Amanda said, remembering what she had heard on the recording. What did you discuss?'

'Nothing much,' Sandy replied, wiping a stray tear from her eye. 'We were both just so pleased to see each other. We had become quite close during the mission. Everyone in the team loved her. She was as tough as a boot, but fussed over us like a mother hen. I told her what happened to Caroline and me after we were separated, and she told me what happened to her and the others.'

Sandy sat for a moment staring silently at her hands, loosely clasped on the table in front of her. David wanted to put his arms around her and comfort her, but with the Director General in the room that was not possible. To cover his feelings he asked, 'What else did you talk about with Badell?'

Sandy shook herself out of her morose state and answered with her voice once more clear and level.

'We talked about Sir Vivian Webber, the previous head of MI6. He had died of a heart attack a couple of weeks before. They were old friends and she was very upset about his death. Upset and angry.'

'Why angry?' asked Amanda.

'She had known him for many years. He never suffered from a heart condition, high blood pressure, anything like that, she said. She was convinced that he had been murdered.'

'Murdered? By whom?'

'She wouldn't say. She refused to discuss it any further and changed the subject.'

'Anything else?'

Sandy shrugged. 'I suppose we talked about the future. She said she was planning to make a documentary about the impotence of the UN Protection Force in Sarajevo. She said she would be arguing in favour of direct intervention, such as air strikes on Serb positions in the hills.'

'That wouldn't explain the need to assassinate her,' Amanda mused.'

'No,' David agreed, 'but Jeanette said they thought she was going to expose the brothel and, presumably, who was responsible for setting it up.'

'It wasn't just a brothel,' Sandy reminded them. 'These were young girls abducted from the streets and from orphanages and forced to work as prostitutes, and some of those abusing them were UN soldiers. They also had very young kids in there to satisfy the perversions of a paedophile ring. That's the big secret that I was ordered never to disclose because of the damage it would do to the reputation of the UN.'

'And if Jane was threatening to do so...' David began.

'It would be reason enough to silence her,' Amanda concluded.

'As we parted,' Sandy continued, 'Jane told me we were both in danger because of what we knew and we needed to be careful. She said I should put the whole Bosnian episode out of my mind and never discuss it with anyone. She also said if anything was to happen to her, I should go to ground and keep my head down.'

'She said that?' Amanda asked, surprised. 'So she knew she was in danger. Did she say what was likely to happen to her or why?'

'No. She wouldn't discuss it any further. She said I was to trust no one, that I should trust only my own instincts.'

'Did you ask her what she meant by that?'

'Yes, but she refused to elaborate further.'

'Did she make any mention of Clermont?' Amanda asked.

'No,' Sandy shook her head. 'No, she never mentioned that.'

Amanda folded her arms and leaned back in the chair. 'We are no closer to knowing who Crane is or whether Eagle knows about Clermont than when we started this conversation. I have to go and see Eagle, and then the Home Secretary. Sandy, I want you to go home, forget about all this and look after yourself and your baby.'

Sandy leapt to her feet. 'I can't do that, Amanda! I've been involved with this since the beginning. Please don't cut me off now.'

Amanda looked at her sympathetically. 'You've done your bit. Now you need to leave it to others to finish off. You're in no condition...'

'I'm pregnant, not an invalid!' Sandy objected loudly. 'I've got another five months to go before the baby's due. I can help the operation.' She saw Amanda start to shake her head and added, 'You wouldn't know anything about this if it wasn't for me!'

'Yes, and for that I am grateful, despite your disobedience of my orders, but can't you see you're too close to this? It's too personal.'

'Of course it's bloody personal, Amanda! They killed my parents and they've gone after my sister. Let me help bring them down.'

'Look,' said Amanda, 'your desire for vengeance is understandable, but I'm ordering you to stand down on this one. David, I want you to arrange Sandy's computer skills training to start A-S-A-P. It will give her something to occupy her mind and prepare her for her assignments after maternity leave. Sandy,' she spoke over Sandy's protest, 'I promise we will keep you informed of progress at every stage.'

Sandy's shoulders slumped. She knew she had to accept defeat. 'What about my sister and her husband?'

'What about them?'

'Well, while all this is going on, won't they still be in danger?'

'I think Sandy's right,' David said. 'Until we clear this mess up, they could still try to use them to get at Sandy.'

'Yes, I see what you mean. That girl, er, Lapwing seemed convinced that Sandy is still alive.'

'Because, quote, *Crane knows,* unquote,' Sandy added. 'How does he know?'

'Eagle,' David hypothesised. 'He has to be connected to Crane. There's no other explanation.'

'None that I want to consider,' said Amanda obliquely, afraid that there might be a mole in her own organisation. Suddenly, she snapped her fingers. 'Oh, something occurred to me regarding Lapwing tailing your sister.'

David and Sandy looked at her quizzically.

'How did they know where to find you?'

'What do you mean?' Sandy asked and then the answer struck her like a thunderbolt. Neither she nor David had considered how Jeanette had come to be outside the Waterloo Inn. 'Oh, my God! They must have planted a tracker on Sam.' Sandy looked at David. She could see in his eyes that he had reached the same conclusion.

'Get onto Manchester,' Amanda said briskly to David. 'Tell them to get everyone out of that safe house immediately.'

Chapter 34

'There,' said Radford. 'That's the one.'

Radford and Duncan remained motionless as a Ford Fiesta pulled out of the cul-de-sac and drove past where they waited. They had sat in the car all night, not showing a light, sitting low in the seats, the tinted windows obscuring them from the view of passersby. Not that there were many of those around on a cold, wet November night. Fortunately for Radford and Duncan, they had had the foresight to bring along a flask of coffee, and an empty four-pint, screw-top milk carton for when the coffee worked its way through. Duncan was using the carton when Radford spoke. He finished hurriedly and picked up the radio microphone.

'Shona? Zulu. Over.'

'Shona receiving. Go ahead, Zulu.'

'White Fiesta heading south on Trojan Way. Index: Delta One-One-Two-Kilo-Yankee-Uniform.'

'Shona. Received. Nothing yet. Wait... Okay, have eyeball. Out.'

Radford picked up the mobile phone and dialled a number. 'Registration check,' he said when they picked up, then read out the Fiesta's registration number. He waited a few minutes before the answer came back. 'Who else lives at that address?' He asked. It took another five minutes before he received a reply. Then he turned to Duncan.

'The car belongs to a Mr Matthew Clark.'

'Transvestite, is he?' Duncan quipped.

'Lives with a Miss Michelle Connor . . .'

'Which is probably who's driving the car.'

'Right. Let's get Dave and Andy to take over here while we go and have a word with Miss Connor.'

'Okay,' Duncan agreed and spoke into the microphone again. 'Masai? Zulu. Over.'

'Masai receiving.'

'Masai, make way to OP now, over.'

'Masai received, over.'

'Zulu. Out!'

Minutes later Duncan saw the other team pass by and pull into the kerb thirty yards ahead. Then he pulled out and turned the car to follow the Fiesta.

'Shona? Zulu. Where is she now? Over.'

'Shona. Just pulling up outside the Co-op on Loxdale Drive.'

'Zulu received. Out.'

Twenty-five minutes later, Michelle Connor, bottle-blonde hair tied up in a scruffy topknot and wearing faded blue denim jeans and a GAP sweatshirt, came out of the Co-op grocery shop and began to load the bags into the boot. She was startled when a male voice spoke from close beside her.

'Miss Connor? Michelle Connor?'

She looked up to see a man of average height, bald, but for a fringe of brown hair around his temples and the back of his head. He was wearing a beige trench coat, open to reveal a shabby grey two-piece suit. He wore a white shirt and blue tie, but the tie was loose and the top button of the shirt undone.

'Yeah, that's me,' Michelle replied. 'Who are you?' It was then she noticed another man hovering close by. He had short black hair, wore a brown leather jacket, tan slacks and a shirt and tie. Her heart sank. Only the "Bizzies" dress like that. 'What do you want?'

'I'm Detective Sergeant Mitchell,' Radford said, flashing an ID, 'and that is DC Wilkins.'

'What do you want with me?' Michelle asked, hoping they would not ask to see evidence that she was insured to drive her boyfriend's car.

'There's a little matter you could help us with, if you wouldn't mind?'

***

'What's happening next door?' asked Petra.

Anthony went to the window, and, standing to one side, looked through the heavy net curtains. The van that had pulled up across the driveway of the house next door, had a roof rack, fixed to which was a long tube.

'Looks like a plumber,' replied Anthony. 'Two men with toolkits going into the house.'

'Is there a name or number on the van?'

'Yeah; John McInnis Plumbing and Heating. Gives a local phone number.'

'Shall we give the number a call?'

'Why?'

'See if they really are plumbers.'

Anthony turned to Petra and raised an eyebrow. 'Aren't you being a little over-cautious?'

Petra had been worried ever since, against her better judgement, they had allowed Samantha to call her husband. 'Can't be too careful,' she said, picking up the phone. 'Call out the number.' She dialled as Anthony repeated the number and then listened for a few seconds. 'Answerphone,' she said, 'John McInnis Plumbing. All right clever-clogs,' she smiled at Anthony. 'Don't say, "I told you so".'

***

'What do you know about the people next door at number twenty-six?' Jerry Radford, alias Detective Sergeant Mitchell asked. The bogus detective was sitting in the living room drinking tea while rest of the team were setting up equipment in the couple's bedroom at the front of the house.

Michelle deferred to her boyfriend, Matt.

Matt shrugged. 'Not a lot. The place seems empty most of the time. A gardener comes every two or three weeks to cut the grass and pull a few weeds. Then every so often people come and stay there for a few days or a week or two. It's always different people.'

'We think it's owned by a company and they put employees up there, temporary, like,' Michelle added.

Sitting on an upright chair, next to the mahogany dining table, Radford nodded and stroked his chin. 'We think it's being used as a safe house by the IRA.' He watched the effect his words had on Matt and his girlfriend. Michelle's mouth dropped and Matt sat bolt upright on the sofa, where, until that moment, he had been slouching.

'You what?' said Matt. 'Look, we don't want to get involved with nothin' like that…'

'They'd come after us, if they knew we 'elped you,' Michelle screeched.

Radford held his hands up placatingly. 'Don't worry. This is part of a much bigger operation. They'll never know we were even here.'

'No,' Matt said. 'I don't want nothin' to do with this.'

'You never said anythin' about terrorists when you asked for our help,' Michelle added.

'Look,' said Radford assertively, 'we're here now and we're going through with it. We're going to keep number twenty-six under surveillance until we've identified all the players and figured out what they're up to.'

'And what about us, in the meantime?' demanded Michelle tearfully. 'That's our bedroom!'

'You'll have to use the back room until we've finished.'

Matt stood up and approached Radford menacingly. 'Now look, you,' he shouted, stabbing the air with his finger, a foot in front of Radford's face. 'You take your men and your stuff and get out of my 'ouse, now!'

Radford remained seated and looked unconcerned. 'Been inside, Matt?' he asked, staring the angry man in the eye.

'What? No. What's that got to do wi' anythin'?' Matt blustered

'Burglary wasn't it?' said Radford, recalling the information that a trawl of the Police National Computer had thrown up about Matt and his girlfriend. 'And there was that little misunderstanding about the cheap fags and booze you tried to sell to pubs and *offies* . . .'

'I never done that,' Matt protested, taking a step back toward the safety of the sofa. 'I wasn't never charged over that.'

'No, of course you weren't,' Radford smiled, 'but we both know you were at it, don't we?'

'Look,' Michelle chipped in, 'what's this gotta do with anythin' anyway?'

'Oh,' said Radford, 'and there was Michelle's little misunderstanding about a jacket she "forgot"' – he used the first and second fingers of each hand to simulate quotation marks – 'to pay for in C and A.' Michelle's mouth clamped shut. 'What would we find if we had a good look around this place, eh? Got receipts for the telly and the stereo, have you? Handling stolen goods is treated very severely by the courts you know.' He smiled at Michelle and added, 'as is driving without insurance.' It was a hunch, based on her body language when they approached her outside the Co-op, but he saw it hit the mark.

'This ain't fair!' Michelle said and burst into tears.'

'I'll tell you what's fair,' Radford said leaning forward in his chair. 'We're going to pay you fifty quid a day to let us use the front bedroom. No one's ever going to know we were here. When we catch the bastards, it will be miles away from here when they're in the act of doing whatever it is they're planning, alright?' Radford watched Matt and Michelle glance at each other. The talk of money seemed to overcome their resistance. Money and the implied threat that their possessions might come under very close scrutiny if they failed to co-operate.

Chapter 35

'They're not in Yellow Pages,' Petra said, putting the directory down on the table. She had a very bad feeling about the situation now.

'What? Who's not?' Anthony asked, looking up from the newspaper.

'John McInnis. He's not here. Not under Plumbers or Central Heating Engineers.'

'Bloody hell, Pet! Are you still going on about that van?'

Petra hated being called Pet, especially in the current circumstances where she was in disagreement with her older male colleague. It made her feel as if he were talking down to her.

'It's Petra! And, yes, I think it's really suspicious. We should call back up.'

'What's going on?' Samantha asked. She had been making coffee for the three of them and had heard the argumentative tones. She stood in the doorway, a tea towel in her hand.

'Petra's worried about the van that turned up next door ten minutes ago.'

'I'm just being cautious. It's probably nothing, but it's our job to check these things out.' She glanced sideways at Anthony. 'Isn't that right, Anthony?'

'Alright, alright. You win,' Anthony conceded. 'We'll call it in. Just to be on the safe side.'

***

'I want you to wait before calling Manchester.'

David and Sandy were in David's office on the Fourth Floor of the Gower Street building. He had the telephone receiver in his hand; the other hovered over the keypad. He looked at her incredulously.

'What are you talking about?'

Sandy looked around the room. She had not seen David's office before. In fact, the interrogation cell, Amanda's office and the corridors and lift in-between constituted her entire knowledge of the building. David's office was a smaller version of Amanda's. The blue carpet was identical, as were the two upright visitors' chairs, as was the wooden freestanding coat rack by a window that looked out, not over Euston Square like Amanda's, but a car park at the back of the building. Thereafter, everything was scaled down. A smaller desk, grey steel instead of oak, one two-seat sofa instead of two, but covered in the same red fabric, and no picture of the Queen. In the latter's place hung a reproduction of Lady Elizabeth Butler's famous painting of the charge of the Scot's Greys at the Battle of Waterloo. Sandy's father had owned an identical one, which had hung in his study at home. Not for the first time she was struck by the many similarities between David and her father.

'If you get them out of that house now, we'll miss the one chance we have to catch Crane.'

'What do you mean? What chance?' He put the receiver back in its cradle.

Sandy started to explain the plan that was forming in her head.

'No! No bloody way,' David responded angrily before she had finished.

Sandy looked dejected and walked across to the window. David felt his anger diminish.

'Look,' he said, 'it's just too dangerous.'

Sandy turned to face him. Her moist blue eyes bored into him.

'You really care about me, don't you?'

David's expression and tone softened even more.

'Yes, you know I do.'

'Then help me do this. I've got no chance of success if you don't help me, but if you do...'

'No, I won't let you put yourself at risk like that.'

The moist blue eyes hardened to steel.

'Please, David!'

'No. And that's my final word on the subject.' He turned back to his desk and reached for the phone once more.

'Damn it, David! I need to do this!' She reached out and grabbed his shoulder and David turned to face her, his body inches from hers.

'And I can't allow you to!'

'I'm sorry, David,' She said and glanced to her left.

David's eyes followed Sandy's. 'There's no need to be sor....' David halted in mid-sentence and gasped in surprise as Sandy brought her knee up into his groin. His knees bent and he doubled at the waist. Sandy made a fist with her left hand and slammed it sideways in a hammer blow to David's temple. It was like being hit with a rubber cosh. He dropped like a stone onto the carpet. Swiftly, Sandy removed David's red silk tie and used it to bind his hands behind his back. Then she slid the leather belt from his trousers and wrapped it around his ankles twice before buckling it tightly. She did not want him to choke on his own vomit so she turned him to lie on his front with his head to one side. This was the nearest she could get to the recovery position under the circumstances. For the same reason, she resisted the urge to gag him. Unplugging the phone from the socket in the wall, she locked it inside one of the drawers in David's desk and put the key into her jeans pocket. She scribbled a quick note and left it on the carpet next to David's nose. Then she took his keys and the clunky mobile phone from his pocket and left the office, locking the door behind her. Unchallenged she rode the lift down to the lobby and left the building.

***

David Richardson had regained consciousness before Sandy had left the building. His head was pounding and his testicles felt as if they had been relocated six inches higher than they should be. The first thing he saw as his vision cleared was the note that Sandy had left on the floor right under his nose, and he read it with mounting despair.

Dear Merlin,

I'm so sorry for what I had to do to you. I hope you can understand and forgive me. I have to see this plan through whether you help me or not. If you don't help me I may die, but at least then they'll leave Sam alone. I told you what I need. Please, please call Tech Branch at Manchester and tell them to meet me at the safe house.

Extract'n of Sam & the others can happen straight after I leave. Attention will be on me by then anyway.

Love, Morgan

PS I've pinched your mobile. I'll switch it on when the op is underway but not before then cos you'd call and try to talk me out of it.

PPS I'll kiss it better when I next see you

'Too bloody right, I'd talk you out of it,' David said aloud.

Loath to suffer the indignity of calling for assistance, David spent fifteen fruitless minutes trying to free his wrists from behind his back before giving up. Then, with an effort, he struggled to his knees. Then leaning first his shoulder and then his hip against the desk for support, he was able to stand relatively upright. His head and his groin ached fiendishly.

With his head spinning, he looked around for the telephone, unable to understand where it had gone. In his mind, he pictured Sandy walking down the hall with a desk telephone under her arm. He shook his head at the absurdity of his situation and lost his balance, falling backwards against his chair, which skittered away on its castors and crashed into a filing cabinet with a bang loud enough to wake the dead. David ended up on his backside on the floor, the impact causing a wave of pain to radiate from his groin throughout his body. He groaned aloud and waited for the pain to subside enough to try again to stand up. Just then, there was a knock at the door.

'David?' it was the voice of Lucinda, a member of David's new section. 'David? Are you all right in there? I thought I heard a crash.'

Before he could answer, David heard Lucinda try the door. It was locked.

'I seem to be locked in,' David said, trying not to sound distressed. 'Get Security to bring a spare key, would you?'

'Are you sure you're all right?' Lucinda asked, concerned and trying the door again, more forcefully this time.

'Yes, I'm fine,' David called back. 'Just get Security for me.'

Lucinda acknowledged and David heard her steps retreating down the corridor. David sank back down to the floor and laughed.

God, but that girl has done me over!

Chapter 36

Sandy shivered as she stepped down from the train at Chester. The platform sported a steel-and-glass-roof, but was otherwise open to the elements and did little to protect the disembarking passengers from the wind-driven drizzle. Sandy hunched her shoulders and mingled with the other passengers making their way to the ticket-barrier and the outside world. Keeping her head down, her eyes surreptitiously scanned the concourse beyond the gates. She was looking for any unwelcome welcoming committee that David might have been able to arrange in the two-and-a-half hours since she left him trussed up like an oven-ready chicken in his office. True, she had left him a false trail by hinting that she was going to Ellesmere Port, but he may well have seen through her ruse and arranged to have this station staked out as well.

She tensed as she squeezed through the gate. If they were going to make a move, it would be now.

However, no one was waiting to accost her. No one paid her the slightest attention and she soon found herself walking briskly away from the Italianate façade of the station, wishing she had another layer of clothing against the cold November drizzle. She regretted leaving her fleece in David's car, along with her holdall, which contained all the clothes and toiletries she had brought back with her from the safe house. Her Glock semi-automatic was in the car as well and she felt naked without it. Fortunately, she still had her shoulder bag with some cash, credit cards and the keys to the Golf, which she left behind at the Waterloo Inn. She hoped it was still there.

Sandy first headed to the nearest sports shop, where she tried on a navy-blue hooded sweatshirt. It was a size too big for her and looking at her reflection in the mirror, Sandy thought it made her look a bit masculine – and that gave her an idea. She picked out a pair of grey jogging trousers, then she added a twenty-five litre rucksack and, to the obvious surprise of the sales assistant, a cricketer's box to her purchases.

When she left the shop to walk to the taxi stand, she was wearing the new sweatshirt and baggy jogging bottoms, having packed her jeans and shoulder bag into the rucksack, which she slung over one shoulder. The cricket box was stuffed into her underwear, the unfamiliar object encouraging her to walk with a masculine, open-legged gait.

At first, the cabbie had thought his passenger to be a young man. It was only when she spoke, that it became obvious that she was in fact female – and a very attractive female at that, he decided after looking at her face in the mirror. He tutted when she asked him to drive five miles out of town to a run-down old pub in the middle of nowhere. He was unlikely to get a return fare from there. Now she had the cheek to tell him to drive slowly past the pub – but not so slowly as to attract attention. Fifty yards further on, she asked him to stop, paid him and declined the change, which surprised him; it was a generous tip.

'Let me get halfway there and then follow,' she instructed. 'Be prepared for me to jump back in. If I do we'll have to move off quickly.'

'What's going on, like?' He asked. 'What's all this about?'

The girl shrugged. 'There's someone I don't want to meet. If they're here, I'll want to get away quick. If you see me getting into a blue Golf, you'll know it's alright and you can drive away. Okay?'

'I could just drop you next to the car and make sure you get in okay.'

Sandy had considered that but decided that it would be too easy for another vehicle to trap the taxi in the car park with her inside. On foot, she was more manoeuvrable. It gave her more options for fight or flight, with the taxi as her getaway car.

'Thanks, but no. Just do it my way, would you?'

'Yeah, alright, luv, if that's what you want.'

The cabbie watched the girl start walking toward the pub as he turned his vehicle around. Taking long, purposeful strides, she had the sweatshirt's hood up, her hands in the pockets and her shoulders hunched forward, with the rucksack hanging from one shoulder. Anyone seeing her would think she was a teenage boy.

Christ! She's probably a dyke. What a tragic loss to the males of the species!

True to his word, the cabbie drove slowly back toward the Waterloo Inn, timing his passing of the car park carefully so he could see that she reached the blue hatchback. He saw her looking all around before opening the door, and then gave him a brief wave as she climbed inside. He waved back at her and headed back to the city centre.

Retrieving the car was the part of her plan that she had concealed from David. She had been far from confident that he would support her and had built in a small, but significant, deception. He could still thwart her at the safe house but she could do nothing about that. Whatever happened there, her very presence would have changed the rules of the game.

Sandy extracted the uncomfortable cricket box from inside her underwear and put it on the passenger seat beside her. Then she turned the ignition key but the engine did not fire. Her first thought was that the car had been tampered with and that concealed assailants were surrounded her at this very moment. She looked around hurriedly but there was no movement of vehicle or person in the car park. A truck thundered past on the road, and she forced herself to control her nerves as she tried for a second time to start the engine.

Nothing.

'Come on you bitch!' Sandy yelled in fury – and the engine fired on the third attempt. With a sigh of relief, Sandy backed the car out of the space and joined the road, heading for Warrington.

From behind the bar, the landlord had a clear view of the car park entrance through the Georgian-style window. It was the red taillights that flickered briefly as the driver touched the brakes that caught his attention. He recognised the Golf as the one belonging to that posh tart who called herself Mrs Jackson. When she had failed to appear at the reception desk long after her checkout time of ten o' clock on Saturday morning, he had gone up to the room and discovered that she had already vacated, leaving nothing behind. None of the staff remembered seeing her leave, but that was unsurprising given all the excitement of the armed police incident in the car park on Friday evening.   He had not been concerned about her unannounced departure as she had paid cash in advance for the room until the Saturday morning and had no outstanding restaurant or bar bills.

He had been puzzled that the Golf had remained in the car park after her departure. However, he decided not to do anything about it until after the weekend. Now he had no need to bother. He returned to his task of taking the glasses out of the washer and putting them on the shelf above the bar.

***

David Richardson sat at his desk and stared at the telephone, now restored to its rightful place on the desk. His headache had cleared but his groin still felt a little tender. He found it incredible that she had actually used violence against him – and so effectively. He just had not seen it coming. Then there was the humiliation of having to be rescued by his subordinate and the security guard. He had declined to offer an explanation to his rescuers as to how he had come to be bound hand and foot and locked in his office. Instead, he had pulled rank and sworn them to secrecy.

David knew he had to tell Amanda as soon as possible that Sandy had gone after Crane, but he knew also that the DG was at Westminster discussing that very issue with the Home Secretary. He had called her office and left a message with Susan for Amanda to call him urgently on her return.

Sandy had told him that she planned to take the train to Ellesmere Port and then take a taxi to the safe house. David called Manchester to arrange for a team to intercept Sandy at the railway station, and, in case she managed to give them the slip, he had another team sent to stake out the approaches to the safe house itself. This, he reasoned, took priority over the extraction of Samantha McNamara and her bodyguards from the safe house. They were not in any immediate danger, he reasoned, but if, despite all his efforts to stop her, Sandy turned up at the house after they had been evacuated, she might walk into a trap with no one there to support her.

Next, he had called Communications and asked them to monitor the mobile phone networks and report if anyone switched his phone on. Almost three hours later, he was still waiting.

The desk phone rang, making David jump in his seat. He snatched up the receiver.

'Richardson!'

'It's Amanda. What did you want me for? Susan says it's urgent.'

David explained the situation in a few abrupt sentences. Then he heard Amanda sigh. Then there was a long silence.

'You'd better come to my office, David,' she said at last. 'Right away, please.'

Chapter 37

'What?' David could hardly believe his ears. 'Amanda, you've got to be joking!'

'The Home Secretary was quite clear on this, David. Unless and until we discover differently, we are to assume this group is working for a foreign power, against the interests of the United Kingdom. The Caesar DG and I have talked this through and we have agreed on a joint operation to round them up and put a stop to whatever it is they're planning.'

'Yes, I fully understand that but...'

'Sandra... Sandy... whatever you want to call her, has taken it upon herself, once again, to disregard my instructions. Well, on her own head be it! I want you to support her in this plan of hers. Madcap as it may be, it's the only one we have at present, and I, for one, can't think of a better one. Can you?'

'But she's vulnerable. She's pregnant. She's...'

'Courageous, determined and resourceful – if somewhat impetuous,' Amanda said.

David struggled to find the words to convince K not to allow this, in his view, foolhardy plan, to continue. 'Amanda, this really is unnecessary. We know where they are. We can send in our own people, or Special Forces, to storm the house. There is no need to... to allow Sandy to put her life at risk.'

'What if we storm the building and Crane isn't there? Or even if he is, what evidence is there of any wrongdoing? We have only the word of this young woman, Jeanette, whose evidence, you may remember, would be inadmissible in a court of law because you interrogated her while she was drugged. Even then we have no actual evidence that they are breaking any UK laws.'

'Apart from the murder of three British citizens you mean?'

'Once again, we have only the inadmissible evidence of this one woman that they were responsible.'

'But…'

'David, you have clearly allowed yourself to become emotionally involved with Sandra – Sandy. That is not a healthy relationship to have with one of your subordinates. It's preventing you from being objective.'

'We are not emotionally involved and I am being objective…'

'Good, then carry out my instructions. Cancel the intercept; arrange for the technician and be prepared to support your officer in the field.'

'But, Amanda…'

'No more buts, David.'

'Shit!'

'Quite.'

David shook his head and strode to the door. He turned to face Amanda, opened his mouth as if to present one more argument, thought better of it and turned, pulling the door closed behind him. He stopped as Amanda spoke again.

'Oh, and David, once you've done that, book yourself onto the first available self-defence refresher course.'

Amanda waited until he closed the door before she allowed herself to smile.

***

By the time Sandy found the cul-de-sac, it was nearly 4 pm. She had driven around the housing estate for half-an-hour trying to locate the safe house, but all the houses and streets looked the same. Eventually she recognised the name of the road as she was driving past.

She continued driving, scanning for any suspect vehicles among those parked nearby. There were several contenders, the foremost of which were three vans, two plain and unmarked, and one with the name of a joinery business stencilled on the back doors and along the side. In addition, several cars aroused her suspicions, one of which had someone sitting inside. She drove around the block again. The vans had not moved, nor had the cars – except for the one that had been occupied. It was now gone.

Whether or not she had correctly identified any of the surveillance vehicles was academic. She was certain that they would be there, but it would have looked odd if she had driven straight up to the front door of the safe house without going through the procedure. Having satisfied herself that anyone watching would have noted the Golf cruising around, Sandy turned into the cul-de-sac and pulled up outside the safe house, just in front of a van parked with two wheels on the pavement. The sides and rear of the van bore the legend "John McInnis Plumbing and Central Heating".

***

In the front bedroom of No 28, Kestrel and Radford were briefing their team leader, Bittern, who had arrived a few minutes earlier.

'We checked out the house during the night,' said Radford. 'There's a service alley at the back with a back gate into most of the properties, including this one, but not number twenty-six. That has just a solid six-foot fence with no gate. We do know the back garden has security lights linked to PIR movement detectors. We couldn't see any obvious CCTV cameras, though that doesn't mean they're not there.'

'Also,' Kestrel added, 'there's no security at all visible in the front garden. No PIR, no cameras.'

Bittern bit his bottom lip. 'But we still don't actually know whether Curlew is in the house?'

Ever since arriving at the property, technicians had been drilling into the party walls in the bedrooms, the living room and the kitchen to create cavities into which they would insert ultra-sensitive listening devices. The work was, of necessity, slow and laborious, using hand drills to minimise the noise so as not to alert the targets of the surveillance, in the house next-door, to their presence.

'Correct,' Kestrel replied. 'But once we get the mics in place we'll be able to ID her voice print as soon as she opens her mouth.'

'Blue Golf pulling up, said Radford. It was the second vehicle to have arrived in the past half-hour.

The first was an unmarked white panel van. The two occupants had unloaded a large buff-coloured carton from the back and taken it to the safe house on a two-wheeled trolley. At this point, the watchers could see the name *HOTPOINT* printed on the carton, which, from the shape, they had assumed contained a new refrigerator or freezer. The delivery men disappeared inside for a few minutes then returned to their van and drove away.

Radford photographed the golf through a telephoto lens, mounted on a tripod sited well back from the window's lightweight net curtains.

'Christ! Is that her?' Duncan spluttered into his coffee. He put down the cup, hurriedly and put his eyes to the binoculars that were mounted on a second tripod alongside the camera.

'Could well be,' Bittern agreed. 'Let me have a look.' He nudged Duncan out of the way so he could look for himself.

***

Sandy could feel eyes on her as she walked up the path to the house. She resisted the sudden urge to scratch an itch between her shoulder blades and kept walking, looking left and right as she approached the front door. She ignored the bell push, knocked twice, paused for two seconds, then knocked three times. The door opened.

***

'She's inside,' said Duncan.

'Is it her?' Bittern asked. In his excitement, his voice jumped an octave.

'Hard to tell with that hood up, but she ticks all the boxes: height, build . . .'

'Blue Golf,' Radford added. 'There was one in the car park at the pub on Friday.'

'Not exactly rare, though, are they?' Kestrel observed.

'Hurry up and get the mics operational,' Bittern ordered. 'I want confirmation that that's her, A-SAP! And,' he continued,

'I want a tracker on that car and two chase vehicles ready in case she leaves again.'

'Blue Mondeo parking,' Duncan said, and then a few seconds later, 'Two males approaching the property. One has a pilot-style attaché case.' He logged the arrivals while Radford photographed both the car and the men.

'Something's going on here,' said Bittern.

'Yes,' Radford muttered. 'I wonder what?'

'They've gone inside,' Duncan reported.

Chapter 38

The radio was playing pop-music loudly enough to thwart most bugs, but not so loud as to alert anyone that might be listening to the fact that they had been rumbled. Sandy sat at the kitchen table and listened closely while Petra quietly explained her unease at the activity next door, involving a local plumber who was not in Yellow Pages. Then it was the turn of Petra and Anthony to listen while Sandy outlined her suspicion that the X-Rays that had traced her to the Waterloo Inn may have been able to follow them to the safe house.

While she was speaking, Justin, one of the two technicians from Manchester, emptied the contents of Samantha's handbag onto the worktop and checked each item thoroughly. It took him less than two minutes to locate the bug behind the mirror in the powder compact. Wafer-thin and circular, the tracking device clearly had been specifically designed for concealment in that location.

'Tracking only,' he said quietly when Sandy had finished speaking. 'No voice recording or transmission functions.'

Samantha was standing beside him, watching with barely suppressed indignation at the violation of the private world that is a lady's handbag.

'Kathy bought that for me!' she said, the hurt and sense of betrayal clear in her voice. 'She said the colour was perfect for my skin-tone, and I agreed with her.' The others in the room looked at her sympathetically.

Justin shrugged. 'It's what people in this game do,' he said offhandedly. 'Don't take it personally.'

Samantha opened her mouth to protest that Kathy's betrayal was *very* personal. Then she saw Sandy's warning glance and remained silent. This was her sister's murky world and Samantha had no wish to be part of it. She folded her arms and sat on the one remaining chair with a sulky expression.

'Now we need to get you sorted out,' Justin said to Sandy. He glanced at the other man that had arrived with him. 'Sunil's all ready to go too.'

'Okay,' Sandy replied, 'but first I want ten minutes alone with my sister.'

'Sam, they're sending me away,' Sandy said, watching her sister carefully for any sign that she might lose control. 'Out of the country,' she added, fighting to control own down her emotions. 'It means we won't be able to see each other for a long time, perhaps never.'

The sisters were alone in the bedroom that they had shared at the weekend. There was no background noise and Sandy did not attempt to keep her voice low. Everyone else was downstairs in the living room.

'But, Sandy,' Sam pleaded, 'you promised me we wouldn't be separated.'

Sandy held up her hands as if physically warding off her sister's emotional outpouring.

'It can't be helped, Sam,' she said. 'All the time we are in contact, you are in danger. If I go abroad, with a new identity, which you won't know, there's no way you could betray me. The opposition will be aware of that and will leave you alone.'

'They might kidnap me to force you out in to the open,' Sam suggested.

'There would be no point. I would be unaware of what was happening. No one in MI5 would tell me or pass on any information. So kidnapping you would hold no advantage for them.'

Sam gripped Sandy's wrists. She was crying openly now.

'Sandy, that means we would never see each other again. I couldn't bear it!'

Sandy put her arms around her sister and held her close.

'Maybe sometime in the future, this will all die down. But right now, our being together places us both in danger; can't you see that?'

***

'Christ, this is breaking my heart,' Radford grinned, listening through a set of headphones. His sarcasm was a front, hiding a genuine emotional reaction to what he was hearing.

'It's definitely her.' Duncan confirmed, looking at the computer monitor. It showed the speaker's voice wave pattern against the one stored on the hard drive.

'This is the fond farewell,' Bittern said to the room at large. 'She's going to do a runner.' He raised a radio to his lips. 'Shona? Masai? This is Nkosi. Stand by. Sierra-Hotel-One confirmed onsite. She's likely to be on the move. Imminent. Will advise. Listen for instructions. Out.'

'So who are the other two guys?' Duncan asked. 'They don't seem to have said much.'

'Bodyguards?' Bittern suggested.

'Whose, the target's or her sister's?'

'The target's,' Radford surmised. 'They must have been covering her when the she went in. When she leaves they'll escort her with the Mondeo as a chase car.'

'That might be inconvenient,' said Duncan.

'We'll have to take them out if necessary,' Bittern said. Then he turned to Kestrel. 'Dennis, find an excuse to go down to the van and plant that tracker on the Golf. Our team might have trouble following her if she has the Mondeo shadowing her.'

'Do the Mondeo too,' Radford chipped in, facing down a glare from Bittern. He shrugged. 'What if they take her away in that and leave the Golf here?'

Bittern cursed under his breath. 'He's right. Do it.'

'Bloody hell!' Bittern muttered. It was two hours since they had eavesdropped on the sisters' conversation. In the interim, they had heard people talking, the washing machine running, the radio playing pop music, but nothing of their primary target. 'What are they doing in there? Masai? This is Nkosi. You still watching the rear?'

'Masai to Nkosi. Affirmative. Nothing doing.'

'Front-door's opening,' Radford said suddenly. 'There she is!'

Sandy closed the door and hurried to the Golf. She threw her shoulder bag onto the passenger seat and slipped behind the wheel. Her mouth was numb but not so much as thirty minutes earlier. Now she could feel the beginnings of a dull ache in her jaw.

She switched on David's mobile phone and put it back in her bag before starting the car. This time it fired at the first attempt and she executed a quick three-point turn before accelerating to the end of the cul-de-sac where she turned left. She looked in the rear-view mirror but there was no one tailing her.

Yet.

Okay, let's see how good they are.

'Shona? Masai? This is Nkosi. Go, go, go! The target is one-up in blue Golf GTi. Tracker in place on channel one-eight.'

'No chase vehicle,' Radford commented.

'They must be the escort for the sister,' Duncan suggested. 'They'll be moving her now.'

Sam watched the door close with a feeling of utter desolation. She glanced at the rucksack that Sandy had left behind containing some personal possessions, including a pretty, gold wristwatch. Justin, the technician from MI5's Technical Branch in Manchester, had handed Sandy a new one that she had put on in place of her own.

Sandy had spent a long time alone in the kitchen with Sunil and Justin, during which time the radio was on, the extractor fan was running and the washing machine was on the spin cycle. When they finally came out, Sandy had been ashen-faced, and when she said her final goodbyes, there seemed to be something wrong with her mouth. She appeared to be in some pain, but she declined to explain when Sam mentioned it.

Two minutes after Sandy had driven away Petra touched Sam's shoulder and inclined her head toward the door. It was time to go. Petra led the way, Sam was in the middle and Anthony brought up the rear, slamming the front door behind him. They carried no luggage, even leaving behind Sandy's rucksack. They all slipped quickly into the Quattro that was parked on the concrete hard standing outside the living-room window and Petra drove off hurriedly.

Alone in the back seat, Sam stole another glance at the folded piece of paper that Sandy handed to her as she left. It said simply, *Remember Andrea.*

'Here we go,' said Radford. 'Second tango and two escorts, one male, one female. They're not the ones that went in earlier.'

'Those others will be the dry-cleaners then,' Duncan said, meaning that the newcomers were there to sanitise the safe house to remove all evidence of the sisters and their minders.

'Or they might just be fitting the new fridge!' Radford suggested with a shrug.

'You going to get someone after the Audi?' Kestrel asked Bittern.

'There isn't anyone,' Bittern replied, 'except us.'

'We have the monitor,' Duncan said.

'Do we care,' Radford asked, 'now we're on to the real target?'

'I think we'll keep tabs on her; just in case,' Bittern replied. 'Paul and I will follow them in Paul's car. Jerry and Den, clean up here. Thank our hosts for their hospitality and tell 'em to forget we were ever here. Then take the van somewhere quiet and get rid of the plumber's signs.'

Paul Duncan led the way down the stairs, with Bittern hot on his heels. They ran outside, jumped into Duncan's car and, while Duncan started the engine, Bittern plugged the monitor into the cigarette lighter socket.

'Turn right,' Bittern instructed.

'They seem to have stopped,' Bittern said ten minutes later. 'Slow down a bit.'

Duncan slowed the car. There was a supermarket car park on the right.

'In there,' Bittern said.

Duncan pulled into the car park and drove around, following the directional arrows.

'We're right on top of them,' Bittern said, looking around. 'I can't see the Audi…. We've passed them, now. Go round to the next aisle.'

'They're inside the supermarket,' Bittern said incredulously. 'They can't just have popped out for some shopping, surely!'

Inside the supermarket, having deposited the tracking bug from Sam's compact behind some tins of soup, Anthony unhurriedly took a few items to the checkout. Then he left the store and, plastic carrier bag in hand, sauntered to the nearest bus stop. He was seen, but not recognised by the two men in the car.

'What do you want to do?' Duncan asked.

Bittern shrugged and thought for a few seconds.

'Park up. I'll have a little look round inside. See what they're up to.'

Another ten minutes passed before Bittern returned.

'They're not in there,'

'Tracker says they are.'

'They must have found it. There's no point in carrying on with this now. I'll get on the radio to the chase team and see where they are. We'll try to catch them up.'

***

Approaching a roundabout under the motorway junction, Sandy indicated right as if to take the southbound entry ramp. Instead of taking the ramp, however, she drove right past it and turned back the way she had come, heading west toward Little Stanney, where she turned south toward Blackford, eventually turning south on Liverpool Road near Upton Heath. When she reached the Chester ring road, she took two consecutive left turns and headed north on the M53 motorway. Smiling at the consternation she must be causing anyone tailing her, she took the slip onto the westbound M56 and drove fast, far exceeding the speed limit, until she reached the junction with the M6. Here she turned north for four miles. Then, taking the Warrington exit, she circumnavigated the roundabout and took the M6 again, this time heading south.

She had made it difficult for anyone to keep a tail on her without being spotted, but not impossible. She only hoped that she had done enough. She let the speed drop back to seventy-five and tried to relax.

Attached to the chassis just in front of the nearside rear wheel, the tracking device faithfully sent out its homing signal.

Chapter 39

It was nearly an hour later that Sandy pulled into the motorway services near the Wolverhampton exit. She parked the Golf in a bay farthest from the services building. No other cars were parked nearby. Most sensible people wanted to park closer to the entrance on this cold, drizzly evening. From the seat beside her, she picked up the Glock that Justin had given her before leaving the safe house and put it in the pocket of her hooded top. With her eyes scanning all around her for any sign of a threat, she walked briskly across the parking area to the building entrance. Once inside, she visited the toilets and made her way to the restaurant, where she sat at an empty table and read a newspaper while drinking a chocolate milkshake through a straw and eating a Danish pastry. In all she sat for a little less than twenty-five minutes. Then she stood up, stretched and headed for the exit.

She reached her car without incident and unlocked the driver's door. At that moment, a black saloon pulled up on the other side of a paved walkway in front of her car. She turned as she saw the movement from the corner of her eye. The driver had his window open; he was thickset, with dark hair and wore a black puffer-style jacket. Sandy turned to face him, her heart racing. It took all her nerve not to reach for the Glock.

'S'cuse me luv,' he called.

'Yes?'

Suddenly, a van screeched to a halt across the rear of Sandy's car, screening her from the view of the rest of the car park and the services building. Sandy turned. The van was the same model as the one she had seen parked outside the safe house, only now the sides were plain; the signs referring to John McInnis were gone. A door in the side of the van slid open and three men, wearing jeans, bomber-jackets and ski masks, jumped out. Sandy reached for the Glock but the men were quicker. Before she could release the pistol from the pocket of her sweatshirt, arms encircled her and pinned her arms to her sides. Someone pulled a hood, made of some kind of sacking material, over her head and several pairs of hands manhandled her into the van, forcing her to lie face down on the floor. The door slammed shut and the vehicle moved off.

One of the men grabbed her wrists and forced her arms up behind her back while another patted her down. He removed the Glock from her sweatshirt pocket and then proceeded to pull off her jogging trousers and underwear, along with her trainers and socks. Then he sat on her legs, pinning her down while the other two forced her arms above her head and dragged off the hooded top and sweatshirt. The hood came off along with her clothing and Sandy caught a brief glimpse of her abductors in the dimly lit interior of the van.

'Get off me, you bastards!' she yelled, struggling ineffectually against the three strong men holding her down. A second later, one of the men covered her mouth with duct tape, cutting off her cries of protest. Then he replaced the hood, plunging her into darkness once more. At the same time, one of the others cut through her bra-straps with a knife and ripped the garment roughly from under her.

She was not surprised that they had stripped her. It was standard procedure, which served to both intimidate the captive and make it easier for the captors to search for weapons or bugs. Expecting and accepting, however, are two different states of mind and Sandy tried her best to resist. Nevertheless, they had clearly planned the whole procedure carefully. Each man knew his part and they had taken just a few seconds to strip her naked, despite her determination to fight them – and they were not finished yet.

Turning her roughly onto her back, they forced her legs up until her knees touched her shoulders. One of them quickly locked his elbows around the backs of her knees to hold her in that position. Guessing what they planned to do next, Sandy struggled and bucked her body violently.

'Keep still and it won't hurt so much!' One of the men advised gruffly. They were the first words spoken by any of the men since the abduction began.

Sandy squirmed and squealed into the gag as he brutally inserted two fingers inside her to search for any device that she might have concealed there. Then he repeated the search inside her anus and her eyes filled with tears of pain, humiliation and rage.

Satisfied that she was hiding nothing inside her body, they pulled her legs out straight again and turned her onto her front once more, forcing her arms behind her back while they bound her wrists together with nylon cable-ties. Then they bound her ankles together in the same manner before backing off, leaving her to struggle hopelessly against her bonds for a few more seconds. Eventually, she realised the futility of struggling and lay still, trying to control her breathing.

In the menacing silence that followed the controlled violence of her capture, Sandy felt vulnerable and exposed. She rolled onto her side, and brought her knees up to her chest. As well as concealing her nudity from the men's gaze, it would offer her body some protection from any surprise assault

Bittern sat on the wheel arch behind the runners for the sliding door. He removed his ski mask and began systematically to check Sandy's clothing for bugs or a tracking device. As he finished examining each garment, he threw it into a heap beside the back doors. Kestrel and Radford, now also minus masks, lounged on the floor of the van with their backs resting against the side. They watched him in silence, ostentatiously resisting the urge to ogle the naked woman lying just a few feet away.

Bittern's face registered disappointment and frustration as he threw the remains of Sandy's bra onto the pile. That was the last item and he had found nothing. He ran his fingers through his hair and drew his hand down across his face. Then, with a knowing expression, he shuffled on his knees to where Sandy lay and deftly removed the dainty gold-plated watch from her left wrist.

Returning to his perch, Bittern used a penknife to open the back of the watch. He saw the transmitter and his face registered triumph. Holding his trophy aloft for his colleagues to see, he rose to his feet and crouching to keep his centre of gravity low, slid the side door open a few inches and dropped the bugged watch onto the road. Sandy felt the icy blast of air on her body and, for a moment, feared they might throw her out of the van, but then she heard the door close again and sighed with relief.

'Just the one?' Bittern muttered aloud, 'or do you have a back-up?' He shuffled back to his seat on the wheel-arch started to check the clothes in the pile for a second time.

This time he paid special attention to the trainers, using his penknife to rip out the insoles. In the hollowed heel of the left one, he found a GPS tracker. As with the watch, he held the trainer up for the others to see before tossing it to Kestrel, who threw it out of the door.

'Welcome, home, Curlew,' Bittern said after Kestrel closed the door. 'Nice to see you again, after all this time.'

Sandy remained silent. The tape-gag would prevent any coherent reply anyway.

Bittern took Sandy's Glock from his pocket and tested the balance. Experience told him that the magazine was full. Pulling back the slide, he saw that there was a live round already in the chamber. He released his grip on the slide and the spring returned it to the firing position with well-oiled metallic snicker. He saw Sandy tense at the sound and, smiling, he dropped to one knee beside her. He yanked the hood off her head then slowly and deliberately, he placed the muzzle of the Glock to Sandy's forehead.

Sandy saw Bittern's finger on the trigger and fought the urge to flinch. Instead, she held her breath and looked him steadily in the eye. He wouldn't shoot her inside the van. There would be too much blood and gore to clean up. Even then, the forensic evidence would remain forever, an indelible presence of what had occurred here. No, if they were going to kill her it would be elsewhere, probably after lowering her into a shallow grave in the woods or on the moors somewhere.

In her peripheral vision, she saw the disapproving looks and body language of the other two men.

'Oi, Martin! Don't be a prat!' the bald one said disparagingly. 'Put the gun away and leave the girl alone.'

Bittern sniggered and replied, 'Keep your hair on, Jerry!' Then he increased the pressure of the muzzle of her forehead and mouthed, 'Bang!'

Radford ignored the snide reference to his lack of hair. He had endured many such taunts over the ten years since his hairline started to recede at the tender age of twenty-five.

Bittern slipped the Glock into the side-pocket of his black bomber-jacket and pulled Sandy into a sitting position with her bare back resting against the ice-cold steel side of the van. She brought her knees up to her chin to cover her body once again.

'Surprised to see us?' Bittern gloated. With his left hand, he ripped the tape from Sandy's mouth. She winced. It felt as if he had taken the skin from her lips in the process.

Instead of answering, Sandy just shrugged and raised her eyebrows. As far as Bittern was concerned, she should be surprised to see him. He might even expect her to be relieved to see him. Had she not already known of his treachery, she might have been hoping that he had infiltrated this group and was planning to come to her rescue.

'You gave us a bit of run around,' Bittern continued. 'We'd almost given up.'

'Who are you people?' She asked. 'What do you want from me?'

Bittern did not play along. 'You know exactly who I am. Stop pissing about.'

'Okay, I remember you,' she said evenly. 'You're Bittern. You were my firearms instructor when I was training. What do you want from me?'

'We have orders, to take you in.' he replied.

'Orders from whom?'

'Crane,' Bittern replied simply.

'Who? Who's Crane?'

Bittern seemed phased by the question. 'If you don't know already, I'll leave it to him to explain.'

'Where are you taking me, Park House?'

'You'll find out.' Bittern said and returned to his seat on the wheel arch, leaving Sandy propped against the side wall.

There was a brief silence.

'How did you find me?' Sandy asked eventually.

'We were watching the safe house. We put a magnetic tracker on your car. You silly little bitch! You didn't even follow the most basic tradecraft. It was too easy!'

Sandy tried to look downhearted. Under the circumstances, it was not too difficult. 'I expected the safe house to be clean. How did you locate it?'

'You should know we have sources everywhere, Curlew,' Bittern replied mysteriously. 'You can't hide from us for long.'

Sandy allowed a look of despair to show on her face. Bittern brightened visibly at her discomfort.

'Can I have my clothes back, now you've checked them?'

'No,' Bittern replied.

'Look, please! It's freezing in here. It's all right for you three; you've got your coats, but I'm stark naked.'

'No.'

'How about untying my hands then? At least I could hug myself to keep warm.'

'No.'

'Bastard! So, where are we going?' Sandy tried again.

'You'll find out soon enough.'

'Oh come on,' Sandy pleaded. 'At least you can tell me where we're going.'

'No.'

'Well, how much longer are we going to be cooped up in this van?'

'Look, just shut up will you? Look, if you're bored . . .' He, lunged forward, grabbed her ankles with both hands and pulled hard. Sandy yelled in protest, but he continued to pull until she was fully stretched out on her back, exposing her body to the other men in the van.

'She needs warming up! If you two guys want to fuck her,' said Bittern, 'now's the time. She won't be around much longer.'

'Leave it out, man,' Radford replied in disgust. 'Leave the girl alone, will you?'

'He's not man enough to do it himself,' Sandy remarked. 'He can't get it up you know. Not with a girl anyway! You two had better watch out, though' she added, laughing scornfully, 'Your arses aren't safe with him around! Isn't that right, Bittern?'

'Shut up, you mouthy bitch! Bittern shouted. He leaned forward and slapped her across the cheek with his left hand. It was not a hard blow and seeing it coming, she was able to roll with it. She turned onto her left side, curling into a ball.

'Stop that, you bastard!' Radford shouted at Bittern. 'There's no need for that!'

Bittern turned his head and opened his mouth to reply. However, Sandy was not as dazed as she had appeared and saw an opportunity for retaliation. Still curled into a ball, she rolled onto her back, tensed her muscles then uncoiled her body like a giant spring, kicking out with both legs. The heels of both feet connected with Bittern's cheek and sent him sprawling on the floor, his head colliding solidly with the rear doors.

'Jesus Christ!' Radford shouted in surprise. Then he started to laugh as Sandy slithered closer to Bittern and proceeded to pummel his body repeatedly with her heels.

Kestrel leapt to his feet, but forgot to crouch and banged his head on the roof. He swore and fell onto his backside, and Radford laughed even louder. Kestrel recovered within seconds, and together he and Radford dragged Sandy away from Bittern, leaving her lying near the front bulkhead wall. Bittern rolled to a crouch and lurched toward Sandy but Radford stopped him in his tracks with hand on each shoulder.

'Leave her alone, you prat! You deserved that.'

'Get out of my way,' Bittern shouted, so angry at being humiliated that his voice jumped an octave. He tried to push past, but the more solidly built Radford was more than a match for him and pushed him back.

For the second time in thirty seconds, Bittern crashed into the back doors. Sandy wished the doors would fly open and deposit the little shit on the motorway – preferably under a lorry – as the van sped onwards, but the doors held fast. The fight went out of Bittern immediately, but he glared murderously at both Sandy and Radford. Radford ignored him and turned to face Sandy who was lying stretched out on the floor, making no attempt to cover herself.

'God, you've got some balls,' he grinned.

'Look again, sunshine,' Sandy replied with a sly smile, 'I don't think you'll find any down there.'

Despite his resolve not to stare at her body, Radford's eyes accepted the invitation on his behalf and flicked to where the balls, if she had them, might be expected to be found. For a few seconds, he was speechless.

Kestrel had looked also – and saw what Radford had just noticed.

'Fucking hell, Jerry, is she pregnant?'

Radford studied Sandy's slight bump in the dim light. 'Are you?'

'What's it to you?' Sandy snarled. She turned her back to the men and lay facing the side wall with her knees up to her chest. To be reminded of her condition under these circumstances was a torment. How could she have been so reckless as to have put her unborn child at such risk?

'Jesus, Martin,' Radford said to Bittern,' she's bloody pregnant!'

'So what?' Bittern challenged, still shaken by Radford's unexpected and forceful intervention. 'We still have our orders. Tape her mouth and put the bloody hood back on her. And don't you ever lay your fucking hands on me again!'

Sandy listened to the exchange and drew hope from the discord.

'Thanks for sticking up for me, Jerry,' she whispered as he sidled alongside her. She did not resist as he gently placed another piece of duct tape across her lips and replaced the hood.

Chapter 40

'David?' New to the Service and still in her probationary period after initial training, Lucinda was the textbook spy – medium height, medium build and mid-brown, shoulder length hair, tied back. She could blend in almost anywhere and no one would give her a second glance.

David looked up and replied, 'Lucinda! Come in. Any news?'

'They found Vixen's car parked at the Sandbach Services on the M6 near Wolverhampton. It wasn't locked and her bag was in the boot with your phone and her car keys inside.'

Vixen was the codename David had assigned to Sandy, though Sandy was not aware of it. He smiled grimly, thinking that Vixen was far more appropriate for Sandy than the innocuous Curlew.

'Thank you, Lucinda. I've just finished speaking to GCHQ. It appears both decoy trackers have gone offline.'

'Where are they?' Lucinda asked.

David looked at the map of Great Britain that he had ordered brought up from the stores, and put his finger on the blue line representing the M6, in the vicinity of Wolverhampton.

'Well, assuming sixty miles-an-hour average speed they'll be around Birmingham now.'

'If they continue to head south,' Lucinda added.

'Where else would they take her?' David grumbled, his concern for Sandy fuelling an unusual degree of irritation. 'They have to be heading for Tadworth. It's going to take them two or three hours, at least, longer if they throw in a few dog-legs to foil anyone tailing them.'

Lucinda wondered if they could count on that, but reluctant to get her head bitten off with the boss in his current mood, remained silent.

'Why didn't we have someone close-tailing her?' David castigated himself, but the answer was obvious. Had a backup team been following Sandy, the opposition may well have spotted them, which would have compromised the entire operation.

***

Sandy was not sure how long it had taken her mind to register the change in motion that signalled they had left the motorway. She had been too intent on the tensions surrounding her abductors and thinking of ways to deepen and exploit the rift she had created between them.

Bittern had played right into her hands when he slapped her and she guessed that any show of spirit on her part would impress the others, especially the one called Jerry; he was that sort. The opportunity actually to retaliate and land a solid blow on Bittern was a godsend. Jerry's physical intervention had put him at odds with Bittern, who was clearly the team leader but appeared to command little respect.   Following the squabble, the three men had lapsed into silence for a long time. Sandy could hear no talking between them – not even a whisper.

She pictured the road network in her head. From the services where they had abducted her it should take an hour-and-a-half to get to where the M6 merged into the M1, near

Rugby. Then it might take another hour to reach the London Orbital motorway, the M25, and a further forty-five minutes to an hour to skirt around the west of London to Reigate where they would take the A217 to Tadworth. Overall, the journey should take three-and-a-half hours or more. Surely, she could not been in the van that long?

Lost in her thoughts, Sandy suddenly realised that the van was slowing; then it came to a complete halt. She heard the sliding door open and cold air rushed into the interior. She held her breath, steeling herself for something unpleasant to happen. She heard the men shuffling about for a few seconds. Someone got out of the van and then back in again and she tensed. It was impossible from the sounds to understand what was happening.

Then Bittern said, 'I'm going to sit up front with Paul for the rest of the way. And leave *her* alone,' he added sternly. 'Leave the hood and the gag on, right?'

There was no answer from the men in the back – at least not an audible one and Sandy imagined the big bald guy giving Bittern the finger. The thought cheered her as the van started to move again.

She could sense his nearness before he touched her. She could smell him; she could feel the warmth of his body as he came closer. She tensed as he touched her shoulder. It was a light touch, not sexual, but reassuring, like a father to his child.

'You're cold,' he said, and she nodded. The floor of the van was cold and she had been shivering almost continuously since the stop.

He pulled her to a sitting position, wrapped his jacket around her shoulders and zipped it closed. She could feel the difference immediately. The jacket retained his smell, a manly smell, musky but not unpleasant. More importantly, it retained his body-heat and the warmth eased the tension in muscles aching from the cold and constant shivering.

'Thank you,' she hummed into the tape gag. The words were unintelligible, but the meaning was clear.

He leaned forward until his mouth was close to her ear. 'Not long now,' he whispered. 'Only another half hour.'

Half an hour – and then what?

Chapter 41

'GCHQ,' said Lucinda, handing David the telephone.

David looked at his watch. It was 9:40 pm and the window blinds were drawn against the autumn darkness. It was about thirty minutes since the last call from the team monitoring Sandy's progress via satellite.

'Richardson here. What's going on?'

'It seems they're not far from their destination,' said the voice on the phone.

'Really? Where are they?' David asked, looking at the wall map. *Surely, they can't have reached Surrey yet.*

'They're heading South on the A3400; they've just gone through Henley-in-Arden.'

David studied the map until he located the village. 'I've found Henley-in-Arden, but I can't find the A3400.'

'You need a new map, old chap. It was renumbered from the A34 last year.'

'Oh, right, got it now. Where are they heading?'

'We don't know that, only that they're about half-an-hour away.' The GCHQ officer went on to explain further. 'One of the gang whispered to her that they had another half-hour to go.'

Whispered? That could be a good sign. She may have somehow turned one of her captors. He stared at the map and wondered how far they would get in half-an-hour on that road.

'Any indication of further violence?' he asked, his voice tense with concern.

'Not since the scuffle we reported earlier,' GCHQ answered. 'We've analysed what happened and we think one of them was giving her a hard time and someone else stepped in to stop it. We heard her speaking quite normally afterwards so we don't think she's been badly hurt.'

Thank god for that!

'Gutsy girl you've got there,' the man at GCHQ continued. 'She seems to be holding up incredibly well.'

'Okay, thanks,' David replied. 'Please keep me informed of any developments.'

'Of course. Speak to you soon.'

David put the telephone receiver down just as Amanda strode into his office.

'How's it going?' She asked.

'They're not heading for Surrey.'

Amanda was as surprised as David had been. They had both been as certain as they could be that the X-Rays would take Sandy to the house at Tadworth.

'Where then?'

'Somewhere within half-an-hour of Henley-in-Arden,' David said, pointing to the position on the map. 'How far can you get in half-an-hour?' he mused.

Standing behind the two senior officers, Lucinda offered an answer. 'On a motorway, I'd say thirty miles; on an "A" road fifteen to twenty; on country lanes, half again.'

David and Amanda turned to look at Lucinda as if surprised she was still in the room. Nervous in the Director General's presence the young woman paled visibly under their scrutiny. David smiled at her reassuringly.

'That's as good a guess as any. They're on an "A" road so . . .' Using his thumb and forefinger as dividers, David measured out about twenty miles south of Henley. That placed them at Shipston-on-Stour. Then he traced an uneven arc from

Evesham in the west through Shipston to Daventry in the northeast. 'They could be heading anywhere within that area.'

'Yes and all our resources are at Tadworth,' Amanda said. 'What do we know about the house there?'

Her confidence bolstered, Lucinda answered the DG. 'Land Registry shows the house is owned by an oil company in Texas. Local council records show Community Charge bill for two residents. Payments are up-to-date. Electoral Role shows no one registered to vote at that address.'

'Surveillance?'

'There have been no comings or goings since A4 followed the tango to the address last night,' Lucinda reported.

'Thank you, er . . .'

'Lucinda.'

'Lucinda,' Amanda repeated, annoyed with herself because the young woman's name had slipped her mind. That should never happen. 'What do you plan to do now, David?'

'We need to get a team on the ground in that area A.S.A.P.'

'Do you have anyone available?'

'No, they're all at Tadworth. It'll take hours to get them to the Midlands, and even then, I'd not want to leave Tadworth open.'

'Okay, I'll call the Home Secretary and get him to order armed response teams from Warwickshire and Thames Valley police to be put on standby.'

'Police? Not SAS?'

'We're not at war, David!'

'I'm not so sure about that, Amanda. What about Tadworth? We need to raid that at the same time we assault wherever they're taking Vixen.'

'Yes, you're right, though I'd lay money on us finding nothing incriminating there. Nevertheless, I'll get an armed response team there too.'

David looked again at the map as if it held the answers to all of their questions.

'Amanda, I need to be on the spot to manage the situation locally. I can probably be there in an hour if I can have your authorisation to take a helicopter from Battersea Heliport. By the time I get there we should know where she's being held.'

'No, David. You need to be here to coordinate the operation . . .'

'No. If the plods go – go stomping in with all guns blazing, San . . .' David glanced at Lucinda and then back to Amanda. 'I mean Vixen is likely to end up dead!'

Amanda half-crossed her arms and cupped her chin with her hand as she thought. She had suspected for some time that David's relationship with Sandy was closer than it should be, and his obvious desperation to get as near to her as possible did nothing to contradict that. She should have taken action earlier, much earlier. She should have moved the girl to another section, broken the professional tie that threw them together. Well, it was too late to worry about that now. She would have to review the situation after this operation. Once the young officer was safe.

'Okay, David, you can coordinate the rescue operation from there. I'll manage the Tadworth end from here. Who will you take with you?'

David shook his head. 'There isn't anyone.'

'I'm here,' Lucinda said hopefully.

David and Amanda both stared at Lucinda.

'Er . . .' David began, hesitantly.

'Please, David.' She saw David's jaw harden and appealed directly to Amanda with big brown eyes.

'Yes,' Amanda said after a moment's thought. 'Take Lucinda with you. But, Lucinda, no risks. You're to stay out of the way and observe.'

'Actually, you can help by managing communications for me,' David added.

'Great,' Lucinda grinned. 'Thank you.'

Amanda concealed an indulgent smile at Lucinda's obvious excitement. Then it struck her that Lucinda was the same age as Sandy, who already had faced more daunting and dangerous situations than most intelligence officers would expect to see in a lifetime. How different those two young women were; one was a prematurely hardened operative and the other, comparatively, an excitable schoolgirl.

'We're still able to track Vixen's movements?' Amanda asked.

'Yes, GCHQ are tracking via a satellite that's picking up the GPS tracker and the voice transmitter.'

'Thank goodness we still have those!' Amanda said.

'Yes, after they found the two decoys, they gave up looking. That's how we know they're near their destination. One of Vixen's abductors whispered to her.'

'Whispered?'

'Yes. Earlier, she was trying to get info out of the three men in the back of the van. They refused to tell her anything. Then one of them seems to have lost it and hit her. Another intervened to protect her and there was a bit of an argument. One of them, we think the one that hit her, transferred to the cab, leaving Sandy with two men in the back. Some while later, one of them seems to have taken pity on her and whispered they had only half-an-hour to go. There's been no audible conversation after that.'

Amanda shuddered at what Sandy must be going through. Even though it was the girl's own plan, it would be on Amanda's conscience if anything happened to her.

'It's incredible they haven't found the other two electronic devices,' Amanda said. 'Do we know where they're hidden?'

Chapter 42

'Our van is here,' said Sunil, turning from the window.

Sunil and Justin had carried out a cleansing operation to remove all trace of the occupants of the safe house. They had cleaned all surfaces with alcohol wipes and vacuumed throughout. They had loaded all used crockery, glassware and cutlery into the dishwasher. They had emptied all the bins into bags to be taken away for incineration. Towels and bed linen had been packed into bags ready to be taken for laundering. Before leaving, the bodyguards and their principal had packed their personal belongings into their own suitcases and holdalls. All of these now stood by the front door, along with Sunil and Justin's equipment, awaiting the return of the white panel-van.

Sunil Pandurangan had been twelve years old in 1968 when political and economic upheaval forced his family to migrate from Kenya to England. They settled in Manchester where his father, Muhesh, worked hard to build up a successful tailoring business. No one, not even Sunil himself, had challenged the assumption that he would follow his father into the tailoring trade, but in 1974, he confounded family tradition and began studying dentistry at King's College, London. It was there, in his fourth year, that he was recruited by MI5.

Racial tensions were running high, with unprecedented numbers of migrants, particularly from Pakistan and Bangladesh, coming to live in the UK. To these were added a large influx of Asians expelled from Uganda by President Idi Amin. The Security Service needed sources inside the Asian communities to identify potential radical elements among the generally hard-working and law-abiding immigrants.

With financial aid from MI5, Sunil duly set up a practice in Oldham, Manchester, and kept his ear to the ground. However, the racial war predicted by Enoch Powell's infamous "Rivers of Blood" speech, in 1968, never materialised and neither did Sunil's fantasy of becoming a kind of Indian 007.

Nevertheless, he and MI5 maintained their relationship through regular contacts with successive handlers. In 1990, they asked him to participate in the development of a new type of covert listening device. Two years later, he would find himself implanting just such a device into the mouth of a beautiful young woman in the kitchen of a terraced house in Ellesmere Port.

Sunil had been reluctant to remove a perfectly healthy pre-molar from the patient's lower right jaw and replace it with an implant containing a sophisticated electronic bug. He was even more disconcerted to discover that he would have to perform the procedure using portable operatory equipment.

Used extensively by armies in the field and by dentists working for medical missions in the Third World, all the equipment necessary to perform complex dental operations came packed into three metal cases that, when stacked and latched together, were comparable in size to a small domestic refrigerator. The cardboard Hotpoint refrigerator carton, in which the cases had been concealed, had been purloined from a nearby electrical retailer and was large enough to contain Justin's toolkit as well as Sunil's mobile surgery.

In order to minimise her recovery time, the patient had insisted that Sunil used the lightest possible anaesthetic. He had obliged with a shot of Lidocaine combined with a whiff of Nitrous Oxide. After removing the tooth, Sunil had screwed a self-tapping titanium post into the root cavity. Into this, he screwed an abutment and finally cemented a false crown, containing the actual device, on top. The result was a firmly seated implant, which would be undetectable except by close examination by an expert. The whole procedure took two-and-a-half hours, and once Sunil had finished with Sandy, it was Justin's turn.

Thirty-six year-old Justin Kemp was an electronics and communications expert who had applied to join GCHQ after five years working for the communications giant, Siemens. Then, in 1990, he had joined the team developing covert listening/transmitting devices, and both he and Sunil had been instrumental in the development of the dental-implant transmitter.

While Sunil was operating on Sandy, Justin fitted a tracking device into the heel of one of her training shoes, and another inside the Seiko watch that he slipped onto her wrist when she emerged from the kitchen, shaking after her ordeal with Sunil. Both of these devices were decoys, intended to satisfy the expectations of the opposition when they captured Sandy. Her safety depended on the dental implant remaining undiscovered, and on the GPS tracker fitted inside a Glock semi-automatic. The device replaced the spring housing at the bottom of the magazine, taking up the space of three rounds of ammunition. Another fourteen live rounds were loaded above. The Glock had been the subject of a further modification and Justin warned Sandy not to attempt to fire the weapon.

Chapter 43

It seemed to Sandy that they had been travelling much longer than Jerry's whispered estimate of half-an-hour. Maybe her mind was playing tricks on her, her perception of time probably affected by her circumstances. Bound hand and foot and hooded, she was sitting on the cold, hard floor of the van with her back against the side wall. At least she had Jerry's bomber-jacket to keep her warm. It was far too big for her and reached to her thighs. If only it would have covered her feet, too. They were *freezing*.

Since replacing the hood and gag, apart from the brief kindness shown by Jerry when he gave her his coat, the two men had ignored her, leaving her with nothing to do but contemplate her uncertain fate. Isolated as she was from her surroundings, she could do no more than listen to the mumbled conversations of Jerry and the other man, who, at one point, Jerry had called Dennis, and the sounds made by the van's tyres and from other vehicles on the road in that other universe outside the confines of the van.

Gradually, Sandy's senses alerted her to another change in the motion of the van. The turns were more frequent, often much sharper than before, and there was more braking and accelerating. It was clear that they had now left the main roads and were following narrower country lanes. Sandy guessed that, finally, they must be nearing their destination. Moments later, the van came to a complete halt, waited a few seconds then started forward again, clattering over a cattle grid. Now the road noise was different, no longer the sound of rubber on tarmac, but the crunching of a gravel surface. Sandy visualised a sweeping gravel drive – and a long one at that! It took a minute or two before the van stopped and the engine was turned off. The cab doors opened and closed and there was the distinctive sound of the sliding door opening, a fact confirmed by a gust of cold air that rushed into the interior. Sandy's heart began to race.

'Get her out of there,' Bittern snapped.

Hands grasped her ankles and dragged her unceremoniously across the ridged floor of the van. They stopped when her legs were outside and her buttocks were on the edge of the doorway. Strong hands took hold of her upper arms and forced her to stand. She flinched, but made no sound as sharp gravel dug into the soles of her bare feet.

'Bring her inside!' Bittern's voice again, and she was dragged forward.

The bonds on her ankles made it impossible to walk and her feet dragged painfully on sharp stones, scraping the skin from her toes. The duct-tape gag muffled her cries of pain but her plight had not gone unnoticed.

'Let me lift her,' Jerry said gruffly and carried her in his arms like a child. They passed through a doorway and he set her down onto a smooth, cold floor that might have been made of quarry-tiles or marble. It was pleasantly warm inside and Sandy detected the distinctive smell of a coal fire. Under different circumstances, it would have been very welcoming.

'I take it that's not her coat,' a new voice enquired, obviously referring to Jerry's jacket. 'Where are her clothes?' The speaker was male, probably middle-aged and had an accent that betrayed an education at one of the top private schools in the country. Was this someone she knew? Sandy searched her memory but could not recall hearing the voice before.

'We dumped them in a bin in a lay-by when we left the motorway,' Bittern replied. 'We found two trackers on her but we couldn't take the risk there might be another one hidden somewhere.'

'Quite, quite. I understand.' There was a brief pause and Sandy sensed that he was looking her up and down. 'Take her in there, please,' he said at last.

To Sandy's surprise, Jerry hoisted her onto his shoulder and carried her through to another room, where he set her down on a hard wooden chair with armrests. Then, without a word, he moved away, leaving her feeling alone and very vulnerable.

She could feel carpet under her feet. The smell of wax furniture polish and leather was strong in her nostrils. The coal-fire smell was stronger too. She could feel its warmth and hear the crackle of the flames. Unbidden, her imagination conjured up the image of a red-hot poker on bare skin. She shuddered at the thought and forced the image to the back of her mind. She tensed as someone approached, but whoever it was merely lifted the front of the hood and ripped the tape roughly from her mouth before letting the hood drop again.

'Good evening,' said the voice she had heard for the first time in the hall. He was standing in front of her. 'Curlew, I presume?'

This was one time where *I'm sorry I cannot answer that question* would be counter-productive. She wanted to provoke a conversation that could be overheard by GCHQ via the transmitter implanted in her jaw – assuming that the device was still working after the knocks it had taken during her abduction and the van journey.

Sandy licked her sore lips then replied, keeping her voice as calm and even as possible. 'And you must be Crane.'

There was a slight pause, which suggested that her mention of Crane's code-name had taken him by surprise. Sandy parted her lips to increase the chance of the microphone in her jaw picking up Crane's reply.

'Interesting you should know of that name,' he mused.

'Bittern mentioned it in the van,' said Sandy, thankful that he had done so. The only other place she had heard it was when she had questioned Jeanette, and she did not want to admit that interview had taken place. 'Are you?'

He hesitated for a second or two before answering. 'That is one of the ways by which I'm known, yes.'

'What's your real name?' she asked pleasantly. 'Mine's Sandy.'

He made a snuffling sound that might have been a snigger.

'Yes,' he replied, 'I know all the tricks. We'll try to keep it impersonal, shall we? We don't want to become too fond of each other, now, do we?'

'Where are we?' Sandy asked. 'Why am I here?'

'Why do think you are here?'

'I have no idea. What do you want with me?' She was surprised that she could keep her voice so level. She sounded unconcerned by her circumstances, which was far from the truth.

'Now, let's get down to business. When did you last see Jane Badell?'

Sandy knew from her questioning of Jeanette that she and Jane had been seen together, but she did not want to admit anything too readily. It would look suspicious. 'Who? Oh, do you mean that TV reporter that got shot a few months ago?'

'Yes,' Crane replied patiently, 'That's the one I mean.'

'Never met the woman.'

'Now, now, Curlew, we both know that isn't true. You met with Jane Badell in Claridges on the last Sunday in August. For what purpose?'

Sandy allowed her shoulders to drop in an exaggerated show of defeat. 'Oh. Okay, you know about that. Yes, we had arranged to have tea together,' she admitted.

'What did you talk about?'

'We hadn't seen each other since... for a while. I wanted to catch up with her,' she ended lamely. It sounded implausible, even to Sandy, but it was the truth.

'Catch up with her?' Crane repeated. 'You're an intelligence officer. You don't meet other operatives for a social chat. You meet to pass on or gain information. I'll ask you again. What did you talk about?'

'Was Jane an operative? I thought she was a news correspondent for the BBC.'

'Don't try my patience,' Crane snapped. 'What did you and she talk about?'

'It's exactly as I already told you. Jane and I became quite close when we worked together...'

'Where was this?'

'I can't answer that,' Sandy replied, knowing that Crane was well aware of the answer.

'You don't need to,' Crane said impatiently. 'I know you were together in Sarajevo.'

'If you say so.'

'Close,' Crane repeated the word as if savouring it. Are you a lesbian?'

'That's none of your business!' Sandy replied. Having been in love twice, once with a man and once with a woman, she had often asked herself that same question.

'I know that Jane Badell was a promiscuous lesbian who indulged her predilections with a number of female partners,' said Crane, still circling. 'The tabloids were constantly speculating about her, a notoriety I believe she rather enjoyed. Were you having an affair with her? Is that what you meant by close?'

'No,' Sandy replied, 'I wasn't having an affair with her. She was an amazing woman. I admired her.'

'A crush you mean? You had a crush on her?'

'No, it wasn't like that. I liked her, admired her, as I said. She was a very strong person, but also very caring. She cared about the welfare of those in her team.'

'Especially the young women, I shouldn't wonder,' Crane suggested cynically. 'Do you think she might have had an ulterior motive?'

'There was never any suggestion of that with me,' Sandy replied then appended a question of her own. 'Do you know who killed her?'

Crane paused as if taken aback by Sandy's question.

'I'm given to understand that agents of the Yugoslav military intelligence agency, KOS, were responsible.'

'What about my parents? Were they also murdered by a KOS hit-squad?' Sandy had decided to keep to herself her knowledge that Bittern and his team killed her parents. If, however she could trick Crane into admitting it . . .

'Why do you say that?'

'I think whoever killed Jane came after me later the same day, and were responsible for the deaths of my parents.'

Crane thought in silence for a moment before answering.

'If what you say is true, then it was probably related to the subject of your discussion in Claridges on that Sunday. What did you talk about?'

'Nothing of any importance,' Sandy insisted. 'We were catching up with news. Personal stuff, you know.'

'Did the subject of General Szopienice come up at all?' asked Crane.

'Who?'

'Oh dear. I do hope you aren't going to continue to be difficult,' said Crane, and Sandy perceived an edge of menace in his voice. The image of the red-hot poker sprang once more into her mind.

'Brigadier-General Antonije Szopienice,' he continued, 'the target of Operation Cevapi. The man that you tracked down, facilitating his capture by Special Forces.'

'How do you know about Cevapi?' Sandy countered, trying to appear shocked that Crane knew of the mission.

'My dear young lady,' said Crane patronisingly, 'I know everything about Cevapi and your role in it. Now, at the risk of sounding like the villain in a B-feature, I will ask the questions and you will provide the answers. Is that quite clear?'

Sandy remained silent, hoping to provoke him into giving away more information. At the same time, she hoped and prayed that the transmitter was working and that someone in GCHQ was listening to the conversation – and knew where she was.

'Well?'

'Well what?'

Crane sighed with exasperation.

'Did you discuss General Szopienice in your conversation with Jane Badell?'

'No, we did not.'

'Are you sure?'

'Yes, I'm sure.'

'I don't believe you.'

'Well, I'm sorry about that, but I'm telling the truth. Look,' she added assertively, 'I'm not answering any more questions until you get someone in here that I know and trust. I don't know you. I've never heard of a Crane in Caesar. I want to see Eagle.'

'You've already seen Bittern and Kestrel.'

'The ones that kidnapped me off the street?' she replied. 'You can't seriously expect me to trust them! I need to speak to someone senior from Park House before I say another word.'

'Is that the case?' said Crane.

He sounded angry and Sandy expected him to hit her. He didn't. Instead, Sandy heard him leave the room. She waited in silence, a myriad fears crowding her mind, each competing with the others to occupy the forefront. The only sounds were of the fire crackling and popping in its grate and from somewhere behind, the monotonous rhythm of the pendulum of a grandfather clock.

Crane returned a few minutes later.

'You said you wanted to see someone from Caesar, that you know and trust,' There was more than a hint of triumph in his voice. 'Okay, I'll grant your request.'

Standing behind her, Crane yanked the hood from Sandy's head. She blinked a few times in reaction to the sudden bright lights and glanced quickly around at her surroundings.

The room was about twenty-feet wide with an ornately carved plaster ceiling, at least twice the height of that in a normal house. To her right, the orange flames of an open log fire danced like phantoms in an inglenook fireplace. Above the mantle was a large mirror in an ornate gilded frame in which animal figures appeared to be climbing toward a summit crested with a coat-of-arms. Dark oak, glass-fronted bookcases, filled with richly bound books, lined the wall to her left Formal portraits from bygone centuries graced the walls, along with hunting scenes and depictions of the sea and ships. This room, Sandy thought, would not be out of place in a grand stately home like Blenheim or Chatsworth.

Sandy's seat faced a large oak desk, behind which were a pair of red velvet curtains, drawn across what might be French doors. Standing beside the desk was a woman of Sandy's age. She was dressed in tight blue-denim jeans and a loose-fitting, pale-blue cashmere sweater, and her voluminous auburn hair was pinned back in a tight bun. She regarded Sandy with a neutral expression and dispassionate eyes.

'Jeanette! What are you doing here? Who are these people?' Sandy's surprise was genuine. She had believed Jeanette to be in the house at Tadworth. Was it possible that she was there after all? How had the journey time passed so quickly? Had she been drugged for part of it?

'Hello, Sandy.' Jeanette's voice betrayed more than her expression. She seemed nervous – frightened, even. 'Please just answer Crane's questions.'

'Well,' said Crane, 'let's get on, shall we? Now that you have seen that Lapwing is here, perhaps you will feel more comfortable about answering my questions.'

Sandy started to turn her head toward the voice but Crane snapped at her to face the front. Then he replaced the hood. Sandy was plunged once more into a world of claustrophobic restriction, making her feel many times more vulnerable. She wondered why Crane was so concerned that she should not see his face. Perhaps he was someone in the public eye; someone she might recognise from television or the newspapers.

'Yesterday afternoon, Lapwing awoke in a hospital bed in Chester,' Crane said. 'She has no recollection of the thirty-six hours prior to that. What do you know of that?'

'Nothing at all,' replied Sandy, trying to sound surprised by the question.

'Really? But you were in Chester on Friday night.' It was a statement, not a question.'

'Was I?'

'You met with your sister, Samantha, at the Waterloo Inn, on the road to Warrington on Friday afternoon. Then on Friday evening, the two of you were taken to an MI5 safe house in Ellesmere Port. Your sister remained at the property but you left, returning this afternoon. Where did you go?'

'Shopping.'

'You didn't go shopping. You were present at Lapwing's interrogation. That's the truth, isn't it?'

'I've no idea what you're talking about.'

'I want to know what information she divulged under questioning and the names of everyone else present.'

'I told you I don't know what you're talking about,' Sandy insisted.

'I think you do.'

'I know nothing about what happened to her,' Sandy insisted. 'This is the first time I've seen her since July. Perhaps you should be interrogating her!'

'What do you mean by that?'

'She goes missing for a day-and-a-half and comes back with some cock-and-bull story about having amnesia? Do me a favour!'

'That's ridiculous!' Jeanette protested. 'It's obvious what she's trying to do! She's covering for herself. Can't you see that? She knows what happened to me and she's trying to make a fool of you.'

'Hmmm, well we'll get to the bottom of it eventually,' Crane said, sounding unconcerned. Sandy had the impression that he was more amused at her clumsy attempt to foster discord than concerned about Jeanette's loyalty. What puzzled her was why Jeanette sounded so insecure.

'I suppose you're hoping.' Crane continued, 'that, at any minute, your white knight will come bounding in on his trusty steed to save you.' He tutted, mockingly. 'Unfortunately for you, the team assigned to rescue you are, at this moment, a hundred miles away, sitting outside the house in Surrey where our decoy car led them yesterday.'

Decoy car?

'What are you talking about?' Behind her calm facade, Sandy's heart was racing. So the surveillance team had been hoodwinked. Once again, the opposition were a step ahead – just as they had been in Bosnia.

'You and your friends from MI5 attempted to tail Lapwing when my people picked her up from the Countess of Chester Hospital yesterday evening.'

'No, that's not true…'

'We had two identical cars in the hospital car park. You followed the first to leave. Lapwing was in the second one, which left ten minutes later and brought her here. Meanwhile the other car carried on to the house in Surrey, which is owned by a very good friend of mine, and your team obligingly followed. They have since been mounting a rather clumsy observation operation, tying up a dozen officers to no effect.'

Sandy's heart sank, but she managed to maintain a neutral expression. 'I really have no knowledge about this. If she was followed, it wasn't by me.'

'We'll come back to that later,' said Crane. 'I will have the truth out of you,' he paused to add menace, 'one way or another.'

Sandy remained silent and tried not to let him see her fear.

'When we picked you up you were found to be carrying two concealed tracking devices. Why?'

Sandy had wondered when he would get round to asking that question, and had prepared her answer. 'I didn't know anything about them. MI5 must have planted them on me. I didn't even know they were there until Bittern searched me tonight. I still don't know exactly where they were hidden. I was blindfolded when Bittern searched me, you see.''

'Why would MI5 bug their own operative?'

'I don't think they trust me, fully.'

'Why do you think that is?'

'Maybe it's because I'm an outsider. Maybe they think I'm some kind of double-agent.'

'A double-agent? Working for whom?'

'I don't know. The Serb separatists, maybe? Anyway, it explains how they found me when I went to see my sister. I had been wondering about that.'

'Do you want to know what I think?'

'Not really, but I expect you're going to tell me anyway.'

'I think you were very well aware of those tracking devices. I think you deliberately trailed your coat with the intention of letting us capture you.'

'That's crazy! Why the hell would I want to do that? All I can expect from you is to be interrogated, probably tortured and then killed.'

'I think you wanted to be captured so you could lead your friends at MI5 to me.'

'You? I knew nothing about you before tonight. I knew someone was after me but I thought it was a Serb hit squad.'

'If that's so, why did you return to the safe house this afternoon without protection?'

'I wasn't supposed to be there, but I wanted to say goodbye to my sister. I'm being – was going to be sent away. They were going to give me new identity and send me to America to keep me safe from... Well, now it turns out it was to keep me safe from you. I didn't expect anyone to be watching the safe house. How did you find it?'

Crane ignored the question. 'Now, let's get back to the subject of Brigadier-General Szopienice. Miss Badell had certain information about the brigadier which, should it become known to a wider audience, would cause a lot of inconvenience to a lot of people.'

'Is that why you had her killed?'

'What are you talking about?'

'You ordered Jane killed, didn't you? Then you set your dogs onto me, but they screwed up and allowed me to escape and ended up killing my parents.'

'Crane laughed, but it sounded rather brittle. 'Oh dear! Your imagination has been running riot, hasn't it?'

'Look, you've practically admitted it. The mere fact I'm here confirms it was your people that have been trying to kill or capture me for the past two months. Why?'

'Now look here…' Crane began to bluster, but Sandy cut across his words.

'Jane didn't mention Szopienice at our meeting but she did tell me she was afraid that someone might try to kill her.'

'Really? How interesting, but tell me, how do you come to equate that with me?'

Sandy took a deep breath; she was about to take a huge gamble.

'She said she was planning to expose the activities of an organisation called Clermont.'

Chapter 44

Clermont.

Crane's reaction to Sandy's utterance of that one word was at once both satisfying and disconcerting. Clearly flustered, his air of self-assured authority and superiority had slipped from him like a discarded cloak.

'What do you know about Clermont?' he shouted. 'What did she tell you?' So close was his face to Sandy's, she could feel his breath against the fabric of the hood.

'She told me that Clermont is orchestrating the mass murder of Muslims in the Serb-held areas of Bosnia.'

'That is utter rubbish!'

'But please,' she continued, ignoring Crane's denial, 'let's call a spade a spade. Ethnic cleansing is just a euphemism for mass murder! How is what Clermont is doing any different to Hitler's final solution to his Jewish problem?' Her intention was to goad Crane into defending or justifying Clermont. Only then would the truth about the organisation begin to come out and GCHQ would hear his confession transmitted via the device in her lower jaw. 'Thousands of Muslim men, women and children are being systematically murdered or sent to concentration camps,' she continued relentlessly. 'Young Muslim girls are being abducted and held in rape camps, forced to work as unpaid prostitutes for the gratification of Serb soldiers, militia and police. And your grubby little organisation is complicit in those atrocities. What I don't understand is why?

'You're quite wrong, you know,' Crane replied, no longer shouting. 'Clermont does not exist merely to conduct ethnic cleansing in Bosnia.'

'Isn't it true that Clermont is an anti-Muslim organisation?' Sandy persisted. 'Isn't the killing of Muslims its prime objective?' The longer she could keep him talking, she thought, the longer she might remain alive – and the more chance David would have of finding her and rescuing her.

'It isn't quite as simple as that,' Crane replied.

'Well you explain to me, then. How simple is it?'

There was a long pause before Crane spoke again. When he did his words were addressed to Jeanette.

'Jeanette, please go and check that someone is watching the security monitors, would you.'

Sandy heard Jeanette leave the room and waited for Crane to speak. When he began, she pictured him perched on the edge of the desk with his arms folded.

'You're quite wrong about Clermont, you know. Its primary objective is not the slaughter of Bosnian Muslims. Its aims are considerably more momentous than that. Clermont is an alliance of intelligence officers from a number of countries on both sides of the Atlantic, formed to counter the threat from Islamist extremists. Tell me, have you heard of *Al Qaeda*?'

'Yes, of course,' Sandy replied. 'It's an Islamic fundamentalist group suspected of instigating terrorist acts against Western interests. Its leaders were members of the Mujahidin that fought the Russians in Afghanistan.'

'That's right. Now listen to this. A year ago the founders of *Al Qaeda* set out their aims in a video recording released through the Arabic television station, *Al Jazeera*. Their aims were, they said:

"To forge all the world's Muslims into one worldwide caliphate, to expel non-Muslims from Muslim lands and to wage *Jihad* on the infidels." Does that not sound to you like a declaration of war on Western civilisation?'

Sandy noticed the similarity with Pope Urban's words, delivered so theatrically by her sister at the safe house. *God! Was that only yesterday?* She felt some satisfaction that she had made the right connection.

'It sounds like a parody of the speech made by Pope Urban the Second when he launched the First Crusade,' she replied. 'I can't remember all the words but he called on people of all classes to get together and drive the Muslims, what he called "that vile race", from the "lands of our friends".'

Crane clapped his hands together three times. 'Bravo! I'm impressed by your knowledge.'

'But that was nine hundred years ago,' Sandy protested. 'What has all this to do with Bosnia in 1992?'

'That is a very pertinent question,' replied Crane. Sandy could tell he was warming to his theme, delighted to have a captive audience with whom he could discuss the finer points. 'Militant Islam represents the greatest threat to world peace today. Greater than Soviet Russia was and greater than an emerging China will be. Islamists resent what they see as the exploitation of Muslim lands by the West, particularly the oil industry. Of course, they conveniently forget whose enterprise and investment located and developed those resources in the first place, but that's another matter.

'They believe the Saudi royal family are puppets of the West, and that the same could be said about the leaders of many other states in the Middle-East. All, according to *Al Qaeda*, are traitors to Islam.'

'You still haven't told me what all this has got to do with Bosnia. The Muslims there are hardly fundamentalists. Their society is secular, tolerant, integrated – cosmopolitan, if you like. If you're trying to exterminate Muslims that are a threat to the West, you've started in a very odd place!'

'Another very good point,' Crane conceded. 'Our American cousins have discovered that *Al Qaeda* views the dissolution of Yugoslavia as an opportunity to gain power in what was until recently the most powerful country in south-eastern Europe, both economically and militarily. They plan to take control, town by town, republic by republic. Their plan is to combine Bosnia, Kosovo and Albania into a single fundamentalist state: The Balkan Islamic Republic, thus bringing hostile Islam one step closer to Western Europe.'

'Is that even possible?' Sandy asked, incredulous at the concept. 'For a start, Albania was never even a part of Yugoslavia.'

'Oh yes,' Crane replied, 'It's possible. Each of them has a significant Muslim population. The majority of Kosovars are ethnically Albanian, and Bosnian Muslims have a rather chequered history with their Serb and Croat neighbours.

'You have to understand,' he continued, 'that what they are doing in the Balkans is part of the wider plan to undermine the Western powers. They advocate attacking Western culture at every opportunity in order to weaken and destabilise it. Their aim is to convert the entire world to Islam under what they call the Worldwide Caliphate.

'Imagine how easy it would be for the United Kingdom to be ruled by a Muslim dominated government. At first, a few apparently moderate Muslims become MPs and, taking advantage of Britain's sense of tolerance and fair play, gradually worm their way up the hierarchy.

'As the Muslim population of our country grows, both through immigration and their propensity to a higher birth-rate, more and more Muslims will be elected to Parliament. Eventually, one of them may rise to be PM. He will pack his Cabinet with his fellows. At first the regime, to all intents and purposes, appears moderate, but gradually becomes more and more radical, strengthening its position, until eventually it gets to a point when it has the confidence to impose Islamic law. Christianity and Judaism are outlawed or at best severely repressed. Women have to wear the veil in public and be covered from head to toe. Alcohol is banned. Those who refuse to embrace the Muslim faith cannot hold public office, perhaps cannot even run their own business. Any Muslim that renounces Islam is executed, as are those that commit adultery. The fabric of our society would be destroyed to a point where it would no longer be recognisable.'

'That's insane,' Sandy sneered. 'You're assuming the vast majority of Muslims in Britain – in all Western countries – are radicals and extremists. That is simply not the case.'

'You are correct, to a point; but there are sufficient numbers of extremists in this country who are bent on radicalising the young, so the number of Muslims with extremist tendencies will grow. They have no desire to integrate, to become a part of our society. They want to force the rest of us to adopt their religion and culture, but that's only the threat from within,' he went on. 'Countries like Iraq and Iran are actively trying to develop nuclear weapons. Pakistan probably has already done so. The former Soviet

Muslim states have access to the nuclear arsenals sited in their countries. We believe that it's only a matter of time before a radical Islamic state uses nuclear weapons to attack the West.' He paused briefly and Sandy smelt the pungent aroma of alcohol in her nostrils. The bugger was drinking whisky! God, what she would give for one right now.

'We believe that the only option available to us in defence of our culture and way of life in the longer term is to launch pre-emptive strikes against those Islamic nations that actively seek to incite attacks on the West, while we are still in a position to win.'

'You mean a pre-emptive strike with nuclear weapons?' Sandy asked, aghast at the very idea.

'Not necessarily with nuclear weapons. A concerted full-blown military attack with conventional weapons would destroy the governments and infrastructure of what we see as enemy countries.'

'With all the attendant loss of innocent lives,' Sandy pointed out.

'It is always regrettable to cause suffering to innocents, but one has to think of the greater good. Such a strike would rid the world of the support and funding of international terrorism and *Jihadism* for a generation.'

'And who are you to decide which lives are worth saving and those that must perish?' Sandy challenged hotly. 'No political objective is worth the death of a single child!'

Crane tutted. 'That sentiment would have had the Nazis goose-stepping along The Mall in the nineteen-forties. It was largely due to the ruthless efficiency of Bomber Command and the American Air Force destroying German cities and industry that saved this country from the subjugation suffered by the rest of Europe.'

'That was completely different!'

'Was it?' Crane contested. His tone was that of a university tutor leading a sceptical student to the one logical conclusion to the argument. 'Then as now we faced an enemy bent on world domination. We sleepwalked our way into that conflict because our leaders were too weak-willed to act before Germany became too powerful. We are in grave danger of repeating that mistake today.'

Sandy shook her head but could not think of a counter-argument. Instead, she returned to the Balkan conflict. 'So how is killing Muslims in Bosnia going to stop the creation of an Islamic state in the Balkans? Surely you should be targeting the *Al Qaeda* leaders rather than thousands of innocent people.'

'Well, you see, if the ethnic cleansing continues unchecked, it will spur Muslim fighters from other countries to come into Bosnia to support their brethren. With a little encouragement, they will inevitably come into conflict with non-Muslim troops of the protection force. When those troops retaliate the more radical Islamic states will protest volubly and, more importantly, send their own forces into the fray.'

'Giving Clermont the excuse to counsel the US and UK governments to escalate the conflict to the home territory of those countries,' Sandy surmised. 'So, World War Three begins in Bosnia.' She shook her head. 'If you think our government would fall for that you're deranged!'

Crane sucked in a deep breath. 'During the Gulf War, last year, Saddam fired Scud missiles into Israel with the intention of goading them into retaliation. He knew that Israel's entry to the war would drive a wedge between the Muslim and non-Muslim states that formed the coalition forces. Many of the former would back the Iraqis against Israel, while the latter would rush to its defence.

The whole thing was our idea, whispered into Saddam's contemptible little ear by some of his closest advisors, who in turn were unknowingly influenced by us. Had we succeeded, we would then have sought to escalate the resulting conflict into a hot war that the West simply had to win. Unfortunately, we failed. We failed because we didn't have enough followers in senior positions in Westminster and Washington to support us, and the Israelis were persuaded by the imbeciles in charge of the coalition forces to stay out of the conflict.

'But, you see, the number of influential people joining our alliance is growing rapidly: government ministers, senior civil servants, officers in the armed forces, etcetera. We are also sponsoring and moulding to our ways ambitious young politicians who are destined for the great offices of state, perhaps even the premiership of this country and the presidency of the United States. When their time comes and they are in power, they will listen to our advice and take any action necessary to defend and protect our civilisation.'

Sandy snorted at that. 'Do you really think you could influence a British Prime Minister to commit our armed forces to ill-conceived foreign adventures on your say-so? Sure, if our country is under real threat from abroad, but you are advocating pre-emptive strikes, striking the first blow, casting the first stone. If we use unprovoked military force against Muslim countries in the Middle-East or Pakistan, what do you think would be their response? You would expose our country to reprisals from terrorist groups. You might even be the *cause* of the radicalisation of Muslims in Western countries that you are so afraid of. Who was it talked about sowing the wind and reaping the whirlwind? That's what your crackpot scheme is going to initiate.' She stopped speaking at the sound of someone coming through the door.

'Jesus Fuckin' Christ, James, what the fuck are you doing?' the voice boomed in a deep, nasal New York accent. 'We're supposed to be interrogating this slut, not having a college debate with her!'

Chapter 45

Sandy recognised the voice immediately. It belonged to Roderick Ekerich, the CIA agent who had posed as a freelance journalist in Sarajevo – the one Jeanette called Roddy. What the hell was he doing here?

'Oh, hello, Rod,' Crane replied, apparently unflustered by Ekerich's aggressive tone. 'We were just having a friendly little chat while we waited for you to join us. I was hoping that she'd be willing to cooperate without the need for the more barbaric methods of persuasion that are your forte. Unfortunately . . .' He left the sentence hanging in such a way as to convey more than a hint of menace.

Ekerich's harsh voice filled the room again. 'What the fuck made you start telling her about Clermont?'

Crane remained unabashed. 'It was she that introduced the subject into the conversation. Apparently, Jane Badell knew considerably more than we had thought.'

'Bullshit! She's bluffing,' the American argued. 'No way! Jane Badell didn't know jack-shit about Clermont.'

The voices receded as the men put distance between themselves and their prisoner and spoke in quieter tones, but Sandy could still hear most of what they were saying.

'Well, she certainly knew something, if not the whole truth,' Crane explained quietly.

'We got her in here to find out how much that bitch Badell told her about Marko, and now you've spilled the whole damn can of beans about Clermont.'

'Look, Rod . . .'

Sandy's ears pricked up. Marko! When questioned on Saturday, Jeanette had said that Marko was the name of Ekerich's Serb contact outside Sarajevo. Crane's questioning of Sandy had seemed obsessed with what Jane Badell may or may not have told her about Szopienice. It was therefore logical to conclude that Marko and the brigadier-general were one and the same. So Ekerich had been running Szopienice and was probably complicit in the ethnic cleansing activities. How far up the CIA chain of command did that go?

Suddenly, Ekerich raised his voice, drawing Sandy's attention back to the present. 'Why are you pussyfooting around with her? We gotta find out what she knows, where she heard it and who she's told. Gimme fifteen minutes alone with her. I'll make her talk.'

Crane's reply was inaudible to Sandy but she heard him leave the room. Then she heard heavy footfalls as the big American approached. He stood in front of her and leaned down until his face was close to hers.

'Okay, honey,' he said. His deep, grating voice resonated around the room. 'You are going to tell me where you heard about Clermont and the names of anyone else who knows.'

'Why, so you can have them murdered?' Sandy snarled. 'Go screw yourself!'

Ekerich laughed. 'Feisty little slut, ain't ya?' There was a momentary pause before Ekerich suddenly ripped off the hood. His big face was inches away. The bulbous nose, the swarthy, pockmarked skin and the cruel, dark eyes filled her vision. He had grown a goatee beard since she last saw him and his lank dark hair had more grey than she remembered. His breath smelled of cigarettes and alcohol. She turned her head away, but he grabbed a handful of her hair and forced her to look at him.

'Do you remember me, honey?'

Sandy shrugged. 'No. Should I?'

'We met in Sarajevo.'

'If you say so. I don't remember.'

'Well I remember you, slut. Fluttering your big blue eyes and wagging your cute little ass at all the guys.'

'You must be confusing me with someone else.'

'Nah, nah. I remember you. Hey, you've changed your hair,' He took a few strands of her hair between his fingers. 'You used to be blonde, I recall. Yes, you sure had them newshounds sniffing around you like hounds round a bitch on heat. How many did you fuck?'

'Not all of them, clearly. You never got your turn.'

He chuckled. 'Well, we got lots of time yet, honey.' He stood up and started to walk around her, circling in the same way Crane had done earlier. Sandy's mouth went dry. She hoped her display of bravado hadn't given him any ideas.

Ekerich reappeared in front of her. 'Sooner or later, sweetheart, you're gonna tell me what I need to know, and the sooner you do, the easier it'll be for you.'

'Go to hell!' Sandy snarled in reply.

The American looked down at her for several seconds before he spoke again. 'Say, isn't it a little warm in here for you to be wearing that coat? Sure, you must be burnin' up in there.' His voice was rasping, now, his breathing heavier, shallow. 'Let me help you some.' He reached out a hand and slowly pulled the zip-fastener down.

Sandy cringed but gritted her teeth and remained silent. There was no point in protesting. She could do nothing to prevent him doing whatever he wanted.

Ekerich continued until the jacket fell open, revealing her body from throat to crotch. Then he pushed the jacket off her shoulders and leered at her naked body. Sandy noticed then that he was packing a Colt 45 semi-automatic pistol in a shoulder holster nestling under the armpit of a plaid lumberjack shirt. Seeing the direction of her gaze, he pulled the pistol out and stroked her cheek with the barrel. She forced herself not to react.

He tutted and shook his head. 'You got yourself a nice little collection of cigarette burns here,' he said, poking each of the little circular scars on her chest with the Colt's muzzle, as if counting them. 'Perhaps we can give you some more.'

Sandy fought to suppress the worm of fear squirming inside her. Although the scars no longer hurt physically, the memory of their being inflicted while she was simultaneously being raped from behind was as raw as if it were yesterday. She quailed at the thought of going through that again.

'You're gonna tell me, everythin', darlin',' he said. 'Before I'm done with you, you're gonna tell me everythin' I need to know.'

'I'll tell you nothing, you fucking pervert!'

'Well, we'll just have to see about that.' Ekerich holstered the Colt and moved behind her. She felt his big, rough hands caressing the soft, smooth skin of her shoulders and shuddered with revulsion. Then, suddenly, his hands slid down and grasped her breasts.

'Stop that! Get your filthy hands off me!'

Chuckling at her discomfort, Ekerich continued to grope her breasts, squeezing and kneading the soft flesh, teasing the nipples. He put his mouth close to her ear, so close that his lips touched her as he spoke. 'I asked you a question, whore, and I want an answer. Who told you about Clermont? Who have you been talking to?'

Before Sandy could think of a suitably disparaging response, she heard the door open and someone entered the room.

'Roddy! What on Earth are you doing?' It was Jeanette's voice, and to Sandy's disgust, her former friend sounded like a jealous girlfriend. How could the lovely Jeanette continue to be mixed up with an animal like Ekerich, especially as she was well aware that he was largely responsible for the death of Caroline? There was a lot about Jeanette's behaviour that did not add up.

'Shut up, Jeanie,' Ekerich snapped. Then he turned his attention back to Sandy. 'Answer, me, slut!'

'I've already told you… Owww!' Sandy yelped in pain as he suddenly squeezed and twisted her nipples. She squirmed in her seat but was unable to prevent the assault from continuing.

'Oh my God! Roddy! Don't do that! Leave her alone!' Jeanette pleaded. She sounded close to tears.

Ekerich interrupted his abuse of Sandy's breasts. 'Look, if you don't got the stomach for this,' he shouted, 'then get the fuck outta here and leave me to do my work!'

'Roddy, you disgust me!' Jeanette hissed and stalked out of the room, slamming the door behind her.

'What's wrong with her – time of the month or somethin'?' He sounded genuinely bewildered at Jeanette's reaction.

'Perhaps she realises what a first class prick you are,' Sandy growled.

Ekerich walked around the chair until he was facing her again. 'You're some smart cookie, aren't you? Well let's see if we can't persuade you to be a little less smart and a little more cooperative.' He reached out and squeezed her nipples again. This time Sandy gritted her teeth and remained silent, refusing to give the bastard the satisfaction of hearing her cry out in pain.

Suddenly, Crane's voice cut through the room like a whip. 'Rod! That's enough of that, old chap.'

Sandy assumed that Jeanette must have told him what Ekerich was doing.

Ekerich let go of Sandy's breasts and rose to his full height. 'What? Oh c'mon, James. I was just getting started.'

Sandy turned her head toward Crane's voice but he had moved directly behind her and she was unable to see him. She wondered at the relationship between these two men. When Ekerich first came into the room it sounded as if he was in charge, but now that Crane had asserted himself, the American appeared to be the subordinate.

'There's no need for this, Rod,' Crane continued. 'We'll do what's necessary downstairs.'

Sandy shuddered, trying not to think of the torments they were planning to inflict upon her. Ekerich saw her fear. He leaned forward and pressed his forehead and nose against hers. Once again, her nose wrinkled at the stale cigarette smell of his breath.

'You'd better smarten up and start cooperating with us, honey. Things are about to get a whole lot worse.'

'Go fuck yourself!'Sandy replied defiantly to mask her fear.

'You stubborn little whore!' Ekerich roared. He stood up and slapped her face viciously, followed by a backhanded blow so violent that the chair almost toppled. Then he leaned down again. 'You want some more like that you just keep getting smart with me.'

Sandy tasted blood in her mouth and her fear turned to anger. She spat in his face. Bright red flecks of blood and phlegm splattered over his cheek and forehead. Ekerich recoiled with a cry of disgust. Still bent at the waist, he half-turned to one side and took a step back, his hand instinctively rising to wipe the blood-flecked spittle his face.

Seizing the opportunity to retaliate, Sandy reprised her attack on Bittern in the van. Drawing her knees to her chest, she thrust out her legs violently, driving both heels into the side of the big American's face. Caught completely unawares and already off-balance he fell to the floor.

Sandy sprang to her feet and launched herself on top Ekerich. Instinctively, he threw his hands up in defence and turned his head to one side. It was no use. Sandy's momentum was unstoppable. Her forehead crashed against his left cheek, causing a hairline fracture, but Sandy wasn't finished yet. She drew her lips back in a snarl and raked his face with her teeth, gouging a piece of flesh three inches long from his cheek.

Suddenly, the door burst open and Bittern rushed into the room, followed by Radford and Duncan.

Chapter 46

Jeanette sat on the four-poster bed and looked disconsolately around the room at the plush wall hangings and antique furnishing. She remembered Crane telling her that Charles II and Nell Gwynn had slept in this very room back in 1668. She could easily imagine the decadent couple frolicking together, if not on this very bed, then one very much like it. She wondered if Nell had enjoyed those encounters. Perhaps, like Jeanette, she was simply performing a role that was expected of her.

Until her arrival at Crane's house, the previous evening, Jeanette had thought Ekerich still to be in Bosnia, or if not, then in New York or the CIA HQ at Langley, Virginia. The last thing she expected was to find him here in this grand house in the heart of rural England. Reluctant as she had been to resume the relationship forced upon her in Sarajevo, Jeanette knew she had little choice if she were to maintain her cover. So she had acted the part, much as she suspected the courtesan Nell had done with her King in this very room.

Returning home from Sarajevo after the tragic conclusion of the Cevapi mission, Jeanette had thought herself free at last from Ekerich's clutches. That hope had been shattered some weeks later when Kestrel approached her and told her he was to be her new handler. Aghast at the thought of being forever under the malign influence of Ekerich and his associates, Jeanette immediately sought an audience with Eagle.

She explained that Grebe had assigned her to work with the CIA operative to identify an alleged traitor within the Cevapi team. As time went on, she told him, she became more and more suspicious of Ekerich, eventually discovering that he was in regular contact with a Bosnian-Serb, code-named Marko, and that it was Ekerich himself that had betrayed the Cevapi team. When asked if she had reported this to Grebe, or anyone else in the team, she said she had not because she was concerned others might be involved. Her fears had been had been justified by Kestrel's approach in the very sanctum of Caesar – Park House. Seriously concerned by Jeanette's revelations, Eagle ordered her to infiltrate the organisation in the UK with the aim of identifying its leaders and other members, particularly any Caesar officers.

Before long, Kestrel said that they were going to engineer an "accidental" encounter between Jeanette and Jane Badell. Kestrel had not told her the purpose of this reunion with her former Cevapi teammate. Her task was simply to establish contact and to arrange to meet at another time when the two women would have more time to chat. By unhappy coincidence, the date chosen for that initial contact was very day that the target had arranged to meet Sandy for afternoon tea at Claridges. After that, events took on a momentum of their own, beginning with Badell's murder and ending with Sandy's capture this evening.

Sandy's capture had been a key component of Jeanette's plan to identify Crane. She knew they would bring Sandy here for Crane to interrogate, and that if she were present at the capture it was likely she would come as well. In the event, Sandy's abduction became unnecessary. As soon as Crane suspected that Jeanette's cover was blown, he had ordered his team to bring her here so that he could assess the extent of damage done to his operations.

Nevertheless, the team had captured Sandy after all and she was now at the mercy of Crane and Ekerich. Jeanette knew that they would kill Sandy once they were satisfied that they had extracted all they could from her. Jeanette was her only hope of rescue, but she could not do it alone. It was time to call in the cavalry.

She glared angrily at the cumbersome mobile phone in her hand. The signal-strength indicator in the top-right of the screen showed not a single bar. The late twentieth century communications revolution was yet to make its mark in this isolated rural backwater and the expensive piece of electronic equipment in her hand was about as much use as a brick. In fact, a brick would be more useful because she could have used that to brain that bastard Ekerich in his sleep. She switched off the phone and replaced it in her bag.

Then it occurred to her that there should be a telephone extension somewhere on this floor, probably in Crane's bedroom, and she decided to go in search of it.

***

'What the fuck's happening here?' Bittern demanded, trying to make sense of the improbable sight of a slightly built, naked woman, bound hand and foot, pinning a man twice her size to the floor and savaging him like a rabid dog. Crane was standing near the fire, apparently transfixed by the scene and watching in disbelief.

'Get her offa me, for Chrissakes!' Ekerich screamed. Having regained his senses, he was squirming and pulling at Sandy's hair in a pathetically ineffectual attempt to dislodge her.

'Help me get her off him,' Bittern ordered the other two men.

He grasped one of Sandy's arms while Duncan took the other and Radford grabbed her ankles. Together the three men lifted her away from Ekerich, who lay writhing on the floor cursing volubly and clutching his face.

Sandy struggled in their grip but she was unable to break free and they forced her to lie face down on the floor. Radford sprawled across her body, holding her down so she could do no more than flap her lower legs up and down together like the tail of a stranded mermaid. Eventually, she stopped resisting and lay panting on the carpet.

'Get her back in the chair,' Crane snapped as he helped a stunned and shaking Ekerich to his feet. Blood was pouring down the American's cheek and spreading across the collar of his check shirt. 'And tie her down properly this time.'

Duncan stood the chair upright and helped Bittern and Radford manhandle her into it. Realising that once they tied her down in the chair she would be helpless, Sandy started to struggle again, kicking her bound legs and trying to jack-knife her body.

'Hold her still!' Bittern ordered, gasping with exertion. Angrily, he slapped her face hard enough to make her head spin. 'Paul, take your belt off. Strap her to the chair.'

Duncan slid the belt from the waistband of his jeans and, while the other two held her still, he passed the belt around her stomach, buckling it behind the vertical wooden spindles at the back of the chair. Radford cut the cable-tie that bound her ankles together and, with Duncan holding her legs still, used duct- tape to fasten her ankles and calves to each of the front legs of the chair. Sandy instinctively squeezed her thighs together to protect her genitalia, exposed now that her legs were parted, but no one made any move to abuse her there. Meanwhile, Bittern cut through the cable-tie that bound her wrists together and taped her wrists and forearms to the arms of the chair. Then he covered her head with the hood and all three men stood back to catch their breath.

'Take her downstairs,' Crane said. 'Lock her in the old wine cellar. We'll deal with her later.'

Sandy's heart missed a beat as Duncan and Bittern lifted the chair and carried out to the hall. They started to descend a creaking wooden staircase.

'Where are you taking me?' she asked. 'What's down these steps, the basement? What are you going to do with me?' She would rather have remained silent, keeping her fear hidden from these bastards, but this was a deliberate, disguised commentary for the benefit of anyone monitoring the transmissions via the electronic bug in her lower jaw. At least they would know she had been taken to the basement. The temperature dropped noticeably and Sandy was unsure whether it was the cold that was making her shiver, or fear.

'Just be quiet. We're not going to hurt you.' Sandy recognised Jerry's voice through his laboured breathing.

'Not just yet anyway!' puffed Bittern. The bastard! God, he had it coming if she ever got anything like a chance.

At the bottom of the staircase, they shuffled along an echoing corridor before passing through a doorway where they put the chair down on a flagstone floor. Then she heard the door slam and a key turn. She was alone.

***

Jeanette crept silently along the landing. She had glanced into three rooms, so far, and none had a phone that she could see. She was about to try the fourth door when she heard the sounds of a commotion from downstairs. She peered over the banister rail in time to see Bittern, Radford and Duncan rush into Crane's study. There was more shouting and the sounds of a scuffle – then an ominous silence. Shortly afterwards, Bittern and Radford carried Sandy, like a queen in a sedan chair, out of Crane's study. As they started down the stairs to the basement, Jeanette changed her mind. Naked, bound and hooded, Sandy looked more like a sacrificial offering than a queen.

Realising her window of opportunity was fast receding, Jeanette focussed on the task in hand. She continued to check the doors along the landing. Finally, she found one with a telephone extension beside the bed. Glancing nervously over her shoulder and listening intently for the sound of anyone approaching, she slipped inside, closing the door quietly behind her. She crossed quickly to the phone and with shaking hands, dialled a number. It was answered immediately.

'Yes?'

'Lapwing,' she announced. 'Condition Red!'

***

Shivering in the cold, dark, dank cellar Sandy's mind finally registered that she had seen Crane. He had been helping Ekerich to his feet right in front her while his thugs were tying her to the chair.

The mental picture she had formed from his voice had been remarkably accurate. He was middle-aged – in his early fifties, perhaps – and a little taller than she was, with a slim build. He was wearing grey slacks and a navy-blue turtle-necked sweater with leather patches on the elbows and epaulettes on the shoulders. He had short, curly silver-grey hair and a bristling moustache to match. She had seen this man before. He had been present at the Operation Cevapi briefing in MI6 headquarters last January. She could recall the face, but try as she might, she could not recall his name.

Chapter 47

'You're joking!' David was sitting alongside Lucinda in the back of a police Range Rover as it sped away from the private airfield where the helicopter had landed. In the front passenger seat, Inspector Burroughs, the armed response team commander, half-turned and stabbed a forefinger at a point on an Ordnance Survey map. David and Lucinda craned their necks to see, but the light from the interior lamp made it difficult to see any detail.

'No, sir,' replied Burroughs. 'That's the grid reference we received from your people.' He tapped his finger on the map again. 'That's Norton Downs Hall.'

David was incredulous. The coordinates were those received from GCHQ pinpointing the location where Sandy's tracker stopped moving.

'And that's the home of the Director General of MI6?' David pressed. 'You're absolutely sure about that?'

'Yes, sir,' replied Burroughs. 'It's been in his family for generations. Landed nobility, you know. A reward for services rendered to Charles the Second, apparently. Chap called Jonathon Featherstone; the King made him Baron Featherstone of Norton.'

By now, they were speeding through narrow, unlit country lanes, blue lights flashing, siren wailing. Burroughs folded the map and turned off the lamp. The interior was plunged into darkness, but it made it easier for the driver to see where he was going

'Tell me more about the property,' David said.

'The estate originally covered several thousand acres, but not now. It's been reduced to about four hundred acres with a deer park, woods and two lakes. A lot of the land was sold off to pay various debts – gambling, mainly, apparently. There's also a fair chunk rented out to local farmers. I don't think Mr Barrington stays there much. He has a place up in London, I understand. We keep an eye on it.'

'You mean you guard the place?'

The driver swung the big vehicle around a tight bend and everyone swayed, restrained only by their seatbelts.

'No, he won't hear of it; says it's a waste of resources. There's some electronic surveillance equipment linked to the station at Chipping. It covers the perimeter and the areas immediately alongside the house and stables, but not the woods and fields because of the deer roaming free.'

'Has an armed response team ever been called there before?'

'Just the once,' Burroughs replied, grinning. 'We didn't find anything. We suspected it must have been a deer that came too close to the house. Surprised it hasn't happened more frequently, considering how many of the buggers he's got around there. He likes shooting them, apparently; holds a licence for several hunting rifles, as well as a few shotguns.'

'What's the perimeter security like?' David asked after absorbing that information.

'The estate's surrounded by an eighteen-foot-tall beech hedge, backed by a wire fence with razor wire on top. At the main entrance there's about fifty-foot of a ten- or twelve-foot-high stone wall either side of electric double gates.'

'Any staff?'

'We know he has two ex-SAS types working for him as security guards and I think he has a live-in housekeeper and some gardening staff.'

'The upkeep of that little lot must cost a fortune,' David remarked. 'How is it funded?'

Before Burroughs could answer, the Range Rover turned into an even narrower lane and pulled up..

'We're here, sir,' said Burroughs.

David looked at the road ahead. Four other police cars and two ambulances were parked there, blocking the lane 'Where's Barrington's place?' he asked.

'We're about a mile from the Hall,' Burroughs replied. 'What do you want to do now?'

David turned to Lucinda. 'Better go and report to Amanda. This is going to get complicated.'

As Lucinda climbed out of the car, Burroughs pulled out a pack of chewing gum and offered it to David.

David waved the pack away. 'No, thanks. So James Barrington is titled, is he?'

'Oh no, sir,' Burroughs said, popping a sliver of gum into his mouth. 'The title expired in 1859 when Lord William Featherstone died. His only son, Henry got himself killed in the Crimea in 1854. He was just eighteen. Mr Barrington is descended from one of Lord William's distant female cousins.'

'Can we come back to the present day, please?' said David, fighting to conceal his mounting impatience.

'Sorry, sir.' Burroughs squirmed with embarrassment. 'I'm a bit of a local history buff.'

'Oh, don't mind me,' said David apologetically. 'Things are a bit tense at the moment.'

Burroughs blew out his cheeks. 'Look, I'm sorry, sir, but what is all this about? We've been scrambled out here with orders from the Chief Constable himself, by all accounts, and with no explanation other than we are to take orders directly from yourself.'

David hesitated for a second or two before deciding how much to tell the inspector. 'Okay, look. One of our undercover officers was abducted earlier this evening in Staffordshire. We've tracked her to that house. They are interrogating her as we speak, probably torturing her. I'm certain that once they have everything they need they'll kill her, so we don't have much time.'

'Fucking hell! Are you sure?'

David bit back a retort. The man's disbelief was understandable. 'Yes, I'm sure.

'Look, sir, I've got six armed officers. That's not enough for a frontal assault on that place,' said Burroughs.

'How quickly could you get some more here?'

'There aren't anymore,' replied Burroughs, shaking his head. 'I told you. We only have three armed response vehicles in the whole of the Thames Valley Force. They're all here!'

'Then we'll have to make do with what we've got.'

'They'll know we're coming as soon as we breach the perimeter, sir. You'd need a company of infantry to get in there.'

David cursed Amanda for not requisitioning an SAS team. Now it was too late. There was no time to get that organised. Sandy could well be dead before the soldiers arrived.

'We're going to need plans of the house,' David said, 'and a better plan for getting us inside than a frontal assault.'

Before Burroughs could reply, Lucinda knocked on the window. David stepped out of the car, shutting the door behind him.

'You've been gone a long time,' David grumbled. He had not intended to criticise her. His manner was simply a manifestation of his concern for Sandy's safety.

'There's no signal on the mobile phone around here,' Lucinda replied. 'One of the plod, er, police officers put me through on the patrol car radio to the station and they patched the call through to Gower Street.'

'What did Amanda say?'

'She just said to await her instructions.'

David clenched his fists in frustration. 'Damn it! We can't afford any more delays.'

Chapter 48

Alone in the cold and musty cellar, Sandy struggled against the duct tape binding her arms to the armrests of the chair. If she could just get one hand free, it would be all right, but pull and twist as she might, nothing budged. There was no give. She cursed Bittern for using a trouser belt to strap her to the spindles on the back of the chair. If not for that, she might be able to use her teeth to free one of her wrists – assuming, of course, that she could have worked the bottom of the hood up far enough to expose her mouth.

God! This is impossible! Damn it!

She had been so sure that everything was under control. She had been certain that they would take her to the house at Tadworth. Then David and the team would have rescued her within minutes of them taking her inside. However, she was not at Tadworth. In fact, she had no idea where she was! What were her chances of being rescued now?

GCHQ should have been able to track her to this place via the GPS device hidden in the magazine of the Glock, but how long would it take to assemble a team sufficient to assault this substantial house? Even if they could, what were her chances of still being alive when they found her?

So what next? Torture? Or would Ekerich and Crane send one of their thugs, probably Bittern, down here to kill her. She wondered what method he would use. A bullet to the back of the head would be the kindest. It would be quick and painless. Of course, they might decide to bludgeon her to death or strangle her. She shuddered at the thought. Well, whatever, the end result would be the same. She would be dead – and so would the unborn child inside her. Tears of self-recrimination pricked her eyes. How could she have been so selfish and stupid as to deliberately place her baby at such risk? However, with Sam in danger from these ruthless bastards, what other choice was there?

If only she hadn't met with Jane! Grace and dad would still be alive, Sam would be safe and none of this would be happening.

It was all because Crane and Ekerich suspected that Jane must have told Sandy that Brigadier-General Szopienice was a CIA mole. That was dangerous knowledge because it implied that the CIA, or some faction within it, was in some way complicit with Szopienice's ethnic cleansing activities. She remembered the conversation over lunch in Szopienice's headquarters in a large villa in the town of Pale, near Sarajevo. She had remarked on his excellent English and he had explained that he had been a military attaché at the Yugoslav embassy in Washington in the late Eighties. Perhaps that was when he was turned, but when the relationship had started was irrelevant. What was clear was that Ekerich was sponsoring Szopienice's ethnic cleansing campaign as part of Clermont's wider agenda to provoke conflict between Islamic states and the Western powers.

Her mention of Clermont had shaken them. Clearly, Ekerich was convinced that Jane could have known nothing about it. Now he and Crane would be desperate to discover the source of her information. They had guessed correctly that someone had interrogated Jeanette and they suspected that Sandy had been present. Sandy could expect them to concentrate on what Jeanette had told her about the organisation – and who else was aware of it.

Just how influential was Clermont? How far did its tentacles reach? The Lisbon Agreement should have prevented the Bosnian conflict from starting. Britain's Lord Carrington and the Portuguese Ambassador to Belgrade, Jorge Cutileiro, had brokered a deal that would see Bosnia partitioned into autonomous ethnic zones. There would be no reason to descend into a brutal civil war like the one that was raging in Croatia. The delegates representing the three major ethnic groups had all agreed and all had signed the accord. Ten days later, however, Bosnia's Muslim leader, Alija Izetbegović, changed his mind.

No one knew for sure why Izetbegović reneged on the agreement, only that he did so following a meeting with the United States Ambassador on 28 March 1992. It must have been obvious that such a move would make civil war inevitable, and that ethnic cleansing would follow as surely as night follows day.

Did the US Ambassador encourage Izetbegović to renege? If so, why? It was difficult to see what advantage America might gain from another Balkan war. Perhaps the malign influence of Clermont was working behind the scenes.

Was it possible that Clermont could hold such influence? Did that influence reach into the upper echelons of the British and US governments? Crane had boasted of the wide and growing circle of membership, including intelligence officers, military officers, senior civil servants and government ministers. In addition, they were grooming prospective future senior politicians, people who, once in power, might be predisposed to taking Clermont's advice.

Sandy despaired. Even if all this was only partially true, it suggested an organisation too large and too embedded inside The Establishment ever to be completely eradicated.

Sandy's mind turned to Jeanette, whose behaviour tonight had been odd, to say the least. She had been jittery and nervous when Sandy suggested there might be some clandestine reason for her missing thirty-six hours. Then there was her continued relationship with Ekerich. Under interrogation on Saturday, Jeanette had said that Grebe had ordered her to sleep with the CIA agent, and he had subsequently tricked her into becoming his mole inside Cevapi. She had been cowed into submission under the threat of being forced into prostitution, chained to a bed in the slave brothel known as Dzenita's.

She could sympathise with the poor girl, but that was in Sarajevo. She was in England now. Surely, Ekerich's hold over her was not so great that she could not escape his control here. If that were the case, would she not have come across as a resentful participant in his schemes, rather than his jealous girlfriend?

Moreover, why would a somewhat shy, sensitive girl with Sapphic tendencies willingly remain the mistress of a brute like Ekerich, whom she knew was to blame for the woman she adored? It did not make sense – unless . . .

Sandy's heart flipped. Unless Jeanette was operating undercover!

The more Sandy thought about it the more convinced she became. The clues had been there in the interview. Despite Jeanette's obstinate refusal to talk about Clermont, she willingly gave up much information about her involvement with Ekerich and her mission to locate the missing Sandy. At the time, Sandy was surprised and relieved that Jeanette's subconscious defence mechanism had not been triggered. Now it made sense. She had only given information that supported her undercover story. She had successfully kept hidden the one thing she should not disclose: the truth – that she was a double agent, a mole inside Crane's organisation. What better revenge for Caroline than to bring down the very people whose betrayal caused her death?

Was Jeanette's hissy departure from Crane's study simply a ruse to whistle-up reinforcements? Sandy could only hope, because the alternative – that Jeanette truly was working for Clermont – was too awful to contemplate.

Suddenly, Sandy heard footsteps on the staircase and voices speaking in low tones. The footsteps came closer. There were men in the corridor outside. The sound of a key in the lock.

They were coming for her.

***

Jeanette put down the phone. The arrangements were made; there was no going back. Crossing the room, she opened the door quietly and slipped out.

'What were you doing in there, Jeanie?' Ekerich's voice sounded strained, but it scared her out of her wits. He had just reached the top of the stairs as she closed the door and started along the landing back to their room.

'What?' Ashen-faced, she turned and gasped with surprise. His expression was malevolence personified. His left eye was already puffing-up and starting to bruise and he was holding a very bloody handkerchief to his left cheek.

'I said what were you doing in James's room?'

'Oh, nothing,' she answered lightly. 'What have you done to your head?'

'My head! It's not my fuckin' head! That crazy bitch downstairs bit half my goddamn face off!'

Jeanette suppressed the urge to snigger. 'She did what? How did you manage to let her do that?'

'She karate-kicked me and then jumped on top of me. I tell ya, it took three men to get her offa me. The goddamn bitch is fuckin' crazy!'

'Well, perhaps it serves you right for groping her tits,' Jeanette snapped. 'It was a despicable thing to do.' She turned her back to him huffily and stalked along the landing, glad of the excuse not to have to explain her presence in Barrington's bedroom.

'Hey! Jeanie, come back here,' Ekerich yelled, striding after her.

'Damn you, Rod!' she retorted, portraying the cheated girlfriend. 'I've had just about enough of your perversions. You can sleep somewhere else tonight. You're not sleeping with me.'

'Aw, c'mon, Jeanie. I was interrogating the bitch. I have my methods.'

Jeanette turned and faced him, her face flushed with manufactured anger. 'Yes, Roddy, I've seen enough of your methods today to last a lifetime.'

'Hey, Jeanie, don't be like that! You have a job to do, just like me. And part of your job is to keep me happy.' He smiled what he thought was an engaging smile, but Jeanette was having none of it.

'Roddy, we are part of one of the most important projects in history. Our overarching objective is to save Western civilisation from Islamist fanatics, I don't remember your sexual peccadilloes being on the wider agenda.'

Ekerich's face darkened. Jeanette turned on her heel and stalked along the landing. She reached the door of their room and pulled down the handle. Ekerich grabbed her arm.

'You'll do whatever I fuckin' tell you to do,' he snarled.

Angrily, she whirled to face him. 'Let go of me!'

Ekerich released her arm but then unexpectedly slapped her face. She reeled backwards against the door in surprise. 'And the first thing you're gonna do is fix up my face!'

Jeanette touched her cheek where he had hit her and looked up at Ekerich, forcing her expression to be one of fear and submissiveness rather than the murderous anger that she really felt.

'Well?' Ekerich demanded.

Jeanette patted her hair and ran her hands down her sweater as if to smooth out creases. 'Okay,' she capitulated. 'You wait in the bedroom. I'll ask the housekeeper for the first-aid kit.'

'Nah, she's out. James gave her the night off 'coz of our little party. I guess you'll find it in the kitchen someplace.

'Okay, I'll take a look.' Jeanette said as she began to walk toward the stairs, but Ekerich stopped her with a hand on her arm.

'Just what were you doing in James's bedroom?'

***

K sat at her desk and steepled her fingers. Already disturbed by the latest report from GCHQ, her mind was now reeling from the information relayed to her by David's young assistant, Lucinda. How could James Barrington possibly be mixed up in all this? Surely, he couldn't be Crane. It was beyond belief.

On the other hand, he was one of the few people that knew for certain that Sandy was still alive and living under a new identity. She remembered the meeting in her office in September. Barrington had suggested that the young woman should be transferred to his care at MI6. How convenient that would have been for him if he wished her harm. She could have disappeared without anyone ever knowing what had happened to her. How fortunate that she had already been seconded to MI5. K scowled as the buzz of the phone on her desk interrupted her train of thought.

'I have Mr Mitchell-Hunter for you, Amanda. He's on the secure line.'

'Thank you, Susan. Hullo Neil,' Amanda said apprehensively. It was only fifteen or twenty minutes since she had given him the news that Sandy's journey had ended at the family pile of the MI6 Director General. In turn, Eagle had apologised for not informing her sooner that one of his undercover officers had infiltrated Crane's organisation and was overdue reporting in.

'Good evening, Amanda. My officer was in contact just a few minutes ago. She has confirmed the location and declared a Condition Red. I've instructed her to do all she can to protect Curlew from harm and to facilitate your team's entry into the house. Here's what I propose...'

A few minutes later, K pressed the intercom button. 'Susan, get hold of Lucinda Barnes-Cooper again for me, please.'

Chapter 49

Sandy listened. People were entering the room. The hood prevented her from seeing how many there were, but she could hear shuffling footsteps on the flagstone floor. The sounds echoed from the bare walls, so that they appeared to be coming from all sides.

Sandy fought to control her fear. She was stark naked and her arms and legs were bound to the chair. She was completely helpless and totally exposed to the whims of Crane and his thugs. She tried not to contemplate what they might do to her. At least rape was unlikely while she was in this position – except perhaps orally, but the first man to try that would seriously regret it.

Suddenly, I'm not half the man I used to be . . . The line from the old song came to her from nowhere and despite the unbearable tension, she almost laughed aloud.

From her left, she heard the sound of running water and remembered the counter-interrogation training at Park House, which introduced the trainees to some of the techniques that they might be unlucky enough to encounter in their careers. All of them were unpleasant but none likely to be fatal. Dead prisoners didn't answer questions, after all. On the other hand, she would not be able to resist indefinitely; no one could. Everyone broke eventually. It was just a matter of time. How much time depended on the subject's state of mind.

Crane's voice intruded into her thoughts and she steeled herself for what was to follow. 'Now, Curlew,' he said in his patient professorial tone. 'Let's start again, shall we?'

Sandy's nose wrinkled. She could smell whisky on his breath. At least it wasn't as foul as Ekerich's.

'I don't believe Jane Badell told you about Clermont,' he continued. 'Tell me how you came to hear of it.'

'I've already told you . . .'

'But I don't believe you. I think that you extracted the information about Clermont from Jeanette when you interrogated her while she was drugged on Friday night or Saturday.'

'No. No I didn't – don't know what happened to her. I told you. You'll have to ask her about it.'

'But she has no memory of that time.'

'So she says.' Despite her suspicion that Jeanette might be a mole in Crane's group, Sandy had to maintain consistency. She had to give the impression of trying to undermine the other woman's story.

'And I believe she's telling the truth, and that you are lying.'

'Suit yourself,' Sandy replied, suppressing the fear that was gnawing at her insides.

'I want to know all of the information you got from Jeanette's interrogation, the names of any others present and those of anyone else you have passed the information to.'

'I keep telling you, I know nothing about that. Jane Badell told me about Clermont and I've told the whole world. You can read all about it in tomorrow's papers.'

'Most amusing,' replied Crane. 'Badell knew nothing about Clermont. Therefore she couldn't have told you about it.'

'Well she did and she did.'

'How do you think she might have come by that information?'

'Perhaps you could have asked her yourself – if you hadn't murdered her.'

'You know, Curlew, you are really not helping yourself. I suggest you start cooperating.'

'I've answered all your questions. I can't help it if you don't believe me.'

'I don't believe your answers because they don't make any sense.' Crane sighed theatrically and continued, 'I've given you every chance to tell me the truth, but still you persist in lying to me. You leave me no alternative than to apply a little . . . persuasion.'

Sandy's blood ran cold. She detected an instant change in the atmosphere. Suddenly, there was an air of almost sexual anticipation. In her mind's eye she saw the men licking their lips, salivating over what they were about to do to her.

Suddenly, she cried out in alarm. Without warning, several men had grabbed the chair and were tipping it backwards. Before she knew it, Sandy was on her back and water was gushing over the hood. It soaked and penetrated the weave so that when she tried to breathe water entered her mouth and nose and was aspirated into her airway. She coughed and retched, trying to purge the water from her lungs. Convinced that she was drowning, her body convulsed. Her limbs thrashed against the tapes binding her to the chair.

The torture lasted for thirty or forty seconds, but it seemed like a lifetime. Sandy was certain she was going to die. Then, as suddenly as it started, the torment was over. They turned the chair onto its side and someone yanked the hood from her head. Sandy lay like a fish out of water, gasping for oxygen. Her lungs burned. She coughed violently and painfully, desperate to purge the water from her airway.

Gradually, her senses returned and her vision cleared. She was lying on her side with her head next to a drain that was set into a grey flagstone floor. The arm of the chair was digging uncomfortably into her ribs. Crane, Bittern, Kestrel and Jerry stood in a circle looking down at her. A fifth man – whose name she did not know – was holding a large green watering can. As her eyes fell upon him, he turned to refill it from a brass tap above an old-fashioned butler's sink.

'Stand the chair up,' snapped Crane.

Jerry and Kestrel stood the chair upright and retreated a few paces. Sandy blinked water from her eyes. Crane was standing in front, looking down at her. There was no attempt at concealment now, confirming her assumption that his plans for her would end in her death.

'Right, Curlew,' said Crane in a crisp, businesslike tone, 'I'm going to ask you again. What did you discuss with Jane Badell when you met with her in August?'

I told you,' she shouted, prompting another bout of coughing. 'It was nothing but small talk.'

'At what point in the conversation did Clermont come up?'

'I don't remember!'

Crane sighed and glanced at Bittern who nodded at his companions. Three men took positions on either side and behind the chair and Bittern approached from the front. Sandy shook her head from side to side, trying to prevent Bittern from covering her head with the hood, but it was no use. As soon as the hood was on, they tipped the chair backwards and Sandy screamed involuntarily. The scream was cut off as the water poured over her face again.

She tried at first to hold her breath, but one of the men noticed and jabbed her in the solar plexus. The blow was unexpected and caused her to exhale. She tried to turn her head away, but someone was holding her, forcing her to remain face-up. Paul Duncan was pouring slowly, a continuous stream of water that gave no opportunity for her to take a breath. The sodden material filled her nose and mouth when she breathed in and once again, she felt as though she were drowning. Again, her body convulsed and thrashed against the restraints. Her head swam and she lost all sense of time, unaware even when the flow of water stopped and they turned her onto her side. The next thing she knew she was sitting upright with the hood again removed. She felt utterly exhausted and disoriented and her head sagged forward, her chin resting on her chest.

'Are you prepared to start telling the truth now?' Crane sounded like a schoolmaster trying patiently to get a troublesome child to admit to scribbling graffiti on the toilet walls.

Sandy knew she could not continue to withstand this treatment for much longer. Perhaps now might be the time to give up some of the information that she had pieced together from Jeanette's interview and from what she had heard in Crane's study. Every minute she spent talking would a minute's delay in the resumption of torture. Every minute's delay gave her more time to recover, and more time for David or Jeanette to come to her rescue.

'Okay, okay,' she gasped. 'I'll tell you. I'll tell you what I know.'

Crane allowed himself a satisfied smirk. 'Good. Good. Let's hear it then.'

'It was Webber,' she said. 'Webber knew about Clermont. He warned Jane of the danger they posed to her.'

Crane stiffened at her response. He frowned and moved away from her, deep in thought, his hand cupping his chin.

It had been a calculated guess. Jeanette had disclosed that Jane and Webber were old friends. As DG of MI6 Webber may well have been aware of Clermont and it was possible that he had warned Jane about them. Crane's reaction suggested that she might have guessed correctly.

What Sandy did not know was that six or seven months earlier, Crane had tried to convince his late chief to abort Operation Cevapi. At the same time, he had sounded him out about Clermont's aims, but had backed off when he sensed the man's lack of sympathy with the cause.

Crane walked across and spoke quietly to Kestrel, who immediately left the room. No one spoke to or even looked at Sandy and she wondered if she had overplayed her hand. Had they decided now was the time to kill her?

***

'Nosy!' said Ekerich, reminding Jeanette of her excuse for being in Crane's bedroom. 'You said you were being nosy. What were you looking for?' He was lying on his back on the bed. His trousers and underwear were around his knees and he had hitched his shirt up above his navel. He was still wearing the shoulder holster, but the Colt was on the Victorian bedside table.

Grimacing, Jeanette spat into a tissue. She was sitting on the edge of the bed, her clothes in a pile on the floor alongside. After she had tended to his facial injury, he had forced her to strip and perform oral sex on him. He said it was to relax him after the incident in Barrington's study, but Jeanette knew it was to reassert his dominance after her earlier show of defiance.

'With all the lovely antique furniture here in our room,' she explained, 'I wondered what wonders might be in the other bedrooms.'

'Crazy bitch,' he said, enjoying watching her put on her black, lace-trimmed bikini-briefs. 'Did you find anything interesting?'

Jeanette sat back on the bed to pull on her jeans. 'Well, I'm no expert, but I'm sure there's a Gainsborough hanging on the wall in there.'

'Yeah? What's a Gainsbro?'

Jeanette knew less about art than quantum physics, but she remembered hearing somewhere that Gainsborough painted portraits. There were a couple of portraits in Barrington's room but she had no idea who painted them.

'God! You are such an ignoramus,' she said and laughed lightly. 'He was an artist – a painter.'

As she spoke, she subtly took hold of the scissors that, along with the dressing gauze and the roll of sticky plaster, she had borrowed from the kitchen. The blades were seven inches long and sharply pointed. Gripping them like a dagger, she continued speaking.

'I think there's a Turner in the study, too.'

'You don't say!' Ekerich raised his hips off the bed to pull up his underwear and trousers.

Jeanette stroked his forehead tenderly with her left hand, the hand that would hold his head still as she drove the scissors through his left eye-socket into his brain. Death would be instantaneous, silent and virtually bloodless. She would then turn him on his side, facing away from the door and pull the bedcovers over him. To the casual observer, he would appear asleep.

She rose to her feet, focussing on his left eye above the large square of gauze held in place by strips of plaster. Tensing her arm, she prepared to strike.

A loud knock at the bedroom door startled her. Cursing under her breath, she slipped the scissors into a back pocket in her jeans. She kicked her bra under the bed and picked up her sweater.

'Who the fuck's there?' Ekerich yelled.

'It's Dennis.' Dennis was Kestrel's Christian name. 'James wants to know when you're coming back down. There's been a development.'

'What sort of development?'

'Crane will explain. You coming?'

Ekerich grinned lewdly at Jeanette and said quietly, 'I just did!' Then louder he said, 'What? Yeah, I'll be right down'.

Jeanette pulled on the sweater and adjusted the hem to cover the handles of the scissors. She opened the door a few inches while, behind her, Ekerich finished adjusting his clothing and slipped the Colt into its holster.

'He'll be with you in a minute, Dennis.'

'Cheers! Tell him to go straight down. I'm going to the security room.'

'What for?'

Kestrel looked at her as if puzzled by the question. 'James wants me to watch the security monitors.'

'Oh, don't worry about that. I'll do that. You'll be more use helping with the interrogation, I should think.'

'Well...'

'Sure, Dennis,' agreed Ekerich. He had come up behind Jeanette and squeezed her waist possessively. 'Jeanie here can watch the monitors. You come back down with me. You can stand behind me and protect my ass from your buddy, Martin.'

Kestrel grinned. 'I don't think you're his type. I think he prefers 'em young and tender.'

Ekerich stepped past Jeanette and the two men began walking to the staircase. In an uncharacteristic show of camaraderie, Ekerich placed an arm around Kestrel's shoulders.

'You talking from experience, boy?'

'Oi,' Kestrel replied with mock indignation.

Jeanette watched their backs until they were out of sight, and then slowly descended the stairs to the ground floor.

***

'This is crap,' Ekerich bellowed, waving his arm around as if conducting an orchestra. 'Webber knew jack-shit about Clermont!' He glared at Crane. 'Unless, maybe you told him something?'

Sandy waited with trepidation while Crane brought Ekerich up-to-date. They were standing alone, away from everyone else, but they need not have taken the trouble; everyone in the room could hear what was they were saying. Ekerich asked again how Webber could possibly have known. Clearly, they had believed that the flow of information was from Badell to Webber, not the other way round. Finally, Ekerich came over to Sandy, leaving Crane watching with arms folded as if resentful of Ekerich's arrogation of the interview and sceptical that he would achieve better results.

'How're you feeling now, honey?' Ekerich asked, his face inches from hers.

'I'm fine, thanks. How's your face, prick?' She spat in his face for a second time, noting with satisfaction his look of surprise and anger. There was a buzz of murmuring and suppressed sniggers from the other men in the room.

He wiped her spittle from his face. The corners of his mouth turned down. His eyes blazed with anger and malice.

'You all really are a stubborn little whore, aren't you?' He touched the gauze square on his cheek. 'Jeanie fixed this up with a couple o' Band-Aids. You're gonna need a whole lot more than that to fix you when I'm done here.' He turned to Bittern. 'Put her under again!'

This time Sandy was prepared. It had been at least ten minutes since the last session and she had worked out the pattern. When the water-boarding was underway she had no control over events. She simply had to endure it until they had exhausted the water in the can. It was afterwards that they applied the most pressure. That was when, terrified of the next partial drowning, the victim was most likely to crack. Now, instead of allowing her mind to panic, she concentrated on what she might be able to say to keep them from repeating the torture again – or worse, deciding she had no more to give and thus have no reason to keep her alive any longer. What could she say, she wondered, that would keep them interested?

'Now tell me again where you heard about Clermont,' Ekerich said, when they brought her up again, gasping and coughing. His nose was inches from hers as if daring her to spit in his face again. 'Who have you talked to about it?'

'I'm not saying anything else unless you give me a way out of this,' she replied. 'I know you're planning to kill me once you've found out what I know and who I've told. Your problem is they already know all about you and that you're holding me prisoner. Kill me and things will get a whole lot worse for you. Let me live and I might be able to help you.'

Although Crane was further away from her than Ekerich, she maintained eye contact with him. Of the two, she thought him the most likely to be uneasy about the consequences of their actions.

Ekerich's jaw dropped and Crane looked stunned by Sandy's declaration and proposition. Once more they put their heads together for a few seconds before Ekerich looked at her angrily.

'You are in no fuckin' position to start dictating terms, missy. We'll get everything we need out of you before we finish here! Put her down again, boys. Let's remind her who's running this show!'

Sandy held out for another five repetitions without offering any more information. Finally, she decided she had had enough. She could take no more, but neither could she allow herself to break. She was never going to disclose her suspicion that Jeanette was a double-agent, nor would she say anything that might lead these bastards to David and Amanda. There was one other way out, however. It might lead to an earlier death for her, but they were going to kill her anyway. Once they thought they had extracted everything from her, death was an inevitable outcome. At least this way she could avoid endangering others. As she lay gasping on the floor after the latest round, Ekerich heard her speaking between coughs. He thought that they had finally broken her and leaned closer to hear what she was saying.

'Yesterday,' she croaked, 'up. . . on. . . the. . . stair, I met a man. . .' *wheeze* '. . . who wasn't there. He wasn't . . .'

'What's this shit?' Ekerich demanded

Crane looked puzzled and ordered the men to pick her up again.

'. . .there again today.

'Curlew?' He shouted into her face. 'Curlew!'

'Oh, how I wish he'd go away!'

'Look, if you think . . .'

'Yesterday, upon the stair, I met a man who wasn't there.'

Ekerich slapped her hard across the face. It made no difference. Sandy barely faltered.

'He wasn't there again today. Oh, how I wish he'd go away!'

'If you're trying to be funny . . .' Crane said, taking her by the shoulders and shaking her.

'James?' Bittern said over Sandy's continuous recital. 'James! She's gone. You won't get her back now.'

'What the fuck's happening?' Ekerich demanded.

Bittern explained about the subconscious anti-interrogation trigger and the only remedy, the keyword on file at Park House.

'That's bullshit!' Ekerich replied angrily. 'She's gotta be fuckin' fakin' it! Dunk her again.'

'There's no point . . .'

'Do it anyway,' Crane shouted at Bittern. 'Keep going until she stops repeating that bloody nursery rhyme!'

'Yesterday, upon the stair . . .'

The men surrounded the chair. Sandy continued reciting

'I met a man who wasn't there.'

'Wait! The hood!' Bittern said. He picked it up and placed it over Sandy's head so that her next words were muffled.

'He wasn't there again today . . .'

The chair tilted backwards.

'Oh, how I wish he'd go away.'

The words died as the water cascaded over the hood. As before, Sandy's body heaved and thrashed against her restraints. After thirty seconds, Paul stopped pouring and turned to refill the can. Bittern pulled off the hood. Sandy's breathing was laboured and she coughed and wheezed continuously.

'See?' said Crane. 'She's stopped.'

'That's because she's fucking drowning!' said Jerry. 'Get her on her side, for Christ's sake!'

They turned the chair onto its side – gently so as not to knock the prisoner's head on the flagstones and render her unconscious – or worse, kill her before they were ready. It took a whole minute before the pathetic figure appeared to recover. She lay there breathing raggedly, but to Crane's relief, not repeating the nursery rhyme. They raised the chair up once again and Crane leaned closer to Sandy. Her eyes were glazed, unfocussed.

'Curlew? Curlew? Look at me.'

The eyes stared into the middle distance showing no sign of recognition.

'Now, stop playing games and tell me who you've told about Szopienice and Clermont.'

'He wasn't there again today . . .'

'Oh, for the love of God!'

'Oh, how I wish he'd go away.'

'You might as well just drown her properly now,' Bittern said callously. 'She'll be no more use to us after this.'

'Look, you asshole,' Ekerich growled, poking his finger into Bittern's chest and ignoring the dangerous expression that clouded the latter's face. 'I need to know everything she knows about Szopienice and Clermont and who she's told! Otherwise we'll always be looking over our shoulders!'

No one noticed that the prisoner had stopped reciting and was sitting quietly, slack jawed, her mouth open. Moments later, a voice from the doorway drew everyone's attention.

'James?' Jeanette walked into the room. She looked at the pathetic, naked figure lolling, apparently unconscious in the chair and gasped. Was she too late to save her? She fought to avoid showing any emotion and said, 'There are two policemen in the hall waiting to speak to you.'

'Police? What do they want? How the blazes did they get through the gate?'

'I buzzed them in.'

'You did what? Why? What were you thinking of, Jeanette?' Crane's face was a mask of incredulity while Ekerich's expression was thunderous. The other men looked totally bemused.

'Are you fuckin' crazy?' Ekerich yelled.

'Sorry, but what else could I do? If I'd refused them entry, they might have got suspicious.'

'Damn it, Jeanette! I'm the head of MI6! Of course you can refuse entry.' He looked around and ran his fingers through his wiry grey hair. 'God, look at me! I'm dishevelled and my clothes are soaking wet.' He took a deep breath to regain his composure. 'Look, go back and tell them I'll be a few minutes. Get 'em a cup of tea or something. I need to go up to the bedroom and change. You men stay down here with her,' he indicated the quiescent prisoner, 'and keep her quiet.'

'Did she tell you anything?' Jeanette asked as they left the room.

'Yes,' Crane replied bitterly. 'She told me about a man she met on the stair. Apparently, he wasn't there.'

'You know what that means don't you?' Jeanette said, 'You won't get anything more out of her.'

'So I'm told. So I am bloody told.'

Jeanette watched Crane climb the back stairs, which, in days long past, the servants would have used to go about their duties unseen by the master's family and guests. She frowned with concern for Sandy and headed for the other staircase and the waiting police officers.

Chapter 50

James Barrington had changed into brown corduroy trousers, a check shirt and a sports jacket with dogtooth weave. He entered the study and eyed the two waiting police officers. They were sipping coffee as they examined the paintings on the walls and the eclectic collection of books on the shelves.

'Good evening, gentlemen. How can I be of help?'

'Good evening, sir,' Burroughs said and introduced himself and his colleague.

'What's this all about, Inspector?'

'Sorry to disturb you, Mr Barrington,' Burroughs replied, 'but we've had some rather disturbing intelligence from our colleagues in Special Branch. They asked us to contact you straight away.' Burroughs had changed out of the black coveralls and presented himself wearing a civilian raincoat that he had borrowed from David, over his uniform shirt and trousers. His companion, one of the local officers from Chipping Norton, was in full uniform. Another uniformed officer waited in the car outside the front door.

'Right,' Barrington replied. 'Please, gentlemen, take a seat. Would you like something a little stronger than coffee?'

'No, thank you, sir. We're fine,' Burroughs answered for both of them.

'Haven't we met before?' Barrington asked, pouring himself a malt whisky from a crystal decanter. He took his glass and perched himself on the edge of the desk, regarding the two men who, he noticed, had declined to take up his offer to sit.

Hands clasped behind his back, Burroughs stood, rocking on the balls of his feet. The other officer hovered slightly behind and a few steps to his superior's right.

'I'm flattered you remember me, sir. We met at a Round Table dinner last year.'

'Ah, yes. Armed Response, right?'

'Correct, sir, but I'm the station duty-officer tonight.'

'Okay, Inspector, what brings you here at this time of night?'

Burroughs glanced at the beautiful redhead seated decorously on the arm of a leather Chesterfield. Jeanette took the hint and stood up.

'If you'll excuse me, gentlemen, I have some things I have to attend to.' She left the room and closed the door quietly behind her.

'Okay,' said Barrington as the door closed, 'shoot.'

'It seems a Special Branch officer, working undercover with the IRA, found your name on a hit-list. It seems the Libyans have contracted out the hit to the Provo's.'

Barrington laughed. 'Well, surely that's no surprise! It goes with the job.'

'The threat appears to be imminent, sir,' Burroughs insisted. 'We have increased the mobile patrols in the area and I've taken the liberty of instructing my men to search the grounds of your house.' This was not entirely true, but it would explain the presence of his men should anyone see them on the monitors as they clandestinely approached the house.

Barrington spluttered into his whisky then looked up at Burroughs. His face was flushed with sudden anger. Burroughs thought the MI6 chief might be about to explode.

***

Jeanette closed the door quietly and crossed the hall to the dining room. At the far end were French doors leading onto the west terrace and the gardens. Glancing nervously over her shoulder, she unlocked the doors and pushed them open. Six black-clad figures slipped silently into the room. Each wore body armour and carried a Heckler and Koch carbine and a holstered semi-automatic pistol. Quickly, Jeanette explained how she planned to lure the targets into a position where they could be arrested, hopefully without bloodshed. Although he had been assured that the young lady was a highly-trained undercover intelligence officer, well able to deal with this type of situation, Sergeant Hooper, Burroughs' second-in-command, had serious reservations. The problem was that she looked far too young and, well, gorgeous for that to be true.

Nevertheless, he followed Jeanette when she led the way into the hall, and his men followed him. Using hand signals, he stationed one officer near the top of the staircase while he and the others followed her down to the basement.

'They are all in there,' she said, pointing to the closed double doors of the wine cellar.

Opposite the wine cellar was the entrance to the old kitchen, now a storeroom, and beyond that, the old servants' staircase at the rear of the house.

Noiseless in their rubber-soled boots, the armed officers deployed themselves into concealed positions in the doorways and on both staircases. Then Jeanette took a deep breath, opened the door to the wine cellar and walked through, closing it behind her.

'What's happening up there, Jeannie?' Ekerich asked.

'They've gone,' Jeanette said distractedly, meaning the police. Her eyes were drawn to the empty chair with the watering can on the floor beside it. She glanced around but there was no sign of Sandy. Also missing were Bittern and Kestrel. 'James wants to see all of you upstairs right away,' she continued. 'I was supposed to stay with Curlew. Where is she?'

'What does he want?' Ekerich asked.

'I suppose it's something to do with the police's visit,' Jeanette replied. 'He didn't say.'

Ekerich shrugged. 'Okay, let's go see what the man wants.'

'Where's Curlew?' Jeanette repeated.

'Your Caesar buddies took her out the back way. With the cops nosing around we had to get rid of her.'

'You mean she's dead?' Jeanette could not keep her voice from betraying her shock.

'If not, she soon will be,' Ekerich replied coldly.

'Where have they taken her?'

'They're going to dump her in the lake,' Jerry grumbled, his regret obvious.

Ekerich looked askance at Jeanette. 'What's your beef? She was no friend of yours!'

Jeanette swallowed. 'No, not anymore,' she managed to say. 'Had you finished interrogating her?'

'She was blown out,' Jerry said, heading toward the door. 'Her mind had gone. We wouldn't have got any more out of her. You guys coming?'

Jeanette held the door open and let Paul and Jerry through. Ekerich was last in line but stopped as he reached the doorway.

'After you, Jeanie,' he grunted with uncharacteristic chivalry.

Jeanette hesitated. It was important to ensure that all the men left the room together. In an instant, Ekerich's instinct told him something was wrong. He grabbed Jeanette's forearm and dragged her aside, at the same time kicking the door shut. At that very moment, pandemonium erupted in the corridor outside.

'ARMED POLICE! Put your hands in the air! On your knees! Down! Down!'

'You treacherous bitch!' Ekerich yelled and slapped Jeanette's face so hard that she fell to the floor. He drew the Colt and pointed it at her head.

Jeanette stared into the muzzle. Would he shoot? He was certainly angry enough to do it. She knew that her only chance was to persuade him to give up. Rising to her feet, she stretched out her hand and spoke as calmly as she could.

'Come on Roddy, hand it over. The place is crawling with armed police. There's no way out.'

The Colt wavered as Ekerich glanced over his shoulder at the door. The police were demanding the occupants of the room come out with their hands up.

'There's no way out,' Jeanette repeated. 'Give me your gun now or you'll end up getting shot. Roddy, please!'

The hand holding the Colt steadied and Ekerich's eyes went cold. Jeanette shook her head in disbelief. Surely, this cold, soulless basement room could not be where her life ended. At first, she felt resigned to her fate, like a mouse facing a python's hypnotic gaze. Strangely, she felt more sadness than fear, but then she shook herself out of her stupor. The training that she had received at Park House kicked in and she knew she should do what Ekerich least expected. Screaming at the top of her voice, she launched herself at him, hoping to unnerve him as she tackled him.

Her desperate plan failed. Without hesitation, Ekerich pulled the trigger. The .45 calibre bullet clipped Jeanette's left ear, carving a deep groove in the antihelix, but it did nothing to slow her momentum. She crashed into Ekerich, knocking him to the ground and landing on top of him. She grabbed his right wrist with her left hand and attempted to gouge at his eyes with her right. Cursing, he turned his head away from her sharp fingernails. At the same time, he wrenched his right wrist against her thumb, the weak point of her grip, freeing his gun hand. Before she could react, he swung the barrel of the Colt into the side of her head. She cried out once, then slumped, a dead weight on top of him

Chapter 51

The track leading down to the lake was just wide enough for one vehicle. Dark woods crowded in from both sides and there were frequent sharp bends where the route skirted around large trees. The almost relentless drizzle of the previous few days had turned the packed earth surface slushy and slippery, made worse by a thick layer of decaying leaves.

Bittern peered out through the rain-splattered windscreen and wondered if even the all-wheel-drive Range Rover, in which they were travelling, was capable of negotiating this treacherous byway.

'There's an old, leaky rowing boat at the lake,' he said, unconsciously clutching at the grab handle above the door as the vehicle bounced and slipped its way along the rutted track. 'It's drawn up on the bank a couple of hundred yards from the slipway. We'll float it and tie her to the thwarts or rowlocks. Then we push the boat out into the lake and shoot a few more holes in it with this . . .' He patted the hunting-rifle beside him. 'When it sinks it'll take her down with it.'

'What a bloody waste!' Kestrel lamented, thinking of the beauty with the clear blue eyes, the long, shapely legs, that lithe, supple body. He took one hand from the steering wheel and shifted the gear selector from L2 to L1 as they tackled yet another steep slope.

'Can't you go any slower?' Bittern grumbled. 'At this rate it'd be quicker to walk!'

Lying curled up in the load space behind the rear seats Sandy listened to their conversation. Her heart was racing, but her mind was working even faster. If she could not think of a way out of her predicament soon, it would be all over.

Twenty minutes earlier, just after Crane and Jeanette had left the wine cellar, Sandy had heard Ekerich pronounce her death sentence. Coldly, the men had discussed how best to kill her. Shooting her would be too noisy and would create a mess that would need clearing up. Bittern had suggested that it would be better to drown or strangle her in the cellar. Kestrel had argued that it would be awkward to transport the body to where they planned to dispose of it. In the end, they decided it would be easier to make her walk to the chosen location and kill her there. No one had defended her in the discussion. No one had argued against killing her. Not even Jerry, dashing her hopes that he might turn out to be her saviour. Jerry had contributed little to the discussion and had not attempted to intervene. Unsurprisingly, once they reached an agreement on how and where the deed was to be done, it was Bittern that volunteered to do the job and roped Kestrel in to help.

Sandy had to work hard to hide her hope and excitement. She knew that she had a far better chance of escape from two men outside the building than from five inside. She maintained her feigned catatonic state when Kestrel cut the tapes that bound her to the chair and she offered no resistance when Bittern covered her mouth with duct-tape and placed the sodden hood over her head once more. She cursed under her breath when he bound her hands behind her back with cable-ties. This would make it more difficult for her to escape.

They took her through an echoing corridor, which was actually an underground tunnel, leading to the old coach house, now used as a garage. There they lifted her into the load space behind the rear seats of the Range Rover, and covered her with a foul-smelling waxed-cotton coat.

As the tailgate slammed shut, Sandy had heard a noise that sounded like someone opening and closing a metal cabinet. She had wondered what it signified. Now, lying in the back of the big four-by-four as it laboured along the rough, slippery woodland track, she understood. The noise she had heard was Bittern taking some sort of rifle from a gun-cabinet. Clearly, if he intended shooting holes in a wooden rowing boat from a distance, a pistol would be useless. He would need a rifle to achieve sufficient accuracy and power over a longer range.

Despite the hopelessness of her situation, Sandy was determined not to make it easy for them. When they came to take her out of the car she would fight like a wildcat until they overpowered her or shot her, but to stand even a glimmer of a chance, she needed her hands free. She had given up trying to slip the cable-ties over her hands or break the one joining them. The next best thing would be to get her bound hands to her front. The two Caesar men should have remembered that during training the recruits had practised getting out of such a situation. Despite her pregnancy, Sandy was still slim and supple. It should be possible. The difficult part would be to do it without drawing the attention of the two men in the front seats.

Already lying in an "S" shape, with her knees to her chest, Sandy forced her bound wrists over her bottom to the backs of her knees. Then she drew her knees up either side of her head and pulled her feet through the loop of her arms.

Now, although her wrists were still bound together, at least they were in front and she could strike a blow or two. She removed the hood and dropped it on the floor, then peeled back the tape covering her mouth. Now she could breathe again. Now for a weapon.

Exploring with feet and hands, she felt around the load space for something – anything – that she might use as a weapon. Her hands found a spare tyre, bolted to the vehicle's side near her head. Perhaps there might be a tyre lever or wheel-jack tucked behind. Awkwardly, she tried to turn the large wing nut that held it in place, but she could not get enough purchase with her fingers. She shifted position slightly and tried again. Still, it would not budge.

Suddenly, the vehicle came to a halt and Sandy knew she was out of time.

Oh God! This is it.

Even with a weapon, the odds of her survival would have been depressingly slim; with nothing but her hands and feet she had no chance. Nevertheless, she was determined to go down fighting.

The interior lights came on as a door opened and she heard Bittern say, 'Wait here. I'll get the boat into the water and bring it closer so we don't have to drag her too far.'

'Martin? Why do you hate her so much?'

'What do you mean?'

'You and her; it's personal isn't it? What has she done to make you hate her?'

'She killed Adrian,' Bittern replied. 'That's enough, isn't it?'

'It was an op and she's a pro...'

'She's not a pro,' Bittern sneered. 'She's a stuck-up, know-it-all little bitch who never knew her place.' He raised his voice. 'Can you hear me back there?'

Sandy remained silent.

'What did she do?'

'Never mind, but I'm going to enjoy watching her see it coming. I might even put a couple of rounds into her legs first, just to make it painful.'

'Don't be so fucking unprofessional, Martin. It's a job. Do it quick and clean.'

The door slammed shut and Sandy was alone with Kestrel. Sandy allowed herself to hope. Perhaps she had a chance after all.

***

David and Lucinda entered via the French doors in the wake of the police officers. Guided by the sound of voices they strode quickly across the parquet-floor of the drawing room and across the quarry-tiled hall to the study. They found Burroughs stoically absorbing a torrent of invective from the silver haired and moustachioed Barrington. Barrington suddenly became aware of the new presence in the room. He turned to face them, taking in David's finely tailored suit and his young companion's black puffer jacket, mid-length skirt and sensible shoes.

'And who the devil are you?' He demanded.

'David Richardson, Security Service, and this is my colleague, Lucinda Barnes-Cooper. Mr Burroughs, if you would be so kind . . .'

Like a dog released from the leash, Burroughs stepped forward and laid a hand on Barrington's shoulder.

'James Barrington, I'm arresting you for offences contrary to the Official Secrets Act, 1989. Also, for the abduction and false imprisonment of a member of the Security Service, and conspiracy to commit murder. You do not have to say anything but anything you do say will be taken down and may be used in evidence against you. Handcuffs, please, Constable Wilcox.'

Barrington opened his mouth to protest but shouts of "Armed Police" from downstairs seized everyone's attention. David strode briskly toward the sound with Lucinda hot on his heels, leaving Burroughs and Wilcox to complete the arrest of an apoplectic James Barrington.

The first black-clad officer that David encountered was a few steps down the staircase. His carbine was at his shoulder, the barrel pointing down toward the basement below.

'What's happening?' David asked.

The officer replied without turning his head.

'Two of 'em are being 'cuffed down there. There's others holed up in a room at the end of the corridor.'

'What about the women?'

'Not sure what's 'appening, there, sir. 'Aven't seen anyone but those two since the redhead went down.'

'Thanks,' David said and brushed past him.

'Hang on, sir, you can't go down there!'

David ignored him and descended the stairs two at a time. Not to be outdone, Lucinda followed him, thankful that she had chosen to wear flat shoes rather than heels today.

'Stop, miss, oh, fuck! You two! Come back 'ere!'

At the bottom of the stairs, one officer watched over two handcuffed men lying face down on the floor of the corridor while three more covered the arched entrance to the wine cellar, barred by solid-looking oak double doors.

'Better stop right there, sir,' Sgt Hooper said to David

'Have either of these two said anything?' David asked abruptly, aware that Lucinda had just sidled up beside him.

'No, sir. Not a word from either of them.'

'How many are in the room?' David demanded of the nearest prisoner.

Jerry shrugged and said nothing.

'Where's the female officer you were interrogating? Is she okay?'

'No comment,' Jerry muttered.

Hooper touched his elbow. 'We think both women are in there with three male suspects.'

'You think?' David repeated, exasperated by the turn of events.

'The young lady said they were all in there. She went in to flush them out but only these two appeared before the door was slammed shut. We've heard voices. They seem to be arguing, so now we'll have to wait and see what happens.'

'Well, do something, man,' for God's sake,' David exploded. 'My officer is in extreme danger in there.'

Hooper shook his head. 'If we go steaming in it could make things worse.'

At that moment came the sounds of a banshee scream and a single gunshot from inside the wine cellar. Everyone froze – everyone except David.

'Wait! Stop!'

Ignoring Hooper's protest, David drew his Walther and ran the few steps to the wine cellar. He turned the door-handle and shouldered the heavy oak door. To his surprise, it was unlocked and he stumbled into the room, instinctively throwing himself to the floor. When he looked up, he was staring straight down the barrel of a Colt 45.

Chapter 52

Bittern pushed his hands deep into the side-pockets of his black bomber-jacket and lowered his head. The wind coming off the lake was driving the drizzle horizontally into his face, stinging his cheeks and clinging to his eyelashes.

Was it personal? Yes, it was bloody personal. He hated that stuck-up bitch. Her and all the other bitches that, throughout his life, had looked down on him, mocked him and made him feel small.

It had been that way since the adolescent Martin Gresham first showed an interest in girls as anything other than alien creatures to tease or bully. Suddenly, he no longer wanted to flick their ears, pull their hair or ping their bra-straps. His hormones drove him to consider other activities with them. Only now the tables had turned. The little bitches that once ran away from him in the playground now laughed at him and mocked his bumbling, tongue-tied efforts to attract them.

'Oh, look at Martin,' they would say, 'He's trying it on.' None of them gave him a chance. None of them wanted to go out with him. They would never let him kiss them, let alone allow him to get any further.

It was not the same for the other boys. They bragged about their conquests, how far the girls had let them go. Some even claimed to have gone "all the way". It simply wasn't fair!

Gresham's anger and frustration boiled within until one afternoon he decided enough was enough. He lay in wait for Susan Duggan, a girl rumoured to be "easy". He dragged her into a service road behind a parade of shops near the school and proceeded to kiss, grope and try to undress her. He had convinced himself that she would be compliant if he used a little muscle, showed her who was boss.

To his dismay, things did not go according to plan. She fought; she screamed; she scratched his face. She fought so hard and screamed so loudly that Gresham lost his nerve and ran away. Inevitably, her parents complained to the school and the miscreant was hauled before the Headmaster. The head gave Gresham a severe dressing down and told him to write a letter of apology to the girl. He was, the Head pointed out, very lucky that he had persuaded Susan's parents not to report the matter to the police.

Of course, Gresham did not blame himself for his predicament. It was that bitch Susan. It was obvious she had wanted it. She knew it; he knew it. There was no need for her to go blabbing to her parents or teachers. A boy would never have grassed him up, no matter what he had done. Of course, girls always have to make a drama out of everything. They're always looking for attention. She had made a big fuss over nothing. From that day forward, he wanted nothing more to do with girls and satisfied his needs in solitary acts, usually with a suitable magazine to hand.

Gresham left school the following year and found a job as a trainee motor mechanic in a garage near his home. Months later, a documentary on TV about the Commandos in the Second World War had him yearning for a life of adventure. He dreamed of storming ashore from high-speed boats or abseiling down vertical cliffs, without a troublesome female in sight.

At the age of eighteen, Gresham joined the Royal Marines. He soon proved to be adept with weapons and a natural at field-craft. He trained as a sniper with Reconnaissance Troop and rose to the rank of sergeant. Later he would become a weapons and tactics instructor.

These were happy times. Few women encroached into this masculine world, and he revelled in the company of men like himself. Where he differed from most of his comrades was in his aversion to women. While his mates frequently went out "on the pull", he would shy away from any contact with the opposite sex. His attitude to women inevitably, but incorrectly, led to the assumption that he was a homosexual, which at that time was illegal in the British armed forces. To make matters worse, pernicious rumours began to circulate that the sergeant-instructor was in the habit of importuning vulnerable young recruits. Things came to a head when an inept recruit, unhappy at being disciplined by Gresham, and being aware of the rumours about him, complained to an officer that the sergeant had tried to coerce him into "unnatural activity". Incandescent with rage at the false accusation, Gresham confronted the boy in a dark corner and beat him so badly that he was hospitalised. The resulting investigation into the incident ended with Gresham's court-martial and discharge on what was euphemistically phrased "medical grounds".

On the recommendation of a former Reconnaissance Troop commander, now a Caesar officer, Gresham joined as an instructor and "black-ops" specialist. Already on the back foot, having been forced out of the male-oriented world of his beloved Marines, the man now designated Bittern found to his dismay that he was once more in the company of females.

Worst of all, these were the type of females that he found most disturbing. They were all beautiful, intelligent, confident and sharp-witted – and, for the most part, from privileged backgrounds. Many of them unfortunately retained the mindset of immature students, prone to practical jokes and mockery. He hated them all. All of them except the disturbingly attractive blonde Curlew.

Disturbingly attractive because of her slim, taut, almost boyish body, her short hair, small breasts, slim hips and long limbs. In Bittern's opinion, Curlew should have been a man. She was tough and determined. She was a crack shot with every weapon in the armoury. She attacked the assault course as if her life depended on it. She waded through the lake and crawled through the mud with as much enthusiasm as the other girls displayed reluctance.

He became obsessed with her; found himself fascinated by her and fantasising about her, attracted to her in a way that no female had attracted him since the incident with Susan Duggan. He wanted her, but he could not even summon the courage to speak to her as an individual, as another human being. He found himself berating her for some imagined transgression on the firing range or unfairly criticising her performance on the cross-country runs. What he really wanted to do was take her to the pub or for a coffee; to get to know her, perhaps even . . .

No, it was never going to happen. She was of a different class to him. She was well spoken and privately educated. She had achieved a Double First at Cambridge. She was beautiful and outgoing, popular with the other trainees. He was a caligynephobic misogynist, ten years her senior, from a Birmingham council-house who left his local inner-city secondary modern with nought but a couple of GCE's.

No, she was a stuck-up bitch, like all the others of her gender, probably worse. In his mind, she would mock him, denigrate and humiliate him. He hated women, but he hated women like her most of all.

Bittern suddenly realised he had walked straight past the upturned boat. He turned around and retraced his steps.

Grunting with the effort, he rolled it onto its keel and pushed it into the water.

***

Sandy could hear Kestrel shuffling about in his seat. Moments later, she detected a faint burning odour. Holding the coat so it covered her head and shoulders, she raised herself to her knees until she could see over the rear seats.

Outside it was pitch black, except for the area illuminated only by the headlights, which showed a concrete slipway sloping down to the inky black water of the lake. To the left a series of small peninsulas jutted into the lake, each forming a platform for coarse fishing. A rustic fence and a wooden gate enclosed the fishing area, which explained why they had not driven all the way to the boat.

The interior lights were still on and Sandy could clearly see Kestrel sitting in the driving seat. He was leaning slightly forward and concentrating on lighting a cigarette. Then he sat back and took a long drag, slowly expelling a cloud of noxious grey smoke, which billowed and eddied around the roof lining. Sandy realised that she was never going to get a better chance than this. Taking a deep breath, she flicked the lever to release the back of the rear passenger seat and launched herself forward. The seat back fell flat across the sumptuously upholstered beige leather of the rear seat and Sandy scrambled forward on her knees.

She saw Kestrel start to turn at the unexpected sound, but he was too slow. Throwing her arms over his head, she pulled the cable-tie linking her wrists back against his throat with all her strength. Yelling with surprise, he slammed his head backwards, intending to smash it into Sandy's nose, but the headrest was in the way and absorbed the impact.

Bracing her bare feet against the back of his seat, Sandy pushed back with all the power of the bunched muscles in her thighs. The cable-tie cut into the flesh of his throat and Kestrel struggled wildly, frantically trying to ease the pressure on his windpipe. He gripped her wrists and dug his fingernails into the soft flesh behind her thumbs. She gasped at the pain and swore with the effort of holding him, driving her feet even harder against the back of the seat. After what seemed an age, his movements became weaker and less coordinated. Finally, he stopped struggling altogether. His body relaxed, his head drooped and his hands dropped into his lap. Sandy kept up the pressure for another thirty seconds before she stopped and withdrew her arms. The lifeless body slumped in the seat and leaned against the door.

Sandy's body was shaking from the exertion and pain. The cable-ties had bitten into the flesh of her wrists as deeply as they had into Kestrel's throat. She curled into a ball on the back seat, clutching her chafed and bleeding wrists to her chest and squeezing her eyes shut against the pain. She lay immobile for perhaps fifteen seconds before her subconscious screamed at her to move.

Sitting up, she looked past Kestrel's slumped form to the dash. The keys were still in the ignition. All she had to do was open the door, drag Kestrel out and then just drive away. Bittern would be somebody else's problem. MI5 or the police would get him.

She shook her head. No. Bittern was *her* problem. Bittern had killed her parents. Bittern had threatened her sister. Bittern had taken obvious delight in Sandy's discomfort at every stage since the abduction. Bittern had said he would "enjoy watching her see it coming". Undoubtedly, he would come after her again. It had to end here. Tonight. Sandy decided that she was going to kill Bittern – or die in the attempt.

He would be back soon. He would be expecting everything to appear just as he had left it. He would be unlikely to shoot her as she lay in the Range Rover's load space. That would leave indelible evidence that she had been killed there. Bittern would have no choice but to do it outside. He would have to open the tailgate and drag her out. He might call to Kestrel to stop being a lazy sod and get out of the car and help, but by the time he realised Kestrel was out of the equation it would be too late. All she had to do was take Kestrel's gun, get back in the luggage compartment and cover herself with the coat. Then, when Bittern opened the tailgate – Boom!

Sandy patted Kestrel's jacket. Nothing. She pushed him forward until his head was leaning on the steering wheel and checked the small of his back. Nothing. *Jesus*! Kestrel was unarmed. Sandy could not believe her bad luck.

Oh, oh... too late!

Bittern had just walked into the cone of light from the headlamps. He was walking along the lake's edge, pulling the old wooden rowing boat along by its painter, coaxing it along the water's edge. He reached the slipway directly in front of the car. Then he pulled the boat far enough out of the water to stop it floating away.

Desperately, Sandy looked around for a weapon and her eyes fell on the rifle. It was in the passenger foot-well, propped against the seat. She grabbed the barrel, pulled it onto the back seat and examined it. It was a Browning "ShortTrac" 7mm semi-automatic, short-barrelled hunting rifle. It had a telescopic sight, a pistol-grip firing stock, and a stubby, four-round magazine mounted in front of the trigger-guard. This was an unsuitable weapon for her original plan to ambush Bittern. It was far too cumbersome. She had just a few seconds to think of something else.

Switching off the interior lights, Sandy hurried to get into position. Her bound wrists prevented her from holding the rifle properly. The best she could do was to rest the barrel on the back of the driving seat and hold the firing stock in a two-handed grip, pulling the butt tight into her shoulder.

Bittern was already walking up the slipway, approaching the left side of the Range Rover. He was too close for her to use the telescopic sight so she simply pointed the weapon in his direction and pulled the trigger. There was a sharp crack, which set her ears ringing, and a neat hole appeared in the laminated windscreen.

Sandy stared at the ground in front of the car. If the shot had hit him, he should be lying on the ground in the glare of the headlights, but there was no sign of him. Bittern had disappeared.

Sandy shook her head in disbelief. Surely, she couldn't have missed the bastard at that range. Perhaps she had seriously wounded him and he was lying somewhere in the shadows, gasping out his last breaths. Alternatively, he could even now be approaching the vehicle stealthily, gun in hand.

She could not stay in the car. He might simply pop up alongside and shoot her through the window. She must get out into the open to give her room to manoeuvre. He had been approaching the passenger side of the car so Sandy guessed that he would have ducked to his right. Therefore, to keep the bulk of the car between them, she would exit from the driver's side.

The waxed jacket had fallen off her shoulders during her struggle with Kestrel. She needed it to cover herself with, otherwise her bare skin would shine like a beacon in the dark, making her an easy target. Keeping her head low, she wormed her shoulders into the coat and used her bound hands as best she could to pull it over her head. When she stood up it should hang like a hooded cape, covering her upper body and leaving only her legs visible.

Crouching on her elbows and knees on the back seat to remain below the level of the windows, she opened the right-rear passenger door. Immediately the interior lights flicked on and she cursed aloud as two shots shattered the left-side window. The rounds buzzed over her head like a pair of bluebottles on amphetamines and exited above her head through the open door.

Sandy gripped the Browning and slid headfirst through the open door, landing on the ground on her hands and knees. Immediately, she rose to her feet and fled, crouching and weaving across thirty yards of open ground to the relative safety of the trees. Three shots rang out before she was able to take cover behind a broad oak tree, but her zigzag run had confused Bittern's aim and all his shots had gone wide.

Chapter 53

The round that Sandy fired through the windscreen had ripped through the padded shoulder of Bittern's bomber jacket. Reflexively, he launched himself out of the area lit by the headlights and drew his pistol as he rolled to the ground. A shadow moved in the rear of the Range Rover and he loosed off two rounds, rapid fire. As the nearside rear window shattered into a million pieces, Bittern rolled to his right to change position before Sandy could return fire, and winced at a sudden burning pain in his right shoulder. He touched the area with his left hand and his fingers came away sticky with blood. The bullet had nicked the top of his shoulder, halfway between the shoulder-joint and his neck. It was merely a graze but it burned like a red-hot poker. He shuddered. A few inches lower or to his left and it would have fatally wounded him.

The expected return of fire did not materialise and he wondered if one of his snap shots had hit her. Cautiously, he got to his feet and approached the Range Rover in a crouch. Suddenly, movement beyond the big vehicle caught his eye and he realised his prisoner was running for the tree line. He fired three more times across the bonnet, but he was shooting at a fast-moving, jinking target, and the pain in his shoulder hampered his aim.

The Range Rover's interior lights still glowed and he could see Kestrel slumped in the driver's seat. The bitch must have knocked the idiot unconscious, but with what? There was a tool kit in the well under the floor of the load space. She must have gotten hold of a tyre-lever or something. How could she have done that without being heard?

Well, it was too late to worry about the how. Now he had to go after her. She had a head start, that was true, but how far would she get on bare-feet in the woods? She would most likely go to ground somewhere. He was an expert tracker and once he'd shaken that idiot Kestrel awake, the two of them would surely find her pretty quickly.

***

Sandy was well aware that she was locked in a deadly duel with one of Caesar's most experienced officers. A former Royal Marines sniper, he had trained Caesar recruits in the art of concealment and movement in the open. He was the expert, she the novice. Her possession of the rifle should have given her the advantage over his handgun, but with her wrists bound together, it was difficult to handle. To make things worse, her bare feet were vulnerable to every stick, stone and thorn on the woodland floor, and she had a coat she could not fasten, draped over her head and shoulders, but open at the front, exposing her bare skin to the cold, damp night air.

Lying prone amongst the wet leaf-litter, Sandy took deep, slow breaths in an attempt to control her shivering. Condensation from her breath wafted in front of her eyes and the musty odour of rotting leaves assailed her nostrils. As before, she was holding the Browning in a two-handed grip, with the barrel resting on the trunk of a fallen tree and the butt jammed into her shoulder. She watched the open ground to her front. Thirty yards away, the Range Rover sat forlornly at the top of the slipway. The headlights shone onto the surface of the lake and the interior lights were glowing.

Bittern was out there somewhere – alive and dangerous. At the last contact, he was shooting from cover somewhere on the passenger side of the Range Rover. She knew that he wouldn't stay still for long. Even now, he might be moving towards her position. A frontal assault over the open ground across which she had fled, would be close to suicidal. He would be more likely to try a flanking manoeuvre and come up behind her.

Briefly, she turned to face the rear and listened carefully. All she could hear was the sound of the breeze in the bare branches high above her head. There was no telltale crackling of branches or soft footfalls on the wet leaves. She turned to the front again.

With any luck, her shot had wounded him, but she could not be sure. Unable to sight properly or to grip the forward stock, the recoil could have thrown the round just about anywhere. She had failed to kill him at point blank range. What chance did she have over a greater distance – especially as he would be moving fast, ducking and weaving? She bit her lip. She had only three rounds left. She could not afford to waste a single one.

She glanced at her bonds. There was one cable-tie around each wrist and a third looped between the two, with two or three inches of slack. The weak-point was the nylon ratchet grip on the linking tie. If she could apply enough outward pressure to stretch the tie, it might break. She pushed the thought aside. She had no idea where her opponent was or from which direction he might come. She could not afford the distraction. She had to remain alert. She pulled the butt more firmly into her shoulder, squinted through the telescopic sight and panned across the ground either side of the Range Rover.

***

Keeping low, Bittern opened the front passenger door and leaned inside.

'Dennis, Dennis! Wake up, you dozy bastard!' As he spoke, Bittern touched his injured shoulder. Blood was still oozing from the wound.

'Dennis!'

When there was no response, Bittern shook Kestrel's arm.

The body lolled forward, the head slipping between the steering wheel and the door panel. It finally dawned on Bittern that Kestrel was dead. He leaned further into the car and pulled the head back up. With disbelief, his eyes took in the contusions on the throat, the bulging eyes and the purple tongue protruding though the open mouth.

'Shit! Shit, shit, shit, shit, shit!'

It was only then that Bittern's mind registered that the rifle was missing. Castigating himself for leaving the weapon loaded, he swore bitterly at the change in fortune.

This was supposed to be a simple job. Two men, one slip of a girl. Bang, bang. Put the body in the boat. Send the boat out onto the lake and sink it. How was he to know the damned woman would break free and kill Kestrel? Kestrel must have been asleep, the idiot. Bittern shook his head and pursed his lips. Perhaps he should have expected something like this to happen. Curlew had something of a reputation for getting out of trouble.

Still, on the plus side, the ShortTrac's magazine held only four rounds, one of which she had already fired. The remaining ammunition was in a box, tucked safely in his left-hand jacket pocket. He cautioned himself not to be complacent, however. Curlew may have only three rounds left in the rifle, but it would take only one to kill him.

Was that her only weapon? Where was Kestrel's Tokarev? He patted Kestrel's body down and, finding no firearm, assumed that Curlew must have taken it. Then, he sighed with relief as he saw it lying on the floor. Part of the handle was protruding from under the driver's seat. He guessed that Kestrel had tried to reach for it when Curlew was throttling him. He must have fumbled and dropped it.

Habitually, Bittern ran his hand through his hair and looked out into the dark woods surrounding him. Where was she? Was she watching him right now? Even now, she might be drawing a bead through the telescopic sight. With an effort, he relaxed. If she was going to shoot she would have done so by now. He convinced himself that he was in no immediate danger. She would have run as far away as possible before her sore and bleeding feet forced her to go to ground somewhere. Bittern knew these woods. He had hunted here with Crane several times in the past year. He didn't need Kestrel – or anyone else. He would track the bitch and he would find her. He would find her and then he would kill her.

Before that, however, he had to sort out his shoulder. God, it was hurting! He switched off the interior lights before easing himself into the passenger seat – there was no point in taking chances, after all!

He pulled a small first aid kit from the glove compartment. Inside were a few rolls of bandages in sealed plastic packs, a roll of adhesive dressing plaster and a packet of paracetamol painkillers. He swallowed four of the tablets – difficult with no water and a dry throat – and then fashioned one of the bandages into a pad the size of his palm. This he shoved under his shirt to cover the wound in his shoulder, using pieces of the dressing strip to hold it in place.

He buttoned his shirt and started to zip his jacket when, suddenly, both side-windows exploded, a nanosecond apart. Bittern cringed as he felt the shockwave of the round brush his face. Instinctively, he threw himself down to the right, his head coming to rest on the fragments of glass that peppered Kestrel's thigh.

Shit! That was close.

Keeping low, he stretched out and opened the driver's door. Then he pushed Kestrel's body out onto the wet muddy ground outside. Keeping his head below the level of the shattered window, he transferred to the driving seat and started the engine. Switching on the headlamp main beams, he reversed the Range Rover, turning the vehicle so that the beams pointed in the direction from which he thought Sandy had fired.

***

The headlamps were pointing straight at her. Sandy squinted, trying to penetrate the blinding glare and see what her adversary was doing. She saw the driver's door open once more and thought she saw a shadow emerge, but she resisted the urge to fire. With only two rounds left, she would have to be 100 percent sure of her target before shooting. Suddenly she realised that the vehicle was moving forward. How could that be? Surely, she had seen Bittern get out; he could not be driving. Then she understood. The Range Rover had an automatic gearbox. He had simply pointed it in her direction and put the selector into Drive before getting out. He was using the big vehicle as cover to cross the open ground.

Damn!

The Range Rover was approaching at a fast walking pace. Was he ducking behind the open driver's door or was he jogging along behind? Or was he even now stalking her in the deep shadows away from the glare of the headlamps? She had about ten seconds to make up her mind, fifteen, maybe. She had to do something, but what? If she stayed where she was, he would soon find her. It would be better to get deeper into the woods where even the Range Rover could not follow, but if she moved from her place of concealment, he would see her in the headlight beams. Finally, she made a decision. She had to move. Using the coat once more to cover her head and back, she crawled rapidly backwards on elbows, toes and knees, wincing at the woodland debris clawing at her unprotected limbs and torso.

There was a metallic crunch as the Range Rover collided with the oak that Sandy had been using as cover. It came to a shuddering halt with the engine idling, the headlamps casting contrasts of light and deep shade that confounded her night-vision. Watching her front Sandy continued to crawl backwards, feeling her way into a narrow animal track between two clumps of bracken. Once behind the cover of those bushes, she could get to her feet and run deeper into the woods.

Suddenly, the breath was knocked out of her by a great weight in the small of her back.

'Nice try, Curlew,' said Bittern. 'Now drop the rifle.'

Chapter 54

David's clumsy entrance into the wine cellar had left him dangerously exposed. The business end of a Colt 45 was pointing unwaveringly at his head. Ekerich was lying on his right side, sheltering behind Jeanette's inert body. David was aiming the Walther in return, but he had no such protection.

'UK Security Service! Put the gun down,' David ordered in the most commanding voice he could muster. 'Let the woman go.'

'Drop yours, asshole. You're in no position to be giving orders.'

David bit off a response as Sergeant Hooper and two other police officers crowded into the room and fanned out around him. Having failed in their efforts to stop him single-handedly storming the room, Hooper had ordered his men through the door in support. They aimed their carbines at the big American.

'Armed Police! Put down the weapon!'

'I am an accredited member of the Embassy of the United States of America,' Ekerich said in a voice that filled the room like that of a Shakespearean actor. At the same time, he was slithering backwards, taking Jeanette with him. Blood from her wounded ear was pouring down her cheek, soaking the neck and shoulder of her pale blue sweater. 'I claim diplomatic immunity and insist you contact the U.S. Ambassador immediately.'

'I am David Richardson of the British Security Service. Put the weapon down and let the woman go.'

'Not until I see someone from the U.S. Embassy,' Ekerich replied pressing the muzzle of the Colt into Jeanette's neck. 'You guys get out of the room and wait until my people arrive.'

'We're not going to do that, Mr Ekerich,' David replied. 'You will come with us now. Your Embassy will be informed of your whereabouts.'

'Well, it looks like we got something of a standoff,' Ekerich replied with grim smile, which was soon replaced by a puzzled expression. 'How do you know who I am?'

'I told them,' Jeanette said groggily. 'They know the whole story, Roddy. Give up. You've got nowhere to go.'

'What have you told them, you two-timing bitch? Who have you told?'

'Where's the other woman?' David demanded. 'Where is my officer?'

'They've taken her to the lake,' Jeanette said anxiously. 'They're going to kill her.'

'I told you guys to get out of here!' Ekerich boomed over Jeanette's words. Keeping his back to the wall, and his left arm around Jeanette's throat, he started to get to his feet, dragging her up with him. Being taller and wider than his hostage, he had to crouch to remain behind her. He waved his pistol at David and the police officers around Jeanette's shoulder. 'Get outta here and wait for people from my Embassy to get here!'

Jeanette lifted her head. 'He's lying. He doesn't have diplomatic status in the UK,' she said. 'He's CIA agent responsible for mass murder in Bosnia and the murder of Jane Badell in London, two months ago,' she added, struggling in his grip. She hoped that the movement would disguise her surreptitiously fumbling for the scissors in her back pocket. 'Just shoot the bastard and go and save Sandy.'

'Don't listen to her!' he yelled, and for a second time, cracked the side of Jeanette's head with the barrel of the Colt. 'Get me someone from the US Embassy!'

Jeanette's knees buckled. Only Ekerich's arm around her throat prevented her from falling to the floor. David's face darkened at the brutal treatment of the young woman.

'As soon as you get a clear shot, shoot him!' David instructed the police. 'We'll deal with the diplomatic niceties later.'

'You know you can't do that...' Ekerich blustered. Then, suddenly, he gasped and his eyes widened in shock.

Jeanette had exaggerated her reaction to the pistol-whipping. Although it hurt her badly, it was not hard enough to make her lose consciousness. She had used the distraction to retrieve the scissors with her left hand and drive the points into the left side of Ekerich's groin, hoping that she had been lucky enough to sever the femoral artery.

Ekerich bellowed like a bull pricked by a picador's lance and he straightened his knees, rising to his full height, towering above Jeanette. He tightened his grip on her throat and rammed the muzzle of the Colt into her temple. David feared he was about to shoot her. Desperately, he lunged forward and snatched the barrel, turning the muzzle away from Jeanette's head. The report from the Colt was deafening and a shower of stone chips exploded from the wall on the other side of the room. David felt the heat of the muzzle-flash in his face as he continued to twist the weapon out of Ekerich's grip. At the same time he rammed the muzzle of his Walther non-too-gently up the American's right nostril.

Jeanette twisted away from under Ekerich's arm and turned to face him. She still held the scissors in her hand and raised them to strike at his throat, but Sergeant Hooper restrained her.

'Let go!' she screamed. 'He's got to die! You can't let this animal out of here alive!'

'Come on, Miss,' Hooper said authoritatively. 'It's all over now. It's all over.'

Jeanette sank to her knees in exhaustion and despair.

David lowered the ashen-faced Ekerich to the floor, with his back against the wall. He was losing a lot of blood and his eyes settled on Jeanette, gradually losing focus until his head lolled forward. One of the police officers shouldered David out of the way and began to try to staunch the wound with a field dressing.

'Get the paramedics in here!' he yelled to the room at large.

'David!' Lucinda called suddenly from the doorway. 'GCHQ called with news of Vixen.'

Chapter 55

Sandy tried to turn over but Bittern had his full weight on one knee in the small of her back, pinning her face down on the ground.

'Leave the rifle on the ground and stand up,' he ordered. To reinforce the message he pressed the muzzle of his pistol against the base of her skull.

To Sandy, his voice sounded strained. His breathing was laboured as if he were speaking through gritted his teeth. Was he in pain?

'Up!' He repeated. 'Don't turn around.'

Sandy obeyed. As she stood, the coat slipped from her shoulders. The freezing drizzle stung her flesh and she tensed her muscles, trying unsuccessfully to suppress her shivering.

'Start walking toward the lake,' said Bittern.

'Can I have the coat back around my shoulders?' she asked, turning to face him. Her teeth were chattering with the cold but her voice betrayed no fear. She was determined not to debase herself by pleading with him.

He was holding a black semi-automatic pistol in his right hand. The Browning hung over his left shoulder on its webbing sling. He was standing slightly hunched and leaning to his right, as if weighed down by a great weight. She realized that he was wounded, but she could not see where. She rejoiced that at least one of her shots had hit him, though she didn't know which one.

'I told you not to turn around,' he reminded her.

'It's bloody cold and I know you have no interest in ogling the female form,' she said. 'Let me have the coat.'

'You won't be cold for long,' he added callously, but then to her surprise he relented. 'Alright, stand away from it and turn around.' When she had taken several steps, he bent down, picked up the coat and draped it around her shoulders.

Sorely tempted to use the opportunity to launch an attack on him, she dismissed it. It was too obvious. He would be expecting her to try and would be prepared.

'Thanks,' Sandy said, holding the coat closed across her front with her hands.

'Don't mention it. Get walking.'

Sandy obeyed. Bittern followed several paces behind, taking no chances on her trying to jump him.

'You're better than I thought, Curlew,' he said, surprising Sandy with the complement. 'You did a good job on Jackdaw at your house and on Kestrel tonight. How did you manage it?'

For someone who was wounded and whose close colleague had just been killed, Bittern seemed strangely detached, almost cheerful. This was surprising. She knew him to be a volatile character, prone to sudden anger – and angry people are more likely to make mistakes. Sandy knew she had to prick his bubble of contentment; fire up his venom again.

'So how did you and Kestrel get mixed up with Crane's little band of merry men? I always thought you were weird but I'd never have thought you'd sink to something like this.'

'You don't understand, Curlew,' Bittern replied. 'We are building an organisation to save the world from being overrun by Muslim fanatics.'

'Oh, come on, Martin! If you think the genocide of innocent Muslim women and kids in Bosnia is going to save the world, you're a bigger idiot than I ever imagined! You're just low-life scum, no better than any other gangster or terrorist. Your gang are the sort that people like us are supposed to be fighting against!'

'Shut the fuck up, you mouthy bitch,' Bittern snarled and shoved Sandy in the back, causing her to stumble and fall to her knees. 'If they get their way we'll all end up living in the dark-ages again. Women like you would all be walking around covered from head to toe in black, nothing but your eyes showing. Do you really want that?'

'I never took you for a feminist, Bittern,' Sandy replied, rising awkwardly to her feet. 'They're not too tolerant of homosexuals either. Is that what you're worried about?'

'I'm not gay,' Bittern snapped. 'Everyone assumes I am, but I'm not. I don't like women, especially ones like you, but I don't fancy blokes either.'

'What do you mean women like me? What have I done?' Sandy was offended, which she knew was absurd in her current circumstances.

'Just shut up and keep walking,' Bittern ordered, clearly not wishing to enter into a discussion. He was doing exactly was she did not want him to do. He was acting professionally. He was detached emotionally from his task. She was no longer human. She was the sheep being driven to slaughter; he was the slaughter-man.

'Are you saying you've never had sex with anyone? Male or female?' Sandy persisted. 'Christ! No wonder you're such a miserable bastard.'

'I told you to shut up!' Bittern shouted. 'One more word out of you and I'll make sure you die slowly and painfully.'

They were only yards from the top of the slipway, now. The boat mutely awaited its final passenger. The persistent drizzle had stopped and the clouds were thinning, allowing through a glimmer of light from the moon.

Sandy's mind raced. Unless she did something now, she would have only a few seconds left to live. She affected to stumble again. This time she stayed down, making no effort to get up.

'Get up, Curlew,' Bittern ordered.

Sandy shook her head and remained on her knees. 'No, Martin, please don't do it,' she pleaded, her voice shrill with terror. 'Please don't kill me! I'll do anything. Just let me go!'

Bittern was unmoved. 'Come on, get up!' he barked impatiently. 'We're nearly there now. Look,' he added, softening his voice, 'if you get up and climb into the boat, I'll make it quick and easy for you, I promise. It'll all be over soon.'

He slipped his left hand under the open coat and grabbed her upper-arm. He started to pull her to her feet but this was what Sandy had been hoping for. She suddenly sprung up, twisting as she did so, and head-butted Bittern's nose. He cried out in surprise and pain, and staggered two steps backwards, clutching at his nose with his left hand.

Before he could recover, Sandy pirouetted on the ball of her left foot and slammed the ball of her right into Bittern's right wrist. The force of the impact opened his hand and the pistol dropped into the mud. Sandy drove her elbow into Bittern's midriff, making him retreat another few steps, then she lunged for the gun.

Recovering from his shock, Bittern aimed a kick at Sandy's head as she bent down, but the rifle dangling from his shoulder unbalanced him. The blow was weak and badly timed and Sandy was able to ride with the impact. Swiftly, she recovered into the basic defensive stance. Bittern was already launching his follow-up attack. Seeing his fist streaking toward her face, Sandy sidestepped, shrugged the coat from her shoulders, to avoid it impeding her movements, then countered with a heel aimed at his solar plexus.

Bittern turned, deflecting the kick with his forearm and reposted with a straight right-handed jab at Sandy's face. She blocked the blow with her forearms, but her bound hands impeded her counter-strike and Bittern seized his opportunity. He kicked out with his left foot. The blow connected solidly with her right thigh, numbing her leg. She staggered back several paces, her bare feet slipping in the mud, but she recovered swiftly and once again adopted a defensive stance. She had expected him to move in to launch yet another strike, but instead he took a few quick paces backwards and retrieved the gun from the mud. He pointed it at her head.

'No more time for games, now, Curlew,' Bittern said, a cruel smile playing smiling triumphantly on his lips. 'Night night!'

Sandy watched him pull the trigger.

Chapter 56

David left the wine cellar and ran up the stairs, two at a time. GCHQ had picked up the signal from the GPS transmitter in the magazine of the Glock and relayed its position via Gower Street to the police. Sandy had been alive then, but that was five minutes ago. Everything could have changed by now.

In his haste, he tripped and stumbled on the top step. Swiftly recovering his balance, he rushed into the study. His eyes scanned the room searching out Barrington. He was sitting on the floor near the French doors. The other two prisoners from the basement were sitting nearby. All three were handcuffed and a grim looking police officer stood over them, holding his Heckler and Koch across his chest. David strode across and, ignoring the police officer, bent down and grabbed the MI6 chief by the lapels of his jacket.

'Where's the lake? Where have your men taken my officer?' he demanded.

Barrington looked up. His lip curled in a calculated display of contempt. 'I have no idea what you're talking about. Which officer?'

David wanted to smash the smug bastard's face in, but by now, two police officers were dragging him away from the prisoner.

'There are two lakes nearby, sir.'

Shrugging off the hands holding him back from the prisoner, David looked around at the speaker. It was the uniformed constable who had helped Burroughs arrest Barrington. He was pointing to an 1825 plan of the estate hanging on the wall of the study between a seascape and a portrait of Jonathon Featherstone, the first Baron Norton.

'Look, sir. This one's visible from the house, just down from the terrace. The other one is much bigger and about, what . . . two miles away?'

David continued to glare at Barrington as he replied. 'That'll be the one. They wouldn't dump a body in the ornamental lake a stone's throw from the house. Inspector,' he said to Burroughs, 'get on the radio to the helicopter pilot. Tell him to pick me up here. We'll find the lake and guide your vehicles in.'

As Burroughs relayed the instruction, David turned to find Lucinda once more at his side.

'Stay here and liaise with the police,' he told her. 'Do anything you can to help the injured woman. Remember, she's on our side. Look after her.'

***

It was light enough for Sandy to see the surprise register in Bittern's eyes. Confused, he checked the safety was off and squeezed the trigger again. Only then did Sandy see that he was trying to shoot her with her Glock – the one Julian had given her. It had always been Sandy's intention to be captured, and clearly, any weapon she was carrying would be taken from her. It would be madness to supply the enemy with a serviceable weapon, so as well as planting a GPS tracker in the magazine Julian had disabled the firing mechanism.

Taking full advantage of her would-be killer's confusion, she quickly stepped forward to launch another attack. Planting her right foot on the ground she attempted to strike at his head with her left, but her foot slipped in the mud and she fought to regain her balance.

Bittern threw down the Glock and retreated a few steps, unslinging the Browning from his shoulder. Sandy hurled herself at him, grabbing the rifle's barrel with both hands before he could bring it up. She held on grimly as Bittern tried to tear it from her grasp. For the first time, she saw the rip in the right shoulder of his bomber jacket and realised that was where her bullet had struck. It was only a flesh wound but the pain was clearly troubling him. He was sweating and straining to maintain his grip. His face was contorted with effort and rage. Sandy suddenly pitched forward and head-butted his wounded shoulder. He cried out in agony and twisted away from her. Sandy went with him and tried again to wrench the Browning from his hands. He raised his arms up high, hoping to outreach her and make her lose her grip, but she stood on tiptoes and hung on desperately. Somehow, in the struggle, her body twisted and she found herself between the rifle and Bittern's body, with her back to him.

He pulled the rifle up to her throat, pulling back against her larynx. She tried to push the barrel away but she was unable to match his strength. In desperation, she threw her head back violently. The back of her head slammed into his nose, already tender and bleeding from the earlier head-butt. The shock caused him to loosen his grip enough for Sandy to sink her teeth into his right hand at the base of the thumb. He cried out and struggled to break the contact, but Sandy held on like a bulldog until finally, he released his grip on the firing stock and wrenched his hand from Sandy's mouth. Instantly,

Sandy grabbed the pistol grip of the firing stock with both hands.

Bittern still had hold of the barrel with his left hand and Sandy lurched forward, trying to break his grip. Then she sensed movement in Bittern's right arm and guessed that he was trying to pull his own pistol from its holster in the small of his back. Twisting her body violently, she drove the rifle's butt into the top of his right thigh, just below the pelvic bone. He grunted with pain and his leg gave way. Sandy threw her full weight backwards and Bittern fell to the ground on his back, dragging Sandy down on top of him.

Winded by the combined weight of their fall, Bittern's left hand slipped off the barrel. Immediately, he wrapped his left arm around her throat. Now unable to draw his pistol, he reached over Sandy's shoulder with his right hand and grabbed the rifle's barrel, trying to yank the weapon from her grip.

'Let go, you bitch! It's all over,' he grunted in her ear as he tried to prise the weapon from Sandy's hands.

'No, you bastard,' she replied through gritted teeth. 'I need it to beat your shitty head in with!'

'Forget it! 'You had a good try but you lost! Give it up!'

Sandy held on desperately, but despite her determination, fuelled as much by her hatred of the man who murdered her parents as the will to survive, she could feel her strength sapping. Her grip was weakening. The rifle was slipping from her grasp.

***

The helicopter rose like an express lift, turning in the ascent to point southwards toward the lake. A glimmer of moonlight was beginning to show through the thinning clouds and as they rose above the trees, the body of water was visible as a dark hole in the forest. David sat beside the pilot. Sergeant Hooper and two other armed officers were crammed in the back like sardines in a tin.

As they neared the lake, David saw the abandoned Range Rover with its front buried in a tree and the headlamps still burning. He felt a surge of hope that Sandy might yet have survived.

'She must have run off into the woods,' David yelled through the intercom. 'Look out for any lights. They might be using torches to search for her.'

The helicopter hovered above the trees but the only lights they could see were the headlights of the two police vehicles coming from the house. They were weaving and jolting along the track through the trees, slowly, far too slowly.

'Put her down there,' David said, pointing to the crashed Range Rover. 'We'll go in on foot while you see if you can see anything from the air.

***

Bittern increased the pressure of the arm-lock on Sandy's throat. Her breath whistled through her constricted windpipe. She could hear a rhythmic thumping, clattering sound and thought it was the sound of her pulse pounding in her ears. She knew she was losing the desperate battle for the rifle. She could barely breathe and her grip on the firing stock was weakening with every second. It was only by trapping the barrel between her jaw and her left shoulder that she had so far prevented Bittern from gaining control of the weapon. She knew that once that happened, she would be dead within seconds.

With nothing left to lose, she took a desperate gamble. Twisting her head to the right, she allowed the barrel to slip across her cheek. The foresight gouged a bloody furrow in the soft flesh, an inch-and-a-half under her left eye, but the pain barely registered.

The rifle was now lying vertically along the right side of her body. The barrel rested on her shoulder, the telescopic sight dug painfully into her ribcage and the trigger was level with her groin. She threw her head back to her left, knowing that Bittern would have to move his to the right to avoid another blow to the nose. Then reversing her grip on the firing stock, she jammed her right thumb onto the trigger and pushed it back twice.

The soft-nosed bullets tore through the skin under Bittern's chin and continued up through his mouth, entering the cranial cavity behind the left ocular orbit. The top of his head literally exploded, spraying, blood, brains and bone over a wide area. The grip on Sandy's throat tightened briefly as the muscles convulsed, but then relaxed. Sandy rolled over to lie exhausted on her back alongside the still twitching corpse of her enemy.

***

David was out of the door the instant the helicopter touched down. Sergeant Hooper and one of the other officers followed. The third remained behind to act as an observer and aerial sniper once the helicopter was airborne again.

With Hooper and the other officer hot on his heels, David gripped his Walther and ran toward the Range Rover. Ekerich's Colt was in his jacket pocket as backup. The helicopter's engine note increased and the machine began to rise into the air. The draft from the rotors battered the ground, scattering twigs, leaves and pinecones all around. So great was the crescendo of noise that they almost missed the reports of two shots coming from their left, the direction of the lakeshore.

'This way,' David yelled and started running.

Hooper matched him stride for stride. Ahead the word POLICE, sewn onto the back of the young constable's coveralls, receded as he streaked ahead. Suddenly he came to a skidding halt and brought his weapon up to his shoulder.

'ARMED POLICE!' he shouted. 'Put down the rifle!'

***

The sound of approaching footsteps slapping wetly in the mud alarmed Sandy and she brought the rifle up to face the new threat. A strong light shone in her eyes. She could not see beyond it. Someone – a man – was shouting at her to put the gun down. She had no idea who it was, but it no longer mattered. She was past caring. The rifle was empty. She was too exhausted to put up any further resistance. Both flight and fight were out of the question. She lowered the rifle and laid it by her side. It did not matter whether the man shouting at her was friend or foe. She was finished.

***

Panting with exertion, David arrived to a scene from a horror movie. A man dressed in dark clothing lay on his back, and where his head should have been was a ball of bloody gore. Lying beside the corpse and looking like a spectre from hell, was Sandy. Stark naked, she was lying on her back with her hands seemingly clasped across her stomach. Blood and tissue plastered her hair, her face and the upper part of her body. The rest of her was streaked with mud.

At first, he thought she was dead but then she opened her eyes. Her beautiful blue eyes, reflected in the light from the torch attached to the police officer's carbine, stared out from the bloody mask of her face. She did not seem to recognise him straight away.

'Put the gun down you fool,' David growled at the constable. 'She's my missing officer.' He ran the last few steps to her side. 'Sandy! Oh God, Sandy, are you okay? Are you hurt?'

The sound of David's voice snapped Sandy out of her stupor.

'I'm alright,' she replied shakily as David helped her to her feet. 'It's his blood, not mine.'

David was too choked-up to reply. He slipped off his suit jacket and wrapped it around her shoulders. Then, ignoring the gory mess that covered her head and upper body, he put both arms around her and held her tightly.

Chapter 57

18th December 1992

Matt Redman looked adoringly at the girl lying on his bed. He simply could not believe his luck. She had skin the colour of milky coffee, prominent cheekbones, a cute, pointed chin and eyes almost as dark as the mass of jet-black hair that covered the pillow behind her head. Nareshma was the most beautiful girl he had ever met, let alone slept with.

'Please, Matt,' she purred in that husky, sexy voice. 'Don't go to work tonight and leave me all alone again.'

Matt finished tying his tie and bent to kiss her. Immediately her arm locked around his neck and she tried to pull him down beside her.

Before meeting her in his local pub two weeks ago, Matt had always assumed that Indian girls were shy and modest. How wrong that assumption proved to be; Nareshma was the living embodiment of the Kama Sutra.

He had been drinking in the White Swan with his mates and fellow prison officers, Charlie and Malcolm, at the end of their shift. All Arsenal supporters, they were discussing a dire penalty decision against the team by the ref, the previous Saturday. Suddenly, this girl, whom none of them had ever seen before, started arguing with them. The referee was right, she said. The Gunner's goalie had fouled the Spurs striker. It was a penalty, no doubt about it.

It was a confrontational introduction, but the three men warmed to her and she just stayed with them, happily discussing football, and being surprisingly knowledgeable too! When first Malcolm and then Charlie left to go back to their homes and families, Nareshma remained chatting to the currently unattached Matt. Only now, the subject of the conversation moved away from football and touched on matters more personal. At closing time, they took the Tube back to Matt's flat in Kingsbury, leaving his scooter in the parking bay near the pub. He had drunk far too many pints to drive anyway.

Insatiable wasn't the word. They tried every position in the book and some that probably had never before been attempted without a safety net. She simply would not leave him alone. When he fell back, exhausted onto the pillow, she found yet another trick to coax him back to life. Never before had he known a woman with such a voracious appetite.

Night after night, she kept him awake with her demands, demands he was eager to satisfy. Regrets for night after night of debauchery came only the following day when he would spend the entire shift yawning and daydreaming about the girl who had all but moved into his flat.

After the first week, his shift pattern gave him several days off work. During this time, they had barely eaten or seen the light of day. Then he started his turn on nights. She had seemed content to let him go the on the first three nights, but this evening, as he was getting ready for his fourth, she was begging him not to go to work.

'Call in sick, Matt. Please stay with me. I'll make it worth your while!'

'Sorry, Resh, I've got to go, love,' he said, reluctantly extricating his neck from her vice-like grip and standing up straight.

'Look what you're missing.'

She threw back the duvet, revealing a long, lithe body with pert, brown-tipped breasts, a flat stomach and narrow hips. The dark thatch at the junction of her shapely thighs drew his eyes and seeing the direction of his gaze, she opened her legs in the most provocative, wanton gesture. At the same time, she reached out to run her fingers over his instantly erect manhood.

'See? He wants to stay. Please Matt, just tonight.'

'Oh God, Resh, I really want to stay, but I can't. I'd be letting me mates down. We're short-handed as it is with Dave off sick.' He kissed her again but when he felt her artful fingers unzipping his fly, he pulled away again. 'Tomorrow, we'll spend all day in bed together,' he promised. 'Tomorrow.' With that, he picked up his coat and motorcycle helmet and left the girl lying disconsolately on the bed.

Nareshma waited until she heard the scooter start up and drive away. Then she got out of bed and padded naked to the phone on the wall in Matt's kitchenette. Tears were rolling down her cheeks as she dialled the number. It was answered on the second ring.

'Myzornis,' she said to identify herself. 'Jailer's on his way to work. No, I tried, but I couldn't persuade him to stay with me. Try not to hurt him too badly,' she pleaded. 'He's really nice. Yes, I know. Yes, okay.'

Using alcohol-saturated wipes, the young woman Matt knew as Nareshma cleaned every surface that she might have touched in the two weeks she had been coming to the flat. Then she placed all the bed linen and towels that might contain her DNA into two black sacks, which someone would collect later. Finally, she gathered up her personal belongings and left the flat, never to return. Despite her entreaty, she knew in her heart that Matt would never be coming back either.

It happened at the junction of the North Circular Road and Golders Green Road. Matt had the green light, but as he crossed the junction, a white van jumped the red and slammed into the side of his scooter, knocking him into the path of oncoming traffic on the other carriageway. The driver of the first car managed to swerve around Matt's body, sideswiping another vehicle in the process. The driver of the car behind had no time to react and ran over the injured man. The white van skirted around the jumble of vehicles and turned right, speeding eastwards along the North Circular. No one managed to note the registration number.

***

'Shit!' Sandy sat up in the bed and stared around her with wild eyes. 'Must I have that dream every bloody night?' She asked the empty room. She looked at the bedside clock. It showed 2:40.

The recurring dream depicted her lying in the boat. She was facing upwards, her wrists tied to the rowlocks. Bittern was standing over her, pointing a pistol at her head.

'No more time for games, now, Curlew,' he said.

She always awoke just as he pulled the trigger.

She lay back and rested her head on a pillow. It was damp with her sweat so she reached behind and turned it over before laying her head down again. Under the duvet, her hands explored the bare skin of her stomach, once flat, but now convex, and she linked her fingers, letting her hands rest protectively around the bump. After a few minutes, she stopped shaking and drifted back to sleep.

She awoke with a start and saw daylight around the edges of the dark-blue curtains at her bedroom window. The clock now said 8:35.

'Time we got up, bump,' she said, patting her tummy. 'He'll be here soon.'

She showered in the en suite and returned to the bedroom where she looked in the mirror, scarcely recognising the young woman that stared back at her. The once blonde hair was now chestnut brown and reached beyond her shoulders. Her breasts were fuller and heavier, and the bump seemed grow larger with each passing day. She smiled to herself. She loved that bump and what it contained with a passion that previously she would not have believed possible.

Her face was softer and rounder than before. Her skin glowed with vitality. She touched the vivid scar that crossed her left cheek from earlobe to nostril. They said it would heal in time, but she might need plastic surgery to remove all trace of it. She shrugged. She was alive. The baby was alive. Nothing else really mattered.

Despite her fears for her unborn child, the baby had proved to be as robust as its mother. Riding out the storm of blows, the waterboarding and the fight with Bittern on the lakeshore, the child had come through with no discernible ill effects. An ultrasound scan at the maternity clinic, the previous day, confirmed everything to be intact. The doctor had declared the baby to be in fine health with a heartbeat strong enough for a regiment of Guards to march to.

A Desire for Vengeance

The walk from the hospital to the railway station had taken Sandy through the busy main shopping mall, which, with a week to go to Christmas Day, was packed with people doing their Christmas shopping. Pausing to look in the window of a jeweller's shop, she had wondered whether she should buy David a Christmas present, but what does a girl get the man who already has everything – including a wife and kids?

Sandy frowned. What should she do about David? They had grown so close in the past three months. There was an affinity between them that some couples never achieve, despite many years together. His feelings for her were obvious, and she loved him as well, but she did not want to be the cause of the destruction of his marriage. Neither, if she were honest, did she want him for her own lifetime partner. They had shared something special, but they could not continue their relationship as it was. She would have to end it and she knew would have to do it today.

How she hated the thought of hurting David. He was always there for her, always on her side, always protecting her. Following the incident at Barrington's house at the beginning of November, she had been taken to the private hospital in Sussex reserved for security and intelligence officers suffering physically or mentally from the rigours of their job. For two days they conducted various tests, dressed her numerous but mainly superficial wounds and extracted a mass of woodland debris from the soles of her feet. David had all but lived at the hospital for those two days and driven her home when they discharged her. Then they spent the whole afternoon in bed together. That was the last time they had made love; *would be* the last time they made love. It had to stop.

***

David arrived promptly at ten o'clock and Sandy took him through to the kitchen. He sat at the table while she made some coffee. She could tell from his manner that something was not right. Something was bothering him.

'What's wrong?' she asked. 'You don't seem yourself today.'

David frowned. 'Barrington was found dead in his cell, this morning.'

After weeks of interrogation, the former Director General of MI6 had been remanded in London's Pentonville Prison to await trial. For security reasons, he was held in solitary confinement.

Sandy's hand flew to her mouth 'Oh my goodness! How?'

'They say he tipped his bed on-end and hung himself from the frame with his shoelaces.'

'Oh dear!'

'He was supposed to be on suicide watch, with an officer checking on him every few minutes. He didn't even have any shoe-laces! They had been taken away from him.'

'So . . .'

'I have no doubt that he was murdered.'

'I thought he was in a top-security prison.'

'He was.'

'So, how . . .'

'Clermont,' David replied. 'They got to him. He'd said throughout the interviews that Clermont's tentacles reached everywhere. Well, that seems to have included Pentonville.'

'Did they get the killer?'

'Not a chance. They were short of staff that night. One of the officers on his wing was killed in a road accident on his way to work; another was on sick leave. There's no explanation from the officers who were on duty how it was possible that someone managed to access his cell, kill him and slip away again. They'll be an investigation, of course, but . . .' He shrugged.

Sandy put the coffee cups down and sat facing David. 'Jesus! So Clermont is still out there.'

'Yes, we may have chopped off one of Cerberus's heads but there are plenty more where that came from!'

'What?'

'Greek mythology. Cerberus was the many-headed dog that guarded the gate of Hades.'

'Oh yes, I remember now. Did we get enough out of him?'

'Barrington? Not really. No other names.'

'What about his cronies?'

'Well, as you know, Ekerich was deported quietly back to the States.' David frowned. When he left the basement on that fateful day, he would have put money against the American's chances of survival. Not for the first time, he wished he'd shot the bastard.

'Yes. One day I'm going to track that bastard down and . . .'

'No, you won't,' David interrupted, glancing significantly at Sandy's midriff 'You've got more important things to worry about now. How's it going, by the way?'

Sandy smiled and rested her hands on the bump. 'We went for an ultrasound scan yesterday. Everything's fine with the baby.'

'We?'

'The baby and me. I could hardly go without her!'

David laughed. 'Oh I see. Her?'

'Yes, they told me it's a girl,' Sandy replied. 'Heard any more about Jeanette?'

'No. I told you she has to have reconstructive surgery on her ear but, I've not heard anything more about her.'

Unconsciously, Sandy fingered the scar on her cheek. 'She saved my life, David. She was so brave, doing what she did. She was playing a very dangerous game for a very long time.' Sandy shifted in her seat. 'I was just so sorry I didn't have a chance to thank her.'

'I couldn't let that happen. Officially, the police got to the lake too late to save you. You're dead. For good this time,' he said, wagging his finger.

Sandy smiled at the mild rebuke. 'What about the police? They know the truth.'

'Yes, and we've sworn them to secrecy. They were all well aware of what you had gone through and when I explained how much danger you would be in if anyone discovered you were still alive, they all readily agreed to go along with the story. We'll have to monitor the situation though. If any of them blab in the future, we'll have to deal with it at the time. For now, though, Sandy Harris is no more.'

'Did you see Sam? How did she take it?'

'Actually, she's one of the few people in on the secret. She knows you're alive but that you can never communicate or see each other.' David watched Sandy's face. She seemed to take that news better than he would have expected.

'We can't take the risk that they'll keep her under surveillance. If you two meet this whole thing could start up again.'

'I think you're being over-cautious. With Crane, I mean Barrington's cell broken up, why would anyone care whether I'm alive or dead?'

'I'm not prepared to take the chance. For a start, Ekerich is still out there. If he got wind you were still alive, he might well come after you.'

Sandy nodded. Ekerich was a real threat. 'That's why I think we should track him down and finish him.'

'What, and start a turf war with the CIA? Come on, Sandy. There's no way that's going to happen.'

'Okay, David,' Sandy said, surrendering to the inevitable.

'We are drawing a line under Sandy Harris,' David added. 'Your sister is in full agreement and is just happy to know you are alive and well. She just wants you to be safe. Maybe later, you'll be able to pass messages to one another using me as a dead-letter-box.'

'Thanks, David,' She said quietly, before changing the subject. 'What about Tom and Jerry?'

'Eh?'

'Sorry, Paul and Jerry, Barrington's minders?'

'They've been taken on by us. They've joined Protection Branch.'

'What? They're not going to be prosecuted?'

'No, they're the sort that do as they're told, no questions asked. 'We need people like them on our side.'

Sandy narrowed her eyes at the thought of them evading prosecution, but she understood the reasoning. 'Did they know anything about Clermont?'

'Not really. They knew very little about Barrington's schemes. He was their boss and they were loyal to him. They certainly don't know anything about the wider organisation.

That's what worries me,' he added 'There must be someone out there pulling the strings, someone in overall control, but with Barrington gone, there's no way we'll find out who.'

'If it was up to me, we'd go after Ekerich. He must know the next person up in the chain.'

David shrugged. 'Not my call, I'm afraid.'

'Well, at least Szopienice didn't get away scot-free,' Sandy said. The Brigadier-General was in detention in The Hague accused of war crimes.

Sandy closed her eyes and took a deep breath. 'David, there's something I need to talk to you about,' she began but he held up his hand to stop her speaking.

'In a minute. First I need to update you on your position.'

'My position?'

'Yes. Look, Sandy, we won't be able to see each other anymore, well not very often anyway.'

'Oh?'

'I'm assigning you to one of the teams in my Section. The team leader, Gary, is a nice chap; he'll look after you. He knows nothing of your past, not even your real name. To him, you are just another new probationer.'

'Oh.'

'I've arranged for your computer skills training to begin on 4th January. You're to report to this address at nine o'clock.' He handed her a scrap of paper. 'You'll continue there until you start maternity leave. Do you have a due-date yet?'

'Yes, 8th March.'

'So you'll be there less than three months. Oh well, can't be helped. Perhaps you can take some stuff home to keep learning when the baby's asleep.'

Sandy laughed. 'Yes, I'm sure I'll have lots of free time!'

'Are you making fun of me?' David asked with mock severity.

'No, Uncle David, I wouldn't dream of it!'

'Uncle David?' He grinned ruefully at the reminder of their argument in October – and the difference in their ages.

'So what about Gary? What contact will I have with him?'

'If it's okay with you, I'll set up a meeting for the three of us in a pub or café near your work during that first week. He'll take it from there.'

'So I won't be seeing you very much after today?' Despite her earlier resolve, Sandy was surprised at how much that thought saddened her.

David looked just as sad. 'We can't carry on as we have been, Sandy,' David said gently. 'My feelings for you haven't changed, but . . .'

'It's alright, David,' Sandy interrupted. 'I had come to the same conclusion. In fact, that's what I was about to say earlier.'

'We're still friends, though?' David said hopefully.

'That will never change,' Sandy replied. 'I hope you will come to see me from time-to-time? Just for coffee and a chat.'

'I'd like that very much,' David replied reaching across to hold her hand. 'I'd like that very much indeed.'

***

It was a cold, cloudy day, threatening rain at any moment. Amanda Gillette walked briskly across Lambeth Bridge. She glanced over the parapet as she neared the southern end and could see him standing halfway between the bridge and Lambeth Pier. He was resting his elbows on the wall of the embankment and gazing down at the muddy-brown waters of the Thames. He seemed unaware of her presence until she was just a few yards from him, then, as if by some sixth sense, he suddenly turned to face her.

'Good morning, Amanda.'

'Hello, Neil. How are things?'

He touched her arm and they strolled slowly eastwards, past the pier.

'Barrington is dead,' Eagle reported tonelessly.

'Yes, so I understand; any difficulty there?'

'No. There's bound to be an investigation but, after several months of digging, they will have to conclude that some fool prison officer mistakenly allowed him to keep his shoelaces. Nothing more will come of it.'

'I should hope not! Pity about the prison officer that died.'

'Yes, it's a shame. My girl did everything she could to stop him going to work but he was adamant he couldn't let his mates down. Poor fool! My girl is terribly upset over it.'

'Couldn't your people have . . .?'

'No. When questioned, he would have mentioned our girl, who, of course, by then would have disappeared off the scene. Someone would have put two-and-two together . . .'

'Yes, of course. Pity, though.'

'Yes.'

'So everything is under wraps, now. We can expect no further fallout?'

'I certainly hope not. What have you decided about Curlew and Richardson? Do we need to mop up there as well?'

'No, I want no further action taken.'

'You're sure? The Clermont project is far too important to be put at risk by ill-founded sentimentality.'

'Yes. As far as they are concerned, the matter is over. They'll be kept busy on other issues. If we use either of them for a Clermont-related operation, they'll not be aware of it.' K stopped and turned to face Eagle. 'What Barrington and Ekerich did went way beyond the limits of what I am prepared to tolerate, Neil. We cannot descend to the level of the people we're fighting. Otherwise what's the point?'

'I totally agree. The cold-blooded murder of operatives and innocent civilians is to be avoided if possible.'

'That's not what I meant. When I became DG, you told me Clermont's objective was to counter the growing threat of radical Islam. You said nothing about igniting a global war, as Barrington claimed. I can't be party to that.'

'Be careful not to rock the boat too hard, Amanda,' Eagle warned, his expression serious. Then he softened and smiled reassuringly. 'However, I can say that Barrington's aim to provoke pre-emptive military action was the polar opposite of Clermont's objective, which is containment.'

'What about the CIA and Ekerich?' K asked as they started to walk again.

'Ekerich far exceeded his remit, which was to monitor the numbers of Islamist insurgents coming to Bosnia to fight on the Muslim side. It was not Clermont's intention that he incite or encourage ethnic cleansing. That could only serve to alienate moderate Muslims. We want them on our side, not driven into the arms of the extremists. The problem is that Ekerich has a pathological hatred of Muslims in general and those of Turkish origin in particular, which, of course, includes those in Bosnia. His maternal great-grandmother's family were Anatolian Greeks who fled to Macedonia in 1922 and ended up migrating to the USA. For Ekerich, what's happening in Bosnia is payback time for atrocities Muslims perpetrated against his ancestors.'

Amanda understood. In the aftermath of the First World War, the Turkish army forced many thousands of ethnic Greeks out of the Turkish province of Anatolia. Many died on forced marches. The survivors told of massacres and of women and young girls being routinely raped by the soldiers.

'His grandmother married an expatriate Serb in New York,' Eagle continued. 'The name Ekerich is an Anglicized version of a Serbian one.'

'So, young Ekerich was brought up on a diet of entrenched anti-Muslim and anti-Turk propaganda,' said Amanda. 'I suppose that explains something about the man.'

'Well, his superiors have had strong words, apparently. Hopefully, he'll toe the line in future.'

'What can we do about what's going on in Bosnia?'

'I don't know if we can do anything to reverse what Ekerich and Szopienice started. The horse has well and truly bolted by now. But on the plus-side, there's a change of administration underway across the pond, and the President-elect is being advised to make finding a way to end the war a priority. It won't happen overnight, but at least it will be a step in the right direction.'

'Ah yes, Szopienice. What are we going to do about him?'

'Don't worry, Amanda. I expect the Americans will take care of that. They won't want him telling tales about his relationship with the CIA.'

By now they had reached the steps leading to Westminster Bridge. K turned once more to face Eagle.

'Much of the problem could have been avoided, Neil, if you had been more open with me. Those two young women were put at terrible risk, which could have been avoided if we had worked together.'

'At that stage I didn't know who was behind it. Crane could just as easily have been you as Barrington.'

'Oh yes, and why did Barrington use the name Crane? Where did that come from?'

Paternal grandmother's maiden name, apparently. He thought it fitted nicely with Caesar's ornithological theme.'

Amanda grinned. 'Dove-tailed, you mean?'

'Oh, very good, Amanda,' Eagle laughed. 'Oh oh! It's starting to rain. Take care!'

Amanda opened her umbrella and climbed the steps to the bridge. Eagle continued through the underpass beneath.

Epilogue
22nd May 1993

Samantha McNamara watched the boats moored in the harbour rocking gently in time to the slate-grey waves that went on to slap feebly against the harbour wall. In a few hours, she remembered, the tide would be out and those same boats would be leaning drunkenly on their keels on the exposed sandy bottom.

For the umpteenth time, she looked at the postcard in her hand. One side bore a sepia photograph taken perhaps in the 1920s or '30s. In the foreground, two men in smocks and straw hats were carrying a basket of fish along the quayside, watched by smartly dressed idlers lounging on the harbour wall. In the background was a church with a square tower, on which the hands of a clock showed 11:15. Samantha was standing on the very spot from which the photo had been taken, and the clock today read exactly the same time as in the picture.

It was nearly two weeks since she had received the postcard. It said the things that one would expect to see on a postcard from a friend on holiday.

Sat 8th May.

Having a great time. Weather not brilliant, but okay for the time of year. As I write, I'm sitting on the harbour wall exactly where the photo was taken and, SPOOKY!!! It's exactly the time that's on the church clock in the picture. Lots been happening and I'll tell you about it all when we meet on the 14th.

Love you lots,

Andrea.

A Desire for Vengeance

Samantha had recognised the place immediately. With its quaint narrow streets, the gift shops and art galleries, big waves crashing onto wide sandy beaches and fascinating rock pools around the headland at low tide, St Ives had always been their favourite holiday destination when they were children.

This was the third communication that she had received from "Andrea" and none of them had included the sender's address or hinted at any way to reply.

The first was a Christmas card containing a handwritten message that said she was "doing fine" and hoped Samantha had resolved her problem with Stephen.

Well, Samantha thought, she had certainly done that. She had not returned to Stephen. After obtaining a *decree nisi* in December, she was now looking forward to the *decree absolute*, next month, which would signal the official end of her unhappy and cloying relationship with him.

With the help of David Richardson and MI5, she had changed her name and moved to Harrogate where she had joined a large legal practice whose dynamic environment was a welcome change from the staid and stuffy world of Brighting and Blount.

As if that wasn't enough to bring a smile to her face, she had no less than three men asking her out on dates, one at work and two at the gym she had joined. Enjoying the attention, she visited the gym regularly and this was contributing to her losing weight and regaining her pre-marriage figure. This too, she found very satisfying.

A month after Christmas, Samantha received a letter in which "Andrea" said that she was expecting to start her "NEW JOB" (those words in block capitals) at the beginning of March, and that she would be so glad for the waiting to be over. This was, Samantha realised, a veiled reference to when the baby was due.

Finally, the postcard in her hand had arrived on May 11th.
It triggered memories of the frustratingly brief conversation in the room at the Waterloo Inn on that fateful Friday six months ago. Sandy had said she would use a code to arrange a meeting, and explained how Samantha should decipher it. She said Samantha should look for clues in the text.

The place and the time of day were blindingly obvious from the picture and from what she had written. The day to meet was given by the reference to the 14th. This did not mean the 14th of the month but the 14th day after the date on the postcard. The card was dated the 8th , hence, the meeting should take place fourteen days later on the 22nd at the time on the clock: 11:15.

Not for the first time, Samantha wondered how Sandy had managed to find out her new name and address without alerting her superiors, whom she knew would forbid the meeting.

According to David Richardson, Sandy was officially dead, killed in an incident involving members of a terrorist cell based in the Home Counties. In reality, she was fit and well and living under a new identity near London. That was a secret known only to a very select few, including herself. With Sandy's demise, Richardson had explained, Samantha should be safe. No longer in any danger from the terrorists, she could get on with her life without the fear of being kidnapped or murdered. The downside, of course, was that she could never see her sister again, but he promised that when he and the head of MI5 considered it safe to do so, he would find a way to pass messages between them.

Nevertheless, true to her word, Sandy had kept in touch using the Andrea pseudonym and now, at last, a face-to-face meeting was imminent. Samantha looked around excitedly. The quayside was heaving with people on this sunny Saturday morning but Sandy was nowhere in sight.

'Hi, Sam.'

The familiar voice came from behind and Samantha whirled round to see a woman she did not immediately recognise. She was wearing a beige waterproof jacket, black Lycra leggings and a knitted woollen hat, from under which, shimmering chestnut-brown hair cascaded around her shoulders.

'Sandy?'

Sandy grinned. 'Andrea, you mean? Yes, Sam, it's really me.'

'Oh my goodness! What happened to your face?' Sam reached out a hand to touch her sister's cheek but Sandy got there first and pulled her hair forward, partially concealing the disfiguring scar.

'You should see the other guy,' she smiled. 'Anyway, forget about that. Say hello your niece.'

Samantha lowered her eyes. Sandy had a blue-and-white-striped baby carrier suspended from her shoulders under the unfastened jacket. All Samantha could see of the baby was the back of a tiny pink head sporting a sprinkling of blonde hair. Sandy turned slightly to one side so that Samantha could see the baby's face as she rested contentedly against her mother's bosom. Choked with sudden emotion, Samantha found she was unable to speak.

'Well, daughter, this is your Auntie Samantha.'

On cue, the baby opened her eyes. They were bright blue.

'She has our eyes,' Samantha said, her own eyes glistening, 'and she's smiling at me.'

'That's just wind,' Sandy replied.

Suddenly, Samantha burst into tears.

'That was my reaction when I first saw her, too,' Sandy smiled happily. 'You'll get used to it. I have!'

Thirty yards away a man stood in a shop doorway, unobtrusively watching the touching reunion. He was in his mid-to-late forties, of slim build and easily six feet tall, perhaps taller. His hairline was receding from the temples, leaving a peninsular of slightly greying fair hair above the middle of his forehead.

David smiled. He could forgive Sandy anything – well almost, but he did not trust her as far as he could throw her.

oOo